ETERNITY FALLS

KIRK OUTERBRIDGE

A RICK MACEY CYBERTHRILLER

MARCHER
LORD
PRESS

Eternity Falls by Kirk Outerbridge
Published by Marcher Lord Press
8345 Pepperridge Drive
Colorado Springs, CO 80920
www.marcherlordpress.com

Cover Designer: Kirk DouPonce
Creative Team: Jeff Gerke, Lisa Lyons

Special thanks to the volunteer acquisitions readers who helped decide this season's books: Rusty Benschoter, Caren Blacker, Morgan Busse, Justin Clarke, Carie Davis, Rachel Davis, Glynda Francis, Eric Futrell, James Jack, David James, Rowena Kuo, Robi Ley, Frank B. Luke, Lisa Lyons, Rachel Marks, Kirsty and Roy McAllister, Jinn McCabe, Carol Parsons, Sarah Sawyer, Glyn Shull, Valerie Smith, and Esther Yi.

Library of Congress Cataloging-in-Publication Data
An application to register this book for cataloging has been filed with the Library of Congress.
International Standard Book Number: 978-0-9821049-7-2

Printed in the United States of America

For my brother, Kevin

June 30, 1972–May 24, 2007

Rest in peace, Big Bro.

I'll see you when eternity falls.

ACKNOWLEDGMENTS

I'd like to recognize all those who helped make this book become a reality. First, to God, who put the gift of writing in my heart. To my wonderful parents and siblings, who support me in everything I do. To my loving wife, Ria, who put up with me hogging the computer for five years straight. To my son, Miles, who brings such joy into my life and reminds me that the best thing I ever created came straight from God and not from me. To all the people on Writing.com, who helped me mold my manuscript with their honest critiques and encouragement. To Jacqueline Argent, my very first editor, who gave me my initial instruction in writing's "dos" and "don'ts." And to Jeff Gerke, my publisher, whose unwavering faith and vision made all this possible.

CHAPTER ONE

Los Angeles—2081

TOO CLOSE.

Horns and screeching tires yelled at him from behind. Rick Macey counter-steered, sliding the silver Lexus sideways before nearly sideswiping a cab. He tuned his neural net to the local traffic satellite, its overhead image minimizing in the corner of his vision as he careened through another intersection in the turbocharged sedan.

Pouring rain turned the city streets into tar-black mirrors. Traffic signals and holographic billboards reflected in a disorientating array of flashing neon and laser light. He forced his eyes to see through it as he neurally shifted gears, plowing through a hazily reflected red light—rain pounding his car top in a snare drum roll.

Artificial adrenaline heightened his senses. He warned slower vehicles with a constant blaring of the horn, weaving restlessly behind them like an Indy car driver waiting for the pace car to pull away. Finally he spotted open roadway ahead on the traffic-sat. He punched the gas, wiper jets barely maintaining visibility as the methanol engine roared and his speed increased.

100 . . . 120 . . . 130 . . .

No way was he letting the killer get away.

Not this time.

Not when he had the location pinned.

Macey locked his comm onto the police band, scanned the channels for confirmation of the kill. His neural net queued up a series of transmissions and he let them play, his AI ciphering through and discarding the impertinent bits according to his search algorithm. A cacophony of voices relayed their various pieces of information.

<confirmed homicide . . .>

<twenty-year-old Hispanic female . . .>

<single head wound . . .>

<20mm shell extracted from wall forty mete . . .>

<shot origin estimated at two miles plus . . .>

Two miles. That sealed it. It was the Streetwalker Sniper for sure.

The traffic-sat marked his destination looming ahead of him, a building towering a hundred stories into the stormy night sky. Macey downshifted and slid the Lexus to a halt at the entrance of the Liberty Tower Complex. He sprinted through the downpour toward the glass front doors.

A lone security guard sat loafing at a duty desk within, but Macey couldn't wait for a proper entrance request from HQ. He gazed upward at the mammoth citadel as rain peppered his eyes. It was nearly a thousand feet tall, multi-terraced and cylindrical in shape—like some giant wedding cake with a cheese grater exterior of windows mapping its outside. Climbing the thing was out of the question. Besides, there were easier ways to the top.

He took a two-step run up and vaulted himself to a first-story window ledge, clinging to it by his fingertips before hoisting himself the rest of the way with a mild grunt. He was already soaked, his hair dripping and matted, water penetrating his trench coat to his shirt, tie, and slacks beneath. He endured the discomfort as he braced himself within the window ledge for safety and bowed his head in concentration.

He accessed the web through his neural net, searched for the building's security system through the data window in the corner of his vision. In seconds he found it and used his encryption keys to gain full access.

He sent an interrupt signal to the security system. At the same moment his elbow smashed the heavy glass. It shattered like a piece of rock candy but stayed fixed to the laminated backing, clattering onto an office desk in a single sheet. He rolled inside after it and tumbled off the desk, his wet shoes slipping on glass shards and office papers before coming to a stand. He sent a fake all-clear signal to the security system right before it registered the breach.

Easy so far.

The internal security system proved even easier. He bypassed it by hacking the device controllers directly. In minutes, he opened the office door, neurally forced the security cameras to scan in the opposite direction as he passed, and hailed an elevator.

As he rode it skyward, Macey drew his Mauser M5 automatic pistol from his shoulder holster and chambered a round. With luck he'd never use it, but at this stage there was no sense being ill-prepared.

The elevator doors opened with a pleasant bing, and Macey stepped onto the top floor. The schematic in his internal view showed that two flights of stairs lay between the top floor and the roof. He hit the stairwell at a run.

As he climbed he kept close watch on the Sniper's position on the internal map. Still stationary—was he seeking another target? Macey doubled his speed.

There'd be no more deaths tonight.

Hurricane-like winds and rain beat against the door to the roof as he forced it open. At a hundred stories up the rainstorm screamed in a banshee howl. Solar panels and satellite arrays rattled with each gust, threatening to break loose from their knee-high mountings and ruin the maze pattern they formed on the roof. A massive sat-dish stood between him and the sniper's position.

He paused to access his remote memory device, retrieving more data on the case. It hadn't occurred to him until now, but the previous occasions the Streetwalker Sniper had struck boasted similar weather conditions. It made sense. At each crime scene, 20mm rounds had been found—and a 20mm rifle made one heck of a bang. Using a silencer would be out of the question as it would lower the accuracy and muzzle velocity, not to mention be ultimately useless as the round itself was supersonic and would cause a sonic boom. A storm provided the perfect cover for the sniper.

Cover Macey would now take advantage of.

He stalked through the whipping rain, which began to abate, forming a stinging mist as he edged closer to the sniper's position. His internal mapper showed a red triangle just around the sat-dish. As Macey shuffled around it, a figure came into view, hunched over the side of the roof's safety wall.

The sniper looked small—under five feet. But Macey didn't let himself underestimate this guy. He'd proven to be a formidable hacker, having accessed the skyscraper's roof most likely in the same way he had. He would also certainly have some military training, judging from his skill, and possibly access to other military weaponry he hadn't yet revealed. On top of that, he was methodical and patient.

The previous rainstorm had taken place over a month ago. The sniper was no raving lunatic on a killing spree. He was an assassin, a rational executioner with a well-thought-out plan of action.

And from the looks of him now that Macey was closer, he was about fourteen years old.

Macey stood for what felt like a minute, gazing at the scrawny white kid decked out in a black jacket, fatigues, army boots, and a baseball cap turned backward. He stood shouldering a tripod-mounted Barrett 20mm cyber-rifle, leaning on the safety wall. The weapon looked twice his size. His white-knuckled hands clenched the pistol grip and trigger while a wire ran from the base of his neck to the Barrett's targeting scope.

Macey took a few steps forward to bring himself within earshot. He blinked away the rain, drew his pistol, and raised his voice above the level of the wind: "Let go of that rifle, son."

The boy jumped, his head turning back to give him a who-the-heck-are-you kind of glare.

"It's over," Macey said.

The kid's lower lip curled into a snarl and he turned back to the scope, tensing for a last shot.

Macey fired a single round from the Mauser. The bullet severed the rifle's control cable with a spark, sending the sniper into a fit of screams as he clenched the back of his neck.

"Coward!" He yanked what was left of the cable from the head. "You're supposed to kill me. Don't you even know that?" He backed against the wall, his young face twisted with all the menace of a high school bully. The stock of the Barrett fell to the floor and dangled from the tripod affixed to the wall.

"Kill you, huh?" Macey kept the Mauser trained on him as he inched closer. "Unlike some I could mention, I don't make a habit of killing people. Especially not kids, even ones as sick as you. Lie down with your hands behind your head. The cops are on their way."

The kid slowly shook his head. "How'd you find me anyway?"

"Your ego."

"What?"

"Think it takes a genius to figure out a two-mile headshot requires a cyber-rifle, smart bullets, and targeting satellite support?"

The kid snorted. "So you hacked the satellite."

"No, but I knew you would." Macey stepped around a solar array. "I gotta admit, you were pretty good when you hit the sat. Quick in and out, just long enough to acquire your target and get your shot off, but . . ." He tapped the neural port on the nape of his neck. " . . . long enough for me to plant a trace."

"Nice one." The kid flicked what was left of the control cable from his hand like a cigarette butt. "Guess you think you're smart, then. Bet you think you're righteous too. Bet you think it's your righteousness that keeps you from killing like I do."

"I don't know what you're—"

"You just fear death more than God."

Crazy little punk. "Just get on your knees."

"I killed those whores in God's name." He tugged at his jacket. "Gave them a chance to repent, but they didn't listen. So I sent them to the judgment—before they can drag any more souls to hell with them with their tempting lusts."

"How can a kid even think like that?" Macey stepped toward him more forcefully. The kid kept tugging at his jacket. Was he hiding something underneath? "Just shut up and hit the floor. I won't kill you but I will shoot you if I have to. And you've seen I'm a pretty good shot."

"Go ahead," the boy said and his jacket flew open. It flapped in the wind, revealing a crucifix dangling from a leather strap about his neck. His torso was packed with what looked like plastic explosives. Perfect. And in his hand he held a trigger, already depressed, a dead-man switch.

Macey backed away, lowering his Mauser and raising his free hand. "Calm down, kid. No one else has to die today."

"You do," he said with a piercing stare, "and so do I." He looked behind Macey toward the door to the staircase. "I thought there'd be more of you when it finally came to it, but if it's just one cop then that's the way God wants it." He leaned his elbows against the wall as if it were a bar and he in a club, the trigger still in hand. "I'll give you the same chance I gave those whores. Will you repent before you die, pig?"

"Why are you doing this?" The kid had gained the upper hand, but there were ways to change that. Subtle ways. "What do you hope to accomplish by all this?"

"Look at you." He smirked, shook his head. "Still so afraid to die, aren't you?"

Keep talking, kid, just a few seconds more. "I guess you've got me all figured out."

"I know where I'm going, man, do you?" The sniper taunted him with a wave of his crucifix. "This is your last chance, little piggy. Repent before God or burn forever in Hell."

Bingo.

"Repent, huh?" Macey holstered the Mauser and strode forward, seized the boy's wrist. "I'll show you repent."

The kid staggered backward, eyes wide, mouth ajar as he sank to the rooftop. His arm shook spastically as he tried to let go of the trigger, his jaw grinding like a vice.

"What is thish?" he said between clenched teeth.

"You're paralyzed." Macey studied the crude detonation device about the boy's waist and quickly disarmed it. "I hacked your neural net while you were busy running your mouth. Don't worry, I just froze your gross motor control. I'll release it as soon as I get a proper cyber-lock plugged into your neural jack."

The kid laughed—as much as he could laugh with a clenched jaw anyway. "You are ferry good." His laughter faded, and despair contorted his features until he sobbed gutturally in jerky breaths. "Preez jush kill me . . . I don't womma liff in dis world no more."

"And just what do you know about living?" He grabbed the crucifix about his neck and showed it to him. "Only this and your hate?"

The boy didn't respond, just kept on crying.

Macey rose with a deep exhale. Kids killing hookers in the name of God. Could it get any worse?

Probably.

The rain had died almost completely now, but the wind still gusted. The police units he had called would be arriving shortly, but he wasn't in the mood for the lengthy explanations they would want from him if they found him here.

"The cops are coming for you. You won't wander off, will you?" He turned from the temporarily paralyzed boy and headed toward the stairwell. "Oh, and just so you know, since you seem to believe in all that stuff . . . repentance alone won't bring you salvation."

An hour later Macey found himself in the place he usually went after a rough day, a dive of a sushi bar called Saban's, in old Little Tokyo. It was little more than a crawl space, shaped like a shoebox with a sushi bar on one side, booths on the other, and an airplane-aisle-sized walkway in between. As usual, Saban's crowd was nonexistent: even at happy hour the place was dead.

Maybe that was partly why he dug it so much: the solitude, the bad air conditioning, the old flat film monitors dangling from the ceiling and covered in dust. A relic like he was. It felt more like home than his bourgeois-approved apartment in the Hills that did little more than serve as housing for his remote memory device.

He sat at the rearmost booth, facing the entrance. In front of him lingered a half order of tuna sashimi he hadn't touched yet and a cup of sake he didn't want to. Memorabilia was their purpose. He took a bite of his real food, a banana-flavored energy bar that tasted more like cardboard than fruit, and sighed.

His mind wandered to the Streetwalker Sniper case. Police band said he was en route to Central. Confused chatter about how he'd ended up in that condition. Macey couldn't make himself turn it off.

An incoming call on his neural net's comm link provided a timely distraction. Even before he checked the ID he knew it'd be Paul Webb calling—he was the only person with reason to.

He maximized the comm display in the corner of his vision, and Paul's face came into full view. Paul was in his fifties, black. His head and face were clean-shaven save for a well-kept mustache that Macey knew he dyed in order to keep jet black.

<*Evening, Major.*> Macey greeted him with his inner voice rather than his actual one, a minor feat he took some pride in.

Most people still spoke aloud while using internal comms. Human nature, he supposed, like the old telephone days when people would gesture while they talked as if the person on the other end of the line could see them. Ironically, now that they had video-feed technology, people seemed to gesture less. Maybe because they knew they were being watched.

Paul was no exception. His shoulders remained square-on but he did manage a smile. <*How long do you intend to keep calling me that?*>

Macey responded with a smile of his own, even though he lacked a camera for Paul to see it. Falling victim to his own statistics gave him an even wider grin. <*Sorry. You know: old habits. Evening,* Colonel.>

Paul laughed. <*And that used to be my line. Old habits do die hard.*>

Macey poked at his sashimi. <*I suspect you're calling about the sniper.*>

<*I am, but I'm also wondering why I have to find out from the police net that the guy's been nabbed.*>

<*Sorry about that too. I should have called you earlier.*>

<*It's okay.*> Paul laughed, lightening the mood. <*I'm just glad we got the guy. Besides, I figured you might be trying to become a superhero or something. Beat up the bad guy and leave him for the cops while disappearing into the night without a trace.*>

He chuckled at the imagery. <*No, no . . . I just . . . The situation got a little messed up, that's all.*>

<*What do you mean? You didn't get hurt, did you, Mace?*>

<*Nah, nothing like that. Just brought back some old memories. Plus the perp turning out to be a kid and all . . .*>

A pause lingered. <*Well, your compensation has already been transferred. Job well done, as usual.*>

<*Thanks.*>

Paul sucked in his bottom lip, glancing sideward.

Macey knew that look. <*What's up, Colonel? You holding out on me?*>

Paul chortled and gave Macey a you-caught-me kind of smile. <*To be honest, the sniper case wasn't the main reason I was calling. But, knowing you had an off night, I feel bad about bringing this up right now.*>

Macey glanced up at the door as a trio of women in business suits strolled in. <*Don't worry about it. What is it?*>

<*A case just came up. Another weird one, but you might find it interesting. It's got some urgency to it, though.*>

<*What's the details?*> Macey took another bite of his banana-cardboard bar.

<*It's too complicated for me to get into. This one is more a referral than a job. CDI can't get involved at this stage, so the client would have to contract with you directly.*>

<No government paycheck, huh?>

<Not for this one, bud. Here's the contact number. The name's Sheila Dunn. If you're interested, check it out immediately.>

<Will do, Paul. Thanks.>

<Try to take it easy this time. Later.>

He signed out and accessed the number. It was a private comm link with voice-only access. It rang a couple times and then a female voice answered.

<Speak.>

<Hello, Ms. Dunn?> He spoke cordially, hoping to encourage the woman to reciprocate on the other end. *<This is Rick Macey. I was given your contact by Paul Webb, concerning some matter of urgency?>*

<It's about time you called. I've been waiting all day. Look, if you want this job, stop screwing around and get to this address in twenty minutes.>

Nice tone, lady. But he forced himself not to react in kind. She was a potential client, after all. He glanced at the address as it downloaded. A private estate. *<Sherman Oaks?>*

<That'd better not be the extent of your deductive abilities or we're in a world of trouble here. When you show up, you'd better aim to impress the life out of me.>

The comm dropped.

Macey mulled over the abrupt conversation before calling Paul back.

<So I called her . . .>

<And? What'd you think?> Paul's mile-wide grin hinted he was resisting the urge to laugh but was on the brink of failure.

<This better not be another one of your gigolo pranks, Paul, I swear.>

Paul slapped his hands together, cackling. <*Come on, Mace, that was funny. But trust me, this has got nothing to do with the gigolo gag. You're probably gonna wish it did once you see her, though.*>

<*Yeah, whatever.*> Macey gave him a grin Paul couldn't see. <*She seems a real piece of work, that's for sure.*>

<*Oh, she is.*> Paul smiled with an overly dramatic widening of his eyes. <*Good luck, Mace. You're gonna need it.*>

Macey loaded the Sherman Oaks address into the Lexus's auto-drive for the short journey north. The navigation computer calculated twenty-eight minutes for the trip—good time, considering the rain.

He let the auto-drive take him there, but not for mere ease. He used the time to run through his normal routine for a new case.

Macey connected to the web through his neural net and began gathering information while the car drove its course through the winding, forest-clad hills of Northern LA. The moon played hide-and-seek behind a smattering of clouds, illuminating the trees with a sparkling glisten as the light reflected off their still-wet leaves.

By the time he pulled up at the Sherman Oaks address, he had stockpiled a fair bit of data about the case and the people involved. Not enough to know all the specifics, but enough to not seem like a clueless idiot when he arrived.

The Lexus stopped before a set of ornate iron gates. Beyond it, the ceramic-tiled roof of a three-story mansion rose in the cloudy night sky. Macey tapped into the comm system, gave a virtual knock, and eventually the security program acknowledged his ID and allowed him inside.

The estate looked every inch the home of a former A-list movie starlet. This one happened to belong to Greta Darling. Macey hadn't heard her name in decades. She had been quite popular in the twenties and thirties but her career had faded near the middle of the century. In her prime, she had successfully made the transition from mere actress to legend of the silver screen. Much like Marilyn Monroe or Julia Roberts, in her heyday everyone knew who Greta Darling was. Though now only old-timers like him would truly remember her splendor, seeing as she was close to ninety years old these days.

The house was the kind you would expect to find in Sherman Oaks: three stories, eight bedrooms, Spanish-tile walkways, an atrium full of exotic shrubbery, and a complement of cheap immigrant labor to man the place on a continuous basis. Ms. Darling apparently preferred Hispanics. This included the butler, who greeted Macey at the carport and ushered him inside.

He handed over his damp trench coat and followed the butler into a large sitting room filled with floral tapestries and expensive teak furniture. Soft yellow lighting shone down from an ornate crystal chandelier dangling from the vaulted ceiling. The scent of burning incense hung in the air.

Moments later a group of people arrived, led by a woman he would have easily recognized as Sheila Dunn even if he hadn't already seen her picture on the net.

She strutted in as if she owned the place, heels clomping on the hardwood flooring, yelling to an unseen person through her internal comm link. She stopped the entire group just so she could emphasize a point with a wave of arms and colorful expletives. Macey suppressed a chuckle as he added Ms. Dunn to his statistics of people who couldn't use an internal comm device properly.

Sheila Dunn looked to be in her early forties. Her raven hair was cut in a stylish bob with sharp bangs, her striking violet-tinted eyes matching a chic purple suit that hugged a body with all the right curves. She could easily be a movie starlet herself. But then, with the cosmetic options available these days, so could anyone.

She strode toward him and met his gaze with a practiced confidence, a talent no doubt honed from years of playing with the corporate big boys. It didn't matter to her that he was a man nearly two heads taller and twice her size. She was the boss, and she would establish that fact right from the start.

"Well, Mr. Macey, you're late." She gave him a quick up-and-down like a drill sergeant. "Your colleague said you were dependable, but so far I'm unconvinced. Nevertheless, you're here and I'm sure you're wondering why."

"Actually, I was wondering who all these other people are." Macey smiled at the two-man, one-woman team with her. Not that he truly cared. It was just a way of deflecting her condescending opening remark.

Her lackeys were all sharply dressed business types. The men: seasoned and white-haired. The woman: a short redhead with an iridescent face tattoo, a lick over thirty, if that.

"Legal representation from my firm, as well as those from Ms. Greta Darling's estate, whose home you happen to be in," Dunn said in one breath before any of them could speak. She then inhaled in what seemed like the precursor to a sigh of annoyance, but instead she continued. "As I was saying, I'm sure you're curious as to why you're here."

"Well, I assume it must have something to do with Ms. Darling and her Miracle Treatment." He paused before risking his next statement. "She isn't dead, is she?"

Ms. Dunn's eyes flashed like a mother hearing her child backtalk for the first time. "Why would you ask that?"

Amazing what a person could reveal through facial expression alone. "So she *is* dead. That would explain your urgency."

"How did you find out? Has the media leaked it already?"

"Just an assumption. You merely confirmed it."

"What assumption? You just got here, didn't you? I haven't told you a thing yet." She folded her arms, fixing her eyes on him over the crest of her sharp nose. "Where did you get your information? I want to know . . . *now*."

Macey exhaled and rubbed his temple. "I just took the liberty of performing a little background checking on the way here. That's all."

"Background checking into what? Explain."

Corporate types. He truly hadn't intended on getting rude with Ms. Dunn, but her persistent glare gave him little choice.

"You," he said finally. "I started with you, Ms. Dunn." He switched to a dictational tone as he recited the information directly from his neural net. "Sheila Rebecca Dunn: Senior Executive Vice President, Gentec Corporation Marketing Division. You've been the highest performing VP for the past eight years, pegged most likely to succeed Roger Boreman as CEO when his contract expires eighteen months from now.

"Your most notable achievement was the hostile acquisition of rival genetics research firm, Heliox Corp, about twenty years ago." He dipped his hands into his pockets and paced like a college professor giving a lecture. "I believe you were only twenty-five at the time, an accomplishment that most agree was due largely to your dual background in genetics and business management. You selected Heliox Corp because of their development of a prototype cellular reconditioning DNA treatment.

"After acquiring the company and its patent rights, you turned this prototype into the product you made famous through Gentec's marketing machine. The treatment was a one-time mutagenic conversion that created infinite cell multiplication without the side effects of cancerous growth. In short: infinite human life extension."

Dunn's rolling eyes prompted him to lay on his act.

"I believe the Fountain of Youth Formula was the product's earliest marketing release, but the skeptical stigma surrounding the name led to poor client interest. It was your business savvy and tenacity, however, that led to the new name, Miracle Treatment, and a focus on a narrow but deep-pocketed target market: celebrities. Which leads to your connection to Ms. Greta Darling, who, in 2060, at the tender age of sixty-eight, happened to be one of Gentec's earliest clients to undergo the Miracle Treatment."

When she kept staring at him he continued, "And finally, Ms. Dunn, your sense of urgency and panicked demeanor, plus the fact that you and your lawyers are here within Ms. Darling's estate at this late hour without her presence, led me to believe she may be deceased. I can only conclude that her death must have been from natural causes, which would not be entirely unusual for a woman of eighty-nine years. However, for a recipient of the Miracle Treatment, natural death is not supposed to be possible.

"Which puts you in the very awkward predicament of having sold someone a 'live-forever' pill for millions of dollars, only to have them drop dead only twenty years later—from natural causes."

Dunn pursed her lips as the entourage of lawyers nodded at his synopsis of the situation. "Very astute, Mr. Macey," she said. "I believe you've redeemed yourself . . . somewhat. You may get this job, after all."

This woman was incredible. "That wasn't my intention. I'm just trying to save us some time by getting the basic facts out of the way so we can move to the real issue. Ms. Darling's death from natural causes would make Gentec's Miracle Treatment the biggest medical fraud of the century, and that's no doubt the reason why you are here, Ms. Dunn. But you still haven't told me why *I'm* here."

"Isn't it obvious?" She cocked her head to the side. "I need someone to prove that Ms. Darling's death was not from natural causes. Or hadn't you already concluded that?"

"Is that right?" He gave a chortle and spun away. "No offense, Ms. Dunn, but I'm in the business of revealing truth, not hiding it. If you think I'm going to help you concoct some murder mystery so Gentec can keep selling a lie, you've got the wrong idea." He started for the door. "You all have yourselves a good night."

"Wait a minute, Mr. Macey, please."

He paused and looked at her.

Dunn turned to the group of lawyers. "Could you give us a moment?"

Once the entourage had departed, she sat on one of the couches and gestured for him to do the same. Reluctantly he took a seat opposite her and folded his arms.

"First, let me apologize." She released a sigh. "Right now I'm under more stress than you can imagine, and sometimes I forget that the whole world doesn't work for Sheila Dunn. I'm very sorry."

Her candor impressed him. "Nice to meet you, Sheila Dunn." He extended his hand. "And I'm sure the other Sheila Dunn, the one who has to throw her weight around the room like a tiger to survive as the sole female executive of a multinational corporation, will appreciate the interlude." He lightened this comment with a wink and smile.

Sheila smirked as she shook his hand. "It's been awhile since someone's had the gall to say something like that to me."

"I don't work for you, you see." He grinned. "Which leads us back to your original offer. Again, I'm sorry, but I won't involve myself in a cover-up."

"And neither will I accept one. I have good reason to believe Ms. Darling's death was not from natural causes."

He rocked his jaw from side to side. "Hasn't an official autopsy been conducted yet? How long ago did she die?"

"This morning. We received the results this afternoon. The coroner's conclusion was heart failure. Natural causes, as you said. But there's got to be more to it than that."

"I hate to say it, Ms. Dunn, but I really don't see how. The official results are the official results. Your efforts might be better spent preparing for the bad publicity than looking for some imaginary smoking gun."

"Bad publicity?" She arched her thin brow. "If only it were just that. I'm afraid this will go well beyond bad publicity. For the last twenty years I've grown Gentec into an international giant by streamlining and perfecting our Miracle Treatment. We've succeeded in lowering production costs and bringing the product to the mainstream market. We have over fifty million clients in the U.S. alone.

International numbers are more than triple that. We're talking trillions of dollars here.

"On top of that, Greta Darling is a celebrity. Already the media hounds and paparazzi are sniffing around. Our CEO is trying to buy us some time with the press, but if news of Greta Darling's death goes public, it will mean the end of Gentec. Clients will lose faith in the product, and it'll probably get recalled—indefinitely, if not permanently. But that's not the real damage this will cause."

"Oh?"

"Think about the billions of lives that will be affected if the treatment is no longer available." She leaned forward on the couch. "This won't just be a blow to Gentec. This will be a blow to all mankind."

"So you still maintain that it works? Even after this?"

"Absolutely," she said with a firm nod. "I conducted many of the initial trials personally. I have faith in our product. What I can't accept is that the human race has finally evolved to the point of avoiding death, and now we're going to throw all that away for this one little incident?" She rolled her eyes. "No way. We'd be setting back our species by centuries. I just can't––no, won't––allow that to happen."

Her resolve seemed intact, at least. "Look, I'm admittedly not a big fan of the whole live-forever concept, but I do understand the implications. Still, what proof do you have that Darling's death was anything but natural?"

"I performed my own analysis on her DNA and found no trace of the Miracle Treatment whatsoever."

Macey glanced up at the chandelier a moment before looking back to Sheila. "Isn't that to be expected?"

"Not necessarily. You see, if the treatment had *failed* she would have died from a cancer or some other mutated form of the treatment. But her DNA appeared completely natural, as if she had never undergone the treatment at all. It's as if . . . as if something had been introduced and somehow negated the Miracle Treatment."

"That, or maybe she'd just never taken it in the first place. Maybe she was only pretending to take it."

"No, the Miracle Treatment doesn't work that way. We call it a treatment because it's actually like a series of spa treatments." Sheila edged forward on the couch as she explained. "Clients receive an injection that reconfigures their DNA to an earlier time period of their lives, and then they spend time in a growth acceleration vat, where they literally age backwards. Depending on what age they want to be, they can take off five to ten years each treatment."

"Interesting. I didn't know that." Macey clasped his hands and rested his nose on his fingertips. "Okay, you said something might've negated the treatment, right? But like what? A virus? Radiation, maybe?"

She shook her head. "Nothing showed up in the autopsy. Besides, we've done extensive clinical testing and found no effect from environmental sources. And if it were a virus, we would have seen traces of that. Not to mention that if she had contracted a terminal virus, then *that* would have been the cause of death, and I wouldn't be sitting here right now."

"True."

"This reeks of some kind of setup." She balled her hand into a fist. Her eyes found Macey's. "I'm not completely certain about this one, but there's another clue. One that answers the question of why I want you, specifically, to help me with this."

"Me specifically?" He wasn't sure he liked the sound of that.

"Let me tell the whole story." She began counting off on her fingers. "First, I tried to talk to the police, but as this wasn't really a crime, they said they couldn't get involved. Fair enough. Next, I tried the Department of Civil Defense and Intelligence, where I contacted your colleague, Mr. Webb, who explained that CDI had similar constraints as the police. However, he did tell me he knew a retired investigator who might be able to help."

"Which would be me."

"But there's more. He said your specialization was in religious-based counterterrorism. He said you pretty much wrote the book on it. Is this true?"

"Well, it was my primary area of concentration for the earlier part of my career." He shifted on the couch. "What does that have to do with any of this?"

Sheila stood. "I'll be right back." She returned moments later with a clear plastic bag containing a small, leather-bound book. "This was lying open on her chest when they found her in bed this morning."

Macey examined the pocket-sized black book through the bag. The leather was worn and cracked. "A Bible? Was she a Christian?"

"No, she wasn't. Not according to any of her staff. None of them knew her to be religious by any means. So I started thinking that maybe this whole thing was some kind of terrorist act by a religious group, and this Bible was their calling card. That's what led me to try your colleague at CDI."

Macey nodded. "Was it faceup or facedown?"

"What?"

"The Bible. When they found it on her, was it faceup or facedown? And what page was it opened to?"

"Facedown, I believe. Not sure of the page."

"Doesn't matter then. If it was meant to be a message, it would have been left faceup. Facedown leads me to think she was reading it."

"But her staff insisted she wasn't religious."

"Maybe she was reading it for laughs. That's what most people tend to do with it nowadays." He chuckled and shook his head. "If you want my honest opinion, Ms. Dunn, this really isn't much to go on."

"Wait, there's one more thing. An inscription on the inside front cover."

Without removing the Bible from the plastic bag, he opened the cover. The inscription was handwritten in faded blue ink: *Remember Utah—June 16, 2027*

He closed the book, as if shutting it would somehow keep his mind from doing exactly as the inscription had instructed.

"I conducted some research of my own," Sheila said.

He barely heard her—his mind already drifting to the past.

"It turns out that a huge standoff took place between the government and a radical church group in Utah," she said. "June 16, 2027, was when the whole thing ended, quite bloodily, unfortunately. But the real interesting part is what sparked the whole incident. Apparently the church group was protesting against—"

"The Freedom from Deity Act."

Her eyebrow rose. "So you know about it? Oh, of course you would, sorry. But you see my point? The Freedom from Deity Act instituted the removal of all religious bias from U.S.

legislation. This act finally made genetic research possible, along with many other freedoms, of course. But without this Act, the Miracle Treatment wouldn't even exist."

"Absolutely . . ."

She touched his arm. "Are you all right? You seem distracted."

"Yeah, fine." He fidgeted to regain his composure. "Look, it's a pretty good theory, but there's nothing that ties this book to any sort of crime. It's a long shot, at best. I really don't think I can help you."

"But there must be organizations you know of that would want to do something like this to us, right? People who maybe know about Utah? Who want revenge?"

Macey forced himself to concentrate. "Sure, there might be some groups that sympathize with what happened in Utah and are anti-Gentec, but to go through them all would amount to drawing straws. Basically we'd have nowhere to start."

"What about the name?"

"What name?"

"Didn't you see it? Oh, I'm sorry—check the next page. It's a dedication to the original owner."

Macey opened the Bible again, turned the page. The second inscription was written in different handwriting. He read it.

Then he read it again. And then a third time, aloud, just to make sure.

"'To Brother Virgil. Love, Brother and Sister Fernandez.'" He examined the cover, back and front. "How old is this Bible?"

"I don't know."

"The copyright should say . . ." After confirming the date, he shut the book again, along with his eyes. "I'll take the job."

Sheila eased back onto the couch, her brows arching high. "Well . . . good. I'm glad to see we could come to such a quick decision. Now let's talk about the contract and compensation. You'll probab—"

"It doesn't matter," Macey said. "How soon can I start?"

CHAPTER TWO

MACEY AROSE FROM THE COUCH as Sheila reentered the sitting room, the trio of executive lackeys trailing behind her. She stopped just in front of him and gestured with a broad sweep of her arm like she was some game show hostess and he the next available prize.

"Gentlemen," she said, "this is Rick Macey. He'll be handling our investigation." She turned to the two old men in the designer silk suits. "Mr. Macey, this is William Boulder and Theodore Marrow, two attorneys from our firm. They'll be putting together your contract for you."

"Bill and Ted?" Macey let out a laugh as he shook hands with the two old men. "You guys serious?"

Ted raised an eyebrow at him. "I'm sorry?"

Macey contemplated filling them in about a low-budget 2D movie involving two teenaged slackers and a time-traveling telephone booth from almost a century ago—but after catching the not so "excellent" looks on their faces, he decided against it. "Never mind."

"And this is Marcia Tullen." Sheila motioned to the young woman with the face tattoo. "She's an actuary from the trust company that holds Ms. Darling's estate."

"I see." Macey shook her hand as well, eliciting a shy but pleasant smile from the youngster. "Nice to meet you."

"Likewise," she said, her iridescent face tattoo glowing in response. "Are you with the police?"

"Civil Defense and Intelligence, actually. Retired."

"Oh, CDI . . ." Her eyes squinted and her tattoo turned a shade darker. "You guys hunt down terrorists or something, right?"

The ignorance of youth. "Yeah, sometimes . . ."

"Shall we get down to business?" Sheila plopped herself on the couch, prompting her entourage to do the same. "Let's get your contract out of the way first, Mr. Macey."

They spent the next hour going over clauses, exceptions, and a mess of other legal jargon he didn't care to understand. They finally agreed to a contract fee, but Sheila had him hold off on signing for the time being.

Next, Sheila began hammering out the legal and financial implications of Ms. Darling's death with Ms. Tullen. Surprisingly, Ms. Darling had named the present household staff as beneficiaries, and what wasn't in the trust was to be donated among several charities. But the trust amount paled compared to the sums Ms. Tullen's company was demanding for compensation.

Macey attempted to lighten the mood by cracking a joke about a ninety-day warranty and no refunds, but it wasn't well received by either party.

He decided to leave them to it and start his own investigation. He took the opportunity to talk with Ms. Darling's staff, focusing on their observations of her home life.

As Sheila had said, none were aware that she was a Christian. Ultimately, that didn't mean much after he discovered that she rarely conversed with any of them. But most of them had noticed a change in her physical condition lately: less active, prone to illness, and generally more out of touch with things. He recorded the interviews and compiled them for later review.

When Sheila rejoined him, she mentioned one final matter to take care of before he could sign the contract and have him officially start the case. "We gotta go see my boss."

"Roger Boreman?"

"Yeah, the CEO . . ." She said it with a roll of her eyes. She stuffed file folders into a suitcase-sized Gucci handbag. "Let's just say he's not exactly *aware* of my plan to uncover the religious conspiracy surrounding Ms. Darling's death."

"Is that going to be a problem?"

"If you want to get paid, it is."

Now it made sense that she'd had him hold off on signing.

"Anyway, I need your help to sell him on the idea." She snapped her fingers at Bill and Ted from across the room and pointed to some banker's boxes by the front door. "Don't forget those." She closed her handbag and looked back at Macey. "So, you up for a visit?"

"You mean right now?" Macey checked the time—it was already past ten at night.

"He should still be at the office. Why? You got something better to do?"

Macey shook his head and smiled. He was itching to get underway.

Sheila announced she would be heading back to the office and sent her team home for the night. To save travel complications, Macey offered to chauffeur her in the Lexus while Bill and Ted took the company car home.

At this time of night, the traffic had eased. Macey opted to drive the route manually, heading south toward the new corporate district.

Two minutes into the ride, Sheila hopped onto her neural net and began making calls to several people at once. "I said by tonight. . . . No, not you, Mark. . . . Sec, Jules, I got another call. . . . Speak!"

Macey endured the comm-induced-schizophrenia for several miles.

Finally she disconnected and let out a sigh. "I'm too stressed." She dug into her handbag and withdrew a small hypo-syringe. She pressed it to her neck and, with a pneumatic hiss, pumped its contents into her bloodstream. She stiffened like a mannequin, then puddled into the car seat.

Sheila caught him looking and then straightened herself. "Anti-anxiety medication," she said, as if it were something legal. She turned her gaze to the window as the drugs took effect. "Man, I'm starving. I haven't eaten since breakfast. Can we stop?"

"Sure, what do you want?"

"Anything that's hot and fast."

Macey pulled the Lexus into a burger drive-through, where Sheila proceeded to order a meal he considered far too large for a woman her size. She asked what he wanted, but he declined. He'd had his fill for the night. Just when he was about to pull away, she stopped him again.

"Hold on!"

"What? They forget the ketchup or something?"

"No. I get carsick if I try to eat while driving."

He waited to see if she was kidding.

Her incessant stare said otherwise.

With a sigh, he parked the Lexus while Sheila tore into her grease-stained bags of goodies. After polishing off her double bacon cheeseburger, fries, onion rings, and triple chocolate shake, she made another call on her internal comm.

"Mike, it's Sheila. . . . Yeah, you too. . . . Look, I need you to send someone over. . . . No, not in the mood for that. A woman. . . . Yes, Yuki would be perfect. I'll be home by twelve. Tell her to let herself in. . . . Yeah, you can go ahead and bill it. . . . Thanks, Mike. Ciao."

Macey tried to pretend he hadn't heard anything. Instead, he debated which side of Ms. Dunn he found more offensive: her professional hostility or her personal indulgences. Then again, maybe he was just being old-fashioned. Her actions wouldn't bat an eye these days.

"What?" she said, as if sensing his thoughts. "Like a guy like you hasn't hired an escort before?"

He spoke without turning his head. "For the record: no, I haven't. But it's your money. Spend it as you like."

"Oh, a virgin—how exciting." She donned a goofy grin, licking her teeth. "Maybe I'll order one for you as a signing bonus." Then in a tone sounding halfway serious, "Or do you want to just share mine?"

"No, thanks." Macey started the car and pulled out of the parking lot.

"Perhaps a man, then?" She uttered a laugh that ended in a snort. After he didn't answer, she tried again. "Okay, okay, so I guess you're the marrying type. Am I right?"

"Was." He pulled onto the highway and resumed his heading south toward downtown.

"Ah, been there, done that. Me too. Divorced twice. They couldn't handle me, the pathetic little wimps. The first one turned out to be gay and the second one I caught cheating on me with the maid. That's why I went for a woman on my third try. But she started spazzing worse than the guys after we got engaged, so I called it off right before the—"

"I didn't mean that," he said. "My wife is dead."

The sternness of his response seemed to sober her up some, or perhaps it was the "anti-anxiety medication" wearing off. Whatever the reason, she remained quiet for a long while. A highway-wide holographic banner flew by overhead, signaling their arrival in the New City district. The city center loomed in the distance, its hundred-story spires populating the night skyline.

"So what's your story anyway, Macey?" she said at last. "You're supposed to be that guy Webb's old boss, but you look younger than he does." She squinted at him with a playful smile. "You aren't a Gentec client yourself, are you?"

"Hardly. I already told you I'm no fan of the live-forever deal."

"And why not? You actually like the idea of dying in a diaper full of your own excrement?"

He tried to ignore the imagery. "It's . . . overrated. Not to mention unnatural."

"Unnatural?" She rolled her eyes. Then she stiffened and jerked her head toward him with a what-did-you-just-say kind of stare. "Can I ask why you accepted this case if you don't like the idea of what our company does?"

"Hey, you're the one who asked the question. I can't help it if you don't like my answer."

"Let's get one thing clear." She jabbed a well-manicured finger in his face. "Personal opinions are one thing, but when they are diametrically opposed to a company objective, I start to get worried. Are you going to fulfill this contract or what?"

"Excuse me?"

"Picture it from my point of view. If you hired some guy to cut down a tree and then, right before he starts, he tells you he's some tree-hugging-Greenpeace activist, how would you feel?"

She had a point, but he felt insulted nonetheless. He downshifted as he pulled off the highway and entered the surface streets. "I believe I can separate my personal opinions from my professional performance, Ms. Dunn."

"You better be able to, because if you're not willing to give this your full—"

"I told you I would. And if you must know, I took this case to find evidence of a religious conspiracy involving Gentec, that alone. The accomplishment of your goal is completely independent of my purpose."

She went quiet, her mouth dropping open.

Nice job. Here he was, not even officially hired yet, and already he was about to be fired. He sighed and prepared himself for her inevitable response.

But it never came. Instead she slumped into the car seat, crossing her arms like a scolded child. He figured there was no sense apologizing to her. After all, he had only told her the truth. At any rate, it hadn't gotten him fired, and it had accomplished at least one positive thing.

Sheila Dunn remained quiet for the rest of the ride.

It was past eleven by the time they arrived at the Gentec headquarters in the new corporate district. The New City sections were nothing like old Los Angeles. They resembled New York with its densely packed high-rises and traffic-filled streets. Even the air suffocated in the noise and commotion. Advertising dirigibles weaved through holographic billboards that lit the sky with an eerie luminescent glow.

Macey much preferred the urban sprawl of Old Town. Here, there was too much traffic, too much stress. Even at this hour the place was a din of chaos. Luckily, Gentec's headquarters loomed near the outskirts and had ample underground parking.

As they rode the elevator from the basement, Sheila broke the silence. "Sorry about all that stuff in the car. I don't normally act like that . . . in front of people."

"Don't worry about it."

"Right," she said succinctly, becoming the corporate tiger once more. "Let me handle the talking unless I ask you to, got it? And whatever I say, back me up one hundred percent. At this stage of the game, confidence is worth way more than substance. This guy is a pushover, anyway."

Soft blue lighting filled the massive open spaces of the Gentec hallways. The translucent walls displayed a nighttime reef motif with shoals of bioluminescent shrimp skating over the tops of swaying indigo fan corals.

As they traveled through the virtual aquarium, Sheila proceeded to bombard him with details of the company's interpersonal dynamics. Who the boss was, who knew who, who was on whoever's side. Every organization had its dirty politics, he supposed, but the mess at Gentec brought the old "corporate backstabbing" adage to life in Technicolor. Before he had a chance to fully digest everything, Sheila led them down a final corridor of circling reef sharks and through a set of double doors, into the office of the Chief Executive Officer, Mr. Roger Boreman.

The office was the size of a small conference room. Floor-to-ceiling windows served as a backdrop to a central black mahogany desk flanked by two Japanese bonsai trees. An oval glass meeting table surrounded by high-backed black leather chairs occupied the rest of the office, and a *Feng shui* sculpture made of three smooth rocks stacked on one another adorned its top.

At their entrance, Boreman glanced up from his desk, as did a younger man standing next to him. Boreman appeared in his mid-fifties, blond-haired with a touch of white matching his full beard. His associate sported dark hair and a hooked nosed. Although he appeared a few decades younger than Boreman, he held a gaze of confidence that betrayed his age.

"What's the story with the media, Roger?" Sheila said. "You haven't contacted me in hours. I need to know what's happening."

Macey recognized the tactic. The same she had used on him when they had first met: strike first to put the other party off balance from the start.

Boreman responded with a stare and scowl. "Sheila, why is it you have to barge in like that? We really don't need—"

"Will you stop it, Roger? The fate of this entire company is on the line, and you're worrying about office etiquette?"

"Fine," he said in a huff, closing his eyes. "Just report."

Sheila strode in from the doorway and into the center of the office. "Before I do, I want you to tell me what's happening with the media. Did you buy us some time or what?"

"A little."

"How much is that?"

"It depends on what it is you have to tell me," he said in punctuated breaths. "And who's this guy with you?" He jerked his thumb.

"My show and tell." She looked to the younger man. "I've already seen yours. How are you, Bradley?"

The man barely nodded in acknowledgement.

Bradley. The name came to Macey now, thanks to Sheila's info dump earlier. Bradley Thomas was Boreman's personal assistant and fairly new to the company. Boreman had parachuted him in to help with "special projects," as he called them. In reality, no one seemed to know what he actually did, besides keeping Boreman company.

"The good news is that Ms. Darling did not die from natural causes." Sheila strolled toward the meeting table and picked up one of the *Feng shui* rocks, tossed it in her hand. "At least, not natural causes alone." She threw the rock back down, knocking over the two others like bowling pins. "She had some help, apparently."

Boreman scowled at the rocks still spinning on the table. "What help?"

"Outside help. There was no trace whatsoever of the Miracle Treatment in her DNA. Somehow it was negated or removed, and I'm going to find out by what and by whom."

"Are you still focusing on that same nonsense from this morning?" He slammed both fists on his desk, blasting an expletive. "I can't believe you've wasted all this time on that ridiculous fantasy of yours. We need to talk about hard facts and damage control, find out where we went wrong with Ms. Darling's treatment and fix it before the media blows this whole thing wide open."

"Nothing went wrong with the treatment." She charged his desk and jutted her finger into his face. "Our product is sound. It was then and it is now. If you were a geneticist, and not just some pencil-pushing bean counter, you'd know that."

Boreman pushed away, flustered, but said nothing. From her prior exposition, Macey knew why. Boreman's biggest flaw as Gentec's CEO was his lack of technical background, a fact she often used to her advantage

"All I know is that one of our clients is dead," Boreman said. "I'm no expert, as you so often like to point out, but I'm pretty sure that the whole purpose of our product is to insure that our clients don't die from old age. It doesn't take a Ph.D. in genetics to figure out that what happened to Ms. Darling isn't supposed to. That's how the media will perceive it.

"You can spout as much mumbo-jumbo genetic techno-babble as you like, Sheila, but the only thing the public, as well as our shareholders and clients, understand is results. Clearly, for Ms. Darling, we didn't achieve them. So unless you're able to bring her back from the dead, I suggest you get on the band-wagon here and start talking damage control."

Sheila bit her lower lip. "Roger, I understand your position. It's probably the best call you can make at this stage, especially with what you've got. It's a safe call, but not one that will necessarily get us out of the woods. I, on the other hand, am willing to take a risk on what I believe—no, not believe: *know* to be true. I can stand by my product. I know it didn't fail. Someone had to make it fail. All that stands between Gentec and complete absolution of this whole mess is finding out who that someone is."

"Really?" Boreman glanced to the side and scratched his head. "And how are we going to find this mystery someone, if they even exist?"

She grinned like a spoiled brat showing off a new toy. "Allow me to introduce Mr. Rick Macey."

Macey blinked and, thinking his introduction was a cue to speak, almost did so before she cut him off again.

"Mr. Macey is a retired investigator for the Department of Civil Defense and Intelligence, and an expert in religious-based terrorism. He has decades of experience solving cases exactly like this.

"In my preliminary investigation, I found evidence that Ms. Darling's death could be connected to the actions of a religious group," she said, "one that's bent on destroying our company and our product. This was all confirmed by Mr. Macey when he arrived at the scene. Therefore, I have no doubt that we will find the person or persons responsible for causing Ms. Darling's death, and clear our product's name before the media ruins it. I'd go into the details of how the connection was made, but perhaps I'll let Mr. Macey speak on the matter."

She smiled up at him.

"Thanks." Macey rocked his jaw from side to side. "Mr. Boreman, I'm going to be honest with you. The religious evidence that Ms. Dunn spoke of . . . The chance of it linking Ms. Darling's death to any sort of crime is . . ." he sought the right wording . . . "feeble, at best."

Sheila's eyes widened. "What?"

"However, she is somewhat correct in that the motive to commit a corporate sabotage of this nature does exist within a few extreme religious organizations. So, while it's still highly unlikely, there is the slim possibility of at least some kind of terrorist activity happening here."

Boreman stared at him over a pair of clasped hands. "Is that it?"

Macey glanced at Sheila, who glared as if she wanted to stab him in the throat. "For now, yes—that's it."

Boreman broke into a chuckle that grew into an outright laugh. "Sheila, have you lost your mind? You honestly think this will get us anywhere? Even your expert has trouble buying it."

"Don't you think you should elaborate, Mr. Macey?" She fumed at him. "The Bible? Utah? Ring a bell?"

"No point in going into specifics," he said coolly. "I gave you my honest opinion of the likelihood of success. It would be unethical of me not to. You both need to understand that the chances of uncovering some kind of terrorist connection are slim, at best, but if they do exist, rest assured they can be found."

She tugged on his coat sleeve and pulled him toward her. "What are you doing?" she said in a forced whisper. "You'd better start talking right now."

Calmly he stepped away from her. "You hired me to investigate a possibility, Ms. Dunn. I'm tempering your expectations with reality. If you don't like what I have to say then you can go ahead and tear up my contract, but I will not stand here and lie about our chances. Mr. Boreman needs to make an informed decision and my professionalism will guarantee that he has that opportunity. Without the interference of your biased propaganda."

Her jaw slackened but she uttered not a word, displaying the same stunned paralysis as in the car.

Across the room, Bradley Thomas whispered something into Boreman's ear, who nodded.

"Mr. Macey, I appreciate your forthrightness." Boreman glowered at Sheila. "It's a welcome change from what I usually get around here." He leaned back in his chair and put his hands atop his head. "But I'm not without an open mind. As farfetched as your idea is, Sheila, I'm going to give you the shot. Mr. Macey, consider yourself hired."

Sheila blinked. "Come again?"

"I do have some stipulations."

"What stipulations?" she said.

"I've managed to broker a few deals with the media giants," Boreman said, "but the most I could get was another forty-eight hours of blackout. After that, they'll be coming for blood. I'll continue working on my own solution, but until that time you can pursue whatever you want. If you come up with your mystery man, fine. If not, we go with what I have. Deal?"

She shrugged. "That sounds fair."

"One more thing. During Mr. Macey's investigation, you'll accompany him personally. I don't want you hanging around here hindering us, got it?"

"Fine." She blew a strand of hair from her face. "Keep your comm open, though. I'll contact you as soon as we have our suspect. Save you all some work."

Boreman gave her a fake smile that ended in a sneer and waved them both out of his office.

When they reached the privacy of the elevator, Sheila let loose. "What do you think you were doing in there?" she yelled. "You made me look like a complete idiot."

Macey resisted the temptation to state the obvious, even though it would have been quite funny. "Don't complain. He accepted your idea, didn't he?"

"Like *you* had anything to do with it?"

"Actually, I did. He would never have agreed to this based on the evidence alone. No sound-minded person would have. I told you both that."

"Huh?"

"Human nature. Boreman hates your guts. By embarrassing you, something he probably fantasizes about doing himself, I became his hero. He probably said yes just because he figured I'd spend the whole time humiliating you."

"Are you kidding me? That's got to be the most ridiculous––"

"Trust me, it's a guy thing. Don't feel offended. It worked to your advantage, didn't it?"

She kept her gaze on the elevator floor, her jaw muscles tensing, no doubt calculating how she could murder him in the next five seconds and get away with it.

He let out a laugh and gave her a nudge. "Take it easy, kiddo, I was joking—about the humiliating part, anyway. The first part was true. Boreman does hate your guts, which probably comes as no shock to you. He's your superior but you outshine him in every way. There's nothing he'd like more than to see you fall flat on your face in the most public way possible."

She eyed him with a raised brow.

"I read the situation," he said. "I knew that no way was he going to agree to something that had a better chance of success than his own efforts, especially if it was coming from you. So I presented the information in a form that would be far more digestible to him."

"So you lied?"

"'Exaggerated' is more accurate." The elevator stopped and they headed into the underground parking lot, their footsteps echoing off the concrete pillars. "By making your proposition seem ridiculously improbable, I knew he'd never pass up the opportunity to accept it."

"That schmuck. He said yes only because he thinks I'm going to fail?"

"Welcome to the world of misinformation manipulation, Ms. Dunn."

Her eyes flashed toward him. "Sir, I believe you have just succeeded in impressing the life out of me."

He chuckled. It felt great to be on a real case again.

"Wait. How much were you exaggerating? How much of a chance do we really have?"

"As for proving your case to the media, that's going to be up to you." He opened the passenger door of the Lexus for her. "As for finding a suspect . . . well, I think the result is inevitable."

• • •

Pooly waddled through the garbage-strewn back alley as if it were his natural element. Not that his body was particularly well built for squeezing through mounds of torn garbage bags and overflowing Dumpsters, but it just didn't bother him to do so. Even if it did, plowing through the rancid stuff would be his only option anyway. At five-foot high and nearly the same dimension wide, Pooly was squat and beefy, as he preferred to put it. Ever since he was a kid he'd been fat, and now, pushing forty, all the more so.

Pooly had never considered himself an unhandsome man, but his double chin and pudgy cheeks had admittedly distorted his features over the years. Add to that his bald head and he could understand his luck with women. Plus he'd traded his real eyes for ebony shaded lenses ages ago, giving his face a remarkably pig-like resemblance. Hence the nickname—Pooly the Pig.

Which had come first anyway? The name or the look? He couldn't remember, or care really. Good looks and fancy names were the stuff of clients. But he had character and smarts, stuff you couldn't buy off some Glitzdoc. And over the years he'd developed something more: power.

Pooly the Pig was no longer a name to be laughed at.

He neared the meeting point, right on time, as usual, but now came the part he dreaded. For some reason the Freak always wanted to meet on the roof of some burned-out hovel of his choosing, and for Pooly that meant climbing stairs, lots of them.

Tonight's rendezvous spot looked like it used to be an apartment complex, now converted into yet another drug den by the cyber-ganger tribes of South Central LA—the particular subspecies responsible was anyone's guess. Gothers, Rudeboiz, Blitzers, Reavers, they were all the same to him.

"Stinking bottom feeders."

He stepped through what had once been the main doorway, the stench of human feces and urine assaulting his nostrils. He gagged but quickly grew accustomed to it, the same way he had with the garbage, and moved further inside. It was pitch black but he didn't need light, not with his lenses. He could spot the heat signature of rat and vagrant alike, and tread carefully to avoid both species of vermin.

He found the stairs and started upward. At least they were concrete and not wooden, like in some of the other joints the Freak had chosen. Pooly was over three hundred pounds, so a set of wooden stairs in an abandoned building was more than just a physical fitness challenge—it was a structural disaster waiting to happen.

The three flights of stairs had completely winded him by the time he feebly pushed open the door to the roof. His leather jacket felt incredibly hot. He fanned it in the night air to dry the sweat-soaked silk shirt beneath.

He rubbed a hand over his dampened scalp and brushed the neural net jacks at the base of his neck, reminding him to plug in to the encryption server in his pocket. No sooner had he jacked a wire into the credchip-sized device than he sensed someone behind him.

"Hello, Gordon."

Pooly never recalled telling the Freak his first name, but somehow he knew it and that was all he ever called him by. Gordon Pool turned about to face his client.

The man's towering height was evident even when crouching atop one of the building's rotting ventilation ducts. His bent knees loomed a good two feet above Pooly's head.

He wore his usual get-up: a pair of camo pants tucked into boots, a matching top covered by a white overcoat, and a pair of close-fitting mirror shades wrapped about his eyes, his face clean-shaven like his head. His skin was of so deep a shade of olive that Pooly never could tell if he was black or Hispanic, or maybe a mixture of the two. But then, he'd never had the inclination to ask.

Pooly held the encryption device toward him, prompting the Freak to pull a neural jack from the back of his own neck and link to it. Once he had tested the software to ensure that neither of them was being hacked or shadowed, he spoke freely.

"It's been a little while. No contact for weeks and then all of a sudden this big rush. What gives?"

"There's been a change," the Freak said, his voice low and even. "Those additional units we spoke of: I have need of them now."

"All of them?"

"Yes."

Pooly whistled. "You do remember the price?"

"Of course. Money is no longer a problem. See here . . ."

Through the encryption device the Freak transmitted a set of account numbers and coinciding balances, the numbers appearing in a display screen in the corner of Pooly's vision. The amounts totaled far more than the price they had initially agreed upon.

"Consider the extra a bonus," the Freak said. "So long as you can guarantee the delivery."

"Not a problem. Where's the drop at?"

"Contact me as usual when the order is ready. I'll let you know then."

"Fine. Hey, you mind me asking you a question?"

"Certainly not, Gordon. Go right ahead."

"What you gonna do with so much of this stuff?"

"I leave that to God's will." He leaned his head back, his mirror shades reflecting the stars. "And if it be God's will, mankind shall again know the truth . . . before eternity falls."

Pooly laughed as a shudder ran down his neck. "You *are* a freak, you know that? But at least you're a rich one."

The giant of a man smiled with subtlety. "That reminds me, Gordon. Have you given any thought to my other offer?"

"What offer?" And then suddenly remembering, he let loose a snort. "Oh, that Jesus-freak bull? No thanks, brotha. I'm a church of one, know what I mean?"

The Freak rose to his full height, the rusted ventilation duct creaking under his weight. "My offer has no time limit. Whenever you may feel ready, I am here."

What a freakin' laugh. "Yeah, okay, man. But you're gonna be waiting a long d—"

The Freak vaulted into the sky, the ventilation duct crumpling with a bang from the force of his launch. His body sailed though the air. He landed on an adjacent roof some fifty feet away, then leapt again and faded out of view.

"Freakin' cyborgs," Pooly muttered. But as he eyed the stairs, he envied his client's greater mobility. "Ah well, at least I'm not crazy like you. Good luck, Bible Boy, may the Force be with you!"

Pooly gave a buffoon-like salute to the darkness and laughed all the way down the stairs.

CHAPTER THREE

MACEY DIDN'T GO straight to sleep that night, but he did have to dodge yet another offer to share Sheila's late-night entertainment when he dropped her off at her penthouse apartment in the New City. It took him two more denials before she finally gave up and agreed to meet him around nine the next morning.

So far, Ms. Dunn was ranking fairly high on his list of oddball women. But he had to be careful what he considered odd these days. In reality she was typical of a woman her age. Vibrant, wealthy, liberal—she could be the poster child for her entire generation. Their view of sex was more like shaking hands. Marriage was like a financial partnership, and "entertainment" was an exploration into sensory overload. Not that he hadn't lived the life in his day, but this decade seemed bent on the whole work-hard-play-hard mentality on a global scale.

It was nearly one a.m. by the time Macey arrived at his apartment in the Hills. He made a pot of coffee and knocked it back while he prepared to connect to his remote memory server to begin his research.

The server was the size of a shoebox. It rested at the foot of a plush black leather easy chair that doubled as a dive couch. Macey sat within it and leaned his head back. The neural jacks in the headrest connected to the ports on the nape of his neck, and his five senses were transported to the piano lounge motif of his workstation. He toned down the "Count Basie" playing in the backdrop and connected his server to the outside net.

He started with the old favorites: the Islamic fundamentalist terror groups. He jacked into the money trails and tapped his normal information brokers, but after a few hours the leads dried up. No surprise there, considering the evidence found was a Christian Bible, but at least he could rule them out.

Simultaneously he checked the security of the media blackout Boreman had arranged. The guy must have paid a pretty penny indeed, because even in the farthest corners of the net, news of Ms. Darling's death were rumors at best, focusing primarily on her celebrity status rather than her connection to Gentec as a Miracle Treatment client.

He investigated the radical Christian groups next. This proved harder, not because there were more of them to weed through, but rather, the opposite. After only an hour his search had led nowhere. Even more frustrating, nothing turned up on the only real lead he felt they did have: Virgil, the name in the Bible.

He sighed and momentarily exited virtual space to pour himself another cup of coffee. Nothing turned up on Virgil by electronic means, anyway. Good old-fashioned street pounding might be the only access to the trail.

Switching perspective, he dissected the recordings of his interviews with Ms. Darling's staff. Finally, somewhere around 6:00 a.m., he found his first solid lead: a long-time friend of Ms. Darling, who visited her once a month.

Her name was Eva Janis, an actress and another Miracle Treatment client of around sixty years old. The staff had said she was about the only person they knew who truly communicated with Ms. Darling. If anyone would know what was going on in Ms. Darling's life prior to her death, it would be Eva Janis.

Gauging the time, he decided to sleep a couple of hours before heading over to pick up Sheila. As usual, he didn't bother retiring to his bedroom but drifted off in the easy chair, listening to soft sounds of jazz from within the confines of his virtual environment.

Macey awoke a few minutes before he had set his internal alarm. He canceled it and disconnected from the server, its image shrinking away as he rose from the chair and made his way to the shower.

The water refreshed and refocused him, and by the time he had selected a new grey suit, his mind was fully alert. He grabbed an energy bar from the fridge and munched it on the way to the garage. He considered upgrading to the Beemer but, after remembering the mess of french fries Sheila had left in the Lexus, opted to stick with it.

No sense dirtying two cars.

He rolled out of the garage and, as soon as he hit the highway, set the auto-drive for Sheila's place. About halfway there he contacted her. Not surprisingly, he woke her up. She groggily assured him she would be ready by the time he arrived.

True to her word, she was waiting curbside at her ritzy apartment complex clutching two tall paper cups.

She looked so amazing in her loose white blouse and tight khaki skirt that he had to force himself not to stare as she entered the car. He did permit himself to inhale her perfume. Melon and peaches? Whatever it was, it smelled almost as good as she looked. Too soon, it was overpowered by the aroma of the freshly brewed coffee.

"Good morning, Mr. Macey." She offered him one of the cups. "Latte?"

"Morning," he said and accepted the coffee, although he'd already had his fill of the stuff. He noticed that her makeup failed to hide a pair of puffy, bloodshot eyes. "Sleep well?"

"Well? Yes. Long enough? No." She tossed back a gulp of caffeine. "So what's the plan, detective?"

He chuckled at his new title as he pulled away and headed for Hollywood. "Before we get started, a little admin." He handed her a tab of paper. "Connect to the address on there. It's a link to my remote memory server. We can route through it as a secure comm channel. Give it a try."

She focused on the paper as she inputted the address through her neural net. "Hello? Testing?"

He heard her in stereo, inside the car and inside his head. "Ah . . . try not to . . . talk when you do it."

"What?" she said in stereo again. "Oh, okay."

<How's this? Can you hear me? Sheesh, this is weird. Am I talking to myself? Is this thing working?>

<I hear you fine.> He responded through the link. *<You're mumbling a bit but you'll get better with practice.>*

"What's the point of this, anyway?" She was talking aloud again. "I mean, if I want to call you I'll just use my comm. And what's the big deal about trying to talk in my head?"

<It has many advantages, as you'll soon find out. For one, this channel is encrypted through my remote memory server. It's nearly impossible to hack. Secondly, when we start interviewing people, we can use this to communicate without them being aware of it. Finally, we can share thoughts and ideas far quicker. Access this directory.>

He changed the permissions of some files within his remote memory server.

"What is it?" she said aloud. *<Sorry. What is it?>*

He chuckled and switched out of the comm. "Don't worry, it's not like you have to use it all the time. Just when you want to tell me something privately. But if you do use it, remember not to talk."

"Ugh, that's a relief. So what's in this directory?"

"My compilation of the case so far." Macey picked up speed as he pulled onto a highway entrance ramp, shifting toward the auto-drive lane. "I've quarantined a section of my remote memory for us to share as a common databank."

"Quarantined?" She craned her neck in mock offense. "Are you *that* afraid of my thoughts infecting you, Mr. Macey?"

"Quite the opposite." He engaged the auto-drive and the Lexus slipped into the automated processing of vehicles headed north. "The quarantine is for your protection, not mine. Which reminds me: don't try to access any deeper into my remote memory than the permissions I've given you, okay?"

"Oh, really?" She rubbed her index finger along her lower lip. "And what would I find if I did try to go a little deeper? Some dirty little secrets, perhaps?"

"You'd find death." He looked at her soberly to make certain she realized he wasn't kidding. "There's an offensive firewall protecting all other areas. If you try to access them, your neural net will be fried, along with your brain. Now, go ahead and access the directory."

She nibbled on her bottom lip, but hesitantly bowed her head and closed her eyes to plug into the directory. Her eyelids fluttered as she made contact, the data from his remote memory synchronizing with her own. After about a second it was done, and she pulled out of the link, gasping.

"Argh!" She pressed a palm against her temple. "My head feels like it's about to explode. How did you compile that much information from just last night? Don't you sleep?" She rubbed her forehead and slugged back another shot of coffee. "You won't ever have to worry about me accessing anything else in your head. I'd probably die even if there wasn't a firewall."

"Sorry. I should have warned you there'd be a lot of data."

"That's an understatement. So . . . this Eva Janis is who we're going to see?"

"Yes. She's shooting a TV movie this morning so hopefully it won't be too much of a problem to get ahold of her."

"Tinseltown—oh, joy." She frowned and reached into her purse, producing the hypo syringe again. "Say, can we stop for donuts?"

He endured the sickening pneumatic hiss. "Sure." He then surveyed the French fries still littering his car. "You don't like sprinkles, do you?"

"Huh?"

He chuckled. "Never mind."

Sheila contemplated grabbing another double-glazed donut as they rolled onto the set of Eva Janis's film. She'd had time to eat only two before Macey had whisked them from the donut shop parking lot. And the place they rushed to wasn't exactly what she'd had in mind when Macey had mentioned a trip to Hollywood.

The warehouse that served as the movie set gave no indication of the film industry at all, save for the lone security officer standing outside in a horrible green uniform. No wonder she had never heard the name Eva Janis before. From the looks of the production quality, her movies probably went straight to download.

As Macey focused on parking the car, she allowed her gaze to linger on him—his chiseled jaw and an aquiline nose, rugged yet sophisticated. His dark hair also showed contrast, peppered with distinguishing grey at the temples. His body wasn't bad, either. He was tall and muscular, although he kept most of it hidden beneath that designer suit of his.

Too bad he had turned out to be such a prude. She still couldn't believe he had declined her offer last night. Few men could. But perhaps it was better that way. Macey obviously had some smarts to him, and it probably wouldn't be to her advantage to distract him. She had to keep him as sharp as he'd been last night dealing with Boreman. She still got a kick out of how aptly he had played him during their meeting. If Macey proved this good starting out, maybe this whole Greta Darling mess would be behind her sooner than she thought.

"Just follow my lead," Macey said, snapping her out of her reverie as he engaged the parking brake with a pneumatic hiss. Before she could respond, he exited the Lexus, slamming the door. As she reached for her own door, it swung upward and he waited with his hand outstretched.

And chivalrous, to boot. This wasn't the first time Macey had opened a door for her. At first she had thought it was him merely sucking up to a new employer, but he had done it enough that it was obviously part of his makeup.

"A girl could get used to this kind of treatment." She grinned as she accepted his hand.

"Sorry, I'm not available for full-time hire." He shot back a grin of his own.

Sheila chuckled and together they started toward the guard—a Hispanic man, probably a retiree, somewhere in his early seventies. Unfortunate that some people still had to endure the indignity of old age. Despite all her efforts to lower the cost of the Miracle Treatment to reach a wider market, it wasn't exactly cheap, and some people didn't know how to plan for the future. This poor old fellow seemed to fall into that category.

Macey greeted him with a nod. "Morning, sir. I need to speak with a Ms. Eva Janis. Is she shooting here today?"

"She's on set already. Who can I say's looking for her?"

"Colonel Rick Macey with the Department of Civil Defense and Intelligence."

The guard's gentle eyes widened, as did Sheila's. She didn't know much about the military but the title sounded impressive.

With the announcement of his classification Macey seemed to carry himself with an even greater sense of authority, or perhaps he always had and she was just now noticing. Either way, she fed into it and straightened up, herself.

"I'll need to see some kind of verification," the guard said.

Macey flashed the back of his right hand with a closed fist. Instantly an image appeared just under his skin, an elaborate military crest along with a silver eagle, the standard barcode ID underneath it. She'd never seen a military ID implant before. Hers had only the barcode, like most people's, but she did have a special Gentec implant that could display her company logo. Maybe she'd use that one.

The guard scanned Macey's fist with a palm-held device, studying the screen before nodding. He looked to her, but before she could offer her hand, Macey stopped her.

"She's a civilian witness. I need her to corroborate some details Ms. Janis might have about a case I'm working on. Due to its sensitive nature, I unfortunately can't volunteer her identity at this time. If it's a problem we can both remain outside while you get Ms. Janis."

"That's okay. I trust you, Colonel." The guard turned and led them toward the building. "You'd better come on in. I'll go talk to the director."

<A civilian witness? You couldn't think of anything better than that?>

<What else do you want me to call you? It was your boss's idea to bring you along, not mine. Besides, it's pretty much the truth, isn't it?>

She twisted her lips into a scowl. Just when she was starting to like this Macey guy, he went and said something that totally put her off, like when he was driving her to the office last night.

That stuff about her goal being independent of his purpose. Sure, maybe being surrounded by people who kissed her backside all day made it seem like everyone should, but some of his remarks bordered on being seriously passive-aggressive.

Why was she so worried about it anyway? This was just business. She didn't have to get Macey to like her, or even respect her. All she needed him to do was his job, and if he had to be somewhat obnoxious to do that, so be it.

The guard ushered them through a side door into the studio, which turned out to be many studios within the one warehouse. The movie sets were divided by partitions that ran to nearly the full height of the three-story ceiling. A garage door-sized entranceway was at the dead center of each one, giving access to the set within.

As they made their way along the shopping aisle-wide corridor that ran between the sets, Sheila noticed at least two other productions going on: a student film project whose participants seemed to be disagreeing on something, and a commercial for some useless device that made peeling onions faster.

At the rear of the warehouse, Eva Janis's movie set buzzed with commotion. Unit directors and prop men bustled with makeup people and stylists while the actors themselves posed repetitively before the holographic imagers, capturing scene after scene with perfection. It looked like a cheap horror flick or something.

The guard told them to wait at the edge of the set. He trotted over to a middle-aged woman wearing a baseball cap, who sat in front of a set of holographic monitors. He drew her attention and whispered something into her ear while gesturing at Sheila and Macey.

"You've got to be kidding me!" The woman lurched from her chair and clomped across the set toward them. "Can I help you people?"

"I need a word with Ms. Janis." Macey addressed her smoothly. "It shouldn't take long. You're the director?"

"That's right." She pursed her thin lips. "Look, I got ten hours to shoot six scenes. You have any idea what that means? I'm sorry, but you people are going to have to come back later."

"I'm afraid we can't do that, ma'am. We're unfortunately under time constraints of our own. We must speak with Ms. Janis. It'll only take a few minutes."

"Don't you know how to make appointments?" She tapped her imaginary wristwatch. "Time is money. I'm sorry, but you'll have to—"

"Not an option," Macey said more firmly. "I don't want to have to invoke any mandatory compliance laws, but I will if I have to. This is a Civil Defense matter."

"Whatever." The director tossed her hands in the air and glanced over her shoulder to an assistant. "Get Eva out here." She scowled at Macey. "You got twenty minutes, Mister Hotshot." She stormed off the set, muttering something about fascist governments.

Sheila smiled bemusedly. At least she wasn't the only one to feel the bite of Macey's tongue.

<Way to abuse your authority there, Mr. Macey. A Civil Defense matter? And I thought you were supposed to be retired.>

<They don't know that.> He cracked a grin, eliciting one of her own.

She definitely liked the way this Colonel Rick Macey handled things. Completely unorthodox, yet totally in control. A lot like herself, really.

<And besides, it's more a semi-retirement.>

<Semi-retirement? What's that supposed to mean?>

<Long story. Anyway, heads up. Here she is.>

Sheila looked to see Eva Janis approaching. There was no doubt that she was a Miracle Treatment recipient. At sixty years old she revealed no trace of her true age. Instead she resembled a woman in her late twenties: radiant honey-colored hair, slim build, toned caramel skin, sparking green eyes. She was exotic—beautiful in the way Hollywood demanded. She wore an 18th century blue corset and black dress. Maybe it was a period piece and not a horror film.

"Yes?" She greeted them with unmasked apprehension, her head angled to the side as she studied them, revealing two fake puncture wounds on the side of her neck.

Nope, it was a horror.

"Colonel Rick Macey with the Department of Civil Defense and Intelligence," Macey said with a quick flash of his ID tattoo. "I need to speak with you regarding a Ms. Greta Darling. Are you a friend of hers?"

"Well, yes." Her eyes widened. "Is something wrong? Has something happened to Greta?"

<Don't tell her that she's dead!> Sheila shouted through the comm—and almost in real life—her words coming out as a muffed slur beneath her breath. Her heart pounded as she cleared her throat in an attempt to cover her mistake. *<Sorry 'bout that.>*

<Don't worry.> He gave her a reassuring smile then turned to Ms. Janis. "She's gone missing, ma'am. I need your cooperation in helping to find her."

"Oh, dear," the actress whispered, her hand covering her mouth. "When did this happen?"

"That's what we're trying to determine. Please try not to be alarmed. As yet, there's no indication of foul play. It might be as simple as her having left on vacation without telling anyone, which is why we need to speak with you. Have you ever known Ms. Darling to do that?"

"Leave without saying anything?" She gave a fervent shake of her head.

"When was the last time you saw or spoke with Ms. Darling?"

"Maybe two weeks ago."

Macey shifted to the side to let some prop men brush past. "Do you recall anything different about her behavior? Was she, perhaps, overly happy or depressed?"

"Happy," she said. "In the last little while she's been very happy. The last time we spoke she said she'd met someone new."

<This could be something.> "Someone new?"

"She met him at Miracles."

<I know that place.> Sheila messaged. Now she could see the advantages of using the comm as Macey had instructed. To Ms. Janis she said, "Miracles—the club?"

"Yes."

<What's this club?> Macey's eyes shifted to her.

<A popular hangout for our clients. We subsidize it to some extent. A social mixer kind of place to get clients back into the swing of being young again. We consider it a post-treatment therapy option.>

"How much do you know about this man Ms. Darling met?" he asked Ms. Janis.

"She was never one to kiss and tell, but she did seem infatuated with him."

"Did she tell you his name?"

Ms. Janis pondered the question. "Virgil. Yes, I think it was Virgil."

"The name in the Bible," Sheila said. Realizing she had spoken aloud again she instinctively covered her mouth. No sooner had she done so than she realized the action only emphasized her error. <*Gah! I'm screwing up. Sorry!*>

Ms. Janis was staring at her now, causing her face to heat. "What did you say?"

"A Bible was found at her home," Macey said. "That name was inscribed within it. Do you recall Ms. Darling being religious or mentioning that this Virgil person was?"

Sheila breathed an inward sigh of relief as Ms. Janis's attention was drawn away from her. Macey was a quick thinker. She vowed to keep off the comm for the rest of the interview.

"Sort of," Ms. Janis said. "She said Virgil was a very spiritual person. Greta was into that sort of thing."

"What do you mean?"

"Well, she did yoga, Buddhism, Kabala. A whole bunch."

"What about Christianity?"

"Probably. I don't really know the difference between any of them. Greta loves all that silly nonsense, though."

Silly nonsense was right. Hard to believe that in this day and age people still got suckered into religion. It was just that kind of self-righteous ignorance that had to be behind this whole mess with Greta Darling—some nut-job wanting to rid the whole world of the greatest invention of the century, just because he believed the myths and fairytales of some two-thousand-year-old book.

"What about you?" Macey asked Ms. Janis. "Did Greta ever try to get you into it?"

Ms. Janis chuckled. "All the time. But unfortunately for her I have no interest in it. It's probably a phase she's going through, a third midlife crisis. She wasn't always into it."

"So she's had these . . . obsessions before?" Macey asked.

"Oh, yes. First it was travel, then studying history. After that it was looking at new homes."

"Would it surprise you, then, if Ms. Darling had left on vacation with this Virgil without telling you?"

"Well . . . I suppose not. If she went on some love getaway with a new guy, she probably wouldn't tell me until she got back."

"We're hoping that's the case," Macey said with a smile and extended his hand. "My thanks, Ms. Janis. You've been extremely helpful."

"Please keep me informed. Should I do anything? Try getting in touch with her or something?"

"Not at this point," he said. "This may all just pan out to be very normal. Don't worry, we'll contact you with any news."

They departed briskly, avoiding the director on the way out. Macey was obviously a pro at this, able to extract all the information they needed without making Ms. Janis any the wiser about the real mess. Despite herself, she was beginning to like Mr. Macey again.

<This was a lot easier than I thought it would be. We have our suspect already!>

Macey cocked a brow at her. *<We have a possible suspect, and we still have to find him.>*

<So how do we go about doing that?>

<That club sounds like a good lead. Maybe the staff or patrons know of him.>

<I can check our client database.> She increased her pace to keep up with him as they walked across the onion peeling set. *< If he frequents Miracles, he could be a recipient of the treatment.>*

<Already done that. There's no match.>

<You did?> Boy, he worked fast and thought way ahead of the game. Wait a minute. *<How'd you get access to our database?>*

Macey grew quiet as she drilled him with a stare. He had obviously revealed more about his information-gathering techniques than he had intended.

<Let's just say you might want to upgrade your company's electronic security measures.>

"You hacked our system?" She couldn't believe he had the gall to admit it, much less accomplish it. Their system was supposed to be impenetrable. And what gave him the right to try such a thing? "You've got to be kidding me. You can't break into—"

"It was in the interest of saving time." He cut her off, but not in a rude way. More how someone would to stop you from defending yourself to tell you they already knew you were innocent. She supposed he was doing the opposite in letting her know he was guilty. "It's not uncommon for CDI work, but I apologize. Sometimes I forget which privileges are within my rights when I'm working on the outside."

She gazed back at him, wondering if Mr. Macey wasn't more rogue than cop. On the bright side, she supposed she should be grateful to him for finding a flaw in their system. She made a mental note to have it looked into by their electronic security team, but she let the issue drop for now. After all, Macey's skills, whether aboveboard or below, had gotten them this far.

"All right, you're getting off with a warning, Mister Cyberhacker," she said with a smirk. "Though I'd appreciate you telling me how you managed to get past my security."

"It wasn't anything special. Here, you can forward it to your security agency or wherever it needs to go." A second later she received an emailed file from him.

As they passed the security guard, he gave them a wave. Sheila considered passing him her business card. But why bother? If he still had to be working at his age, no way could he afford the treatment.

It was almost criminal. So many people still had to end up in state-run retirement homes, their twilight years dwindling in obscurity, loneliness, and insignificance. Merely because they lacked the resources to afford the better life the Miracle Treatment could provide. Before this whole Greta Darling mess had broken, Sheila had been well on her way to brokering a deal with the federal government to spend social insurance funds on Miracle Treatment vouchers rather than Medicare and seniors' homes.

It was financially viable, she had proven that. But, as with any government, the political wheels needed a lot of greasing before they would turn. A goal she couldn't even dream about achieving if news of Greta Darling got out. They needed to find proof of this conspiracy. Only then could people like that guard have a chance of an endlessly healthy life.

Macey punched the general direction of the New City Center into the auto-drive and reclined his seat so they could converse about their next plan of action. The club was a good lead, but there were other avenues he wanted to explore.

Sheila beat him to the punch. "That club won't open for a while. What's our next move till then?"

He smiled at her eagerness. "There's another angle I want to explore, but I need your input."

"What's that?"

"There's one sure way to track a terrorist. Through his tools."

"Tools?"

"Your average terrorist rarely possesses the background to create the tools of his trade. Terrorists love nukes, for example, but you're not likely find one who's a nuclear physicist. This case is no different. If we uncover a religious conspiracy surrounding Ms. Darling's death, they would have needed help making a drug or toxin to make her death seem natural, right?"

"Of course. That's what I meant when I said it was as if *something* had been introduced to somehow negate Greta Darling's Miracle Treatment."

"So my question to you is this: who would have the capability of developing something like that?"

She stared at the dashboard. "Besides Jules and myself . . . probably just our internal R&D team. Since yesterday I've had them trying to synthesize an agent that could nullify the effects of our product. We're calling it a negating agent."

Macey rocked his jaw. "Guess it was somewhat presumptuous of me to assume you hadn't thought to check this avenue already. Who's this Jules?"

"Oh, I'm sorry. Doctor Julian Hague: the original designer of the Miracle Treatment. He worked for Heliox Corp before we took them over. He's retired from our firm now, but we keep him on retainer. He was the first one I called when I heard the news about Greta Darling."

"I see. And what was his reaction?"

"He was totally shocked, of course. At first he didn't want to believe that there could be an agent that could wipe out our Miracle Treatment. But after he considered the alternative, that the Miracle Treatment had failed, he set to work on his own substance."

"So you wouldn't consider him a suspect?"

"Jules?" She glanced at him from the corner of her eye with a you've-got-to-be-kidding sort of expression. "This was his baby. That'd be like the pope actually admitting the Koran isn't real or something."

"The Bible, you mean."

"What?"

"The pope would admit the Bible isn't . . ." He shook his head. "Never mind. What about your other staff? Would any of them have the motive to do something like this?"

"Extremely doubtful. I went to great lengths setting up profit-sharing for all our research staff for this very reason. No way was I going to let someone steal our golden goose. I know these people personally. This stuff is their life, literally."

The mid-morning sun beamed through the windshield as the Lexus crested an overpass. "You mean they're all clients?"

"Yup."

He drummed his fingers. "There's always the chance that one of your employees is being blackmailed."

Her brow creased. "I didn't think of that."

"Is it possible for a single person to create something like this negating agent?"

Sheila leaned against the car door. "It'd be extremely difficult. Of the same order as what it took to create the Miracle Treatment itself. And that took a team tens of years. I seriously doubt it."

"So unless your entire team has been blackmailed for the last few decades, it's more likely that a rival genetics firm is behind this."

"I thought of that too, but the motive doesn't make much sense. Gentec holds the patent rights on the Miracle Treatment for another twenty-odd years, so until they expire we basically have no competition. Doing something like this would bring no one else any gain, just us great loss. This would be purely out of spite, which is why when I saw that Bible I knew there had to be some whack-job religious cult behind it."

"But even if that's true, it doesn't answer the question of how this 'whack-job cult' gained the capability to do this."

"You're right." She pursed her lips. "Let me call Jules. Maybe he's found something by now."

As she connected via her neural net, Macey gazed out the window at the hills in the distance. A thick column of smoke was billowing atop one of them. Fire season again.

"Jules, what do you have?" Again she spoke into her comm aloud, her expression puckering as she listened. "Well, what is it? Okay, I'm on my way." She disconnected. "He's found something, but refused to discuss it over the net."

Macey snapped the car's controls to manual. "Where to?"

Forty-five minutes later they were at the entrance to Dr. Julian Hague's private lab in the center of the Old Town's warehouse district.

Since the last quake, much of the Old Town area had been deemed non-feasible to rebuild. Decaying buildings and all kinds of rusted equipment littered lot after lot for miles. Not the place you would expect to find a fully functioning genetics lab. Then again, if you were spending your own money on a private facility, the lower property values made sense.

Still, as Sheila repeatedly keyed the antiquated buzzer on the door, Macey was almost expecting no one to answer. Finally, the garage door they were standing in front of hummed upward and a man stood within.

A young man.

Dr. Julian Hague was nowhere near the "man" Macey had anticipated. Although he knew not to expect a stereotypical full-bearded scientist with Coke-bottle glasses and a balding head, Doctor Hague's appearance was startling nonetheless. He had taken his use of the Miracle Treatment to an extreme. Now he appeared no more than eighteen years old.

The sight of him gave Macey a flashback to the Streetwalker Sniper. It hadn't occurred to him to check if the Sniper had been a Miracle Treatment recipient. He had no idea people actually opted to look so young.

Dr. Hague wore jeans and a T-shirt. His hair was a ruddy brown mop parted in the center. The bright blue gaze of his steely eyes was the only part of him that conveyed any sense of his true age, which Macey figured would have to be somewhere in the seventies.

Hague stiffened when he spotted Macey. "Who is this, Sheila?" He gave a jerk of his head.

"Relax, Jules." She strolled inside. The garage served as a laboratory, filled with computers and equipment. "This is Rick Macey. He's a private investigator helping me with the case."

Macey nodded in greeting, but Hague retained his rigid posture.

"Wish you would have said something." He keyed the garage door to close behind them. "I have sensitive equipment in here."

Macey took note of the contents of the lab, but little of it made sense to him. He could barely identify the stacks of laboratory apparatus amid the numerous computer workstations that scrolled data across their holographic screens. In the rear of the garage, against the back wall, was a kennel, which he imagined housed animals for testing.

"Dr. Hague," Macey said, "you said you had some information you weren't willing to share over the net."

Doctor Babyface shot an agitated glare at Sheila.

"It's all right, Jules," she said like a mother soothing a troubled teen. "You're too paranoid. He's on the case with us. Go ahead and tell us what you found. A negating agent, I hope."

He folded his arms and sat on the corner of a desk covered with glass vials. "I wish."

"So?"

Again, Hague eyed him suspiciously. "I'm sorry if I appear lacking in manners, Mr. . . . Macey, was it? But as you can probably tell, I'm not in the best of moods."

"No apology necessary." He tried to lighten the atmosphere with a smile. "I understand the situation you're in here."

"What's your background, if I may ask?" Hague slipped his hands into his jean pockets.

"Civil Defense and Intelligence," Macey said. "Retired."

"Counterterrorism?" He arched his eyebrows and looked at Sheila. "Do you really think there's terrorism going on here? There's some evidence of this?"

"It depends more on what you have to tell us, Jules," Sheila said. "So what did you find?"

"If that's the case, you may not want to hear it. We may have a really big problem here, Sheila."

"Such as?"

"Well, I've been up for over twenty-four hours and haven't been able to come up with anything that could work as a negating agent."

"C'mon, Jules. It's only been one day. Give yourself some time." She grinned with encouragement. "Have you been in contact with the main lab? I'm sure my guys are eager to hear what you have so far. Maybe you can collab—"

"That's not it." He sagged against the wall and slid into a crouched position, looking every bit the college student agonizing over a final exam. "I've . . . found a flaw."

Macey shot a glance to Sheila, who blinked several times.

She crouched to Jules's level. "A flaw? What do you mean?"

"In the Miracle Treatment itself." His hands clasped over his nose and mouth as if reluctant to utter anything more. "There is a chance there could be a flaw."

"What are you talking about? There is no flaw!" She shouted at him the same way she had at Roger Boreman, jumping to her feet and jabbing a finger into his face. "You need to take a break, Julian. This isn't going to help us. Just start again. There's no chance of a flaw—"

"There is," he said calmly. "A strong possibility anyway."

Macey didn't even want to think where this could lead them.

"Stop this nonsense." Sheila threw a hand in his face. "How many tests have we run all these years? How many models? All of them prove our product."

"They're all old models!" He raised his voice to match hers. "The same old models I created. Same old parameters."

"So what's changed then?"

"This . . ." He threw his hands into the air non-descriptively. "This whole idea of a negating agent. It caused me to rethink the whole process, try new parameters. And when I applied them to the model . . . I saw the possibility of the treatment failing, on its own."

"You saw a possibility? Where? Show me." She started toward the mass of computers and lab equipment.

"Don't touch anything." He scurried after her. "I'm running another simulation right now. It won't be finished for another six hours."

She wheeled about. "Jules, you're not making this easy." Her eyes went wide. "Wait! Did Boreman call you and put this idea into your head?"

"No. He hasn't contacted me at all."

"Good. And don't you call him either. And if he tries to get hold of you, don't tell him about this possible flaw."

"Why not?"

"Just . . . don't worry about it right now." She waved her hand as if batting away a fly. "Look, Jules, I know how much this means to you. It means a lot to me too. But I think you're just under a lot of stress and probably burned out. Go home, get some sleep. And when you come back, concentrate on finding the negating agent. That other stuff with the flaw is probably an error."

"An error? Are you telling me *I* made an error?"

Sheila cocked her head to the side with one hand on her hip. "Well, either you made one now or you made one back then, right?"

Hague grew silent. His chest heaved and his eyes glazed over with a mixture of indignation and contempt.

Macey took a step closer to stand in between them. <*Think you better calm him down, Sheila. This guy looks ready to rush you.*>

"Okay fine." Sheila raised her hands in surrender. "I didn't mean to insult you, all right? All I'm saying is check your work. We both know how stringent our testing parameters were. It's not likely that something could have slipped by all these years, is it?"

"I have my results," he said detachedly, "but I will retest if you want me to, and I will continue to search for a negating agent."

"Fine. Is there anything else?"

He shook his head and keyed for the garage door to open.

<*Guess that's our cue to leave.*> Macey glanced toward the door. <*I think you ticked him off.*>

Sheila headed for the doorway as soon as it was open. Macey hustled after her to keep up. They climbed back into the Lexus just as the garage door began closing itself again. He waited for it to shut fully before starting the car.

"Where to now?" He noticed Sheila sat staring into space, her violet eyes glassy and shimmering. He killed the engine. "Hey, are you okay?"

She blinked a few times. "This can't be happening." Her voice was a hoarse whisper. "What if I'm really wrong?"

"Wrong? About what?"

"The treatment. Everything."

"What are you talking about? You said yourself the guy's burned out and made some mistakes. He'll probably call you later confirming—"

"I said that more for myself than for him!" Sheila leaned her forehead against the dash. "Jules understands the Miracle

Treatment better than anyone else possibly could. He created the thing. And what he said in there was true. He doesn't make mistakes. If he says he might have found a flaw, there's a real good chance there is one." She gently banged her head on the console. "What am I going to do if it really is true?"

The cool and confidant demeanor he had come to expect of Sheila Dunn was dissolving. Her brows were furrowed, her eyes glistened. "What if I've messed up?" She gazed up through the windshield, her eyes fixed on nothing. "What if I've gone and marketed this stupid thing to the whole world and it doesn't even work?"

She remained quiet for a long while, a single tear trickling down her cheek, her bottom lip quivering, her knee bouncing. In that moment she looked like a little girl, lost and afraid for the first time.

"Hey, easy, kiddo." Macey took hold of her hand, squeezed it firmly. "Don't lose faith in what you believe in, all right? This was only one angle, remember? We have a whole other avenue to explore, and a good lead to boot. We're going to find our suspect, Sheila. I promise you that."

She looked up at him, her eyes reddened but without any more tears. She nodded and he released her hand. As he restarted the car and pulled away from the warehouse, Sheila wiped her face and sniffled. "I must look a mess." She laughed a little and pulled down the vanity mirror.

Macey smiled at her.

Still look good to me, he wanted to say.

Smeared makeup and all.

CHAPTER FOUR

ON THE WAY BACK from Hague's lab, and against his better judgment, Macey suggested they get something to eat. From what little he knew about Sheila, he knew she enjoyed eating. She perked up at the idea and, as they had some time, she picked a high-classed French joint located in the New City.

Traffic and finding a parking space proved a nightmare, especially during the lunch-hour rush, but eventually they found a spot and were escorted to a table on the top terrace of the restaurant, thanks to Sheila's VP status.

Macey managed to get by with a light appetizer without drawing too much protest from Sheila, who was convinced his meager meal stemmed from her picking up the tab. After a few glasses of wine she seemed to forget about it. He managed to sneak off to the restroom to wolf down an energy bar on top of the shrimp cocktail he had already eaten. Back at the table he kept the conversation light while they waited 'til early afternoon for Club Miracle to open.

He hated waiting, especially on a case with a timeframe, but it couldn't be helped. As always, he made good use of the lull. Between interjecting words of affirmation into Sheila's monologue-like conversation, he snuck a peek at the official police report on the Streetwalker Sniper case and lifted the kid's real name—Philip Walden.

He then hacked back into Sheila's company database and cross-referenced the name, finding a match. As suspected, the kid wasn't a kid at all. He was close to eighty, and on top of that a war vet. In a sense he felt relieved. At least the pieces finally fit together, and Philip Walden gave him a halfway decent lead in the current case: military background, a Miracle Treatment recipient, and, most of all, religiously motivated to murder.

"Time to go," he told Sheila.

"Already? Is the club open, you think?"

"We need to make a quick stop before that."

"Where?"

Macey grinned. "Jail."

An hour later they entered the old Hollenbeck Police Division in downtown LA. The place never seemed to change.

Flickering halogen lamps hung from loose mountings, their dull blue light painting the thirty-by-thirty entranceway in a dingy hue, like a morgue. A checkerboard motif covered the vinyl floor of the jail's public area, though the colors were now black and yellow instead of black and white. Rows of steel chairs were bolted to the floor.

Scores of cyber-gangers of all creeds thronged the entranceway, clashing with cops in tactical gear. The din of their shouting matches added to the general chaos of the cramped confines and graffiti-strewn walls.

As Macey approached the plexisteel-shielded duty desk toward the back, a bronze skinned, seven-foot-tall *Rudeboi* with five-foot dreadlocks, white eyes, and dual Krueger claws careened into it ahead of him, manhandled by three cops from behind. The reek of marijuana smoke and unwashed hair followed, almost triggering his gag reflex before he had a chance to filter it out. He spotted a cyberlock jutting from the side of the Rudeboi's neck, keeping his body immobilized, but apparently it lacked the ability to curtail his speech.

"Police brutality!" Spit flew from his goatee, followed by a string of Jamaican patois. "Chichimon babylon dem."

"You want brutality?" One of the cops slammed her rifle butt into his kidneys. "Bantu rapist mother—"

Her verbal and physical assault continued for several more blows, eliciting howls of pain and rage from the cyber-ganger before one of her partners finally decided to intervene.

"All right, all right; don't kill him. Should've done that before we got here, like we told you to. Now we gotta do the paperwork."

Macey tuned out the rest of the cop's lecture as he wandered to the far side of the desk. Sheila clung to the back of his suit jacket like a frightened child.

<Macey, did you just see all that?>

<Tried not to. Take it you don't experience this kind of thing too often.>

<And you do?>

More than he'd like to admit, but that didn't make him enjoy it any more than Sheila did. Sadly, this was the true face of Los Angeles: bloodthirsty gangs versus burned-out cops. It was a far cry from the façade of the New City, where the wealthy worked and played.

"What you doing here, Mace?"

He glanced up to see the duty officer grinning at him from behind the plexisteel shielding, so scratched it now looked frosted. But even that couldn't hide Reggie Braxton's thousand-watt smile. Reggie was a pretty black girl in her thirties, her real thirties, with a bubbly personality to match—so long as you were on the right side of the law.

"To have you brighten my day." Macey mirrored her smile. "You look as radiant as ever, Reggie. How you been?"

"Same ol', same ol', as you can see." She laughed and gestured toward the Rudeboi now groaning on the floor next to a trio of spindly Gothers. "What you need, baby?"

"To see that sniper suspect you got locked up. Got another case I'm working on that might tie into him."

"Come on," she said without a second thought and led them toward the cell blocks. "Least I can do for the guy who nabbed the sick little freak."

<She an old friend of yours?> Sheila asked.

<New one, I'd say. Reggie's good people. Honest.>

<Thought that was supposed to be one of the job requirements. What are we going to say to this guy anyway?>

<Don't worry. I'll handle it.>

Reggie led them through several security doors and finally into the isolation cell block.

Philip Walden, the Streetwalker Sniper, sat on the edge of his cot, Bible in hand—the good little Christian boy. He barely moved as Reggie opened his cell door and let them inside.

"You know what to do if he gets out of hand," Reggie said. "The guard's just down the hall and he can hear you through the comm."

"Thank you, miss." Sheila nodded to Reggie, jumping as the cell door banged shut.

<*Stay by the door.*> Macey took position directly in front of the Sniper. "I want to ask you some questions, Philip. Do you recognize me?"

"Sure," Philip said not looking up. "You're the cowardly pig."

<*What did he just call you?*>

<*Never mind.*> "Nice memory. Let's test it some more. Tell me . . . why did you get the Miracle Treatment?"

"What's that got to do with anything?" Philip set aside his Bible and made eye contact. "And why do you expect me to cooperate with you? I'm not looking to lessen my sentence."

"That's well understood. And if it's any reassurance, you'll most likely get what you're looking for. The death penalty. But I'm not here regarding that. I only want some information you might be privy to. From where I stand you have nothing to lose from telling me, and everything to gain."

"Gain? What can I gain from helping you?"

"Purpose."

"What's that supposed to mean?"

"Right now the media has you pegged as a psychotic nut-job. That's all you'll be remembered as. No matter how much you claim a righteous cause, people won't see you any different than any other psychos who claimed 'God told me to do it.' Was that your true purpose? To be labeled a psycho? As I recall, on that roof you had quite a different vision."

"So what?"

"So I can tell your real story. People won't believe you, but they'll believe me."

"What makes you so special, pig?"

"For twenty years I was head of CDI's Religious Terrorism division. My testimony can mean the difference between you dying a simple murderer or a religious martyr. Which do you choose? Or rather, which do you think God would want you to choose?"

Philip, the old man now made a boy, chortled at the idea. "So what do you want to know?"

"Virgil. You ever heard the name?"

"Poet wasn't he?" Philip said with a quiet laugh.

<This guy doesn't know anything.> Sheila rolled her eyes. *<He's just going to jerk us around.>*

"I was thinking of a more recent incarnation," Macey said. "Someone who perhaps shares the same ideals as you?"

"Not a chance."

"All right," she said aloud. "We're wasting our time. Let's go."

"Not a chance that he would share the same ideals." Philip clarified his statement and smirked at her.

"So you do know him then?" Macey said.

"I've run into him here and there. As I said, we don't see eye to eye. I'm actually a bit intrigued. Has Mother Teresa finally struck a bold blow for God?"

"What do you mean by that?" Sheila asked. "Are you saying he's a terrorist like you? An extremist?"

"I don't like those terms." Philip looked away from her and back to Macey. "Virgil is a spook, always hanging in the shadows. He's no Christian soldier, not like me. He's more like the poet than you think, Pig-man. A coward, like the rest of you."

Sheila edged back toward to cell door. <*This guy is nuts. You know that, right, Macey?*>

"What's he look like?" Macey asked.

"Big bald black guy. Wears shades all the time."

Sheila snorted, bemused. <*Well, that narrows it down to half the guys in LA.*>

"Where can I find him?"

"I wouldn't know. He always found me."

"What about this place called Miracles, you ever known him to frequent there?"

"Like I said, I wouldn't know. Me and him weren't exactly friends, understand?"

<*Okay, I think we've got enough. At least we know Virgil is in the city.*> Macey called for the guard to release them. "Thank you, Philip. Actually, I have another question for you."

"Shoot."

"What made you change your mind?"

"About what?"

"Life. You got the Miracle Treatment but now you want to die. Seems a waste of perfectly good money to me."

Philip rolled onto his cot and stared at the ceiling, his scrawny kid-arms clasped behind his head. "Your type would probably never understand this, but I'll try to explain anyway. Life isn't what you think it is. It's like this." He gestured to his surroundings. "If you people want to stay here and rot in this jail, that's fine. But me, I've had my fill."

<*What a nut-job.*> Sheila frowned. <*Can we please leave now?*>

"One last question," Macey said. "With the treatment, you could become any age you wanted to. So why a kid?"

Philip the Streetwalker Sniper smiled at him and shrugged. "Guess I wanted to feel innocent again."

"Quite a challenge. I don't think any of us can truly feel innocent after Utah. I can only imagine how it must have been for you, a sniper. At least I didn't have to see their faces half the time."

The smile dropped from Philip's lips and he sat upright. "What the hell do you know about Utah?"

With a buzz the door rumbled open. "All done?" the policeman asked.

"Yeah. We're done."

"You get back here," Philip shouted, jumping from his cot and lunging at him with a closed fist. Macey blocked the attack with his forearm, quickly palmed Philip's hand within his own, and forced him to the floor.

"Macey!" Sheila cried and stumbled backward out of the cell and into the policeman.

"This can't be real." Philip stared upward at him, awe on his face. "You're just like him, aren't you?"

Macey tossed him aside. "Let's go, Sheila."

"What did he mean by that?" she asked as he stomped by her and the policeman. "Macey?"

He didn't answer. Neither did he stop.

• • •

Pooly was early, as usual. This time the Freak had picked an old parking garage, which he was actually quite thankful for since it allowed him to *drive* to the top. He'd parked his jet-black Bronco near the center of the deserted rooftop and was now surrounded by four of his guys he'd brought along for added protection.

The extra security was necessary. Not that it mattered to the Freak, but the location he had picked happened to be deep in cyber-ganger land, and Pooly wasn't well liked by any of the factions.

The roof was the size of a football field. Its faded concrete surface was littered with a smattering of decade-old cars—their rust-drip paint jobs now bathed in the warm orange glow of the fading sun.

From near the edge of the twelve-story structure, he had a good view overlooking the burned-out core of the old downtown. Already, pockets of cyber-gangers were congregating as twilight neared.

"Just like cockroaches." He couldn't wait 'til he didn't have to rub shoulders with the likes of them. This deal offered a good chance of that.

As if to emphasize his point, a pack of Reavers suddenly burst from an abandoned building below, their tell-tale white trench coats becoming capes as they chased down some punk caught in the wrong place at the wrong time.

It was no contest really. The Reavers used their speedhack boost, outpacing their quarry by miles. In seconds the dozen white trenches cut the punk off and encircled him, looking like the reflection in a fun house mirror with their identical bald heads, tech shades, and black Glock handguns, which they pulled from their coats with synchronized unity.

The poor sod was on his knees, hands raised, begging. Again the Glocks moved in unison, this time lowering to an executioner's angle. Twelve muzzles flashed at once, their thunderous report sounding a half second later across the distance. The punk fell and shuddered twice before going still. The Reavers peeled off, strolling back toward their haunt in a V formation.

"Man, that was cold," one of Pooly's guys, Troy, said. "Hope those psychos don't come up here."

"Yeah, me neither," Pooly said. Then he noticed all four of his men were peering over the wall with him. "Hey, how you supposed to keep lookout if you're all—"

The concrete trembled beneath his feet. A cue that, somewhere on the roof, his client had touched down.

"Never mind."

Pooly turned about to see the Freak approaching them from behind. His white overcoat billowed to reveal his usual GI Joe getup beneath. It hadn't hit him until now, but that was probably why the Freak creeped him out so much. He looked just like one of them stinkin' Reavers. Probably even took the coat off of one. And that was no easy task.

The Freak jumped on top of a car and sat on its roof, his weight causing the rusted metal to groan. "You brought company, Gordon. What's the occasion?"

Pooly held out the encryption device for him to jack into, then answered. "You're the one who picks the spots. If you want to keep these deals one-on-one, stick to more civilized territory."

"Your men do not concern me. Are the units ready?"

"That's why I contacted yah. Where and when do you want the drop?"

The Freak hopped off the car top with a metal squeak and scanned the surroundings. He approached the ledge, peered over it to the empty streets below. "Here seems nice. Make it tomorrow, same time."

"Fine. Just so you know: I'll be bringing my guys again." He looked down at the punk's body. It was now being hacked up and looted for parts by organ-rippers. "Maybe even a few extra."

"If you deem it necessary."

"Hey, have you been checking the nets? There's a whole lot of hoopla starting up about this stuff in the media. You'd better watch out. I heard there's some CDI investigation going on too."

"CDI?" he said. "That's a name I haven't heard in a very long time."

"Well, you'd better check it out. I don't want anything going down on this deal. I want this to be clean, understood?"

"I'll look into it. It is probably simply all part of the plan."

"What plan?"

"His." The Freak pointed skyward. "'For as the heavens are higher than the earth, so are my ways higher than your ways, and my thoughts than your thoughts.' Who can know what purpose God has planned, Gordon?"

"Whatever, yo." What a psycho Jesus freak. "Just be here on time and let's—"

Again the Freak didn't wait for him to finish. He just leapt off the roof like a giant cricket.

Pooly didn't bother waiting to see whether he lived or died when he landed. The Freak was one client he couldn't wait to be rid of.

"One more day," Pooly muttered, shaking his head as he returned to his car. "One more freakin' day."

• • •

Macey and Sheila arrived at Club Miracle around 7:00 p.m. It was located in the western section of the new downtown, which meant it was less crowded than the city center. Lower buildings here, and more pedestrian-friendly streets. The club itself stood one story high and was situated at the corner of the block, bearing the words "Club Miracle" in a simple white hologram on an otherwise completely black façade. Macey parked across the street and they made their way inside.

Inside, the air was artificially chilled and tinted with cigarette smoke wafting from the handful of patrons at the bar. The layout was typical of these places: sunken dance floor, several lounges to the side, bars at both ends, and a roped-off VIP section toward the back. The music was an eclectic mixture of oldies from the twenties and thirties. A comfortable place. Macey could see why Gentec's clients would like it here.

Macey stepped into the club interior just ahead of Sheila. "How come I haven't heard of this place before?"

"They don't advertise," Sheila said. "A deliberate tactic to keep it exclusive. Many of our clients are celebrities."

"Does it work?"

"No idea. I never come here. This place is way too old-fashioned for me."

Macey smiled. "Let's start with the bartender."

The bartender looked out of place in the swanky club. He was in his twenties, sporting tattoos, lip-piercings, and a shaved head. He was adorned with the trademark of the Blitzer crowd, a new-age version of the classic punk: several external memory devices screwed directly into his skull, designed to look like vacuum tubes in a sort of retro-chic fashion statement. The bartender had made a vacuum-tube Mohawk out of his.

Macey had to hide his disdain for the fashion trend as he sat at the bar and drew the young man's attention.

"What'll you 'ave?" he asked in a British accent.

"Tonic water with lime." Macey looked to Sheila for her order.

"A Manhattan, please."

He waited for the drinks to arrive before beginning his questioning. "I was wondering if you could help me with something."

The bartender paused, his vacuum tubes sparkling as he gave a nod. "Sure, mate. What is it?"

"Looking for a friend of mine I haven't seen in a while. I heard he might hang out here. Bald black guy, wears shades all the time. Name's Virgil."

The bartender nibbled on the silver hoop jutting through his bottom lip and sized him up. "I might've seen him a few times, yeah."

So the punk knew, but he wanted something for his information. Irritating. With a decent RF transmitter he could hack into the Blitzer's neural net through his exposed vacuum-tube hairdo and extract whatever information he wanted directly from his brain. Luckily for the bartender, such actions were not only illegal but against Macey's personal code of ethics. Although if it were legal, he would be tempted to make an exception in this guy's case.

"Know where I can find him?" Reluctantly he drew a few bills from his pocket and slid them over the bar.

The Blitzer's shaved eyebrows rose. "Dunno where he is. But I know someone who might. There's this German guy, Kestler, comes in here all the time. Knows everybody in the place. He's a . . . well . . . he gets people things they want, yeah? I'll leave it at that. I used to see him with Virgil. Think they were in the same kind of business."

"Where do I find this Kestler?"

"He shows up most nights around eight or nine."

Macey reluctantly offered a bit more cash. "I'd appreciate it if you could point him out to me."

"Sure thing, mate." His grin showed off his steel-plated teeth as he tucked the bills away.

Macey suppressed a frown as he collected his drink and pointed to the nearest lounge. "We'll be over here." He led Sheila across the bar to a couch with a small glass table in front of it.

"So are we just going to wait for two hours?" Sheila asked as she sat down.

"Can't think of much else to do." He eased back in the comfortable couch and took in more of the place.

It was starting to fill now. Mostly office types catching the happy hour after work. The music was good and he could almost relax, but he knew the inevitable was coming. It had been a silent trip from the police station and it was just a matter of time before the subject came up again. It took about five minutes.

"So what did that sniper guy mean earlier?" Sheila said. "About you being just like someone else."

"Who knows? The guy's nuts, you said it yourself."

She fixed him with her violet stare. "Look, if you don't want to tell me, you can just say so. I need to know if this will have any bearing on the case, that's all."

"A negative bearing, you mean?"

"I didn't say that."

He took another sip of his tonic, stalling for time more than anything else. "'I have yet many things to say unto you, but ye cannot bear them now.'"

"What's that supposed to mean?"

"It's in the Bible. John, sixteen twelve."

She leaned into the couch, folding her arms. "You're really starting to freak me out here, Macey."

He chuckled. "If you want the truth then yes, there's more going on here than you know about. Will it affect the case any? I don't think so."

"Why the big secret then? I thought we were supposed to be partners on this case. We should share information."

"We're not partners," he said. "You are my client and I'm providing you a service. I already told you I had other reasons for taking this case and I'm not under any obligation to reveal them to you."

"Why wouldn't you?"

"Because it's personal."

Sheila grabbed her Manhattan and tossed it back before slamming the empty glass on the table between them. "I'm getting another drink."

Macey sighed and rubbed his temples. It was going to be a long night.

As the hours went by and the club got louder, Macey tried to reestablish friendly communications with Sheila. But she wasn't biting. It had been a long time since he'd had to deal with a woman. He'd forgotten how quickly their feelings got hurt, even a tough-as-nails broad like Sheila.

All he'd done was reinforce their professional ground rules, but now she was taking the concept to the hilt: no idle chit-chat, just the plain facts. That was fine by him, but he could tell she was hating every minute of it—and growing even more annoyed because he wasn't.

As the place filled, he suggested they mingle and try to pick up some leads. She warmed to the idea and quickly took off on her own, hitting the bar to flirt with some twenty-something-looking guys in business suits.

Macey stayed within the lounge area to keep an eye out for the bartender's signal in case the Kestler guy came in. He spotted a trio of ladies sitting together and ordered them a round of drinks before heading over to introduce himself. The art of social interaction was a skill he hadn't used in quite a while but, like riding a bike, it returned with ease.

He befriended the three women quickly, discovered their names and learned they were all Gentec clients. They ranged in age from sixty to eighty, but all looked about thirty, of course, and dazzling at that. The youngest and most jovial, Gina, was approaching retirement and was full of plans to travel. The two older women, Susan and Beth, had already done almost everything Gina mentioned, so they spent most of the conversation commenting on how much better things used to be. Before the conversation became too depressing, Macey asked about Virgil, but none of them had heard of him.

After repeating the process with different groups around the club, he mused on the sampling of the demographics. Eighty and ninety-something Gentec celebrities cavorting with hot supermodels a fraction their age. Goths and techies created a morgue-like silence within their booths. They were plugged in, enjoying the virtual side of the club in an extravagance of debauchery that made even the most X-rated possibilities in the real world seem like Sunday school. He spent as little time as possible in that area of the club.

But even the real world was becoming a bit sickening. It was nearly impossible to tell who was a Gentec client and who was not, with everyone looking so oh-so-thirty-something-TV-gorgeous. The revolving door of pretty plastic people began blending into a homogeneous mass of nauseatingly sweet eye candy.

A new distinction within the group began to emerge. The newer Gentec clients were full of energy and zeal, excited about their new lease on life and keen to waste it on whatever sensory excitement they could afford—cars, houses, travel, food, alcohol, drugs, sex. Whatever was within their reach. The older ones reminded him of high school burn-outs, jaded and unimpressed by anything. Sadly, that was something he could identify with himself.

Despite the head-swimming exposure to the lifestyles of the rich and immortal, he managed to dig up a few more leads on Virgil. Some people knew of him, a few even remembered seeing him with Greta Darling. Almost all knew of Kestler, and that was a promising sign.

By the time he and Sheila rendezvoused at the lounge again it was close to 10:00 p.m. She began to relate the number of embarrassing sexual advances she had received and how funny she found them, but then seemed to remember she was mad at him, and suddenly clammed up again.

"Will you stop with the emotional embargo, Sheila? There's no reason we can't talk openly."

"You have a reason, apparently."

He released a sigh and then sat forward on the edge of his couch, resting his tonic water on the glass table in front of them. "All right, I'll make a deal with you."

"A deal?"

"Everything you want to know is in my external memory. I'll drop the firewall for five minutes and you can have a look. How's that?"

She nibbled her bottom lip. "Are you serious?"

"The wall's down now."

"How do I know?"

"You don't and that's the deal. If you can't trust me that I've dropped the wall, then I can't trust you to find out what's behind it."

She tapped her lower lip with her index finger. Eventually she smirked and threw a napkin on the table. "Fine, you win. Keep your little secrets to yourself."

He chortled when she smiled again. "Had your chance."

"So what did you find out from the schmoozers?"

He told her. Not surprisingly, she had collected much of the same information, plus a few pick-up lines that had them both laughing and feeling at ease again. Eventually she apologized for prying into his personal life, and he reassured her that what he couldn't share with her would in no way impact the case. At least he honestly hoped it wouldn't.

From the corner of his vision he noticed the bartender gesturing. As he made eye contact, the punk tapped a man at the bar—a lanky fellow with a blond ponytail and a trimmed goatee. Kestler. The bartender said something to him and pointed in Macey's direction. When he and Kestler locked eyes his features contorted with anxiety and panic. He shot a glance at the door and back to Macey, then bolted.

Great. "Kestler's running." Macey leapt from his seat. "Let's go!"

"What?" Sheila dropped her drink and followed him across the dance floor. "Where is he?"

<*Head for the door.*> Macey pushed patrons out of the way.

By the time he made it through the entrance and onto the curb, Kestler was diving into a blue Chevy sedan parked near the end of the block. Sheila emerged from the club behind him just as the Chevy's headlights lit and its motor revved, pulling away with a screech of tires and locking into an immediate U-turn, peeling off in the opposite direction.

"Come on!" Macey dashed across the street, unlocked the Lexus, and jumped into the passenger seat. "You drive."

"What? But I don't—"

"Drive!" He flung open the driver's door. "Don't think, just drive."

She clambered in and he hit the ignition for her. The seat and steering wheel auto-adjusted to her height. She tapped the accelerator and pulled out of the parking bay shakily, almost hitting the car in front of them before taking off in the same direction as Kestler.

"Speed up! Speed up!" He jacked a wire into the back of his neck.

She leaned hard on the gas. The powerful car accelerated rapidly, the side streets streaking by in a blur as the Lexus ate up the road between Kestler and themselves. Ahead a traffic light changed color and she began to slow.

"No, go through it!"

"What?"

"Go! Go!"

She screamed and half closed her eyes as she pegged the gas at the last minute and punched the Lexus through the intersection.

Amazement dawned on her face as they came through unscathed on the other side. “Macey, this isn’t funny,” she yelled at him. “Why am *I* driving?”

“Shut up. Turn right.”

“What?”

“Now!”

She tugged the wheel and the Lexus spun sideways. Beams from the oncoming traffic glared through the windscreen as the air filled with the alarm of blaring horns. With another scream she nearly let go of the wheel, but Macey grabbed it and yanked it in the opposite direction, causing the Lexus to straighten and swerve, avoiding a collision.

“Keep going,” he said to her calmly. “If that happens again, counter-steer.”

“What?”

He stared dead ahead as he tracked their quarry.

“Macey?”

“Straight.” He tried to tune her out. “Just keep going straight.”

She kept on the gas. The road was deserted, not another car for blocks. Eventually he spotted the Chevy.

“Make a right here.”

Sheila worked the wheel sloppily but managed to keep the Lexus on all fours through another power skid. She regained control and they slid into a side street that led almost immediately into an onramp.

“The highway?” Panic tinged her voice.

“Almost there.”

"Almost where?"

He pointed to the left and the merging traffic. Slightly ahead of them, Kestler's blue Chevy was swerving in and out of the lanes. "Don't try to catch him. Just keep pace."

She nodded and sped up.

The Chevy dodged other vehicles, making its way haphazardly toward the slow lane. Suddenly its brake lights lit and its tail end lifted as the car went into a nosedive. A puff of white smoke emitted from the tires as it halted on the shoulder.

"Stop behind him," Macey said.

She did so just barely, causing a massive tire screech of their own as she brought the Lexus to a stop inches from Kestler's vehicle.

"Good job, kiddo." He pulled the jack from the back of his neck.

Sheila breathed like an asthmatic in need of a pump.

"You okay?"

She nodded wordlessly and let go of the wheel, wrapping her trembling arms about herself and curling into a fetal position. "Think . . . I'm gonna be sick."

"Come outside." He helped her out through the passenger door, leaned her against the car.

She doubled over, rubbing her back. "Ugh, it feels like my kidneys are bruised."

"It's not your kidneys," he said, "it's your adrenal glands. They've probably never been worked this hard. Relax. You'll be okay in a while."

A frantic thumping permeated the air, emanating from the window of Kestler's vehicle. The Chevy was shaking as Kestler pounded on the window.

"Is he locked in there or something?" she asked, still rubbing her lower back.

"Yeah."

"How did that happen?"

"I hacked his auto-drive." Macey approached the driver's side of the Chevy. "It's not easy, takes a lot of concentration. That's why I had you drive."

"That's what you were doing? You could have let me know." Slowly she followed him. "I was having a heart attack."

"Wasn't time. Besides, all you had to do was keep him within range. You did fine."

With a mental trigger he popped Kestler's door open. He hauled him out by the collar and pinned him against the Chevy with his forearm. "Why did you run?"

Kestler cursed at him in German, spittle flying from his mouth.

Macey repeated the question. "Warum sind Sie geflohen?"

Kestler blinked. "I'm not speaking to you cops without a lawyer," he said in German. "I know my rights."

"We're not police. And speak English. I know you know how."

"What do you mean, you are not polizei?" His English bore a Swiss accent. "Who are you with, then? Bruno's guys? Are you one of them?"

Cars and trucks whipped past on the highway behind them, stirring up dust and debris as they flew by. Macey shot a quick glance to Sheila, made sure she was out of harm's way, then turned his attention back to Kestler.

"I don't know any Bruno. Look, calm down. I'm a private investigator working on a missing person's case. I just need some information. We could have had this conversation in the club if you weren't so impatient."

Relief swept across Kestler's face as Macey unhanded him. "Oh, man." He smiled widely. "When I saw you I was sure you were a cop."

"Well, I used to be, sorta. The bartender was telling me you're the kind of guy who can get people things. I take it you're some kind of fixer?"

Kestler glanced sideward at the dubious title.

"It's okay. I told you I'm not a cop. I'm not here to bust you. Anyway, I'm looking into the disappearance of Greta Darling. I heard she frequents the place. You know her?"

"Yah, Greta, I know her. She is missing?"

"I heard she used to hang out at the club with this guy named Virgil. The bartender said you know him. I need to find out where he is."

Kestler rolled his eyes in a sort of oy-vey expression. "Virgil. I always knew that guy would be a problem."

"Why do you say that?"

"He was always coming to me for my clients. He says he is wanting my old clients, the ones that are depressed and want nothing. So I send him to the people and always something strange happens to them."

"What do you mean?"

"Some clients I send him to, they no longer come back to the club. Like Greta, I haven't seen her for weeks. Then this other guy, he's a millionaire, sells everything and lives like a bum now in Old Town, opened some soup kitchen. So when Jimmy is telling me you are looking for Virgil, I'm thinking, oh, man, he's some kind of serial killer or something and he's pinned a murder on me somehow. . . . So I ran."

"Why do you think Virgil could be a murderer?" Sheila asked.

Kestler swiveled his head to Sheila, who was now leaning over the back of the car, both hands on the trunk. Kestler looked back to Macey. "I'm not saying nothing, he's just a really weird guy. I never liked him."

<*Two out of two peers who don't seem to get along with this Virgil guy.*> Sheila put a smirk on her lips.

"Do you know where we can find him?" Macey asked.

"He lives on the streets. I don't know where. I haven't seen him lately."

"You said one of your clients he spoke with sold everything?"

"Yah."

"Could you tell me how to find this guy?"

Kestler explained that Steven Grant, a former music producer, was a Gentec client around eighty years old. After meeting with Virgil, Grant had liquidated his estate, giving most of it to charity. With what little he kept he opened a shelter in the mission district of . Kestler told him exactly where.

"Thanks, man." Macey shook his hand, at the same time pressing a few bills into his palm. "For your troubles."

A grin lit up Kestler's face. "Cool."

"And let me have your contact, will you?" Macey passed him a data chip to download his information. "In case I need your services again."

They made the transaction and then headed to their respective cars.

"So next we're going to find this Steven Grant guy?" Sheila asked as they climbed back into the Lexus.

"Best lead we have. I believe we're getting close."

"How do you figure?"

"'Sell all that thou hast, and distribute unto the poor, and thou shalt have treasure in heaven: and come, follow me.'" Macey winked. "Luke eighteen, twenty-two."

"Who's Luke?"

Macey smiled. "It's from the Bible."

"Will you stop with the Bible verses already?"

"Sorry. I'm enjoying your reaction to them too much."

"What's it supposed to mean anyway?"

Macey hit the auto-adjust, repositioned the car's seat and steering wheel to his height. "In the Bible there's a passage where a rich man asks Jesus what he must do in order to enter heaven. That was the answer Jesus gave him."

She seemed to replay in her mind what he'd said. "Give it away, have some other treasure. . . . And you think that's what happened to Grant? He asked Virgil that question and Virgil gave him the same answer?"

"It's a possibility. In the story the rich man couldn't bear to part with his wealth, but Grant apparently has."

"No doubt thanks to Virgil's influence."

"Exactly." Macey started the engine. "To convince a man to do that, Virgil had to have known him well, gotten close to him."

"Who said he had to talk him into it? From the way this Virgil guy is coming across, Grant could easily have been coerced."

"Only one way to find out." He pulled back onto the highway. "Hope you like soup for breakfast."

• • •

"Fine, Julian, thanks."

Roger Boreman, the CEO of Gentec Corporation, disconnected and rubbed his forehead with an open palm. Seated across his desk, Bradley Thomas waited for him to say something.

"You heard everything." For security purposes he knew Bradley would have tapped into his call to Doctor Julian Hague. "What do you think?"

Bradley sat on the edge of his desk. "It's been twenty-four hours. With this new information from Dr. Hague I don't see how else we can proceed. You need to make a decision, sir. If we wait much longer we'll be at the mercy of the media. But if we act now we have a chance of controlling the outcome."

Roger let out a sigh and fiddled with a pen. "Everything is in place, correct?"

"We can commence as soon as you give the word."

Roger stared out his office window at the glittering neon cityscape, preparing to make the biggest decision of his career.

"Fine," he said. "Make it happen."

CHAPTER FIVE

AT EIGHT THIRTY the next morning, Macey and Sheila drove into the Mission District within the heart of Old Los Angeles. The address Kestler had given him lay near the eastern section, amidst a block of three-story buildings that looked to have once been a strip mall.

The scenery was a melancholy collage of broken windows, rusted fire escapes, and graffiti-strewn walls. Cars balanced on concrete blocks littered the streets. A few lone souls shuffled along the sidewalks around them. Other people holed themselves up in doorways and open windows, sporting lifeless stares as they sucked on cigarettes, booze, or whatever else they could get their hands on—which probably wasn't much around here.

The mission district shared the same fate as the old warehouse district following the quake: too expensive to repair and, thanks to the accuracy of modern seismology, not viable enough to reclaim. Abandoned apartment blocks had become homes to those too destitute to live elsewhere. It was a modern third-world slum in the heart of a first-world nation.

"Amazing there are people who have to live like this in our city," Sheila said.

Macey grimaced at the dingy laundry hanging on dead power lines crisscrossing the street above them. "Yeah . . . And can you believe we're only twenty minutes from your apartment?"

Sheila folded her arms. "Not like they can't change all that."

Maybe she'd taken offense to his statement, but he hadn't meant anything by it. He let it rest. No sense starting an argument.

As they neared the end of the block, he spotted a cluster of people gathered outside a building that stood out from the rest of the neighborhood in two ways: it had been freshly painted—in banana yellow—and signs of life came from inside.

"Guess that's the shelter." Sheila turned toward him from the passenger seat. "So how we going to do this?"

Macey parked the Lexus a half block away and killed the engine. "I've been thinking about that all morning. Our next move can either make or break this case."

"How do you mean?"

"We know this Steven Grant must have some kind of relationship with Virgil, but we don't know to what extent. We've been fortunate so far in that our first leads were people who had no interest in Virgil's well-being. That may not be the case with Grant. If we take the wrong approach he could clam up or, worse yet, tip Virgil off."

"So what do you suggest?"

"The best forms of subterfuge employ as much truth as possible." He engaged the car's security system and opened his jacket to make sure the safety on his Mauser was set. "We'll tell him Kestler sent us."

"What?"

Macey explained the rest to her and made certain she understood before they left the Lexus.

As they approached the shelter, the aroma of bacon and coffee mixed with the scent of freshly baked bread. The few people outside leaned against the building with breakfast bowls and cups of java in hand. Macey greeted them as he passed and reached into his pocket to hand a few bills to whoever asked, which, after the first, turned out to be all of them.

Sheila rolled her eyes as he dug into his wallet for more cash. *<Is this really necessary?>*

<I dunno. Why don't you ask them?>

She let out a huff. *<Fine, whatever.>*

After declaring bankruptcy to the crowd, Macey moved inside.

The shelter resembled a cafeteria with picnic tables and benches placed throughout and a kitchen in the rear. He counted fifty-two people, some seated, others in line for food. A half-dozen people served them. The white interior walls boasted symbols of God and Jesus, and displayed messages of hope. The place had an eloquent yet humble charm. Easy to see why anyone would feel instantly secure within such an environment.

With Sheila close by, he approached the kitchen counter and gave a pleasant smile to the crew. "Good morning."

The gang returned his smile and greeted him with a series of hellos. They looked to be volunteers, ranging in age from retirees to high school students. They all wore T-shirts in the same bright banana yellow as the building exterior, emblazoned with the words "Christ's Kitchen" front and back.

"I'm looking for Mr. Grant," Macey said. "Is he about?"

A plump black man who looked to be in his early forties, with a thick salt and pepper goatee and matching hair, brought himself to the front. "I'm Grant, Steve Grant," he said with a mild Georgia accent. He outstretched his hand. "God bless you. What can I do for you all this morning?"

Macey shook firmly. Sheila did likewise, adding a pleasant smile of her own. "We're friends of . . . Mr. Kestler," he said. "He gave us your address, hope you don't mind. I was wondering if we could have a few minutes of your time to discuss something he mentioned."

Grant returned a blank stare.

Maybe he'd done too good a job of leaving his inquiry vague.

Sheila smiled again. "He mentioned a Mr. Virgil. Do you know him?"

"Oh . . . ?" Grant folded his arms apprehensively. But then his expression changed as if a sledgehammer had hit him: "Oh! Come on back here a sec. What did y'all say your names were again?"

"I'm Tony and this is June," Macey said.

"Pleased to meet you." Grant turned to his staff. "You guys take over for a bit. I'll be right back."

Grant ushered them through the kitchen doors, down a corridor, and into a comfortable office cluttered with papers and notebooks. He sat behind the desk and gestured for them to take a seat opposite.

"So you know Kestler . . ." He gave a wide grin and clasped his hands. "I ain't seen him in ages. How is he?"

"He's good . . . I suppose," Macey said. "I have to admit I don't know him very well. I've only seen him at the club."

"Oh, right, so . . . he sent you to come looking for me, did he?"

"Not you directly," Sheila said. "Mr. Kestler mentioned someone named Virgil, but said you could tell us more about him. He said you were one of his clients."

"Clients? I suppose that's one way to put it." Grant's soulful laugh filled the small room. "What are you two looking for exactly?"

"That's the thing." Macey leaned closer. "We don't really know. Kestler said this Virgil might have something we may be interested in, but couldn't tell us what it was. So we got curious, asked him some more. Finally he said just to come here and ask you. And . . . here we are."

"I see." Grant nodded, looked up at the naked light bulb dangling from the ceiling. "You said you met Kestler at the club, right?"

"Yes, at Club Miracle," Sheila said.

"Right." Grant licked his lips. "You all had the treatment then?"

Macey tried his best appear uncomfortable. "Why do you ask?"

Grant grew silent, as if battling with something internally.

"Have *you* had the Miracle Treatment?" Macey asked.

"Yes," he said quickly. "I'm sorry . . . it's kinda unusual for Kestler to just send people here to me . . ."

<I think he knows something's up.> Sheila flicked her eyes to him.

<Don't get jittery.> "To be completely honest with you, Mr. Grant, Kestler didn't exactly send us. He told us about you. And after we heard what you did, we had to know more and so we went looking for you ourselves."

"What do you mean 'what I did'?" He leaned back in his squeaky office chair, raised an eyebrow.

"This." Macey gestured to the surroundings. "You opened this place down here and sold everything else. You were worth millions, weren't you? What made you go and do that?" He added a smile, hoping to convey approval. Luckily Grant smiled back.

"Look, man, if you want it in a nutshell, there it is." He pointed to a poster above his head. It read *Jesus Saves.*

"You found religion?"

"Pretty much." Grant beamed at him.

"But how do you live now? You gave everything to charity, right?"

"Yup. Money isn't everything, man. And neither is living, if you ain't doing it right."

"How's that?" Sheila asked.

"I'll break it down for you guys." Grant clasped his hands atop his desk. "Up until about a year ago I was one of the richest men in this city, maybe even the country. I shelled out for the Treatment, thought it would be the answer to everything." He shook his head and rolled his eyes. "I have to admit, it seemed like it was for a while. A good long while.

"But if you would have met me last year, you would have thought I was the most lonely, depressed man on this earth." He enjoyed a reminiscent chortle, and Macey tried to laugh with him. "I felt like an idiot. Going to that stupid club every night, trying to act the age I looked. Can you imagine? Me? Eighty years old in that club trying to impress some twenty-year-old girl?"

That *did* make him chuckle. "I can relate to that."

"After a while, it don't make any kind of sense." Grant's tone became defeatist. "I've been to every corner of this earth. Lived a life most people only dream about. Money, women, cars, drugs, you name it. But after twenty straight years of living like that, having everything you want, whenever you want. . . . After a while you don't know what to want anymore. At least that's how it was for me. Do y'all ever feel like that?"

"Every day." The speed of his response surprised even him. "Well . . . sometimes."

Grant smiled knowingly. "You're not alone. A lot of us start to feel like that after a while. When life's got no limits, no boundaries . . . it loses its purpose. Like anything else."

"Life's purpose?" Sheila said. "In my book, life's purpose is to live as long as you can."

"A lot of people feel like that, I guess." Grant shrugged and gave a whimsical smile. "But it's pretty silly once you really think about it."

Macey glanced at Sheila, who was now sporting a disgusted smirk on her face.

"So what happened a year ago?" Macey asked.

"Hmm?"

"You said you were feeling this way until a year ago?"

"Oh, right. That's when I met Virgil."

<*Bingo.*> Sheila glanced at him.

"What happened when you met him?"

"He showed me things. About life, about the truth."

"The truth?"

"The Gospel plan of salvation." Grant smiled wide, plumping his cheeks. "Faith, repentance, confession, and baptism into Christ for the remission of sins."

"Interesting." He nudged Sheila with his knee. <*Go now.*>

"Wait, isn't all this Bible stuff supposed to be about going to heaven when you die?" she said. "What good is it if you've already gotten the Treatment? You've got everlasting life already, don't you?"

Grant rocked back in his chair. "A very good question. Next to the Gospel, the solution to that dilemma was probably the most important gift Virgil offered me."

"And what was that?" Macey said.

"Death."

Macey cleared his throat and adjusted his tie. "How do you mean?"

"Well, first Virgil taught me about salvation through Christ. After I believed, I got baptized. Then I changed my life. You see, I realized that now I really was never gonna die. That's when Virgil told me about it."

Sheila tilted her head. "It?"

"Virgil said he found a way of making the Miracle Treatment disappear for good."

<*Double bingo!*> Sheila squirmed in her seat. "And how was he able to do that?"

"He had this injection. I can't believe I can even say this now, but . . . would you believe I was happier the day I took that injection Virgil gave me than on the day I stepped out of that Gentec clinic with the Miracle Treatment for the first time?"

<*Triple bingo! This Grant guy, what a wacko. Virgil sure knows how to pick 'em.*>

"Amazing," Macey said. "And, if I'm honest, a bit hard to swallow."

Grant leaned back with a deep belly laugh. "I suppose. A lot of people don't understand. Just like they don't understand when I tell them I'm a happier man today—to wake at 4:00 a.m. to come run this kitchen—than I ever was getting up at 4:00 p.m. just to run to some club. But you know what I say to those people who don't get it?"

"What's that?"

"Just keep on living. You'll understand eventually."

<*Please. Can he get any more self-righteous?*>

<*Just relax, will you?*>

Sheila shot him a glare, her eyes conveying both anger and hurt. <*What? What did I say?*>

<*Nothing. Forget it.*> "Mr. Grant, I need to tell you something. My name isn't Tony and I'm not here because Kestler sent me."

Grant's smile faded. "Huh?"

"My name is Rick Macey and I'm a private investigator. The woman next to me is Sheila Dunn, an executive for Gentec Corporation."

Grant stiffened. He looked as if he would run straight through the wall behind him if he could.

"Please relax, Mr. Grant. The reason I'm telling you all this is because we desperately need your help."

"W-what for?"

"Do you know Greta Darling?"

"The actress?"

"The same. Two days ago she was found dead from natural causes."

Grant's eyes bulged and his mouth fell open. "Greta's dead?"

"Yes. And, like yourself, she was a Gentec client and also in contact with this Virgil character."

"So, you mean it works?" Grant's anxiety suddenly boiled over into elation. "Thank God! It really works?"

"It's nothing to be happy about!" Sheila lurched forward across the desk, jabbed a finger in Grant's face. "This little experiment you people are running is killing people! Not to mention that it could cost our company billions."

<Easy, Sheila. Back down or we may lose this guy.>

"I'm sorry." Sheila raised her hand in surrender and slowly took her seat. "It's been a stressful period for me. Please, forgive my outburst."

"Not at all," Grant said sheepishly. "Look, I still don't understand all this. What does this have to do with your company losing money or killing people?"

"Ms. Darling's death has been deemed natural," Macey said. "There's no evidence of this serum that Virgil gave you, and possibly her. Can you confirm that Greta received the same injection from Virgil as you did?"

"Of course she did. I saw her take it myself."

<Well, at least the mystery of Greta Darling's death is solved for certain now. Your Treatment does work. Works as well as it ever did. It's the negating agent that did her in, and she took that voluntarily. A fact for which we now have a witness.> Macey shot a glance at Sheila before looking back to Grant.

"I'm glad to hear you say that, Mr. Grant," he said. "However, to the media, it will appear as if the Miracle Treatment simply doesn't work. I don't think I need to explain the impact that will have."

Grant exposed the whites of his eyes. "I'm sorry if your product and your company are suffering, Ms. Dunn. But you know, folks like me who seek help from Virgil have decided we don't *want* to live forever." He smiled. "And it's not like it's some suicide pill killing people. The injection just takes the Treatment away. I'm gonna die when God calls me now. Virgil was only meeting a need, just like any person or company marketing a product."

"Except that the product Virgil's marketing isn't legal," Macey said. "You're the only witness who can lay some claim to there being another cause, besides the obvious, for Greta Darling's death. We need you to testify that it is this injection that allowed Greta Darling to die and that the Miracle Treatment works perfectly well."

Grant's hands fell to his sides. "But what about Virgil? He showed me the way to life everlasting in Heaven."

"That may well be, but this is not about Virgil. It's about revealing the truth about this serum you received from him. All we're asking for, Mr. Grant, is your honesty."

Grant's eyes flashed upward, the way Macey expected they would. He knew that, as a Christian, Grant answered to a higher authority when it came to telling the truth.

"Your honesty and the truth, Mr. Grant. That's all we need from you. Testify the same way you just did to us. We're not here to persuade you to implicate anybody. We just need evidence that this serum actually exists. And right now, you're the only person who can provide that."

Grant sat near motionless, fighting some inner turmoil that Macey figured had to be about Virgil. A few seconds later he confirmed it.

"If I do this, what will happen to Virgil?"

"I really don't know. There's a lot left to uncover on this case. What I can tell you is that your statement will have little to do with what happens to Virgil. Like I said, to save Ms. Dunn's other clients we need proof that this serum exists. Will you help us?"

Grant sighed and looked away. "Mercy. I thought this was something that would only affect me." He mulled it over some more. "But no matter. There's no shame in Christ or in telling the truth. If that's what you need me to do, then fine. I gotta be right before God before anyone else."

"Thank you, Mr. Grant." Macey gave as warm and reassuring a smile as he could muster. "We'll try to make this as quick and easy as possible. Would you be willing to make a statement with an attorney right now?"

"Yeah, I suppose. Mercy."

<Will his statement alone be enough?>

<Enough for now. It'll keep the media at bay and will definitely be enough evidence to get CDI involved officially. After that, it'll only be a matter of time before you have your man and then it's case closed.>

Sheila's face lit up with an ecstatic grin. *<I could kiss you right now.>*

He stood. "Shall we go?"

They waited as Grant collected a few belongings and gave some instructions to his staff before heading out of the shelter. It was a little after nine. The sun was already beaming down full force.

"We're just down there." Macey pointed to his Lexus at the end of the block. "So tell me about this Virgil. What's he like?"

"Virgil?" Grant shook a few hands of the shelter's patrons as he passed by. "He's like . . . what I think the apostles must have been like."

"How do you mean?"

"Full of the Holy Spirit." Grant skipped to keep pace with Macey's long strides. "Peaceful, loving, patient, charitable, all that. Full of it, I tell you. Full of it!"

<*You can say that again.*> Sheila snorted a laugh. "Does he have a full name?"

"If he does, I don't know it," Grant said. "'Brother Virgil' is all he's ever asked to be called. People respect that. We never pry. He's done a lot for this community."

"Like what?" She gestured at the dilapidated surroundings as they walked.

"You see the shelter?" He jabbed a thumb behind them. "That was his idea. He's built several of them throughout this area. He's built schools and churches too."

"What do you mean 'built'? How does he 'build' anything?"

Grant chuckled. "Well, I was a millionaire, don't forget. And so was Greta Darling, I presume. He'd use the money to get contractors to come in. Fix places up. Tear bad ones down. Give people proper homes again."

"And no one notices? What about the authorities?"

"No one cares about these folk. Society has disowned them. An ambulance wouldn't come here if you called it. Virgil is like the hand of the Father caring for the forgotten sons and daughters of this city. I'm just glad to be a part of it."

"Sounds noble," Macey said.

<*Don't tell me you're falling for this nonsense. This Virgil guy is a corporate terrorist!*>

He deemed it wiser not to respond.

<*I'm going to call ahead to Roger. Tell him to get our legal team ready.*>

<*Bill and Ted again?*> Macey cracked a smirk.

<*Who?*>

<*Never mind.*>

As they neared the Lexus, he turned to Grant. "I don't suppose you'd want to tell me where we could find Virgil?"

Before Grant could respond, Sheila stopped short. "I just got cut off. I can't get a signal at all."

Macey tested his own connections and was met with an error message. "Something's up. I think we're being—"

Jammed was the thought in Macey's mind as the shrilling screech of tires filled his ears. The blare of automatic gunfire came next, followed by the metallic ring of high-caliber rounds tearing into the Lexus five feet in front of them.

"Get down!" he screamed and lunged toward Sheila. He pulled his Mauser from its holster and, grabbing hold of Sheila's waist, turned his back to shield her. Her shrill screams matched the terror on her face, rivaled only by the thunder-like gunfire hailing down upon them.

Rounds thumped into his back and legs, their force keeling him over.

In the corner of his vision he saw a white Mazda sedan speed away from them. He crossed his arms, drawing Sheila deeper to his chest as he fired a few aimless shots. The car moved too fast to get a license number. Probably wasn't one anyway.

Sheila trembled in his arms, screaming, crying, but unharmed. Macey looked to Grant.

He lay in a heap by the bumper of the Lexus, his head split open from a shot to the temple. Eternity started now for him.

Instinct and training kicked in next. Macey looked to the Lexus. Whatever caliber rounds the attackers had used, they were powerful enough to turn his car into a useless heap in seconds. He heard the sound of squealing tires echo down the street. They needed to get out of there and fast.

Sheila gasped for breath, her face pale, her lips trembling. "What happened?" She spotted Grant and let out a yelp before burying her head into his shoulder. "Oh, no. Is he dead, Macey? Is he dead?"

"Come on." He hoisted her over his shoulder in a fireman's carry. "We need to move."

Macey didn't stop running. He lost track of how far he had gone—three blocks, five blocks, ten? But he dare not stop yet, not until he was certain they were safe. Not even Sheila's protests to put her down slowed him. Only after she threw up from all the jostling did he concede.

He ducked into a building that looked like a former department store and rested Sheila against a concrete pillar within. She gagged a little, a strand of saliva trailing from her mouth. Maybe he'd pushed her too hard. He looked around for something to wipe her mouth and, when he didn't find anything, took off his tie and used it instead.

"I'm sorry, Sheila." He stooped over her. "Are you okay?"

She shook her head, looking as if she was going to throw up again—and she did. He waited for her to finish and then cleaned her up a second time.

"Macey, you nearly killed me." She sat up weakly, holding her stomach. "How can you run like that? I've never seen anyone run that fast before."

"Let's get away from this mess." He helped her to another pillar far away from the first. She shook as he set her down, her eyes darting back and forth in shock. "Try to relax," he said. "We're safe now."

She leaned her head against the pillar, staring upward at the half caved-in ceiling, and abruptly began to cry. Tears streamed down her face in a torrent of jerky sobs. "I have no idea what's going on." Distress filled her shimmering violet eyes. "We were almost killed back there— Wait, weren't you hit?"

"Nah, must've missed me."

He took hold of her hand and sat next to her. She rolled toward him and nestled against his chest. Wordlessly, Macey wrapped an arm around her and held her close. Eventually she slept, the mixture of emotion, shock, and adrenaline overcoming her. He didn't move for twenty minutes.

Then she stirred abruptly, as if awoken by a sudden noise. She looked up at him and quickly pulled away, but he took no offense.

"How do you feel?" he asked

"Like I look. What time is it?"

"Close to ten o'clock."

She sighed and leaned again against his chest. "I keep seeing that guy, Grant, in my head. Just lying there. I've never seen anyone get killed before . . . especially not like that."

"Try not to think about it. We need to start concentrating on our next move."

"Next move?" She looked at him as if he'd just asked to crucify her first child. "There is no next move, all right? We nearly got killed today. It's time to call the police!"

"Don't try to connect to the net," he said quickly. "We need to stop and think for a minute."

"What are you talking about? This is it, Macey. Game over. I just saw a guy's head get blown off right in front of me. You might be used to this kind of stuff, but I'm not. This Virgil is obviously some sick individual who's willing to kill just about anyone to get away with what he's doing."

"You think it was Virgil who attacked us?"

"He killed our only witness, didn't he? Who else would have the motive to do something like that?"

"Look," Macey said, resting his hand against a rusted clothing rack, "in his mind, he's saving people from the curse of eternal life on earth. And, given all the good he's doing for this community, I seriously d—"

"Like you know him." Sheila snorted. "Don't tell me you were buying into Grant's story about him. It was all lies—and look at what good it did him, huh? Virgil was manipulating him. Anyone capable of tricking people into thinking it's better to die than to live is a sick-minded freak. And he just proved that to us."

Macey rose to his feet. "So what are you going to do now?"

"What?"

"This is your case. The call is yours."

"What's this 'you' stuff?" Her eyes darted back and forth. "Are you abandoning the case?"

"I might as well, if you don't want to listen to me."

"Fine." Sheila crossed her arms and leaned her head against the pillar. "What now then?"

"The police aren't going to do anything. All we have is a guy who was gunned downed in the middle of the mission district by unknown assailants. Do you realize how far down the bottom of their priority list that will end up? What do you hope to gain from contacting the police anyway? For them to take over the case? If that's your goal, then go ahead and call, because that's exactly what will happen once they get involved."

"Then what am I supposed to do? Wait for this psychopath to realize I'm onto him and come kill me next?"

"I know you're upset but we need to think logically here." He crouched to her eye level. "We've been tracking Virgil, but there's no reason to assume he knows that. Only a handful of people even know we're on this case. Besides, if it was him . . ." He stopped.

She leaned forward. "What?"

"Never mind." He stood again. "What's most important is that what happened out there wasn't a random act of violence. Whoever it was, they were hired to do it."

"So, who else would have a motive to kill Grant?"

"Who says they were after Grant?"

Her face grew pale as the realization finally hit her. "You think they were after us?"

"Who knows? Maybe all of us." He tried to downplay it. "What I do know is that they jammed our comms right before the attack. Those aren't run-of-the-mill street tactics. More like military, if you ask me. And if they're sharp enough to do that, they could probably track us through our net usage. So until we know anything for sure, I want us to stay off it, all right?"

Sheila ran both hands through her dark hair, raking her scalp as she let out a sigh. "What do we do now? Our only witness is dead, we don't have any other leads, and now this . . . . I'm not going to get myself killed over this, Macey. I'm not."

"I won't let that happen. I promise you. But you can't give up now. You stopping won't make any difference to whoever sent those guys after us. It'll only make their job easier."

"What do we do then?"

"First things first. We need to get out of here and use a public terminal so we can't be traced. There are some things I need to check." He helped her to her feet.

"Just don't carry me this time."

"Deal."

They hiked through the endless blocks of abandoned buildings that made up the mission district. Finally they entered the "civilization" of the New City, where Macey hailed a cab and gave the driver an address.

Minutes later they were in the center of New Chinatown, its narrow streets crowded with people and street vendors selling anything from food to clothing beneath makeshift tents. Usually he loathed the stuffiness of the New City. But, under their current circumstances, the sight of people was comforting.

"Why'd we come all the way out here?" Sheila crinkled her nose as they exited the cab. "Couldn't we have found a terminal closer?"

"You'll see."

At the end of the block he took a right that led to a street of tightly packed tenement buildings. Through his neural net he keyed a trigger, and the garage door to one of them opened, revealing a black Hummer tucked within.

"Get inside, quick." They hurried in, and he closed the door behind them.

"Where are we?" Sheila marveled at the large garage, spinning in a circle. "Is this where you live?"

He unlocked the inner door to the house and let her inside. "Not really. This is one of my safe houses."

"Safe houses? You have safe *houses*? Plural? How often does stuff like this happen to you?"

He chuckled and showed her around the place. It was a cramped one-bedroom apartment with low ceilings, tacky furniture, and a lousy view. Worth nowhere near the amount of rent he paid for it, except in times such as these. He made coffee and scrounged up some tinned soup and crackers while Sheila rested on the couch. He served it on the coffee table and turned on the holo-feed while they ate. He was glad to see the food return some of her color.

After they were finished, he brought a small holo-terminal from the bedroom, set it up in front of them, and jacked into it.

"Hey, wait up." Sheila shuffled next to him on the couch. "I thought you said we needed to access the net from a public terminal."

"I am. This one's a remote. I have it patched into a public terminal in the restaurant next door."

"What are you, some kind of government assassin or spy or something?" She leaned closer to him to get a better view of the holoscreen. "What are you doing now?"

"We've been so caught up in what we're doing that we've been ignoring a really big aspect of the case."

"What's that?"

"Tools," he said.

Sheila furrowed her brow. "Tools?"

"Remember I asked you who would be capable of producing a negating agent? What did you tell me?"

"Me, Jules, and maybe our internal R&D team, but—"

"But it would take years, right?" He leveled his gaze at her. "What if Jules has been working on it for years without your knowledge?"

"Jules?" She dismissed the idea with a wave of her hand. "That's absurd. Why would he do that? And he's already tried to synthesize an agent and couldn't make one."

"Or so he said. Remember, we found a witness who said otherwise. Regardless of the fact that Grant is now dead, we still have the information he gave us. If a negating agent exists, it had to have been made by someone. And that list of someones is really only one item long: Dr. Julian Hague. So if we apply what Grant told us, it leaves only two possibilities: either Dr. Hague is truly incapable of making a negating agent and Grant was lying, or—"

"The opposite." Sheila's eyes went blank with morbid realization. "You really think he could be involved?"

"If he is, I have an idea for how we might be able to prove it." He connected through the remote terminal onto the net and, within seconds, had his destination locked. A face popped onto the holo-screen.

"Who is this?" Paul Webb answered.

Macey keyed on his own camera, and a relieved expression came across Paul's face.

"Mace? What are you doing calling from a public terminal?"

"Long story," he said with a chuckle. "Paul, I need your help with something."

"Name it."

"I need my O-6 clearance temporarily reinstated."

He burst into laughter. Then sobered. "You're not kidding, are you?"

Macey smiled but maintained the seriousness of his stare.

Exasperation then flashed across Paul's face. "You know I can't keep doing this for you, Mace."

"You know me. I wouldn't ask if it wasn't warranted."

Paul sighed and fidgeted in his seat. "You were always the one that handled stuff like this. I sure wish I could pass the buck to you, like in the old days."

"I'll make copies of the data and prepare a letter to General Tamarack for you. How's that?"

"You'd better start that private investigator's office you keep talking about—and make sure it has two desks. 'Cause as soon as I get fired I'm coming for my job, understand?"

Macey laughed in the way only Paul could make him. "Thanks, man."

"Give it a few seconds to update," he said and signed out.

"You two seem really close."

He had nearly forgotten that Sheila was there. "Yeah, we go a long ways back."

"So what's this O-6 thing?"

"My old rank in CDI. I asked Paul to temporarily reinstate me. It'll grant me the authority to check personal records of private citizens."

"What are you going to do with it?"

"Watch."

He opened several connections simultaneously and soon the holo-screen was jumbled with popping icons and scrolling text.

Sheila leaned back. "Man, you're fast . . ."

He barely heard her, his concentration fixed on his task. "There it is," he said and pointed to the screen.

"Where what is?"

"I followed a lead that Grant hinted to when he talked about where his and Ms. Darling's money ended up. Officially, both their monies went to charities. But Grant mentioned that Virgil was using the money to rebuild the district. Somehow he had to have access to it. So I ran a trace on the charity accounts. They turned out to be fronts for some offshore financial instruments. I noticed some pretty big withdrawals and tracked them to the receiving bank. Not surprisingly, they ended up in another offshore account, and guess who owns it?"

She read the name of the account. "Dr. Julian Hague?"

"The one and only."

All color drained from her face. Then she shook her head fervently as if trying to wake from a bad dream. "But why would he get caught up in something like this? Why would he lie about being unable to make a negating agent, about there being a flaw in the Miracle Treatment itself? It doesn't make sense."

"Only one way to find out." Macey clicked off the terminal. "We need to pay the good doctor another visit."

CHAPTER SIX

DR. JULIAN HAGUE groaned apathetically at the third ringing of his door buzzer. He seldom invited people to visit him at his lab, and frequently had uninvited guests trying to lure him out of it, so ignoring the thing was always his first course of action.

On the fourth ring he reached over to his holo-terminal and keyed the security camera. Outside stood a squat, pudgy man in a black overcoat. Julian's skin bristled with anticipation. About time you showed up.

He triggered the garage door and headed toward the entrance to greet his visitor. As usual, he had to suppress his urge to laugh. Round as a soccer ball and with a head resembling a potato and buttons for eyes—there stood Pooly the Pig.

The first time he had heard his name, he had literally laughed in his face, eliciting death threats. Now he made certain to laugh only on the inside.

"Pooly," Julian said with a smile to hide his contempt. Dealing with this low-life was a marriage of necessity. Today would be the end of it, though, and he couldn't wait to get the divorce papers signed. "You have the money?"

"I got confirmation," Pooly said gruffly. "Where's the stuff at?"

Julian sighed and headed toward the back of the lab. "Follow me."

Pooly did so, keeping a bit too close for comfort, but a quick halt and glance downward sent the message.

"What? Sorry." Pooly tossed his hands in the air.

"Just keep your distance."

Pooly gestured like an usher with a sweep of his arm. "After you, sir."

Julian resumed his trek at a quick pace, choosing his path carefully to accommodate the girth of his business partner. Not for Pooly's comfort, but to prevent him from knocking over his gear, as he had done on a previous visit. Reaching the back, Jules came to a piece of equipment that would probably look like a giant cake mixer to the pig man. About where the mixing bowl would be was a sealed glass cylinder the size of a soda can, brimming with clear liquid.

"There it is. The amount you wanted, liquefied to 100ccs."

"Whatever, man. It can do the job, right?"

Julian sighed before responding at a level of complexity his companion could understand. "Yes."

"Good." The pig man opened his jacket. "Let's get this over with. I can't wait to be done with your freaky kid doctor face."

Macey decided to use a stack of his emergency cash to buy Sheila some new clothes before they headed for Hague's lab. Her skirt and blouse hadn't fared too well through their ambush earlier and she'd broken one of her heels. At first, Sheila complained about spending his cash, but after he reminded her that any form of electronic transaction could be used to track them, she relented. She did make him write a receipt. They hit the shopping district in New Chinatown, and Sheila picked out a navy tracksuit, matching sneakers, and an Angels baseball cap.

In the Hummer they headed South toward the warehouse district. Within minutes they were turning on to the side street that led to Julian Hague's lab.

Macey had to admit, the excitement of linking Hague to the charity money had propelled him to rush to confront him. But now apprehension nagged. He slowed the Hummer.

"What's wrong?" Sheila asked.

"We haven't talked about this yet, but we haven't considered who else could have been involved in that attack this morning."

She looked out the window. "Who else could there be?"

"Like I said, only a handful of people know we're on this case. Hague was one of them . . ."

"That doesn't mean he hired someone to kill us."

"He's already in far deeper than you expected. We can't underestimate what we might find or what will happen when we get to his lab."

"What are you saying?"

"This car is armored. We'll try and park inside his garage, but if anything happens you get back in here and stay inside, understand?"

She bit her lower lip. "Macey, you're starting to scare me here."

"I promised I wouldn't let anything happen to you, right? I intend—"

He jammed on the brakes, barely missing a black Bronco barreling around the corner in the opposite direction.

"Idiot!" Sheila gave the driver a none-too-pleasant finger gesture.

"My fault, wasn't paying attention." He sped up again. "Anyway, stay close to me when we get there."

"You don't have to tell me twice. I can't wait for all this to be over."

"It will be. Hague can be as good a witness as Grant if he confesses."

"And what are the chances of that?"

"Don't worry. If he's guilty, he'll confess."

Thankfully she didn't probe further. CDI had its methods—many of them questionable because of their use of neural nets—for extracting information from people. Concentrating on his driving, he pulled into the parking lot outside Hague's lab.

The garage door stood open. His instincts sharpened. Considering Hague's earlier paranoia about security, this was a bad sign.

"Was he expecting us, you think?" Sheila asked.

"Doubtful." He drew close enough for a full view of the interior. He could see no movement inside. "Something's not right." He took the Hummer all the way into the garage and parked, then drew his Mauser.

Sheila gasped.

"Don't worry. Just stay in the car."

He chambered a round and slipped out of the Hummer, mentally keying the doors to lock. Pointing the Mauser toward the ground, he headed toward the back of the lab.

Bright red bloodstains peppered the floor. Fresh. It took mere seconds to see where they led.

Not thirty feet away lay the teenaged body of Dr. Julian Hague, crumpled against a set of lab equipment in a pool of blood. Hague still moved, but only slightly, his shirt stained crimson.

Macey swept the rest of the lab for signs of the doctor's assailants, but found no one.

<Sheila, get in here!> He rushed toward Hague. *<Jules has been shot.>*

<Oh, no . . .>

As he checked Hague's vitals the man stirred, his pulse weak from blood loss. No telling what internal injuries he had sustained from the single bullet wound now painting his lower abdomen red.

"Jules!" Sheila exclaimed from behind. "What happened? Who did this to you?"

"Please . . . help me." He struggled to prop himself up against the lab equipment.

Macey helped and Hague's breathing eased.

<He's lost a lot of blood. I don't know how much longer he's going to hold up. Better call for an ambulance.>

<What about being traced?>

<We'll have to risk it. We can't let him die. Talk to him. Keep him alert. I'll try to find a med kit.> He stood, began scanning the lab.

"Jules, stay with me," Sheila said. "We're calling for—"

"Don't you dare talk to me, woman!"

Macey glanced back down to see a sudden malevolence enter Hague's eyes. "You're the one who did this to me!"

Sheila lurched back.

Macey dropped to her side. *<Keep him talking. What's he going on about?>*

"Jules, you think I did this to you somehow? Why?"

"Shut up." Blood and spittle flew from his mouth. "As usual, you don't have a clue what's really going on. You're so ignorant."

"Why don't you tell us then," Macey said. "We already know you've made a negating agent and that you've sold it on the black market to a guy named Virgil. I have the banking records to prove it. Or perhaps you already knew that I was onto it and that's why you called a hit on us."

Hague's top lip curled into an indignant scowl. "What do you think I am? I'm no murderer—"

"Shut up!" Sheila's voice cracked with emotion. "Why would you do this, Jules? Make this stupid thing! Why would you destroy our company? Our research? Our product?"

"*Our* product? It's my product, Sheila!" His chest caved in and out as his breathing increased. "You stole it from me. My whole life, you stole it all. You took my research, slapped a name on it, and sold it as your own."

"That's not true. Your name is on the patent."

"But whose name will be in the history books? Whose picture is on the cover of *Time*? You stole my recognition, my significance . . ."

"Is that why you made the negating agent?" Macey said. "To prove you could do what she couldn't?"

"In a way . . ." He turned his head to the side, gazed down at the floor now glazed in his blood. "But more to destroy everything she represents: the company, the commercialism. My treatment was supposed to benefit all mankind, but what does she turn it into? A centerpiece for the lifestyles of the rich and famous."

"Jules," Sheila said softly, her hand resting atop his. "I . . . I had no idea you felt this way. Why didn't you say—"

"Would you have listened? Would you?" His eyes darted as he gazed into Sheila's. "No, not greedy little you. You're worse than the rest of them. I was going to bury Gentec in humiliation and remake the formula the way it was intended, but you screwed it all up. Just like you always do."

"Is that why you sold the negating agent to Virgil?" Macey said. "For him to use on people, so you could blame it on Sheila?"

"Who's Virgil?" Hague looked up at him angrily. "I don't know who you're talking about."

Did he really not know? "Who did you sell it to, then?"

"The fat little pig that shot me."

"What's his name?"

"Pooly. That's what he calls himself, anyway." Hague coughed with a pneumonia-like hack. "He was greedy, just like you. One last deal, that's all it would have taken. I almost had all the money I needed to start my own company . . ."

"One last deal?" Sheila said. "How much of this stuff have you been selling?"

Hague laughed in a way that reminded Macey of the Streetwalker Sniper. "Not much at first. But this last time he wanted a ton of it. Gave me a challenge too. Wanted it dispersible by air."

Sheila's mouth gaped. "How could you do something like that? How much did you give him?"

Hague shrugged, a gesture well suiting his teenage appearance. "Enough to take out the city initially. Over time it'll spread virally. Once someone's been exposed, there's no chance of the Miracle Treatment ever working again. Your legacy is over, Sheila, and in more ways than one too. Just wait. You'll see."

A fire lit in Sheila's eyes as she snatched him by the collar. "What do you mean by that? Answer me."

"Watch the news." He gave her a blood-stained grin. "You'll understand. I didn't even plan that part. Maybe there's justice in this world, after all." He coughed more violently this time, blood erupting in clots from his mouth. "Look at me . . . I invent the cure for death and here I am dying anyway." He turned to face her. "What a laugh, eh, Sheila? What a l . . ."

His stare grew glassy and fixed.

"Macey, I . . . I think he's dead."

He checked his vitals and stood. "Come on." He helped her to her feet. "Let's move outside."

Sheila trembled, her face creased with anger, remorse, grief—he couldn't tell quite what. He wrapped an arm around her shoulders and she responded by clutching his waist, sniffling.

"I always looked up to Jules. I had no idea he hated me so much . . ."

"People rarely show their true selves. A dead man tells no tales, but a dying man tells all."

"Is that the Bible again?"

"No, I don't know where I picked that up from." They left the lab interior and began toward the garage door.

"What do we do now? If he's truly made this stuff to disperse virally, once it's released, it'll be the end of the Miracle Treatment, the end of Gentec. Once people start dying, there might not be any way to prove that it's from the negating agent at all, because it didn't show up in Greta Darling's DNA. I bet he designed it that way too. People will assume the Miracle Treatment was a fraud and, clinically, they'd be right."

"We still have a chance to stop the negating agent from getting out there." Macey quickened his pace. "Remember that black Bronco earlier?"

"What about it?"

"How many vehicles do you see around here? This place is a ghost town. And from the looks of things, Hague couldn't have been shot more than a few minutes ago. So that could have been—"

"Sheila?"

Beyond the hood of the Hummer a man in a dark suit stood outside the garage. It was the younger man he'd seen with Roger Boreman that first night of the case. His personal assistant.

"Bradley?" Sheila said. "What are you doing here?"

"I could ask you the same thing. I was coming to check on how Jules was making out with his research. Where is he?"

She shook her head. "He's dead."

"What?" Bradley stepped toward them. "What happened? Are you okay?"

"Not really. Jules just admitted that *he* was the one who made the negating agent and was selling it to some psycho named Pooly. Sounds like he made enough of it to wipe out our product permanently."

"You're kidding." He began a wide arc toward the Hummer. "What happened to Jules?"

"Someone shot him. We think it was the guy he was cutting the deal with. It's a good chance he just left too. We need to get after him. There might be time to recover the agent. We need to tell Roger right away. Is he with you?"

"Back at the office."

"You alone then?" Macey said.

"Yes . . ." Bradley's paced slowed to a stop. "Why?"

"No reason." He tried messaging Sheila through the comm but, as he expected, he was met with another communications error. He glanced behind Bradley to see a white Mazda sedan parked outside the garage.

Macey could make out two or three silhouettes within it. He clenched Sheila's shoulder, trying to snag her attention, but she merely buried herself deeper into his side.

"Unbelievable," Bradley said. "This is awful."

Macey edged closer to the Hummer. "Sure is. You never know what a person is really into."

"Isn't that the truth." Bradley leveled eyes with him.

He suspected something. The façade would soon drop.

The doors of the Mazda opened and men in suits stepped out.

"What's going on?" Sheila stiffened against him.

"Tell me something, Bradley." Macey stared him down. "Do you *really* think it was just bad luck that you weren't able to kill me earlier?"

Bradley's face went stark white. The split second of hesitation he had hoped for.

"Get in, Sheila!" He flung open the Hummer door the same instant Bradley whipped something from beneath his jacket. He pushed Sheila and she tumbled headfirst into the driver's seat, letting out a scream.

Bradley ran toward the front of the Hummer, pistol in hand, aiming over the hood. Macey ducked behind the door just as Bradley opened fire and sent the window cracking into a spider web of broken glass, the bullet lodging in the ballistic-resistant resin beneath.

"Move over!" Macey jumped behind the wheel. He closed the door just as Bradley fired again, a flurry of sparks and broken glass erupting as the bullets impacted.

He punched the gear shift into reverse, spinning the huge tires with a screech only slightly less strident than Sheila's screams. As he pulled away, Bradley reloaded and let loose a magazine from dead center in front of them. Patches of shattered glass exploded onto the windscreen like snowballs as the rounds hit.

More gunfire filled the air as the men from the Mazda opened up with what sounded like automatic rifles behind them. The heavier caliber rounds burst through the back window, zipping past them and out through the front.

"Get down!"

Sheila screamed and lodged herself between the seat and the dashboard. He didn't let off the gas, his eyes focused on the rearview mirror. He could see the white Mazda and three men in suits surrounding it, assault rifles at the shoulder. The muzzle flash from one of them preceded a round hitting the rearview mirror and shattering it. But he needed it no longer.

He kept the accelerator pegged. Predictably, the rifle fire stopped milliseconds before he plowed into the side of the Mazda with an earsplitting bang. The force threw him into the air and his head hit the roof.

Macey shifted into first and stung the gas again, pulling away from the wreckage of the cheap Mazda now compacted to half its size. The gunmen fired from the sides, setting the Hummer alight with sparks.

Fifty feet in front of him Bradley stood with pistol raised firing continuously through the weakened windscreen. A round punched through and hit his arm. Another hit his chest. Macey kept on the gas. Bradley stopped firing as the three-ton Hummer bore down on him.

Macey cut the wheel and pulled the emergency brake, sending the back of the Hummer sliding about and slamming into Bradley with a thud, tossing him onto his rear about ten feet away.

Macey steered toward the road, hit the gas again, and pulled away. In what was left of his side mirror he saw Bradley stagger to his feet.

Sheila was still huddled under the dashboard, her hands atop her head.

"It's okay," Macey said, leaning forward to see through a grapefruit-sized hole in the windshield. "We're safe now."

She made a low whine and he knew she was crying again. He let her be for the time being and focused on the road through the damaged windshield. He would have to ditch the Hummer, but it had served its purpose. If they had been in the Lexus, it would have been a different story. They'd need another vehicle to track down this Pooly person, but first they needed time to sort things out.

Macey stuck to the side streets as he drove back to Chinatown. He had no idea what the Hummer looked like from the outside, but it would assuredly draw unwanted attention from police. Twenty minutes later they were back at the safe house, the Hummer concealed inside the garage.

"Do you think they followed us?" Sheila asked.

"Not unless they had another car. I think we're safe for now."

He served Sheila some coffee as she sat on the couch. "I don't think I can go on, Macey," she said after a while. "I can't handle this."

She didn't have a choice, but he couldn't tell her that. "We'll get through it." He joined her on the couch and handed her a mug. "We have to stay focused. For now, just put out of your mind what happened. We're here and we're alive. That's all that matters." He punched keys on the remote terminal and accessed the news media feeds.

"Why are you fiddling with that thing at a time like this?"

"Remember what Jules said about you? About checking the news?"

"Don't you ever stop? We were nearly killed. Again! Doesn't that bother you?"

He took a sip of his coffee but didn't say anything. She needed to vent her emotions, and he was prepared to endure them in whatever form they took.

"We need to call Roger," she said. "Maybe I can talk to him, find out what's going on. Maybe he doesn't even know about Bradley or any of this."

"Do you really think that's plausible?"

"I don't know, okay? I'm not a genius like you. I just don't know." She rested a palm against her forehead, her features twisted with grief. "I don't understand any of this," she said in a whimper. "Why is this happening to me? I'm a normal person. Things like this don't happen to normal people . . ." She stared at the floor, her eyes darting, glassy.

"Come here." He reached out to her. After a moment's hesitation she took his hand and nestled closer. He pulled her into an embrace. She went limp in his arms and began to cry. He held her there, silently consoling her.

Eventually her sobbing stopped and she pulled away, gazing up at him, her violet eyes tearstained. She looked beautiful. Then she gave him a smile that increased the sparkle in her eyes.

He cupped her slender jaw, caressing her cheek with his thumb. Gently, he tilted her chin and she responded with a slow close of her eyes. He leaned inward, kissed her, her mouth opening as she kissed him back.

But he forced himself to stop, breaking off with a turn of his head. "I'm sorry. That was . . . inappropriate of me."

She withdrew, brow creased. "What? Why?"

"You're upset right now. I shouldn't have taken advantage. Besides, this is a little . . . unprofessional, don't you think?"

She lowered her gaze, managed a nod.

He cleared his throat and repositioned himself on the couch. "I know this is a lot for you, Sheila, but whether you want to believe it or not, this *is* happening to you. And I need you to focus. What are your thoughts?"

When she said nothing, he wondered if what had just happened between them had made things worse. Most likely. Such things always did.

He could see Sheila's mind at work as she pondered his question, her eyes steadying until she looked more like her normal self. It was the result he had hoped for. Asking for her input had forced her to think about their predicament rather than their emotions.

"Maybe Jules told Roger about the negating agent," she said. "If Roger knew I might have a chance of succeeding with my religious-conspiracy theory, maybe he . . ."

"Decided to kill you?"

She looked back at him, mouth trembling. "I still can't believe he'd do that."

"Actually, I agree. As much as he dislikes you and the threat you represent to his career, he dislikes even more the idea of Gentec failing. I don't think he would give up on any real chance to salvage Gentec. Besides, let's look at this from Jules's point of view. He wanted not just you, but all of Gentec to go down in flames. He wanted people to think the Miracle Treatment had failed. He would never have told Boreman he'd made a negating agent. He would have lied to Boreman, the same way he lied to us."

"That makes sense." Sheila took a sip from her mug. "So we have to assume that Roger knew nothing about what Jules was up to. But what about Bradley?"

"Maybe . . . . I've been wondering how Bradley managed to show up at Jules's place so conveniently."

"Could he have tracked us from when you called the ambulance?"

"I didn't get a chance to. Jules started spilling his guts too soon. No pun intended. Which helps us narrow things down a bit. Really there are only two possibilities why Bradley was there. One, he was there to see Jules, like he said. Or two, he's been following us this whole time. My intuition leads me to the latter." He angled the remote terminal toward her. "I checked some of the media feeds, found headlines about Greta Darling and Gentec all over the net."

"Already?" Her chest heaved and her eyes darted wildly with fright. "But what about the media blackout? It's been nowhere near forty-eight hours yet!"

"That's why we may find answers here. Boreman may have cut the blackout short for some reason."

Macey accessed a headline entitled "Gentec Scandal," and a female reporter came into view on the holo-screen.

"Authorities today confirmed the death of actress Greta Darling, who died in her Sherman Oaks home two days ago at the age of eighty-nine. Rumors that her death was a result of natural causes has sent a shockwave through the halls of Gentec Corporation, producers of the well-known Miracle Treatment, of which Ms. Darling was one of the earliest recipients. Earlier today, Gentec CEO, Roger Boreman, had this to say on the matter . . ."

The camera switched to a press conference with Boreman at a podium topped with a bouquet of microphones. "The report of Ms. Darling's death has come as a shock to all of us here at Gentec. We have begun an internal investigation into the matter and can now share some initial findings."

The screen flashed back to the reporter. "Mr. Boreman goes on to allege that Ms. Darling's death could be the work of a disgruntled Gentec executive, the current Vice President of Marketing, Sheila Dunn."

A picture of Sheila flashed onto the corner of the screen.

Sheila stood so fast she spilled her coffee. "What!"

"Gentec sources claim that Ms. Dunn has had a long history of dissatisfaction within the company and has stated openly her willingness to resort to extreme measures if certain company changes were not made, most notably the removal of Roger Boreman as CEO. Dunn was turned down for the top job two years ago."

"This is nonsense!" Sheila shouted at the screen. "How can they air this?"

"Dr. Julian Hague," the reporter continued, "one of the original inventors of the Miracle Treatment, has been closely involved with the ongoing investigation and had this to say."

The late Jules Hague appeared next to Boreman in the next scene, dressed in a dark business suit. He took over the mics. "Since the start of the investigation we have uncovered evidence that Ms. Darling's Miracle Treatment had been tampered with. It is unknown at this point whether other clients may be at risk."

"Dr. Hague," an unseen reporter sang from the crowd, "what do you have to say about allegations that Ms. Dunn might be responsible for Ms. Darling's death?"

"Although I do not wish to speculate too much at this point, I can only say we have strong clinical evidence of tampering. Certainly Ms. Dunn's motivations have been taken into consideration. All this information has been passed on to the police."

"Jules . . ." Sheila said his name like a curse and followed it with a volley of actual curses.

"Based upon this new evidence," the reporter said, "earlier today police launched an investigation into Ms. Darling's death and have since issued an arrest warrant for Sheila Dunn on suspicion of first-degree murder."

Sheila's mouth hung open, her eyes glazed. "This can't be happening."

"Police fear that Dunn may be eluding authorities. They have begun a citywide manhunt. They urge the public to make contact with any information that may lead to her whereabouts."

The news file ended and an option to replay appeared.

Sheila stared at the screen, her emotions unreadable. "How can this be happening? Roger, Jules, Bradley . . . they've all turned against me. But a manhunt? They're trying to pin murder on me?"

Macey rested a hand on her shoulder and pulled her back down to the couch. "They've bought the media, that's all."

"What about the police?" She jutted her chin at the screen, her eyes wild with rage. "I'm . . . I'm a fugitive now? How are they believing this stuff?"

"Circumstantial evidence, probably. The need to blame someone and assure everyone that the Treatment itself is still working."

"What happened to hard facts?"

"They probably won't need them." He keyed off the terminal. "They're going to make up their own facts and buy the rest, because they don't expect any opposition when they put forward their version of the truth. In other words, the only way for their story to be true is if you aren't around to say it isn't."

She blanched. "Wait. I told Bradley that Jules had admitted he'd made the negating agent and was selling it to Pooly. What if I can convince Roger that there's another way out of this? That what happened to Greta Darling had nothing to do with the Miracle Treatment failing. That this was all Jules's doing, not mine."

She was still thinking like a normal person, still seeking to resolve conflict with logic, reason, arguments, the law. But he knew better, knew what blind ambition and fear could drive men to do, even honest ones.

"You saw that news broadcast. Jules seems to have convinced Boreman that you're the guilty party, and now your boss is gunning for you as a scapegoat. If you make contact with him, the police manhunt will be over. There's only one way out of this, Sheila. We need to uncover the truth and blow everything wide open. Once we get some sort of evidence, we take it to CDI. Paul will handle the rest."

"Guess that means I should steer clear of Bradley too, then." She rubbed the edge of her mug with her thumb. "Wait . . . if we find this Pooly person, couldn't we get hold of the negating agent ourselves? That could be our evidence."

"*Their* evidence, you mean. They'd claim you made it. You'd be caught red-handed, so to speak. No, even with the negating agent, we'd need Virgil as well, make him testify to CDI that he gave the negating agent to Greta Darling. That's the only way to clear your name."

Sheila stared into her coffee mug for a minor eternity, her face blank. "This is about me now . . . not the treatment, not Gentec . . . me."

Macey remained quiet as the reality finally set in for her.

"Okay, you mentioned Pooly, right?" She shook her head tiredly. "But how do we find him? We've been trying to do that this whole time. Nobody we've spoken to has had a clue where he is. Where do we even start?"

Macey shut down the holo-terminal on top of the coffee table. "With Pooly, of course. He's most likely the one supplying Virgil with the negating agent. If we track him down, he'll lead us straight to him."

Sheila arched a brow. "Really? How you figure that?"

"Remember, Jules was paid by money from Greta Darling and Steven Grant's charities. Money that only Virgil had access to. Pooly's just the middleman here."

"But even if it was Pooly in that Bronco, he's long gone by now. How do we even find out who he really is?"

"Find out? I already know who he is."

Sheila's eyes widened. "You do?"

"Of course. You can't be in my line of work without running into Pooly the Pig."

"Pooly the Pig?" Sheila let out a laugh. "Are you serious?"

"Don't laugh." But he failed to hide a grin of his own. "The guy could destroy your entire life with a single hack."

"Well, tell him he's too late." Sheila smirked with a cynical smile. "Now, where do we find this guy?"

CHAPTER SEVEN

SHEILA WAITED while Macey removed the rest of his emergency cash from the bedroom safe and packed a bag. He led her by the hand as they wove through the teeming sidewalks of Chinatown.

The traffic, vehicular and human alike, had thickened as rush hour neared. Good time to make a break for it, she supposed. If Bradley had followed them to Macey's safe house, maybe they could lose him in the crowds. But that all depended on where they were going—which she still wasn't quite sure of yet.

"So where exactly are you taking me?"

"The Metro." Macey pushed past a food vendor trying to offer him a sample of chicken on a toothpick. "We need to get to my other safe house and pick up a car."

"Two safe houses and another car?" Sheila took the vendor up on his offer, savoring the sweet taste of teriyaki as she popped it in her mouth. "How 'oaded are you, any-ay?"

He smiled but didn't give her an answer.

They hustled a few more blocks to the Metro station and caught a train into the Old City. Macey kept glancing at the doorway as passengers entered and exited the carriage. Only after the doors closed and the train started moving did he sit down next to her.

"Don't think we were tailed," he said, taking one last look at the door. "We can relax for awhile."

"Sounds good to me."

Sheila eased back against the chair's hard plastic headrest and, despite the discomfort, found the gentle rock and sway of the carriage soon lulling her toward sleep. She let her mind drift, trying to avoid the constant looping of the news program that had left a permanent carpet stain in her mind.

Boreman, Bradley, Jules—she didn't want to think about any of them. That left only Macey to think about. That was something she didn't mind thinking about at all. Her guardian, her protector through this mess that had become her life. It was amazing how much he was doing for her, risking for her, far beyond anything even close to normal. That caused another thought to surface, one she needed an answer to.

"Macey, can I ask you something?"

He answered without opening his eyes, semi-dozing as she was. "Sure."

"Why are you still doing this?"

One eye popped opened and he arched a brow. "What kind of question is that?"

"Don't get me wrong," she said. "I appreciate it. I just mean . . . . Well, you saw the news. It's not like I can honor your contract anymore."

"Hey, don't worry about it. Remember, I have my own reasons for taking this case."

"Oh . . ." So *that* was the reason. She felt silly for even asking now, but she should have known. Apparently that kiss had meant nothing to him. Just as well. Emotions were messy things. It was enough that he was willing to help her, whatever his reasons. She should be happy with that.

"I won't abandon you, Sheila," he said suddenly. "You don't have to worry about that, okay?"

He took her hand and held it. Her heart rose in tempo to match the click-clack of the tracks. Maybe she was wrong about that kiss after all.

At least she hoped so.

They spent the rest of the trip in silence. Eight stops later they emerged at the old Firestone Station in Watts.

The heart of the Old City reminded her of the mission district where Grant had set up his shelter, except here it was not so far gone. Shops and businesses still thrived, albeit with security bars across every window. Even now, during the middle of the day.

Cyber-gangers skulked along the narrow sidewalks in packs. She didn't know the names for the different groups, mainly because she never really cared before now, but the ones here looked different than the "Rasta" she saw get beat up in the police station.

These people looked Latino, with colorful, shape-shifting bio-tattoos across their bare chests and backs, even the women.

A few were big like Macey, bigger even. Augmented with cheap genetics, probably. Others had weapons protruding right from their skin: blades on the forearms, spikes on the shoulders.

Revolting.

<*Why are we here?*> Sheila asked.

<*My safe house is here.*>

She stiffened as they headed toward one of the groups.

<*Don't worry, they won't bother us.*>

She fixed her gaze straight ahead as they passed a cluster of them. Macey practically dragged her by the arm as she clung to him.

A beefy teen with a glowing crucifix tattoo on his chest separated himself from the pack, eyeballing them with a grin to reveal a set of filed steel teeth.

Sheila stopped dead, her heart stuck in her throat. Macey kept her moving with a push, veering around the youth. The kid blocked their path again, and her heart all but came out of her mouth. "Macey, what t—"

"Oye! Salga de su manera," another gang member with a plaited grey beard and a set of permanent shades for eyes called out. "Él es el poli del hierro."

Sheila remained quiet.

The youth eyed Macey with a hint of disdain, his chest crucifix flashing from yellow to deep red, then finally shook his head and stepped out of the way.

Macey sped up and her blood pressure dropped a few notches. After a good while, she risked a glance over her shoulder at the crew, thankful to see the kid had not followed them. "What did that guy say to him?"

"Who knows? Come on, it's just ahead."

They continued to an auto garage on the corner of the block. Within the lot, several cars lay dormant in various states of dismantlement and repair. Within the twin-door garage behind them sat a few more cars on jacks, mostly old junkers that looked to cater to the "ghetto fabulous" gang clientele in the area.

From underneath the hood of a yellow Mustang, a Latino man in grey coveralls caught sight of them and rose from his work, a broad smile on his face. He looked to be in his early twenties, with a close-cropped haircut and trimmed goatee. His nametag read Hector.

"Hola, jefe," he said to Macey, wiping his hands on a rag.

Macey shook his hand. "How are things, Hector?"

"Good." He then shot her an appreciative glance. "New girlfriend, Mace? She's pretty, this one." He chuckled and gave her a wink. "I like to pull the old man's chain when I get the chance. The name's Hector." He stretched his hand toward her.

She felt like an idiot for blushing a little, but managed to shake his hand with a smile. "Sheila."

"She's a client," Macey said. "We're going to need to use the apartment upstairs, and I'll need a car as well. Can you help me out?"

"Sure thing, Mace. Any preferences?"

"Something that won't get me pulled over." He surveyed the gaudy chrome-and-glitter plated monstrosities surrounding them. "Could you put it around the back for me? We'll be heading out soon."

"Sure thing, jefe."

Macey led her toward the back of the garage, where a set of stairs led them up to a corridor, which took them past an office to a locked door. He keyed it open, revealing a living space containing a bed with a silver trunk at its foot, a computer terminal, a closet, and a small bathroom.

"Well, this is it. Sorry, it's a bit of a downgrade."

She chuckled. "Dibs on the cot. So you rent this room from that guy?"

"I own the garage. It belonged to my wife's family. I took it over after she died."

Right: dead wife. "Oh." She didn't know how else to respond to that.

"Hector looks after the place for me. He's a good kid. Sorry about the girlfriend thing. He's not known for his tact."

"It's all right." Her cheeks grew hot again. "Is he family?"

"More or less." He stooped to the trunk and fiddled with the digital lock. "We need to equip ourselves a bit before we head out."

"With what?"

He tossed open the lid and rummaged among an assortment of clothing and personal effects. He withdrew a plank of wood that served as a false bottom. Beneath lay a cache of weapons and other armaments she couldn't begin to recognize.

"You've got to be kidding me." She'd never seen so many guns before. "We're actually going to need all this stuff?"

"Just this." Macey produced a revolver that looked nearly two feet long.

"What *is* that thing?"

"A twenty-millimeter handgun," he said, although that didn't make it any clearer to her. He popped open a barrel the size of a soup can and put three huge bullets into it. He slapped it back in place and jammed the revolver into a holster, which—she saw as he put it on—went on his shoulder. He tucked his regular gun behind his back.

"Don't worry, it's not for you." Next he went to the closet and sorted through some clothing, settling on a black nylon jacket.

"*This* is for you." He tossed it to her, nearly burying her with it.

"Eesh, this thing is heavy." She pushed it off to examine it at arms' length.

"It's armored. It'll probably look like a raincoat on you but be ready to wear it. It could save your life. Why don't you try it on?"

True to his prediction, the waist came to her knees and the elbow patches to her wrists. He helped her to fold the sleeves until it looked somewhat normal.

"There you go."

She took a glance in the mirror. "I look like a schoolgirl in this thing."

He laughed. "Yes, very cute, little Sheila."

"Spare me, Versace."

They both laughed and sat, she at the foot of the bed and he on the trunk opposite her. As their laughter died, they were left staring at one another. She wished he would kiss her again and, for a brief moment, she could sense the same longing in his eyes.

"Where are we going with this, Macey?"

His gaze quickly dropped to the floor. "Somewhere we shouldn't." Then raising his eyes again, he cracked a smile. "Was I that easy to read?"

"At least some things about you are. Why is it you play so emotionally hard to get?"

He licked his lips. "There's a lot you still don't know about me."

"I know enough. I know you're a pretty decent guy." Probably the most decent I've ever met. "Once you get past all that machismo, that is."

He laughed and took her hand, squeezing it gently as he stood. "Let me try and live up to that, then."

Forever the gentleman. She beamed up at him and he helped to her feet.

"Come on," he said. "Let's go find Pooly."

Twenty minutes later, Sheila found herself wrapped in the armor jacket and nestled within the plush leather seat of a '78 matte-black Viper. Hector had managed to round it up for them earlier. Macey had complained about its chrome rims and souped-up engine, but he'd finally conceded it was the least conspicuous choice on the lot. As Hector had put it, they would only get stopped if they caused reason to. Unfortunately, Macey seemed to be having a problem sticking to the speed limit. The throaty engine echoed between the buildings as they roared through the old downtown neighborhood.

He hadn't told her their exact destination, but he had mentioned Koreatown. Try as she might, she couldn't notice anything that differentiated it from Chinatown. The streets were packed with the same vendors and colorful displays, clogged with the same amount of traffic and tourists. Macey didn't seem to be heading for the market area though. Within a few minutes the shops began featuring live women as window dressing, displaying their bioenhanced bodies for sale.

"We headed to the red light district?"

Macey didn't answer. Eventually he pulled the Viper over in front of a hole in the wall with an open garage door entranceway and rows of private terminal booths set within. A flickering neon-pink holographic display above the door read: Jackson's Net Café. Macey exited the Viper and then, as usual, skirted around the hood to open her door. She took firm hold of his arm before following him inside.

Still the gentleman—but would a true gentleman take a lady to a place like this?

The air reeked of cigarette smoke and cheap beer, the dim fluorescent lighting against the black walls enhancing to the claustrophobic ambiance of the place. A handful of patrons were using the terminals: sweaty, balding old men with potbellies and five-day-old shaves. They were probably filling their heads with smutty sim-dreams or hacking some poor woman's neural net to watch her use the toilet or something.

Totally disgusting.

Macey paid them no mind as he passed through, pressing toward the back of the café. Sheila spotted a slim Asian man in a tight black suit leaning against the back wall, which she then noticed was actually a door.

As the man caught sight of them, he stiffened. "Hey, what do you want?"

"I want to see Pooly," Macey said. "And make it right now, please."

The man tilted his head and blew out a laugh. "Let's see a warrant."

"You know I don't need one, Troy." Macey fixed eyes with him. "Open the door or I'll do it for you."

Troy smirked and began laughing again. "You got no—"

Macey drove a fist into the door with a *blam!*

Sheila jumped—as did Troy, who leapt to the side.

"Hey watch it!" He glanced back at the door as if expecting it to be broken, but it remained intact.

"Next time it'll go straight through." Macey showed him the back of his fist now illuminated with his CDI tattoo. "Open it."

Troy muttered something in Korean, and the door slid open with a pneumatic hiss.

Inside lay a darker room, made even more so by the half-dozen men in black suits pointing handguns at them. Sheila's heart hit her chest and she screamed. A crack of gunfire reverberated as the men within reacted in a domino effect of confusion and panic.

Her world spun as Macey dove into her, pushing her to the ground.

Gunfire filled her ears. She clenched her eyes shut, barely opening them to glimpse Macey standing above her, his shirt popping with the impact of bullets.

Her screams and the gunfire sparked a further chain reaction of panic from patrons in the café, who fled in a disorganized mass.

Troy yelled something in Korean, repeating it several times before the men finally stopped shooting, their faces painted with as much panic and shock as hers must have been.

"Macey!" She rushed to his side to examine him. How was he still standing?

She searched his chest rapidly, patting him down, trying to find where the bullets had hit. But she didn't see any blood at all. Someone burst into laughter.

"What do you think you're doing, lady?" It was Troy, looking at her as if she were trying to clean a window with a hammer. He glared at his men. "And you trigger-happy noobs, thanks for scaring the customers away."

"I don't understand." She looked at her hands, expecting them to be covered in blood. "Macey, what just happened? Wait . . . are your clothes armored too?" Yes, that had to be it. Armored, just like her jacket.

"Let's talk inside." Macey pushed through the doorway, Troy's men parting like a school of fish. She stumbled in after him and Troy shut the door.

Immediately the gunmen trained their weapons on Macey.

"Drop 'em, you idiots," Troy said. "Don't you know who this guy is?" In a mixture of English and Korean, he muttered something about rookies. "If you want to threaten him, aim at her." He pointed at her and his men followed suit, training on her with their pistols.

Sheila's breath left her and her heart rate soared.

"Relax," Macey said. "They won't hurt you."

"Oh, are you speaking for us now, Mace?" Troy cocked his head. "I doubt she's built like you, buddy boy." He thumped on Macey's chest with the bottom of his fist. "I bet she doesn't know, does she?"

"Know what?" Sheila heard a squeak of panic in her own voice, which served to only heighten her fear. "Macey, what's going on?"

Troy laughed, clapping his hands. "Oh, this is going to be fun." He pulled a pistol from his jacket and aimed it straight at Macey's head. She tensed, her knees shaking. "Now don't move, Mace, or my boys will smoke your little honey there in more ways than one." He cocked the hammer for emphasis, grinning wildly.

"Please! Don't do this." This couldn't be happening. Not now. Not when everything was going so right. She sank toward the floor, curling into a ball. Her eyes flushed fresh with tears. "We just want to find someone named Pool—"

"Shut up," Troy shouted.

Casually, he pulled the trigger.

The pistol exploded in her ears, stealing her breath. She watched in slow motion as Macey's head jarred to the side as if hit with a baseball bat. His body convulsed in spasms and he hit the ground in a crumpled heap.

"No!" Her stomach left her as a shrill scream escaped her lips. She fell backward onto her heels, hands cupped over her mouth in a surrealistic daze. "This can't be happening. Macey!"

"Aim for the head," one of the gunmen said, a sick grin on his face. "Makes sense . . . no armor up there."

"Shut up," Troy said and then whirled on her. "And you shut up too."

She barely heard him, her eyes fixed on Macey. Something was wrong. He couldn't be dead. "Macey, get up. Come on, wake up."

But his body remained still. Lifeless. The image of it mocking her. Macey, the only person she had left to rely on, her only hope for salvation in this entire mess. Why did this happen? How? Why had they come here? For this?

She screamed in an uncontrollable sob, pain and rage consuming her. How could they kill him? How could they just kill him like that? She balled her hands into fists and pounded the floor as hot tears streamed down her face. "This can't be right! This can't be happening to me!"

Troy edged to where Macey lay and stooped to inspect his handiwork, tapping Macey's head with the tip of his gun barrel. "Man . . . that was easy."

"You sick freak!" She was losing all sense of herself. "You sick—"

"Hey! Will you please shut the—"

A hand caught him by the throat, severing his words as Macey sprang up, lifting Troy into the air in a single bound.

Sheila screamed, now as afraid of his reanimated body as much as anything. What was happening?

Macey and Tony hit the wall in a crash, both flying straight through it in a shower of plaster and splintering wood into the next room. Troy slammed, back-first, into a row of terminals as Macey landed a punch to his chest, solid as a sledgehammer driving a stake.

Sheila shook as she watched it all unfold in what seemed like barely a second. Her knees buckled as a deathly silence took hold, the only sound being that of debris crumbling from the wall.

Macey forced himself to ignore the freight train running through his head. The pain from the bullet impact still pummeled his brain.

He glanced back at Sheila, saw her staring at him, blank-faced, shaking. The gunmen threw glances between themselves as the silence permeated, broken by a wailing moan as Troy came to. Macey grabbed him by the collar, dragged him back through the makeshift opening they had just made, and pressed him against a wall with his forearm.

"No way, man," one of the gunmen said. "I think he's a freakin'—"

"Cyborg," Macey finished for him. "That's right. Your boss here should have known better than to try toying around like that. Isn't that right, Troy?"

Troy gurgled something inaudible between his blood-soaked teeth.

"Call your goons off. Now!"

Troy managed to wave his arm in a "drop it" sort of motion, and his men backed away.

<You okay, Sheila?> He tried contacting her through the comm but, as he expected, she didn't respond. He couldn't look at her right now—didn't want to see the horror on her face, the disgust in her eyes. Now she knew. He focused his attention on Troy instead.

"We came for Pooly. Where is he?"

"Nuh here man."

Macey shook him against the wall. "I can see that for myself. Where is he?"

Troy looked toward the ceiling and then at his feet, now a foot off the floor. "I dunno."

"Try again." He leaned inward. "Or do you want another flying lesson?"

"All right." Troy spat up some blood that rolled down his chin and over Macey's wrist. "He had a big transaction to make later. I got stuck here babysitting the new recruits." He glared at the gunmen. "Stupid f—"

"Who's the transaction with?"

"Dunno the guy's name. Pooly calls him the Freak."

"Where's it taking place?"

"A parking garage in old downtown." Troy gave him the address. "Look, man, I dunno what you're after but we don't want no beef with you."

"You should've thought about that before you shot me, huh, punk?" He looked to the gunmen. "And don't any of you even consider trying to warn Pooly. Pigman's going down for murder and more. If you have any sense you'll bail on that loser before you get pulled into it."

With that, he dropped Troy, who collapsed against the wall, breathing heavily. Sheila stood on the other side of the "doorway" he had made, her expression unreadable. Shock? Anger, perhaps?

As he stepped through the wall he couldn't bear to look at her. <*We're leaving now.*>

She walked in front of him as they departed the café and returned to the Viper. Reaching for the ignition, he stopped and risked a glance across at her, stomach tight with anxiety. She stared straight ahead, biting her lower lip.

He inhaled deeply and let out a sigh. "Sheila, I—"

"Don't."

He waited for her to speak first. It didn't take long.

"So, this is your big secret . . ." She threw her hands in the air. "That you're not human. That you're some kind of cyber machine?"

"Not human? Will you listen to yourself?"

"Sorry, I'm in shock here." She shoved a palm toward him. "I can't think right now."

Macey drummed his fingers on the steering wheel, kept his head straight. "I'm as human as you are, Sheila. The only difference is that you still have your original body. I only have about five percent of mine."

"So your entire body is—"

"Prosthetic, a shell made to look like me. But even if the only part of the real me that's left is my brain, I'm still a person. The same person you've come to know."

Her response was an all-too-familiar stare, a stare of aversion, distrust, and plain old pity. It was the look he'd come to expect whenever he revealed the truth to someone.

"I understand if you want me to stop." He turned away from her.

"What?" Her brows arched. "Oh no, Macey . . . . I'm sorry. I just . . . . I mean, I've heard of this before, but I didn't think it still happened. I thought they did away with prosthetic body transplants ages ago."

"They did. I'm obsolete technology. I'm sure your genetics firm could probably clone me a fresh new body to transplant into."

"Absolutely, we could. Why haven't you—"

"Personal reasons. Besides, this body does have its advantages, especially in my line of work."

"So I saw." She gazed at him as if for the first time. "It all makes sense now . . . why I barely see you eat anything, how you were able to run so fast that time. What about at Jules's lab when Bradley attacked us? Couldn't you have done what you did just now? Why did you run then?"

"Those guys had assault rifles, not handguns like these clowns. My body is fairly well armored, but those rifle rounds would tear me up eventually. Besides, I didn't really want you to . . ."

"To know?"

He sighed and wiped his face. "It's not something I like to advertise, okay? I mean, look how you reacted."

"Me? Macey, I thought you were dead. That upset me more than anything else. Do you know what was going through my mind when I saw you hit that floor?"

He honestly hadn't thought about that. "I'm sorry. I needed some way to throw Troy off. I knew he was going to do something stupid like that. Besides, it wasn't all fake. That bullet might not have penetrated my skull but it hit hard enough to knock me out for a few seconds. Got the headache to prove it too. I can still get concussions, internal hemorrhaging. I can still die from a head wound. I just played possum a little longer to sucker him in."

She pulled her lips into a frown. "Well, you certainly suckered me in."

He couldn't help but let loose a chuckle, but he dare not push it. "I'm really sorry. I honestly didn't mean to upset you so much."

"Macey, look . . ." She turned herself toward him. "I admit I'm a bit surprised, but I'm okay with it. I mean, it's not like your body is that different. I wouldn't have even known unless you told me, or maybe if we had tried to— Oh, my. Is that why when we almost . . . you know . . . is that why you never wanted to . . . ?"

"Huh?" Then he understood what she was getting at. "Oh, no."

"So you're a . . . *full* man then, right?"

Macey smirked. "Is that all you're worried about?"

"Well?"

Was she for real? "Just don't expect any kids, all right?" He sighed with embarrassment. "I can't believe I'm even having this conversation."

Her giggle eased his tension. "Are you blushing?" She shook her head slowly at him, her eyes filled with awe. "All this time . . . During the shooting in the mission district, you were hit, weren't you? And you protected me, didn't you? I thought it was just luck that I didn't get shot. How many times have you saved my life without me even knowing it?"

Thirty-four. "Come on, we need to get moving." He started the car.

"Wait." She leaned over the handbrake, grabbed him by the collar, pulled his head to hers, and kissed him thoroughly on the lips.

Finally she released him and sat back in her seat with a mischievous grin. "That's to let you know how much I hate your body. And don't you forget it, okay? Now drive."

Macey chuckled, fully aware that she really had made him blush. Even more surprising was that he didn't mind.

Bradley watched the matte-black Viper pull away from the curb and started his own car.

<They're moving again.>

<Do they have it?>

<Don't think so. We'll see where they go next. They seem to be taking off in a hurry.>

<Make sure you do a better job this time, Bradley. I want this business over with as soon as possible.>

<Don't worry, Mr. Boreman.> Bradley checked his rearview mirror to make sure his two vans were shadowing him. *<I have plenty of help this time.>*

CHAPTER EIGHT

MACEY HAMMERED THE GAS. He steered the Viper down the onramp and onto the freeway. But then he had to ride the brakes. The rush-hour traffic barely moved, trudging forward like a troop of weary soldiers at a slow march. He had to slow almost to a stop before he found a gap to merge into.

Sheila sighed and rubbed her temple. "We'll never get through all this. Maybe we should have stuck to the back roads."

He tried to ignore her negativity as he continued merging toward the auto-drive lane at the far left. When he finally reached it, he keyed the auto-drive and slipped into the queue.

"What are you doing? This is gonna be worse. We should stay in the manual lanes and try to weave our way through."

"Trust me, this will be faster."

"Yeah, right." She folded her arms and slumped into her seat. "By the time we—"

In unison the traffic in front of them began pulling to the edge of the slightly wider auto-drive lane, leaving an opening just wide enough for the Viper to fit through.

"Oh ye of little faith," he said with a grin, "wherefore didst thou doubt?"

Her mouth hung open. "What did you just do?"

"Hacked the traffic control satellite. The other cars think we're an emergency vehicle now."

"You can do stuff like that?"

"Pretty easy if you know how. I'm surprised more people don't do it. But we'll need to get off here before the real authorities notice."

"Maybe this is a bad idea, then. The last thing we need is that kind of attention."

"You have a better solution?"

She twisted her lips and gave a shrug in her oversized jacket. Taking that as consent, he disengaged the auto-drive and pressed on the gas. With a roar the Viper accelerated with a force that pushed them deep into their seats. Peeling through the gears, he brought the Viper onto a straightaway, where he dropped into top gear with the pedal pegged to the floor. The scream of the engine became a constant high pitched-drone. The traffic on either side blurred into two solid walls as they sped through, streaking past close enough to touch.

Sheila sat white-faced, her hands digging into the leather seat as she stared through the side and front windows. "How fast are we going?"

"You don't want to know." He held the wheel tightly as he navigated through their slim pathway. It was a little like threading a needle in the middle of a hurricane. Even with the Viper's fine-tuned feedback control linked to his neural net, he couldn't risk losing concentration, not for a second. As if to drive the point home, something caught his eye in the rearview mirror, and he eased off the gas immediately. Barely visible, maybe a football-field length behind them was a black sedan. He enhanced his vision, magnifying the rearview.

"What's wrong?" Sheila said.

"Something's in our wake."

"Our what?"

"The traffic moves out of our way for up to a mile ahead and there's a delay before it moves back again. Another vehicle can slip in and take advantage of that gap, so long as it can keep up."

"Is it the police?" She peered behind.

He checked the traffic satellite. "No."

"Who is it then?"

He had a few ideas, but he didn't want to alarm her any further. "Could be some street-racing punks. Vipers attract that kind of attention."

"Oh . . ." She sounded unconvinced.

He let the topic rest and returned his attention to the road. He hit the gas again, to make certain taking advantage of their wake would not be an easy task.

• • •

Pooly marveled at the object that would soon become his key to success. A glass vial the size of a soda can, nestled tightly within the foam cushion of the silver case on the hood of his Bronco.

The clear genetic goop inside it was pressurized, or so the kid doctor had told him, warning that if the container broke, the stuff would go off like a grenade. Pooly had made a mental note to be careful while handling it and, after thanking the good doctor for the information, had wasted him with a gunshot to the gut—just to make it more painful.

The late afternoon sun was blocked by the Freak standing next to him. His long shadow stretched across the concrete of the parking garage roof. The sun painted the rest in a dull orange glow.

It still bothered him that he'd had to double-cross a client. That wasn't his style. A fixer lived on his reputation, after all. If word ever got around that Pooly the Pig killed his clients, his career would be over. But the sum to be made off this last deal had made killing Dr. Hague well worth the risk.

Enough to make it to the big leagues in one easy transaction.

All he needed to do was stop being the middleman and start delivering the goods directly, which meant getting rid of the seller. In this case, the seller had been a straight-up chump from the mundane world, and an annoying one at that. No one in the right circles would know him, much less know the size of the deal going down. Or care that he was dead. To the people that mattered, Dr. Julian Hague didn't exist. And now, he really didn't.

"So, Virgil?" Pooly glanced up at the ebony giant standing next to him. His mere presence always brought on a sense of anxiety within him. He had heard stories of combat cyborgs slipping into psychosis after a while, flipping out. And as much as he knew about Virgil, the guy had to be well on his way.

Pooly glanced about, making certain his entourage of five bodyguards had stayed with him. They were still here, loafing against the roof's safety wall and keeping watch on the riffraff below. Not that they would stand a chance against Virgil—he'd once seen a combat cyborg take out a tank. But his bodyguards would serve as great cannon fodder, giving him a chance to escape. The prospect made him chuckle.

Virgil took the canister and stared at it in silence. The amount of time he spent doing so caused another worry—could the kid doctor have stiffed him with a dud? Suddenly Virgil pried the cylinder from the foam, rolled it within his palm, then bounced it up and down as if weighing it.

"Hey, don't drop that. If that thing breaks it'll blow up."

Virgil's lips curved into a smile below his mirror shades, and he rested the cylinder back in the case. Pooly's blood pressure dropped a few points.

"This will be fine," Virgil said. "I'll transfer the funds to the account now."

Pooly opened his access to Dr. Hague's offshore account and watched the transaction take place in the corner of his vision. He failed to restrain a grin of utter delight as the final sum lit up. "Very nice."

A call came through on his internal comm, tagged urgent. The ID checked as Troy.

<*What is it?*>

<*Pooly, it's Troy.*>

<*I can see that, you moron. What do you want? I'm right in the middle of this.*>

<That guy Macey came poking around here.>

<What did he want?>

<He was looking for you.>

Pooly rubbed his scalp as a fresh film of sweat sprung forth. *<What did you tell him?>*

<Nothing. Well, I didn't say nothing, but Macey got hold of one of the new guys and the dumb kid spilled his guts about the whole deal.>

"What!"

"Something the matter, Gordon?" Virgil peered down at him.

"Nuffin'." Pooly waved him away and turned his back to the giant. *<What are you talking about, Troy?>*

<The kid told him where you were headed, but don't worry. I already took care of that little punk for you. I took his—>

<I don't care about that. What happened with Macey?>

<I think he's on his way to you. He looked kinda ticked. I think you better jet.>

Pooly cursed as he disconnected the call. Virgil hovered over him, as if expecting to hear what the call was about.

"We need to wrap this up," Pooly said. "We got some company coming."

"Company?" The Freak remained cool as ever. "The authorities?"

"Something like that." He closed the case containing the vial, since Virgil hadn't bothered to do that yet. Finally he handed it to him. "Come on, man, take it."

"What's goin' on, Pooly?" one of his men called.

"We're splittin'." He opened the door to the Bronco and clambered inside. "Every time I get so freakin' close to something big, something like this happens."

"I sense your anxiety, Gordon." Virgil stood outside like an idiot. "I wish there was something I could do for you. Perhaps I still can. My offer stands—"

"Will you just get outta here, man? I already told you I don't need no Jesus bull—"

Wait a minute.

It was true, he didn't need Jesus or whatever else Virgil was trying to pawn off on him, but he could sure use something else he had to offer. His heart raced at the mere thought of it. Macey had been a pain in his side for years. Granted, he didn't hustle him like some of those other crooked cops he knew, but Macey had a way of poking his nose in the wrong place at the wrong time. Not unlike now.

Usually his first reaction to hearing that Macey was paying a visit was to turn tail and run. A perfectly sane response, considering Macey was a full-blown cyborg.

But then, so was the Freak.

"Hey, hold on a minute," he said to Virgil, then turned to his men. "You guys get back out of the car. We're staying."

"Changed your mind, Gordon?"

"Sorta. How'd you like to earn yourself a little cash-back discount on the price?"

"What do you mean?"

"There's this guy on his way here. Works for CDI. He's built like you, if you know what I mean."

Virgil removed his mirror shades, the first time he'd ever seen him do so. Now Pooly understood why he kept them on. His eyes were two completely black spheres, like giant black olives. The sight of them sent a chill down his spine.

"That's freakin' scary, man," one of his men said.

Virgil leveled his face to Pooly's, his hollow black eyes looking like the pits of hell itself.

"CDI, you say? I'm listening . . ."

Macey pulled out of the auto-drive lane and onto the exit ramp, nipping through the traffic. He kept his speed up as he entered the narrow surface streets, using the traffic satellite as a guide to the parking garage and Pooly's deal. Behind them, the traffic clogged again, hopefully trapping whoever it was who had been following.

Dilapidated buildings and cars lined the streets. Cybergangers congregated in packs. He wouldn't have to worry about the police chasing him here—this neighborhood was on the same "do-not-service" list as the mission district was. It made sense for Pooly to have chosen this area for the deal to take place. Within a few turns, the designated parking garage came into view, looming like a monument before them.

Macey slowed the Viper to a stop. "Troy said they'd be on the roof."

"And I'm guessing we don't just drive up there?" Sheila craned her neck.

"The car stays down here. So do you."

Her gaze hardened. "You're kidding, right?"

"It's too dangerous. This could be a lot worse than anything you've seen yet."

"But it's just two guys, right? Pooly and Virgil. I mean, you're indestructible. I'll stay out of your way but—"

"You're not hearing me. You are staying here."

She glanced about. "Macey, you see the type of crowd hanging around here? I'd feel safer with you than staying down here by myself."

Macey exhaled. She was right. Even now he could see some Gothers slinging neurostims from just across the block. No, leaving Sheila alone in the Viper created a temptation even the most reformed criminal would be unable to resist, much less these freaks. He hadn't counted on the neighborhood being so bad, but neither had he anticipated taking her with him all the way to the roof.

"I can move faster on my own," he said.

Her face reddened. "I . . . ah, no problem. I thought you were . . . . I feel stupid now."

"What are you talking about?"

"I thought you were trying to protect me. I didn't realize I was just slowing you down."

"Hey, don't think like that. It *is* to protect you. I honestly don't—"

Something in the rearview mirror drew his attention. It was the same black sedan, bearing down on them at high speed, two white vans close behind it. He grimaced inwardly. So much for losing them on the highway.

The two vans cut away in opposite directions, leaving the sedan on its solo path toward them. He read the tactic immediately. A pincer maneuver—they were trying to surround them.

"We need to go."

"What? Why?"

He didn't have time to explain. He jammed the Viper into gear and hit the gas.

The tires spun as he poured on the acceleration to keep ahead of the sedan and the two vans attempting to outflank them.

He thought about pulling them into a chase, trying to lose them, but that would take time they didn't have. About now, Pooly would be concluding his deal, handing over Hague's negating agent for citywide dispersal. No choice. He headed straight for the parking garage.

Sheila peered through the rear window. "Is that the car that was following us?"

He shifted forcefully through the gears. "I doubt it's Troy. It's probably—"

"Bradley," Sheila said it for him, spitting out his name like cod liver oil. "I bet it's him. You can fix him the same way you did Troy. Little punk." She smirked like a bratty little sister who had just gotten her big brother into trouble.

"Look, I'm not Superman, okay? Don't get complacent. You can still get killed, and so can I."

"But you're—"

"I mean it." He plunged the Viper through the garage entranceway. "Just because my body is prosthetic doesn't mean it can't be damaged. There's no telling how this is going to pan out."

She opened her mouth as if to say something, closed it again.

He felt bad for chastising her, but he couldn't dwell on it, She needed to know the truth. He concentrated on driving, the tires chirping on the smooth concrete as he jerked the Viper toward the narrow access ramp. No sooner had he reached it than an answering chirp of tires came from the sedan behind them.

They were too close. He sped up as much as he could within the confines of the ramp, but the Viper's length and tendency to lose traction on the concrete worked to their disadvantage.

He could barely get out of first gear before having to slow down and negotiate another turn.

"He's gaining on us. Speed up!"

He felt like reminding her that they were heading to a rooftop—speed up to where? Worse, he had no idea what he'd find there. He had envisioned making his way to the top solo, stealthily, taking in the situation and formulating a plan to deal with it. But that was impossible now. Whatever they would find, however Pooly and his client would react to a Viper tearing onto the roof, he would have to be ready for it.

The moment came all too quickly. He rounded the final bend and met the crimson glare of a sinking sun.

He took in his surroundings while holding the gas. His vision enhanced automatically, magnifying the targets. Toward the far end of the roof sat a black Bronco. Pooly and several men stood in front of it, pistols drawn.

They fired.

Macey pulled the emergency brake and slid the Viper's driver side to face them. Sheila screamed as a bullet blew out the rear window in a glass-shattering pop. A shower of debris sprayed inside, bouncing off the leather seats like hail.

"Get out your side." He pushed her.

They scrambled from the Viper as more bullets tore into it. For a split second, ridiculously, his only thought was that this was the third car this week destroyed on this case. Wiping the thought from his mind, he rushed to shelter Sheila. He grabbed her by the waist and rolled to bring them behind the engine.

He hadn't seen their attackers wielding anything more powerful than handguns, so the engine block should be able to shield them. As the firecracker pops of small arms filled the air, he managed to draw his Mauser from his waist, though returning fire would mean exposing Sheila. Sparks flew overhead, bringing a torrent of broken glass. The world was closing in on him.

"Macey! What do we do?"

The roar of an engine and the squealing of tires drew their attention: the black sedan making its entrance.

Pooly's men turned their fire to it. The sedan slid to a stop and reversed, sparks pinging off of its hood.

Pooly's ambush had come in handy for something at least.

But the air of relief evaporated as the two white vans joined the melee. They drove to shielding positions ahead of the sedan and halted with their broadsides facing front. Macey tensed in preparation for whatever would come flying out of them. But so far nothing did. The gunfire died away and a piercing silence filled the void.

"Macey?" Sheila whispered.

"You okay?" He couldn't see her face, but from her voice he knew she wasn't crying. In a way he wished she were, but her tone held steady, calm, matter-of-fact. The tone of someone resigned to a bitter fate.

"We're going to get out of this," he said, even though he had no idea how. He glanced toward the roof's edge. He could easily reach it without catching a bullet, could easily survive the fall. But not while carrying Sheila. Even with him cushioning her landing, the impact would probably kill her.

They were pinned down. Pooly and his men on one side and, on the other, Bradley and whatever arsenal he had brought.

The silence stretched into an eon. The lack of movement brought his nerves to a razor's edge.

And then it occurred to him.

Pooly wouldn't have stopped firing merely from the shock of Bradley's arrival. Pooly had no idea who Bradley was. If anything, Pooly would most likely assume the vans belonged to Macey. That thought sparked him into action.

"Give it up, Pooly. C-D-I!" he shouted through enhanced vocal chords, his voice magnified as if through a megaphone. Sheila's mouth gaped but he couldn't spare time to explain. "We have the roof surrounded. I suggest you toss down your weapons."

"What are you doing?" Sheila said in a squeal.

"Now!" He was playing a gamble and so far it was paying off—both sides had hesitated. In any battle, information held the key to victory, and knowing who held what information could turn the tide in even the most desperate situation.

His only true goal was to reach the other side of the Viper and find more protection from whatever Bradley had hidden in the vans. His body could take anything Pooly could dish out, but he didn't want to take that chance with Bradley. The kid had already proven he liked big guns—enough to be accused of overcompensating for something. With the car as a shield, he could keep Sheila safe. He hoped.

Bradley just needed to hesitate long enough for Pooly to lower his weapons. Then he could make a break without the risk of Pooly shooting Sheila. He prayed his unorthodox oratory had achieved that.

Or something.

"Hold on," he whispered to Sheila. And then in his booming voice: "Drop it now, Pooly, or we open fire."

Metal clattered on concrete as pistols fell to the ground, mere seconds before a mechanical click signaled the van doors opening. He waited no longer. Grabbing Sheila tightly about her armored jacket, he vaulted into the air and flipped into a back somersault over the Viper's roof. His feet touched ground and he spun his back to the Viper, his eyes to Pooly.

His sudden move must have caused yet another hesitation from Pooly's side. In front of the Bronco, Pooly stood alongside his five men, faces contorted with twisted brows and hanging jaws. Although the image would probably imprint in his memory for an eternity, it lasted but a moment.

A terrible sound like the revving of an un-muffled chainsaw assaulted the air in an ear-shattering burst. A water-cannon like stream of bullets chewed the Bronco into a smoldering wreck. Instantaneously, Pooly and all five of his men literally exploded in a cloud of red mist.

Sheila screamed horrifically. "What was that?"

Macey knew the answer but his mind had scant chance to comprehend it, much less utter its name. Somehow Bradley had gotten hold of a rotary cannon.

As successful as his ploy was in getting them to the other side of the Viper, now he knew it had done nothing to save them. A rotary cannon would tear the Viper in half and himself as well. He clutched Sheila close, preparing for another inevitable cannon-blast.

The ground shook beneath him. Next the chainsaw sound of the cannon shattered the air into a million pieces. He tensed against the cannon blast.

But nothing came.

The blare sounded again and a patch of concrete some twenty feet away from them became a three-inch pothole. The firing continued, but nothing came close. Bradley couldn't be shooting at them.

Macey risked a glance over the hood, a swift twist and turn that revealed only a glimpse of the action, but a glimpse proved all he needed. They were shooting at someone but not him.

Instead, they were targeting someone new to the party. A tall black man dressed in camos, a white overcoat, and mirror shades.

"Macey?" Sheila said as he plopped back down. "What's happening out there?"

His mind was reeling.

"It's Virgil." He let his Mauser drop to the floor in a clatter and pulled the 20mm revolver from his shoulder holster, cocked the hammer. "When I stand up I want you to get directly behind me, understand?"

"What for?"

"Just do it!"

He sprang to his feet, whirling to encompass a view of the battlefield and absorbing the details. The black sedan had left the roof, the two vans remained, their side doors wide open, each revealing a tripod-mounted rotary cannon inside. A single gunner controlled each of the monstrous weapons. Presently they seemed to have their hands full trying to get a lock on their elusive target—Virgil.

He was built like an NBA star. But he moved with the agility of a gymnast, bounding and somersaulting from one end of the roof to the other, stopping long enough to goad both gunners into committing to an attack and at the last second bounding away so quickly he became a blur.

"I've never seen anything like that," Sheila whispered from behind him. "Is he a—"

"Yeah. Stay down."

The display of acrobatic skill and power was mesmerizing, even for Macey. Virgil's leaps and bounds were more than just random dodging too. With each jump he inched toward the vans. Now the gunners were not so much trying to shoot him as trying to keep him away from them.

Thanks to Virgil's distraction, Macey had a chance to turn the tables. He aimed the 20mm revolver at the barrel of one of the rotary cannons, braced himself for the heavy recoil, and pulled the trigger.

The revolver went off with a thunderclap. The heavy slug flew true to its target, and the rotary cannon collapsed in an explosion of sparks, leaving the gunner sprawling.

Before Macey could take aim at the other gunner, Virgil launched his own assault, jumping in a criss-cross motion so rapidly the gunner barely had chance to swing the barrel, much less get a shot off. In a final leap, the giant of a man plunged inside the van and tore the cannon from its supports before turning his head toward the gunner, who now cowered with his arms raised.

Virgil said something to the gunner he couldn't quite hear, and the gunner leapt from the van and ran down the exit ramp. The other gunner and the drivers followed suit. Virgil then lifted the huge rotary cannon to his side, wielding it as easily as a rifle within his broad arms.

"Oh, no," Sheila whispered, "he's coming for us next. Can your gun stop him?"

"Yeah . . ." Macey aimed his large revolver at the giant. "It can." He lined up his shot, locking his arm to prepare for the recoil.

Virgil turned to face him with the cannon.

Macey's nerves stood on end. Would he simply open fire on them? Perhaps he saw them as no threat, not realizing he held a 20mm revolver in his hand.

Whatever the case, the ebony titan chose to stride toward them, cannon raised, white overcoat billowing behind him like the wings of an angel of death.

"Shoot him!" Sheila said. "What are you waiting for?"

"You see what this is, don't you?" Macey called out to him. "Fires 20mm rounds. You know it can penetrate your skull."

"Indeed," Virgil said, his gait unabated. "Is that what you came here to do?"

Shakily, Macey reset his grip on the revolver, trying to ignore the sweat coating his palms. "I don't want to kill you."

Virgil tossed the rotary cannon to the ground with an almighty crash, presenting himself with palms open. "If you don't mean to kill me, you know where to aim to immobilize me." He tapped his throat, indicating the best place to separate his human brain from his cyborg body. "Go ahead, if you think your cause is just."

Macey smirked. "And what makes you so certain that yours is a just cause?"

"We are all meant to die," Virgil said, looking at them through those reflective shades. "'The days of our years are threescore years and ten; and if by reason of strength they be fourscore years, yet is their strength labor and sorrow; for it is soon cut off, and we fly away.'"

"Psalm ninety, verse ten."

Virgil dipped his chin. "I'm glad to see you've not grown weak in the Scriptures, Brother Macey." A broad grin spread across his face. "When I heard that CDI was involved, I prayed I would find you again. God truly answers prayer, doesn't He?"

<*What did he call you?*> Sheila's voice needled him through the comm, her eyes burning holes into him like lasers.

Macey examined him. "You look different. At first I wasn't sure it was really you."

"I inherited this body from an Egyptian man." Virgil stopped just a few feet from him. "Closest thing I could find to my old body. But when you're a cyborg living on the fringes, you take what you can get. You, on the other hand, look very much the same."

"I got a good maintenance plan."

The big man let out a laugh. "Ever the joker. I've missed your humor a great deal. And who is your lady friend, Macey? It's rude not to introduce."

"She's none of your concern." He tightened his grip on the 20mm. "And I didn't come here to tell jokes."

Virgil clasped his hands in front of him. "So tell me, Macey, why *did* you come? Did you truly wait all these years just to find me now?"

"I've come to stop you from releasing that negating agent Pooly gave you. Where is it?"

"It's a shame to hear you say that. I've already hidden it in a safe place." He paused, looked up at the sky. "I also have no intentions of stopping. If you truly want to try to prevent what God has ordained, I give you the opportunity now."

"It's not your right to take all those people's lives, Virgil. Thou shalt not murder, remember? You do realize that the negating agent will destroy the Miracle Treatment worldwide? You will be responsible for the premature deaths of billions of people. Is that what God has ordained?"

"I do nothing more than what God has already willed." Virgil tucked his hands into his overcoat pockets. "All men must die. Man's pride has disrupted that simple plan. I would think you of all people would understand this, Macey. Are we not both victims ourselves? I am simply setting the course straight."

"You're killing people."

"I kill no one. I am merely giving them back the fear of death. Is it not the fear of death that drives men to seek God? But with this illusion—this Miracle Treatment—man has fooled himself into believing he has defeated death. And now he believes he has no need for God. But man's will cannot supercede God's will. Death still exists, my old friend, and it will seek all out eventually."

He glanced to where the bodies of Pooly and his men lay. "Sometimes violently. And then where will their souls be? But don't we both know this already, Macey? Why would you want to doom these people to our fate? Artificially long life is no blessing. Or have you fallen prey to the illusion as well?"

Things he had ignored for years flooded to the surface of his mind. He closed his eyes tightly, trying to force them out of his head.

"If you still feel I am wrong, then take your chance now." Moving a step closer, Virgil took the barrel of Macey's revolver and stuck it to his own throat. "Stop me while you have the chance."

He could barely bring himself to look at Virgil. So many years, so many memories. He turned away from him and glanced at Sheila.

Her eyes were shimmering puddles. Helplessness, confusion, and despair marred her angelic face. His own eyes welled as guilt consumed his soul. Slowly he lowered the revolver and sank to his knees.

<I'm sorry, Sheila.> He messaged her through the comm, unable to meet her violet gaze, much less speak over the tightness growing in his throat. *<I'm so sorry.>*

"Praise God," Virgil said and he extended his hand. "Come with me, brother. Let us do the work of the Lord together. Like old times."

He stared at Virgil's hand intently, wanting it to disappear. "I . . . I can't go with you," he said hoarsely and took another glance at Sheila. She had wandered toward the edge of the roof, her arms wrapped around herself as she stood with her back to him. "I . . . I have—"

"I see." Virgil followed his gaze toward Sheila. "You have some decisions to make. I'll wait on you then, old friend."

"Just go, please." He could bear Virgil's presence no longer.

"Next time, I shall be the one to find you." With that, he bounded into the air and soared off the garage roof.

Macey stared at the revolver in his hand, thought about placing it to his own head. But he just stuffed it away in his holster. He dragged himself to his feet and lumbered toward Sheila. If not for the situation, he would leave her be. But he had to get her to safety first.

Get her to safety? He could have ended her whole ordeal moments ago with a simple pull of the trigger. Such a useless hypocrite he was. Yet he pressed on with the façade anyway.

"Sheila," he called to her ramrod spine, "we need to leave."

She didn't respond.

He waited a while before trying again. "Sheil—"

"Don't say my name," she said with enough venom to kill. "Don't even come near me. You . . . you . . . I don't even know what you are anymore."

Macey took her words in silence. He deserved every one of them, and more.

Finally she did turn to face him, a mocking smile on her face. "You know, Macey, I really thought you were doing all this because you actually cared about me. I'm so stupid."

"I—"

"To think you really were doing this for yourself from the start. Just like you said. You were never out to solve this case, to help me. All you wanted was to find your old . . . church buddy or whatever he is."

"It's not like that."

"Isn't it?" Her small frame shook and her eyes pierced him. "I trusted you with my life. Macey, you're all I have left to believe in. My life is gone. Everyone I know has betrayed me . . . hates me . . . wants me dead." Her brows dropped into deep arcs of sorrow. Tears ran freely. "Now even you've betrayed me . . . abandoned me. You said you'd never do that. You lied to me, Macey."

The ball in his throat grew to the point of choking him. He wished he could find the words to fix this. Once, he could always find words to fix anything. But not now, it seemed, not when he was so dead wrong.

He deserved every minute of the agony he felt.

"You know what the worst part is?" She sniffled, wiped her cheeks with the sleeves of the armored jacket. "The reason why this hurts me so much? Do you?"

When it looked like she actually wanted an answer, he managed to shake his head.

"I was really starting to have feelings for you." She said it with a disdain that ate at the core of his soul. "And I thought maybe you had feelings for me too. Do you know, at one point

I pretty much resigned myself to this whole thing? I told myself that no matter what happens to me in the end, no matter how it all turns out, it would all be worth it if in the end all I got . . . was you."

He paused, almost unable to respond. "Sheila, I'm still here . . ."

Her face twisted into a mask of pain and grief. "No, you're not," she said in a sob. "Why is my life like this? Every time I think something good has happened, it turns out so messed up. My career, the Miracle Treatment, and now you . . ."

"I never meant to lie to you, Sheila. But I never planned on what's happening between us either."

Her eyes lifted and he held her gaze.

"I didn't plan on a lot of things. I didn't plan on how things would turn out today. To be honest, yes, I did take this whole case in the hope of finding Virgil again. But I had no idea what I wanted to find him for. Maybe I wanted to finally confront my past. But in these last few days I've lost focus. Sheila, I have feelings for you that a man in my position just shouldn't."

"Why? Why do you say that?" She stepped toward him, pleading with her hands. "Why do you keep closing yourself off from me?" She stopped a few feet from him, just in front of the burned-out Viper. Her form was silhouetted against the fiery light of the setting sun.

"I'm not. Not anymore. I want to tell you everything."

Sheila swallowed visibly, waiting.

"Not here," Macey said. "We need to go someplace. Bradley could still be around."

"No." She shook her head, dark hair swinging. "I'm not going anywhere with you. Not until you tell me something, anything. Make me trust you again."

He leaned against the Viper next to her. “What do you want me to tell you?”

“Anything!”

He glanced over his shoulder into nothingness. Sighed. And then looked back at her again. “How old do you suppose I am?”

The question sent her brows snaking upward. She shrugged. “I don’t know. Forty maybe? You said you’ve never had the Treatment, right?”

“Never. And I probably won’t ever need to either.”

Her eyes squinted.

“Life extension might have been made popular by your Miracle Treatment, Sheila, but it wasn’t the first method to achieve it.”

“W-what are you talking about?”

“Most cyborgs were created with military intention in mind. Few survive combat long enough to see the full extent of their normal lives. If they did, they’d soon realize that, without a normal body to pollute it, the human brain can survive a very long time.”

“What are you saying?” She stepped closer, eyes darting. “Just how old are you?”

Macey inhaled deeply and released a lengthy breath. “I was born in 1970, Sheila.”

Her eyes grew wide as her jaw fell slack.

“I’m one hundred and eleven years old.”

CHAPTER NINE

BRADLEY THOMAS SCANNED the top of the parking garage from three blocks away. He tried to catch a glimpse of his quarry through his multi-optic shades. His subordinates wisely kept their distance from him as he searched. They crammed themselves into the back seat of the black sedan while he remained outside, the bunch of them looking every bit the little boys that they were.

Pure incompetence.

He couldn't blame them only, though. Bad intel was also a culprit. He hadn't expected another party to be present, nor for them to attack on sight. Then that cyborg had showed up, putting an end to the entire production. None of that was in the plan. He hadn't ID'd the new cyborg yet. Ironically, they had come especially equipped to handle a cyborg—just not two of them.

He'd done his homework on Rick Macey after Macey had knocked him flat on his rear outside Julian's lab. The official files he could lift on him were sparse, but after a small amount of snooping via external means, he found Rick Macey was well known in certain circles to be a full-body prosthetic, and a combat cyborg at that. He'd have to check if there was a link between Macey and the other cyborg that showed up. Far too improbable for coincidence.

Bradley scanned the parking garage floor by floor with his shades in telescopic mode but could see no movement. And what could he do if he did find them? Let Macey bust his chops again? He needed to stop wasting time and come up with another plan. Besides, tracking Sheila wasn't a problem.

"This mission is a wipe," he said to his men. "We won't be heading back to HQ either. We're taking another shot at this."

His goons went quiet—a silent protest to his statement.

"We've wasted too much money on this op to go back to Boreman empty-handed. We *will* get this right."

While Bradley was looking for Macey, Macey was watching him. He watched from concealment as Bradley jumped into the black sedan and drove off. Then he waited for it to disappear into the distance before finally feeling secure enough to reveal himself.

"He's gone." He stood from behind the roof's retaining wall.

Sheila dusted off her knees while he took in their transportation options.

The Viper was a wreck. So was Pooly's Bronco. The two vans looked tempting, but he didn't trust them not to be traceable by Bradley. Any other cars in the garage had long ago been scavenged of any working parts.

"What now?" she asked.

"We'll have to walk. Seems the safest bet."

"Are you serious?" She jerked her thumb toward the vans. "Let's take one of those."

"Thought about that. Too much risk that Bradley can track us if we use them."

"Who cares?" She was already walking toward the closest one, her armored jacket clinging to her like plastic wrap. "He seems to manage that no matter what we do. Besides, we can ditch it and grab a cab somewhere, right?"

He smiled. Sheila was way ahead of him.

An hour later they returned to the safe house in Watts, stopping for something quick to eat on the way. They passed Hector on the way inside. Macey dodged the obvious question as to why they had returned in a taxi and not in the Viper. He gave a simple "Don't ask" and Hector knew him well enough not to pursue it after that.

Inside the tiny upper room, Sheila found a seat at the foot of the bed. Macey sat opposite her on the trunk. He knew she was probably wary of both Bradley and Virgil and what they would do next, but they would be safe for now. It would take some time for Bradley to mount another attack. And when it came to Virgil, the ball was in his court, it seemed.

A pause weighted the air. As the inevitable moment of confession approached, Macey found himself hesitating, at a loss for words.

"So how do you know Virgil?" she asked.

The question was simple enough, yet he contemplated his response. He didn't want to get any of the details wrong. "We met during the war in Iraq. We were in our thirties at the time, both lieutenants, platoon commanders in the same company. After that came the Iranian conflict, and we served together there as well."

"So you've known him for . . ."

He spared her the calculation. "Over seventy years. In those days we were close friends. No . . . much more than friends. We were brothers . . . literally."

She arched a brow.

"Virgil was one of the best field commanders I've ever known." Macey smiled as he remembered it all. "I'm not sure how much you know about the Iraq War, but when Virgil and I entered the conflict, things were in a terrible state. The invasion was over and our mission was to restore peace, but a civil war was brewing between the Sunni and Shiite sects.

"Each day was a nightmare. Car bombings, urban warfare—we didn't know friend from foe. But each day Virgil would face it all fearlessly. No, not fearlessly." He sought a more appropriate word. "Peacefully. He got scared like anyone else. That was normal. But Virgil had a way of overcoming that fear, despite the worst.

"One day I asked him what kept him going. He told me that it was because he was a Christian. 'My life is in God's hands,' he would say. 'If I perish, I perish.' He always used to smile when he said it too. Just shrug with a big toothy grin.

That really encouraged me back then. Virgil got me through some tough times."

"So you became a Christian too, I assume?" Her tone hinted that she didn't approve, but he wasn't going to try to hide anything from her now.

"Eventually. After Virgil taught me the Gospel, I believed, got bap—"

"Now it makes sense. Why you and that Grant guy were so chummy. You both had the same teacher." Her voice filled with venom. "Macey, how could you keep all this from me? I feel so lied to."

He retained his composure. After all, he deserved her aggression. He hadn't been fully honest with her. "I had my reasons, but please let me finish."

She inhaled sharply. "Go ahead."

"Being brothers in the faith helped maintain and strengthen our relationship, especially during wartime. In peacetime we stayed close as well. Our families spent time together." The images returned the smile to his lips.

"Tell me about your family." Her tone softened some. "You had a wife, right? How about kids?"

"My wife's name was Sophia. We met in high school, not too far from here."

"So this is where you grew up?"

"Sort of. My dad was a marine so my family moved around a lot when I was a kid. Overseas mostly. Japan, Guam, Germany."

"That where you learned German?"

"Huh?"

"That guy Kestler—I remember you speaking it to him. Or was that language software?"

"Oh . . . . No, that was me. I got a knack for languages, I guess." He punched numbers absently into the trunk's digital lock. "Anyway, my dad settled down here when he left the Marine Corps. I was just entering high school then, so I guess you could say this is where I got Americanized."

"And what was your wife like?"

He chuckled and looked at her slyly. "Feisty. Too smart for her own good most of the time. Sweet and beautiful. We never had the easiest of marriages, with me being in the military and the wars and all. But we made it work somehow. Our love for each other was strong."

She shifted her position. "And your kids?"

"One daughter. Maria."

"Where is she now?"

"She died about ten years ago in a car accident."

"My God, I'm sorry, Macey." She rested a hand atop his.

"Thanks." He cleared his throat. "These things happen. Besides, she'd lived a full life. She was seventy-two."

Sheila shook her head, maybe trying to imagine him with a daughter who looked like she could've been his mother. "What about your wife? How did she die?"

"Breast cancer. She was sixty-two."

She blinked. "Wait, that would have been around 2030, right? Why didn't she get the cancer vaccine? It was widely available by then. And a few years later our Miracle Treatment was available. I mean, if she had she could still be . . . I'm sorry. I didn't mean to go there."

"I know what you're saying. We talked about it. But she refused any treatment for it. It wasn't long after I had gone through my transplant surgery, see? In a way, I blamed the transplant for her death. She never said it, but I think she resented it. I don't think she could handle the idea of me staying young while she grew old." He swallowed the lump in his throat. "I think she actually wanted to die. Wanted to remove herself, to make room for me and my new life. She never understood that was the last thing I wanted."

Sheila went quiet for a while. "Do you have any grandchildren?"

"A few. And more great-grands than I can count. From that generation onward I tried to stay out of their lives. It seemed a bit ridiculous. Well, there's one exception."

She pointed at him. "Hector?"

He smiled at her intuition. "My great-grandson."

"Does he know that?"

"Yeah."

She let out a nervous laugh and rocked back on the bed. "Whoa, that's kind of weird."

"Tell me about it." He laughed with her. "But you must be used to this sort of thing, right? Dealing with Miracle Treatment clients? They must go through the same problems."

"Honestly, I don't get involved in that part." She fiddled with the corner of the bed's comforter. "I just market the stuff."

Macey nodded and tapped his heels against the trunk as a silence took hold.

"Can you tell me about the transplant surgery?" Sheila said eventually. "Why did both you and Virgil get it done? Were you in some kind of special cyborg unit or something?"

"We were, but not 'til later. At that point, they did full cyborg transplants only when soldiers lost their bodies in combat. What caused me and Virgil to need it . . . well, that's an event at the center of a lot of things."

"And that would be?"

He moistened his lips. "Utah."

"The same Utah you mentioned to that Streetwalker Sniper kid in jail? And in Greta's Bible?"

"The same."

"So you were there." She leaned closer, her eyes squinting. "What happened?"

He paused to collect his thoughts. "After the Iranian War, Virgil and I joined CDI. Civil Defense and Intelligence had recently been formed from what used to be the Department of Homeland Security. It was a good option for people like us: officers with combat experience, able to work actively in the military without the risk of being recalled to war. Those were good years, probably the best of my life.

"Anyway, we were in our late fifties and thinking about early retirement when the incident in Utah broke out. By then we were both majors, division commanders. I ran the Religious-Based Counterterrorism Division here in LA. Virgil ran the same division in Seattle. But to really understand the whole thing about Utah, you need to know how it started."

She propped her elbows on her knees and cradled her chin upon her knuckles. "You mean the Freedom from Deity Act, right?"

"Yeah . . . When it was passed, a small town in Utah—town called Jasper—objected openly to it. The mayor of Jasper, Pat Harold, who was also an evangelical minister, decided to civilly disobey the new Federal law. In what started as an almost tongue-in-cheek protest, Harold proclaimed that the city of Jasper was a sovereign nation and they were no longer bound by the laws of the United States."

Sheila chuckled. "Are you serious?"

"A lot of people laughed at first, but as the media picked up on it, some big church groups started paying attention. Even some splinter groups like Mormons and Amish got into the action. They started to push the idea within their congregations. People started moving to Jasper and began camping there in demonstration."

"Sounds idiotic."

Macey shrugged. "It went on pretty quietly for a few months. But the next time the media picked up on the story, the number of people camping out in Jasper had grown to over 100,000. A figure like that was big enough to make the national news. What was more, Mayor Harold stuck to his resolve.

"He had the city boundaries marked and barricaded. They were getting pretty serious about Jasper being another country, crazy as it sounds. By the time CDI got involved, the population of Jasper had grown to over half a million people. It became a spotlight for the media and a thorn in the White House administration's side. That's when they called us, the heads of the religious-based counterterrorism divisions, to formulate a plan to diffuse the situation."

"They treated it as terrorism right away?"

"I don't think it ever got called that, but it was obviously a civil protest that couldn't be broken up with a couple of tear-gas canisters. The mayor was demanding that either the Freedom from Deity Act be revoked or the U.S. acknowledge Jasper's sovereignty. The White House ignored it, of course, but soon the public was demanding that something be done about Jasper."

"So what did you do?"

"Not much at first. Our initial job was to ascertain the reality of the situation. Virgil and I led teams of agents who worked undercover as moles gathering information. The news that came back was bad. The people really did consider themselves no longer part of the United States."

"That's so nuts. What did you do next?"

"Well, the first plan conceived wasn't ours. It came directly from the White House. They tried to stop supplies going into the city in an attempt to starve people out. That quickly backfired."

"How so?"

"In a way, it was unofficial acknowledgement by the government that they considered the people of Jasper separatists. In short, trying to stop trade was a move that only escalated the tensions. The army was used to enforce the trade embargo too, which was another big mistake. Tanks and ground troops deployed on U.S. soil—against U.S. citizens. It was something I thought I'd never see happen. Jasper had become an international news story. The White House placed more and more pressure on us for a solution."

"So how did you resolve it?"

"We tried a subtle approach. Infiltrate the community, work agents into positions of authority and influence within Mayor Harold's inner circle, and steer him toward a peaceful solution."

"Sounds like it would take forever."

"It did. We were almost eight months into the operation before we started to see any significant results, but by that time another operation was up and running and having much better success.

"We never officially knew about it until later, but the White House had decided to use the CIA to incite violent protest within the Jasper community. It wasn't until near the end that we began to suspect that another team was causing the tensions and violence we started seeing."

"The end? What finally happened?"

Macey shifted his weight on the trunk, cleared his throat. "The CIA op had worked a good chunk of the population into a minor militia. They were sitting on a razor's edge. Slogans like 'Be ready to die for God and country' were rampant. The reaction from the outside populace was no better. Soon clashes were breaking out between civilians along Jasper's borders. There were lots of injuries and even a few unreported deaths. That summer, the tensions rose to a boiling point. Finally the government decided to pull the plug on our operation—and pull the trigger on Jasper."

"'Pull the trigger'?"

"The CIA assassinated Mayor Pat Harold. Sniper shot him through the window while he was at the dinner table, right in front of his kids. They rigged the media to cast the blame on an extremist group from the anti-Jasper side. But they peppered it with bits of the truth and started rumors that it was, in fact, a government-led execution.

"That was enough to set off the powder keg that had been building for almost two years. The militia groups the CIA had been supplying with weapons and training struck out at the Army forces surrounding Jasper. That was all the justification the government needed to launch a retaliation strike. And sure enough, they did . . . ."

He suddenly became aware that he was shaking, and that Sheila had moved from the bed to sit next to him. She had an arm draped around his shoulders. "You don't have to go on," she said softly.

He shook his head. "No, I need to get this out." His vision blurred with tears. "CDI was ordered in as part of the regular forces. We were ordered to treat the situation as normal combat. Everyone was deemed a combatant. Our troops were killing people in the streets. It was Iraq all over again, only this time it wasn't Baghdad, it was Main Street U.S.A. Then . . . they bombed the place, Sheila. They actually bombed it. A-10s. F-18s. Predator drones. That's when it happened to Virgil and me . . ."

"When what happened?" she asked slowly.

"For the past eight months we'd been living there as part of the community. We knew families, had friends. In truth, those were some of the most decent people I've ever met. Once you got past all the politics and looked at the people living their normal lives, Jasper was like a little slice of heaven on earth."

He savored the memory. But, like so many things in Jasper, it was soon gone.

"Virgil and I were helping evacuate a busload of school children when we were caught in an explosion. A bomb taking out a transformer station struck just as our bus was passing it. Virgil and I both survived the blast but had third-degree burns over ninety percent of our bodies. The forty children with us didn't have the armor we wore—they were burned alive."

"Oh, my . . . ." Sheila covered her mouth with her hands. "I've heard of Utah—some battle, and all. But I've never heard stories like that."

"Of course not. The government took care of the media censoring. On the news it looked like another Waco. In reality, it was our own Tiananmen Square."

"I had no idea it was so bad." Her eyes watered. "What happened to you and Virgil?"

"We were taken for treatment. At that time, an immediate prosthetic body transplant was the best option for survival for a full burn victim. So that's what they gave us." He rested both palms on the trunk. "As for the conflict, it was over in three days. The fighting only affected a small section of the town, thank God, but the casualties were in the hundreds. The people who had come to Jasper left in droves. The whole thing died out in a shameful whisper."

"That's so awful."

"Official blame for the incident was placed on the dummy militias the CIA had started. In a show of appeasement, several of the agents posed as militia leaders and were tried and convicted. But it was just another dummy act. They were all secretly released under new identities less than a year later."

"How do you know all this stuff?"

"I made it my job to know. After all I went through, I wanted to know the exact truth about what happened in Jasper. Besides, I was in recovery and rehab for years because of it. What else was I going to do, play cards?"

"So why don't you tell the truth? Write a book or something."

He smiled. "Many have. But Jasper, Utah, might as well be Roswell, New Mexico. The government has their official version of the story sealed tight. Any other version is labeled quackery or the work of some conspiracy nut. I gave up trying to tell the truth a long time ago. In the end, no one wanted to listen. No one wanted to believe the truth ever really occurred."

"This is so messed up . . ."

Macey looked up at the bare ceiling but didn't really see it, his mind still awash with memories. "Virgil and I were never the same after that. I'm not talking about our bodies. I'm talking about our relationship. As the CDI operation progressed, we began to feel differently about the situation surrounding us.

We both felt genuine compassion for the people of Jasper and, as Christians, we identified with their rejection of the Freedom from Deity Act. But we differed on how they reacted to it.

"Virgil felt they were doing the right thing, standing up to a government that had turned its back on God. I felt they were going about it the wrong way, causing unneeded strife and fueling the hatred that led to the final outcome. We never did see eye to eye on that point. After the surgery, we recovered and went through rehabilitation together to learn how to use our new bodies, but it wasn't long after that when Virgil and I had our last conversation."

"Your last?"

"It was almost three years after Jasper. Virgil and I had gone back to work. Those first few months were hard. Everything was different. Back then, prosthetic bodies were nowhere near as good as they are now. It was tough for both of us. I was dealing with Sophia and her cancer, and Virgil was going through a divorce. His wife couldn't accept what he'd become after Utah."

"His body, you mean?"

"No . . . what he'd become inside." Macey thumbed the edge of the trunk. "I was *interested* in Utah, trying to find out what happened. But Virgil was obsessed with it. He wanted revenge for what the government did. In the end she left him. It was about a month after that when Virgil confided in me that he was planning to leave the country. He didn't want to live in a nation or serve a government that had no respect for God. He asked me to join him."

"But you didn't . . . ?"

"For a combat cyborg, leaving the country is a big deal. After the surgery we had been reenlisted in a special cyborg unit and went back to active duty. I think we saw more combat in those few short years than in our entire careers put together. Anyway, our bodies officially belonged to the military. We were no longer soldiers. For all intents and purposes, we were weapons. Able to be deployed wherever the military needed a big stick. By taking off AWOL like that, Virgil was committing treason. I tried to talk him out of it, but his mind was made up.

"I heard he headed toward South America. I got one postcard from him, from Belize in 2035. That was the last time I ever heard from him. After that, I stopped thinking about Virgil. Consciously, anyway." He paused again, licking his lips. "Over forty years and barely a thought . . . . Until the night you handed me that Bible and I saw his name written there."

"I was wondering about that. Why you were so concerned about its date?"

"To see when he might have written it. That Bible was printed in 2077, which meant there was a good chance he'd survived his travels and returned to LA, where he must've met Greta Darling."

"So *that's* what made you take the case . . ." She closed her eyes in a failed attempt to hide her resentment. "You wanted to find him."

A little shame crept in. "Yeah."

Sheila blew out a breath, as if trying to relieve the weight of the story she had just heard. "I need to ask you some questions, Macey."

"Go ahead."

"Now that you've found Virgil, what do you plan to do?"

He sighed. "I don't think I know the answer to that right now. I've been asking myself that question since we started this case. Until now I've let myself stay preoccupied in the chase, ignoring it."

"I see," she said coolly, as if marking off a checklist. "When he offered himself up to you to be captured, why didn't you? Why did you let him go?"

"I really don't want to—"

"Macey, please. I think you owe me this much, don't you?"

He rocked his jaw from side to side. Would telling her the truth make things worse? Probably, but he couldn't keep lying anymore. "Okay, but you're not going to like my answer."

"Try me."

"Sheila, I'm not entirely sure I believe that what he's doing is wrong. At least, not all of it."

"I see." Her lack of emotion left him cold. "Why's that?"

How could he put this in a way that made sense to her? "After Virgil left, after Utah, I lost a lot of my faith. After Sophia died I think I lost it all. A couple of years later I stopped attending church, stopped reading my Bible. Finally, I even stopped praying . . . . I don't know when I actually stopped believing."

He ran a hand over his face as if somehow that would stop the memories from flowing back. "I haven't been a true Christian for over fifty years. When this case started picking up and we started learning more about Virgil, I felt a chasm open inside me that I had tried to cover for decades. My brother in the faith, Virgil, was still alive, still out there doing God's work. And here I was, ashamed to even admit to anyone that I had once believed that Jesus Christ was the Son of God.

"When we met on that roof, and he confronted me, confronted my faith, I . . . I just couldn't handle it, Sheila. I look back fifty-some years ago, when Virgil told me he was leaving the U.S., and I told him he was making the biggest mistake of his life. Now I wonder which one of us really made the mistake."

She stared at him coolly, remotely. "I see."

He cleared the dryness from his throat. "When we were on the roof, Virgil said that he was going to wait for me."

"Meaning what?"

"Meaning he's not going to release the negating agent or do anything else until we meet again. So that buys us some time, anyway. I think he's asking me to join him." He smiled. "Same as he did fifty years ago."

"Will you? Join him?"

He didn't know how to answer that. He gazed through the tiny window in the room, watched the moon rising in the night sky. He checked the chronometer on his neural net and saw the time was stretching past nine.

Finally Sheila looked him squarely in the eye. "I need to ask you one last question. Are you still going to help me? Answer me honestly."

Tears formed in her eyes as she waited for his response, tears that matched his own. No way could he talk, not now, not yet. He rubbed them away with a shaky hand.

"It's all right. You don't have to answer."

He opened his mouth in an attempt to protest. But nothing came out.

She stood, as if to leave.

He rose after her. "It's getting late, Sheila." He rested a hand on her shoulder. "You stay here. Take the cot. I'll sleep downstairs. We both need some rest. We can talk about this in the morning."

She sat back down on the bed, stared at the floor.

He couldn't leave her like that. "This has nothing to do with the feelings I have for you, Sheila." He managed to get out. "I still have them. Please understand that."

She didn't raise her head. "I know."

He waited for her to say something else, but she didn't.

"Good night, Sheila."

Macey left without a reply and closed the door behind himself.

CHAPTER TEN

MACEY COULDN'T BRING himself to sleep that night. Not that he normally required much sleep, but tonight's bout of insomnia was anything but normal. He checked the chronometer in the corner of his vision: almost 5:00 a.m. He hadn't managed to drift off for more than an hour at a time. It felt as if he'd been awake all night. Memories old and new clogged his mind, too vivid to be ignored.

He arose from the easy chair where he had been trying to sleep and wandered into the semi-darkness of the garage. The collection of vehicles stared back at him, their brightly colored affectations mesmerizing in the dull light. The greasy tang of motor oil filled his nostrils and turned his stomach. The place suddenly felt cramped. Or perhaps it was just his state of mind superimposing itself on his surroundings.

In either case, he needed some fresh air.

He ventured upstairs, past the hallway and the door to Sheila's room. He had heard crying coming from behind it. He contemplated knocking but decided against it. Part of him felt like bursting through the door, taking her into his arms and promising her that everything would be all right, that he would stand by her, protect her, save her.

But that wasn't reality.

The truth was he had no idea how he was going to handle things with Sheila now that Virgil had entered the picture. A choice between his best friend of over seventy years, his brother in arms and in Christ, and a woman he'd just met but cared for greatly, maybe even loved.

He fixed his eyes on the door again. He needed to talk to her, to know exactly what she was feeling. It had been her silence in the face of all that he had revealed that had torn him up inside. What was going on inside her head? Had she lost faith in him? Did she hate him? Had he sunk to such a state that he could no longer make a clear decision about Virgil without caring how Sheila felt about him?

"I suppose you have," he said aloud, just to hear it come from outside his head. "I suppose you have."

Climbing the last flight of stairs, he emerged onto the rooftop of the garage, his skin bristling against the coolness of the early morning air. It was a relatively quiet night. A crescent moon hung low in the predawn sky, the jagged outline of light speckled skyscrapers set against a cool indigo hue. He blanked his mind as he focused on the coming sunrise, mental relief from the relentless onslaught of his thoughts.

A car passed below. A tune from its stereo knocked him back into reality. This wasn't going to work. He eyed the building across the street. He couldn't remember exactly what business was in it, but it didn't matter. His interest lay in its height.

Breaking into a sprint, Macey launched himself off the rooftop, vaulting across the two-way street with ease. His feet touched the edge of the opposing building's roof and he turned to face the garage again, now several stories below him. He felt like a gargoyle here, sitting out in the weather. But he felt more at ease at the higher vantage, better able to watch the garage and avoid the traffic.

As if on cue, another vehicle drove by, this one screaming by at top speed. Wild laughter burst from the occupants as the car veered around a bend, tires screeching. Reckless idiots. Sirens wailed. Macey half expected a squad car to emerge next, but the sounds emanated from too far away. Just the normal backdrop of the city, permeating the waning night.

He closed his eyes and let the distant hubbub soothe him, felt himself finally relax. Perhaps he could even sleep. Numbness embraced him, his senses giving way one by one to the fatigue of his exhausted mind.

"You're up early," someone said. "Or is it late?"

Eyes flashed open as he jerked his head toward the voice.

It belonged to a figure at the far end of the building, now striding toward him through the shadows. Panic straightened his spine. How could he have let his guard down so easily? He forced himself to react rationally. He took quick note of his surroundings and focused acutely on his senses.

The siren had faded. In fact there was no sound at all. The entire world stood still, as still as a photograph: no wind, no movement, no sensation. He tested his internal comms and met a host of error messages, but it wasn't jamming this time. The realization finally hit him and it brought on a sense of calm. There was only one explanation for what he was experiencing, and he knew of only one person capable of achieving it.

"So, you managed to hack my neural net," he said appreciatively. "I didn't even notice you make a connection attempt."

Virgil, or rather the virtual image of him, grinned as he emerged from the shadows. "Don't act surprised, Macey. I always was the better hacker."

He chuckled. "Not according to my memory. I think you got lucky."

"Perhaps. I found you asleep."

"So, I did doze off." His friend wore what his mind recently remembered him in: combat fatigues and a white overcoat. "And to what do I owe the honor of this visit, Virgil?"

He stepped up onto the lip of the roof to stand next to him and they both stared into the simulated night sky. "I told you I would be the one to find you next, didn't I? I hope you don't mind me choosing this method. I didn't feel like jumping across half the city trying to find you in real space. Didn't seem very practical."

Macey chuckled. It felt good to laugh with Virgil again—something they used to do a lot of. Laughing, cracking jokes, it all seemed a lifetime ago. A lifetime ago indeed. The humor quickly evaporated and the reality of their contact began to sink in. "I'm really not prepared to talk to you right now," he said truthfully. "I have a lot I need to think about and, frankly, I'd rather do it alone."

Virgil slipped his hands into his pockets. "Is that right? And here I was, thinking you probably needed someone to talk to by about now."

He let out a grunt. "You know what the sad part is? You're probably the only person I *could* talk to about all this."

"So talk," Virgil said with a shrug. "We're still friends, aren't we?"

"A lot's happened since those days."

He stooped into a crouch, his mirror-shaded eyes overlooking the city. "Yes, a lot has. Many years have gone by. I'm sorry I never tried to contact you before now. I should have."

"So why didn't you?"

"I was afraid, I suppose."

"Of what?"

"Of how you would react. And now that we have met again . . . I can't say my fears were totally unfounded."

A flame of indignation lit inside Macey. "What did you expect, man? You disappear for fifty years and the next time I see you, you're a borderline terrorist?"

"Is that how you think of me? A terrorist? Please tell me you understand what I'm trying to do here." He glanced away. "It's very important to me that you do, Macey. You're still my brother. If there's anything more I could pray for in this life, it would be for you to be by my side again."

"Is that why you came back to LA? Looking for me?"

"Honestly . . ." He paused. "No. I don't know why I came back here. I guess it's true what they say: the older you get the more you long for the things of your past."

"So what led you down this path you're on now? What made you decide to destroy the Miracle Treatment?"

"I stumbled upon it, saw its effects firsthand. The irony of it caught my attention, I suppose. I couldn't understand why people would willingly subject themselves to what we were forced into in order to survive. Can you?"

Not fully. "Look, I understand what you're trying to achieve, but I'm not sure I can accept it."

"But why?" Virgil's brows twisted with concern. "Surely you can't think that this life extension should exist. Look at us. How many lifetimes have we lived? Haven't you grown sick of it? To linger on while you watch your family grow old and die? We're cursed, Macey." His mirror lenses scanned the cityscape. "The people of this world are too young to understand. We'd be sparing them this agony."

Virgil's words touched the pain that still lingered within Macey's soul—his wife, his daughter. "I don't disagree with you. I'd be lying if I said I didn't get tired of living sometimes." He bit his lower lip. "You know how many times I considered putting that 20mm to my head and ending it? Or wondering if I could crack my titanium skull by jumping off a building? I think about dying more than you can imagine. But now it just seems like . . . like I'm just . . ."

"Afraid of dying?"

It wasn't what he was thinking at all, but that didn't make his statement any less true. "I wasn't going to say that."

"But I'm right, aren't I?" Virgil latched onto his weakness like a vice. "Tell me honestly, Mace: after all these years, have you lost hope in your salvation?"

He looked down to the street below. He didn't want to think about it, much less talk about it. "Look, if you came here to poke holes in my faith, you're wasting your time. The world did that to me a long time ago."

"Is that the reason you haven't decided to join me? Do you no longer believe in the will of God?"

Macey ran his hands through his hair. He had purposely tried to leave God out of the equation. So far he had thought of this as a choice between Virgil and Sheila. But deep down, he knew it amounted to far more than that. This wasn't about choosing between two people. It was about choosing between what he wanted and what God wanted. It was a decision he didn't want to make, a decision he was terrified to make.

"Does it have anything to do with that woman?"

"No," he said quickly. He wanted that answer to be the truth. But then he shook his head. "Yes . . . . She's a big part of it, I think."

Virgil smiled. He walked to the edge of the roof and stepped backward off it, floating on nothing. "Who is she?"

"Her name is Sheila Dunn. She's the woman who created the Miracle Treatment. Well, marketed it, anyway. She hired me to protect her company from what you're about to do with that negating agent."

"Are you in love with her?"

He glowered at Virgil's simplistic rationalization. "She's about to lose more than her career over this, all right? The company is trying to pin the whole thing on her and take her out at the same time. You've destroyed her life."

"Oh?" He stepped further back in midair. "I'm sorry. I had no idea."

"Or concern." He huffed in disgust. "You may think you're doing the work of God, Virgil, but do you *really* care about what happens to the people you affect?"

"I'm caring for their souls." His voice rose sharply. "What greater 'thing' can one care for?"

"If you truly cared for their souls, then why not shepherd them like you did Greta Darling and Steven Grant? Let them make the choice, not make it for them. Like with forcing the negating agent on everyone. Do you really think that eliminating the Miracle Treatment will send the whole world repenting to God?"

"One would hope. Why not take yourself as an example?"

"What?"

"Why have you lost your faith after all these years?" He cocked his head. "More importantly, why haven't you done anything about trying to regain it? Could it be that because you fear no death, you've grown slothful and complacent?"

"What are you talking about?"

"You no longer seek God because you know you can avoid Him. You're hiding from God behind your thin veil of immortality, the same way these other people are." He snorted a laugh. "It's no wonder you seek to stop me from destroying the Miracle Treatment. You sympathize with these people—not because you care for them, but because you're one of them."

His hands balled into fists. "Don't you judge me. I don't deserve that from you. If you could gift me with death right now do you think it would magically bring back my faith?"

"I'd hope you'd at least have the motivation to try and regain it. But these days I sense your motivation lies elsewhere. Fleshly lusts, perhaps? Tell me, would you be willing to defy the will of God to save this woman? Would you choose your own selfish desire for her over the God that gave you life? Not only life but eternal life through the Cross, which you've tossed aside as if it were nothing."

"You dare to preach to me, Virgil? You of all people? You don't know what I'm going through, man, what I've gone through. And don't you dare accuse me of being selfish either." He pointed at him viciously. "Do you realize what it was like for me after you left? Skipped the country like some draft dodger. You turned your back on me when I needed you most. My wife was dying, man! I lost everything. My family, my faith. And you come back here fifty years later preaching to me like you're so bloody righteous?"

"Now who's preaching?" Virgil slowly shook his head. "I've never claimed to be righteous, Mace, but I know I'm far more righteous than you are right now, my friend."

"What did you say?"

"Scripture says you can tell a tree by its fruits. What fruits have you produced these last fifty years? How bright has your light shone for Christ? Or has it shone at all? I left back then because of my love for God. Did I think it would hurt my family? Yes. Did I think it would hurt you, knowing Sophia was dying? Yes. But did you really expect me to place anyone or anything else, even my own feelings, above God?"

Macey's skin grew hot with anger. He felt like cursing Virgil, punching him. But for all their sting, Virgil's words came seasoned with the truth.

To any Christian, the priorities of life followed a simple plan: God first, then wife and family, then friends, then job. Perhaps Virgil had broken no law in God's eyes, but knowing that did little to ease the pain his departure had caused him all those years ago, and apparently was still causing him now.

"You know what? I don't think I ever forgave you for leaving," he said. "Maybe I still don't."

"Macey, that was half a century ago." Virgil stretched out his hands. "For what it's worth, I am sorry for the pain I caused you. I'm sorry that Sophia died. I'm sorry that I haven't been there to support you. But please, don't let something that I did cloud your judgment about a decision you need to make today."

"What are you talking about?"

"'The heart is deceitful above all things, and desperately wicked: who can know it?'" Virgil quoted to him. "Can you truly trust your heart right now? Trust what it's been telling you to believe in? Trust what it's telling you to do?" His tone softened. "God may no longer be leading your life, Macey, but He's still in control. He knows your desires. Your faults. There's no shame in baring yourself to Him.

"Do you think it's just coincidence that we've met again after all these years? God has placed me here to help you. To help bring you back to Him. You're still a child of God. You confessed Christ as His Son, buried yourself in baptism, and accepted His grace. There's no longer a sin on this earth that you can commit that God won't forgive, if you simply repent and come back to him now. Trust what I say. It's never too late—never, before eternity falls—to regain your soul."

Each word stabbed at him. He wanted to believe Virgil, but he couldn't feel the same conviction. How could he? He had turned his back on God for so long. There had been times he had doubted God's very existence. Questioned whether the Bible wasn't just the fictional work of men. Or that the concept of God itself was not some by-product of human evolution that man had now outgrown.

It was so easy to buy into all of that, especially in this age of wonder and technology. Such questions he had tried to avoid by bottling them deep down inside. Not wanting them answered one way or the other. Trying to pretend that God didn't exist, while secretly unwilling to admit the possibility. He rode the fence pathetically, void of all conviction. No way could he return to God with a clear conscience after having doubting Him as deeply as that. And now, on top of everything, he had these feelings for Sheila to deal with.

His insides twisted with uncertainty. Was Virgil right? Was his heart deceiving him? If he had never met Sheila, would he still be trying to stop Virgil?

"After all these years I finally meet a woman who gives me the hope of living again." His stared into nothingness as he recalled her image: her angelic face, violet eyes, fiery spirit. "And now you're asking me to give her up? How can I make a decision like that?"

"I'm not the one asking you to make it. God is giving you the chance to make this choice."

Macey held his tongue. He didn't want to hear any more about God. If there really was a God, how could he ever please Him now?

"Abraham prepared to sacrifice his son for the Lord as a test of his faith," Virgil said. "Maybe He's asking you to sacrifice this woman to regain yours."

"I don't want to hear this."

"Trust in God, Macey. 'Seek ye first the kingdom of God and his righteousness and all things shall be added unto you.' Choose God, and the rest will come."

"Please, Virgil!" He couldn't let anymore seep in. "Just leave me be."

"Your soul is in torment," Virgil said calmly, compassionately even. "I can see you need more time. I'll wait for you still. Here is where you will find me." He left an address registered on his net. "Come when you are ready, old friend. Until then, I'll be praying for you."

The world returned in a rapid burst of motion and sound, like a fast-forwarded recording being played at normal speed again. The bright yellow sunlight of dawn met his gaze full-bore, forcing him to squint. He checked his chronometer. Past seven already.

He was still standing on the ledge of the building. But not for long. He dropped to his knees, mentally and physically drained, his conversation with Virgil looping over and over in his mind like a bad recording. So many emotions filled him that he could no longer bear it. He heaved shakily before releasing a deep sob that caused his eyes to tear.

He needed strength, yet he felt so weak. He wanted to save Sheila, yet he couldn't bring himself to betray his friend. He wanted to believe in God again, yet all he could think of was his doubt and disbelief.

He tried to focus his thoughts. He ran his hands fiercely over his scalp until he nearly bled. Virgil had indeed preached to him. Preached to him words he had not wanted to hear. But the pain he felt was evidence that he'd needed to hear them.

Life, for all it was worth, the entire world and its possessions, his loved ones, his wife, his daughter, Sheila—what did they all amount to in the end? The sad truth was that, when the end finally came, nothing mattered. Nothing except the only true possession you ever really had. Your soul.

For him, there existed only two possibilities when it came to death. Either God did not exist and death was inconsequential, or He did exist and the consequences of death were real and grave. Terrifyingly, his belief or disbelief in God's existence made absolutely no difference in whether He truly existed or not.

The odds ran fifty-fifty, a binary possibility, a simple yes or no that would only be answered after it was all too late to matter. The scant amount of faith he had left simply wouldn't allow him to take the risk of dying without knowing his soul's final destiny for sure. He understood Virgil's phrase perfectly now.

"When eternity falls . . ."

Macey looked down into his hands, saw tears fall upon them. He would die one day. So would Sheila. So would everyone. That was the only certainty in life. Everyone would die eventually, and before that time you would have to make a choice.

A choice to either follow God or not.

He thought of Sheila, of how much he cared for her, wanted to protect her, desired her. Would he be willing to give her up to return to God's side? If his faith in God caused him to lose her forever, would it be worth the price? He contemplated the question painfully, but in truth he already knew the answer.

"'For what shall it profit a man," he whispered the Scripture, "if he shall gain the whole world, and lose his own soul . . .'"

He knew the words he had to speak next, the words that would reconcile himself to his Creator. He ought to know them well, he had taught them to so many others himself, but that seemed more than a few lifetimes ago now. Still he couldn't muster the courage to utter them. His tongue felt stiff against his jaw. He felt ridiculous. Ashamed. He glanced upward at the rising sun, the power of his God self-evident within it.

Macey raised his hands toward the glowing orb, squeezed the tears from his eyes as he shut them and whispered words he had not spoken in decades.

And for the first time in too many years, he prayed.

• • •

Bradley Thomas surveyed the rundown neighborhood in the middle of Watts. The abandoned lot he had parked in was surrounded by a rusted chainlink fence—choked with weeds and random pieces of garbage, serving as a visual barrier to the mobs of cyber-gangers cruising outside. Across the street, an all-night liquor store was the only source of light, its patrons sauntering in and out of the darkness like vampires to an all-you-can-eat blood bank buffet.

He'd already seen two people killed on this street tonight. And at this early in the morning he didn't fancy having to blow some poor punk's head off just to prove a point to the rest of his loser friends. Luckily he hadn't encountered much more than a bum and a jacked-up hooker all night. Be fine if it stayed that way too, and by the look of the sun cresting the horizon, it probably would.

He kept his eyes fixed on the auto garage at the far end of the block, alert to any signs of movement inside. The place looked dead enough, but it was too early to tell if anyone was in there or not. Fortunately he had patience. He had waited this long. He could wait a little longer.

As if on cue, a call request came through on his comm. He answered. *<What do you have?>*

<Confirmation, sir. She's alone.>

<Are you certain? We can't afford to screw this up.>

<Positive, sir.>

Bradley pondered the best plan to move forward. *<Wait for me.>* He started the sedan. *<No one does anything until I get there.>*

• • •

Macey knelt penitently on the roof, his arms spread wide, his palms facing the sky. He didn't know how long he had prayed or even what he had prayed for. But by the time he finished, he felt as if his spirit had been pulled through turmoil and turned inside out.

He breathed heavily as he reopened his eyes, saw the sun, enjoyed its heat on his face. He felt peace. He felt relief. Most of all, for the first time in years, he finally felt the strength of his belief.

He remained upon his knees, descending from his spiritual high. It felt good for a while, but as his mind refocused, reality set in. He still had no idea what he was going to do about anything. He had not prayed for that. He had prayed for the people involved: for Sheila, for Virgil, even for Boreman and Bradley, and for God to direct his path in whatever outcome was His true will.

The thought brought about a sense of calm and a smile to his lips. In reality, he was no further along in solving his dilemma than when he had jumped upon the roof this morning, but the difference was in his perspective. And it was a contrast as stark as the night that had passed and the new day that had dawned.

At last he could be fully honest about his feelings for Sheila. Despite everything he had just experienced, he retained the deep desire to protect her, to love her. And Virgil remained his best friend, his brother who, in the end, had saved his very soul.

No way could he betray either of them.

When it came to the Miracle Treatment, his opinion had not changed. Part of him agreed with Virgil that it should not exist. It was true that the fear of death could draw people back to God. He had just experienced it himself. Yet when he tried to envision himself joining Virgil and destroying the Miracle Treatment, he couldn't justify such an action.

His thoughts disturbed him. They seemed contradictory, illogical. Was he still using his love for Sheila as a motive? He exhaled deeply, considering the grim possibility that he was already deceiving himself again.

"No," he said firmly. He had already willingly given Sheila up when he'd made his choice to follow God. He had removed her from the equation. And yet still his decision to stop Virgil stood firm in his mind. He clasped his hands pensively. Was this truly God's will? For him to side against his brother? His brother who had led him back to God? The prospect pained him. It made no sense. Immediately he wanted to reject it. But then, like a lifting fog, its meaning formed in his mind.

It was enough to make his jaw drop open.

Ironically, Virgil's own words had cleared his vision. Virgil had been right about his heart: it had been deceiving him, but not with lust for Sheila as he had accused. It'd been clouded with his own self-doubt and guilt regarding his loss of faith. Every time he had stood against Virgil's ideals, his own lack of faith had buckled his courage to stand for what he believed to be right. But now he had restored his faith and at last he could feel the conviction of his beliefs without shame or guilt.

Virgil was wrong.

He knew that with certainty now. And he had the righteous conviction to believe it. The destruction of the Miracle Treatment was not about choosing between Virgil and Sheila.

It never had been. It was about much more than that, something far more fundamental.

He jumped to his feet. He knew what he had to do. He looked once more to the morning sun, felt God's presence radiating from it. His Father had answered his prayer. "God led you to save my soul, Virgil," he said solemnly, "and now He's leading me to save yours."

He leapt off the rooftop and plummeted to the garage below. He landed in a crouch to dissipate the impact of his fall, though he still shook the roof with a thud. He arose hastily and started for the door, thinking about Sheila. He couldn't wait to see her face again, tell her with confidence that he could stand by her, protect her, even love her.

God had re-proved His existence to him in leaps and bounds. He'd had scant time to consider it until now but, as Virgil had said, God had been testing his faith. His willingness to place God before his love for Sheila had resulted in God giving Sheila right back to him. Now he could love her with a pure heart, a heart unmarred by guilt or regret. He had to force himself to calm down as he dashed through the hallway and knocked on her door. Bad enough that he was feeling like a goofy, love-struck kid all over again. The least he could do was not act like one.

"Sheila," he called softly. "Sheila, are you awake?"

He tried the handle.

"Sheila?" He coaxed the door open gingerly, took a look inside. He expected to see her asleep in the cot, but found the bed neatly made. Had she gotten up already? He didn't hear her in the bathroom, but he checked anyway. Not there.

"Sheila?" he called into the air, heading downstairs.

Laughter and talking drifted from the garage. A woman's voice as well as a man's. He grew apprehensive at first, but relaxed as the familiar ring of Hector's voice conveyed a story about getting drunk last night.

When he entered the garage, he spied Hector and Sheila toward the far end, eating breakfast on the service counter. Hector caught sight of him and waved.

"Wassup, Mace," he sang out.

Sheila faced the counter, had her back to him. She didn't turn as he approached, but he didn't expect her to. Probably still upset with him from last night. He had to remember to take things slowly. *He* might have just had a life-altering spiritual experience, but she hadn't. It would take some time to gain her trust back, explain everything to her, and he was willing to wait.

To his surprise, as he stepped behind her she turned to face him, smiling widely.

"Hi there."

Macey froze. "Who's this?" He gawked at the brunette in front of him. Latino, about thirty. She looked nothing like Sheila, save for from behind and even then it was a stretch.

Hector grinned as he introduced the woman, who still wore the wide smile. "Mace, this is my friend Angela. Angela, this is Macey."

"So you're Uncle Macey." She stuck her hand out in greeting. "I'm so glad to finally meet you. Hector talks about you all the time. I feel like I know you already."

He shook her hand, but his mind wasn't on her. "Where's Sheila? I didn't see her upstairs."

"Oh, she left already."

His heart nearly stopped. "What! You let her leave?"

Both of them to gaped at him. "I . . . I'm sorry, Mace," Hector said. "Did I do something wrong?"

"What time did she leave? And how?"

"I don't know." His eyes darted back and forth. "About an hour ago? She took a cab. I saw her getting in the cab as I got here."

"Did you speak to her?" How could he have allowed this to happen? Hector's terrified expression suddenly registered in his mind and he lowered his voice. "Sorry, Hector. I didn't mean to shout at you. It's not your fault. Did Sheila say anything to you when she left? Anything at all?"

"Yeah, she said she was going home and to—"

"Home? Are you sure?"

"Yeah, and she said to tell you not to worry about the case. Said she could handle it from here or something like that. She said you'd know what she was talking about."

He pressed his palms against his temples. He tried accessing their private channel on his memory server but, as expected, she wasn't online.

"I'm sorry, tío." Hector rested a hand on his shoulder. "I didn't know where you were. I didn't know she was supposed to stay here and wait for you."

"Don't worry about it. It's not your fault." He then noticed Angela sitting stiff as a board. "I apologize, Angela. I didn't mean to startle you."

She didn't reply but managed a mousy nod.

"I should have said something to you earlier, Hector." He raked his hands through his hair. "How could I have been so stupid not to expect her to go and do something like this?"

Hector stared back at him as if trying to figure out if he wanted an answer or not.

No time to lay blame, to consider how he could have done things differently. Sheila was out there, alone. Easy prey for Bradley or the police. He had to find her—quickly.

"I need another car."

"Yeah, ah, sure thing, Mace." Hector moved from behind the counter. "I'll go find something low-key for you, okay?"

"I don't care what it looks like. Get me anything. Just make sure it's fast."

CHAPTER ELEVEN

SHEILA HUNKERED INTO the back seat of the taxi as a police car passed in the opposite direction. The cab driver's eyes flashed at her in the rearview mirror, and she feared she'd reacted too obviously. She must already look like a stereotypical fugitive with her dark shades, baseball cap, and raincoat-like flak jacket. Best not to act like one as well. But he didn't seem too interested in her otherwise and, thankfully, didn't talk much either. The last thing she needed right now was a chatty cabby.

The solitude gave her time to think, time to plan what to do next. In truth, she didn't have much of a plan at all, but the ball was rolling, no turning back now.

She watched the city pass by through the window. People going about their daily lives, heading to work, taking the kids to school, shopping. She envied them. It wasn't long ago that she too had preoccupied herself with the routine worries of a mundane life, but that seemed an eon ago. Now her problems seemed far more basic—survival. A wave of depression swamped her, but she forced herself not to dwell on it.

Her thoughts reverted to the situation she had just left. Or, more accurately, the man she had just left. Like a recurring dream, Macey permeated her mind, finding his way to the center of her attention regardless of how hard she tried to ignore him. He had come to mean so many things to her in such a short time—Rick Macey, the man who had first impressed her with his intellect and wit, then protected her with his strength, comforted her with his compassion, and seduced her with the promise of his love.

In the end, though, he'd proven himself no better than the rest of the men in her life. He had abandoned her. Her last hope of salvation, gone when she needed him most. But she shouldn't have been surprised.

As much as she hated the fact, she had only herself to blame. She'd opened herself up to this man, let her guard down. She had relied on him for everything, for things she had promised herself she would never rely on any man for. Her weakness disgusted her. She should have known better. If life had proven anything to her, it was that the only person she could truly rely on was herself. She had broken that law with Macey, and now she was paying the price.

But that was all over with now. She would solve this problem on her own, as she should have done from the start. Her destiny would be decided by no one. Especially not by a man who couldn't decide whether he wanted to live in the future or grovel in the past. Probably better this way, for his sake, at least.

If Macey couldn't make the decision, then she would make it for him. Perhaps he had made it already. After all, she'd seen no sign of him before she left the safe house this morning. Perhaps he had already gone to join Virgil, leaving her behind.

She bit her lower lip as tears stung her eyes. It was not merely heartache she felt now, but anger. Who was she to him anyway? Macey was old enough to be her grandfather. What kind of perverted relationship could they share? And had he really left her without saying a word? Was he so cold? So weak?

"Here you go, ma'am," the driver said, bringing the taxi to a stop. "You sure this is place?"

The cab stood outside the desolate warehouse that had been Julian Hague's lab. She almost reconsidered, but where else could she go? "Yes, this is fine." She paid the driver in cash and stepped out of the cab.

She waited for the taxi to depart, the driver stalling as he studied her through the rearview, probably wondering if he should leave a woman alone in a place like this. Probably not, but he did anyway. As he drove away, uncertainty and fear hit her for the first time. Her bleak surroundings did little to ease her anxiety. Even the wind seemed to whistle a sinister tune.

"Strength, Sheila," she told herself as she put on the mask again. She would decide her own fate. No man would to do that for her.

She strode toward the warehouse, unsure how to even get into the place. The garage door was probably locked, so she would have to find an alternate entry. Scanning above, she spotted some windows beneath the roof, about thirty feet high.

“Forget that.” Too bad she wasn’t a cyborg. She returned her attention to the door, focusing on the digital lock plastered into the wall. It had a keypad as well as a neural jack. She had to force herself not to think about how easily Macey would probably overcome the device, but he wasn’t here. She had to do this herself.

She tried the keypad, punching a few codes and hitting the Open button. Zeros, Jules’s birth date, Gentec’s telephone number, the patent number for the Miracle Treatment. Nothing worked.

“Stupid thing.” She banged the open button. The door lurched and began to open. She jumped back. Had someone opened it from inside?

She pinned herself against wall, her heart racing. Surely no one could be here. As the door reached its limit, she honed her senses. She couldn’t hear anyone inside. Perhaps it had just been left unlocked.

She edged an eye around the doorframe. Dark inside, a good sign. No one worked in the dark, did they? And the place looked deserted. But what if someone lay in there waiting for her? A river of fear flowed through her stomach. Too late to hide now. They already know her presence.

She glanced toward the road, contemplated running, but what sense would that make? She’d come here for a purpose and she had to see it through. She made a decision, even if it would be the last decision she would ever make. Taking a breath, she rushed through the door.

“Come on and get me!” she yelled, her eyes clenched, her body braced for the impact of bullets, however they would feel. After a few seconds of nothing happening, the idiocy of her action set in. Thank God no one was there to witness it. If someone had been here, perhaps a bullet would have been a welcome deliverance from her embarrassment.

She laughed out loud at herself. Maybe she *was* going crazy from all this, but at least she had now determined that the place was empty. She found the door switch and closed it, engaging the lock. Then it dawned on her. If Jules had been the only person to know the combination, whoever had closed it previously would not have been able to lock it from the outside. Even more, now that she had locked it from the inside, no one else would be able to gain access.

Content with her security, she turned her attention to the lab. As she had expected, the place had been ransacked. Many of the terminals lay toppled over, some hard-copy files sat opened and scattered. She spotted some chocolate-colored stains on the floor—Jules's blood, now dried and discolored.

What if his body was still here? The possibility sent a shudder through her. She had not prepared herself to handle that. She didn't smell anything decomposing, but her mind would not rest until she knew for certain. Slowly she climbed the stairs to the upper level and looked down to where she remembered last seeing Jules alive. A wave of relief washed over her as she saw only another stain upon the pillar of lab equipment where he had expired.

Thankfully, someone had taken his body. But who? The police? It didn't seem logical, especially the way the place had been torn up. And if the police had gotten involved they would have the place secured with police tape and a shiny new padlock. It had probably been Bradley.

She headed toward the cluster of computers in the back of the lab, satisfied she could get started on what she had come for. She hastily keyed the terminals and poured through Jules's hard-copy files while she waited for the systems to come online. With the amount of information left, it had to be Bradley who had searched the place. The little idiot had left her a ton of data to use.

The main terminal came alive and she jacked into it neurally, activating the lab equipment and searching for more files within the database. Her plan could prove a long shot, but it was a chance she had to take. She might not be able to stop Virgil from releasing the negating agent, but maybe if she knew exactly how the agent worked, she could develop an agent to counter it.

Well, not counter it exactly. That would take far too long to achieve, but if she at least knew how it attached itself to DNA, she could produce a dummy agent with the same coupling mechanism that would block the receptor, thereby blocking the agent. An inoculation was perhaps the best way to define it. All she needed were more details on Jules's negating agent, and she could most certainly design an antidote. A negating agent to negate the negating agent.

That would be the first step to getting out of this mess.

The second could prove a bit trickier. Next she would have to face Boreman. He controlled Bradley and was thus the one who controlled her fate. If she could convince Roger that there existed another solution, another way out of this, perhaps she could get him to call off the police hunt. He had *some* brains, after all.

But to do that she needed an edge, an alternative he could accept. That's where the inoculation came in. It was a poker chip, a chance to buy back her life. No matter how much it disgusted her to make this kind of deal with Boreman, it was the only thing that made sense, the only thing she could do.

She raced through the files with a reinvigorated sense of purpose, her confidence returning. All that lay between her and a return to normality was the creation of this inoculation agent. Her plan would work. She could do this.

After all, she was still a geneticist, and a good one too.

Macey twisted hard on the throttle as he leaned the Buell toward the exit ramp. The tricked-out motorcycle responded with a surge of torque to the rear wheel, lifting its front in the air. He struggled to pull it down to earth as he flew toward the gridlocked traffic ahead. Squeezing the brake lever, he downshifted a couple gears, causing the engine to swoon as the bike decelerated to a stop, his front tire emitting a screech as it barely missed a passing car. The driver flung an insult, making him appreciative of the full-faced helmet and tinted visor he wore.

He hadn't ridden a motorcycle in years. And, frankly, the Buell was a pure embarrassment to be seen on, especially at his (apparent) age. But Hector's supply of fast vehicles had been limited to the Buell or a race-tuned Mitsubishi with a turbine engine. Not that he had anything against Japanese sports cars, per se, but he had picked the bike over the car for a very practical reason.

Picking up the front wheel, he launched the bike in first gear and sped alongside the standing traffic, slipping between it. He probably looked like a complete hooligan, swerving the obnoxiously loud motorbike in and out of the long lines of cars, buses, and trucks. But he ignored it and focused on reaching his destination—Sheila's apartment.

Even on the bike it took longer than he would have liked, but eventually he pulled up to the sidewalk opposite her building. Shutting off the engine, he balanced the motorcycle between his legs and performed a scan of the area. It seemed unlikely she would return to her apartment. Surely she would know that the police would be staking it out, waiting for her, but he had to check.

Within minutes, his trained eye spotted an unmarked car containing two detectives parked not far from him, scoping the apartment building's entrance. Probably a third cop somewhere inside the lobby, but he didn't need to verify that. He had all the information he required. If Sheila had tried to come back here, the police would have long since nabbed her, and they wouldn't still be sitting here watching.

That was good, but now he had no idea where she was. In truth, it would probably be better if she had been caught by the cops. The prospect of Bradley finding her worried him more.

Where could she have gone? He hoped not back to Gentec to try to work out some deal with Boreman, but the idea had crossed his mind more than once. Where else? Out of the city? Out of the country? The options became too numerous after that. He needed some way to find her, and fast.

He homed in on the facts thus far. Sheila had left early this morning, told Hector she was heading home. But why? Did she want to stop Macey from following her? Most likely. She probably didn't consider him much of a friend right now. Still, she had to have left some trace of where she had gone. Come on, Macey, are you a detective or what?

An idea struck him.

He might not know where she had fled to, but he did know how she would have gotten there. Hector said she had left in a cab and she must have called it from somewhere. She probably wouldn't have used her comm, fearing detection, which meant she had probably used the land line at the garage.

Macey leaned his elbows across the Buell's large fuel tank, ensuring he wouldn't tip over into the passing traffic as he dove into his neural net. When he accessed the web, he found Paul hadn't bothered to strip him of his O-6 access yet. He'd have to thank him later. He hacked into the phone company and searched the records listed under the garage. In a few minutes he had isolated Sheila's call to the taxi company. No voice. Just an electronic message that automatically sent a cab to the caller's address. And the name of the cab company.

Next he hacked the taxi company's database, breaking through its digital security with ease. He found the ID number of the cab that had responded and accessed their GPS tracking system to plot a route of the taxi's course. After obtaining a map, he superimposed the route and the destination become clear.

Julian Hague's lab . . . ? Why on earth would she go there? Worst of all, it lay in an isolated part of the city. Bradley had struck there once already, and he didn't put it past him to try again.

Macey started the Buell and stomped it into gear. Sheila was in as vulnerable a spot as he could imagine. He just prayed he would get to her before Bradley did.

Sheila focused on the results from the latest test run. More garbage. Twisting her lips, she keyed the sample for deletion and prepared to start over. Another disappointing failure.

But she wasn't discouraged. Not really. Jules must have taken months, maybe even years, to develop the negating agent. But she couldn't start thinking like that. No way could she spend months at this. She had only hours. She had to make this thing work, and she had to do it now.

She leaned back in the old office chair and released a sharp sigh. She couldn't remember the last time she had felt so pressurized to produce results. Back in university, maybe. Finishing her doctoral thesis had to come close, or during the launch of the second-generation Miracle Treatment. She smiled at the memory. She'd driven her team relentlessly, herself even harder, but in the end she'd come through.

Sheila Dunn had overcome the impossible, just like always.

From a kid she'd done just that: overcome incredible odds no matter what. People she knew now would probably never believe it, but life had not always been easy for her.

Home for Sheila was a dead-end town outside Chicago, where she grew up never really knowing her father and dealing with a mother who was stone drunk half the time. Somehow she had kept her head straight, determined she wasn't going to end up a statistic like her mom: broke, busted, and disgusted because she'd opened her legs to some man she thought loved her, only to spend the rest of her life cursing him like a dog while she crawled into a bottle. She had made it her mission to get out of that house, and like all her goals she had accomplished it with flying colors.

Something wet ran down her cheek. Crying again.

She thought of Macey, about his life, his family. How impressive it all seemed, especially compared to hers. He still didn't know much about her. How would he react if he knew the whole truth? Knew how cold and selfish she could be. The terrible family she had come from. Would he still desire her?

Maybe they were too different to make things work between them. After all, here he was, having some sort of religious dilemma while she didn't even believe in a god. She hadn't had the courage to tell him that, didn't know how that would make him feel. More precisely, how it would make him feel about her.

Maybe that explained why she had run from him. She supposed some people still needed to believe in some sort of supreme being, but she wasn't one of them. Her mother had seen to that. Not by neglecting to teach her about all that rubbish, but the opposite. One year her mother had decided to get all spiritual and started dragging her to some church across town. The people there used to try to force that garbage down her throat, but even at that age she knew not to believe it.

One Sunday after church the preacher came over to the house and she found out the real reason her mom kept going to his services. Although she was only ten or so at the time, she knew what they up to when they locked themselves in her mom's bedroom after supper. Even now she could hear her mother's groans through the door, churning her stomach with nausea.

The preacher would come over to "counsel" her mother on weeknights too, until his wife found out. Then suddenly church became a bad thing, a place for hypocrites and liars, and her mother never took her back there.

That was just fine with Sheila.

Religion was a sham, a mechanism designed by power-hungry men to give them control over the weak. People too lazy, afraid, or stupid to think for themselves. It shook her that a man like Macey, so intelligent, so sophisticated, could believe in something like that. And that's when it started to eat at her, when she lay awake last night: that maybe Macey couldn't make the right decision.

As much as she hoped he would come through for her, she knew the idiotic decisions religion forced people to make, and she couldn't handle the idea of him making a decision about her life based on some stupid myth or legend.

It was exactly that kind of thinking that made the Freedom from Deity Act all the more important. A modern society couldn't operate based on the nonsensical ideals of religion, and neither could she. As much as she wanted to believe in Macey, this time she had to rely on herself.

Overcome the impossible, just like she always had.

Keying up the terminal, she punched in a new set of variables and set the simulator for another run. She would beat this thing. She would beat Virgil, she would beat Boreman and Bradley. Maybe then, after all this ended, she could work things out with Macey. She would show him, prove to him that she could solve this problem on her own, without him having to sacrifice anything for her, prove to him there could be another way.

She glanced about the lab as the terminal hummed away. Jules's desk was on a raised upper area of the warehouse, overlooking the garage door entrance below. A metal banister ran the edge of the platform, serving as a safety rail. Dull lighting came from ancient yellow sodium lamps hanging from the ceiling. It would've been barely enough to see, but the holoscreen provided plenty of light on its own.

She rummaged through the drawers of the old wooden desk, looking for something to nibble on. She wished she had eaten something before she'd left this morning. Already her stomach was growling and it was barely ten o'clock.

The simulation stopped, spat out an error. So much for that attempt.

Maybe she had entered the data wrong. As she turned to look for Jules's notes, something caught in her peripheral vision. She stiffened, looked again. It was a shadow, cast from the dull florescent light behind her. Oddly shaped, slender.

And then it moved.

Her heart dropped though her stomach. Someone was standing behind her. She had to force herself not to scream as she searched the desk for some kind of weapon. She found an ashtray made of plastic, too flimsy, the only other option a slightly less flimsy pen. It'd have to do. Her hand crept toward it as she held her breath, her heartbeat a galloping racehorse within her ears.

Releasing a scream, she leapt out of her chair, twisting at the same time to strike out at whoever stood behind her. Her plastic pen cut the air as she whirled and she stood breathing in gasps. Facing no one.

She scanned the room to spot where the shadow had come from and started feeling silly. Had she overreacted? Could it have been an animal? A rat or something passing in front of the light? She looked down and the shadow was still there. She followed it, saw it split into two, like a pair of legs, and where the feet should be, she saw nothing.

"Easy, Sheila," a voice said.

She screamed again. The voice had come from right in front of her. She threw herself on top of the desk, trying to back away from whatever it was. "What is this?" she cried out, hearing the trembling in her own voice. "Where are—"

Something grabbed her by the throat, cutting off her wind and making her gag. A split second later she was struck hard across the face, her head jarring to the side. Her vision blurred.

She couldn't scream, couldn't breathe. Her hands went to her throat and found something there, something invisible gripping it. It felt like a hand covered in leather, squeezing the life out of her. It pulled her up off the desk and hung her in the air, her feet barely touching the floor.

She kicked her legs at her unseen assailant, her lungs burning. She tore at the unseen glove, wishing she hadn't dropped the pen. Her body thrashed as her brain screamed for oxygen. Seconds felt like days. Her vision tunneled. Her neck strained against the pull of her own weight.

Her mind entered a state of disbelief. Someone was killing her, strangling her. Her body heaved upward, her diaphragm caving in and out like a paper bag.

Abruptly the hand released and she crashed to the ground.

Air flooded into her lungs with a harsh, painful gasp. Her eyes streamed pools as she coughed and gagged.

"Did you enjoy that, Sheila?" the voice said from somewhere above her. It was Bradley's voice. "You were about ten seconds from dying. How did it feel?"

She scuttled across the floor, getting as far away from his voice as she could, her mind reeling. She wiped her watering eyes but still she could not see anything. Her throat felt like it had been in a vice. Her cheek burned and it felt like her face was beginning to swell. Her jaw throbbed.

The air shimmered in front of her, and the outline of a figure emerged. It was oddly shaped, transparent, like looking through a piece of thick glass. Then Bradley Thomas appeared, his body materializing amidst a kaleidoscope of colors as he pulled the hood of what looked to be a poncho from his head.

She cringed. He had used some kind of camouflage device. The thought that he could make himself completely invisible chilled her soul.

"You . . . . How? How did you know I was here?"

He stared at her as if she'd just asked him how to spell her own name. "Don't you remember your implant? Or perhaps you became an executive so long ago you forgot about that little company policy. Good thing I didn't."

Her mouth dropped open. Indeed she had forgotten. It had happened over twenty years ago. A GPS locator had been installed in her body, the same implant that held her flashy company ID tattoo. All senior VPs had one. It was supposedly a safeguard against kidnapping, but in reality it was just a means of reducing their company insurance premiums. She'd never thought about it as anything other than that.

So that's how he kept finding her. Her throat felt sore, raspy. "If you knew where I was the whole time, why didn't you just come and get me?"

"I did." He indicated the present circumstances with a wave. "I just needed you to leave your boyfriend long enough for me to do it. Thanks for helping me out with that." He stared at the hollow rib ceiling as if contemplating a thought. "Still haven't figured that part out. What possessed you to leave the garage alone? Didn't you realize Macey was the only thing stopping me from getting to you?"

"The garage? You were there?"

"Of course. I've been with you everywhere you've gone. I stayed at that garage after you left, just long enough to make sure Macey wasn't following you. Then I caught where you told the taxi driver to head to. And all we had to do was wait for you to show up."

"We?"

Bradley turned to look behind him. "Yeah, these guys."

One by one, men in the same hooded ponchos materialized like specters, four of them in all. Had they truly been in here with her the entire time? Silently observing her every move? A shiver coursed down her spine.

"Nice entrance." One of them grinned like an ape. "Honestly, man, you should have seen it. She ran in here screaming like a freakin' banshee. I nearly shot her."

The rest of them burst into laughter and jeers.

She would never have let any man talk to her like that, but she could only stare at them now, helpless while they mocked her. Joked like buddies on some camping trip. What was this to them? A game? Just another day at the office?

"You think this is funny? Some kind of joke? This is my life you're playing with!" She had had enough of this. "If you plan on killing me, Bradley, you'll be making a huge mistake. I have a way to get us out of this. I can save this company."

"Can you now?"

"Don't blow me off. I'm making a formula that can counter what Jules made. I can stop all this. Just get me in touch with Boreman so I can speak to him."

"Is that what you were doing here?" Bradley pushed a stack of files off the desk, grinned as they clattered to the floor. "You think your little genetic gimmicks will save you?"

"Don't be an idiot." Why was she dealing with him anyway? "Look, you won't understand. Just let me speak to Boreman. Please."

"I have my orders, Sheila."

"What orders? Can't you make a decision on your own? Can't you see that I can change everything that's—"

He launched a kick so fast it blurred. His boot slammed into her bottom jaw and sent her head reeling into the desk behind her.

Briefly she lost consciousness. Then a stabbing pain brought her to and she tasted blood. There was something hard in her mouth. She spat it out. One of her teeth landed on the floor in a red puddle.

"I'm setting the ground rules from now on, okay?" Bradley stooped down to her, grabbed her by the chin. "That demonstration was to let you know playtime is over. No more psycho-feminist-control-freak babble out of you. I'm the one in control now, understand?"

He increased the pressure on her jaw. "You think we haven't done our own research already? Think we're just sitting helpless, waiting on you to come save us with your scientific genius?" He leaned toward her, his mouth so close to hers she feared he might try to kiss her. "You're no Jules." His taunt came with reeking breath. "Never were, never will be. Not even close."

She jerked her head from him, breaking his grip on her jaw.

"Oh? Hurt your feelings did I? Maybe I can make it up to you somehow."

He mulled her over, a carnal leer in his eyes that reminded her of her mother's boyfriends and how they would ogle at her whenever she was alone with them. He grabbed at her blouse, tugging her forward as he pulled on it. A rip tore the silence.

"No!" she cried.

Laughter erupted as she tried to cover herself with her arms. But he grabbed those next, pulling them apart. A grunt escaped her lips as she strained against him. He was too strong, too barbaric. A malicious grin crept onto his lips as he forced her arms wide, his eyes gorging on her body.

"Oh, nice, Sheila," he said in a sickening whisper. "Come on, let's see what else you got going on down there . . ."

"No!" She squirmed to free herself. She couldn't stand him touching her, looking at her. Her mind blanked out the depravity that would come next, refused to accept it. She screamed so loud it hurt her own ears. "Don't! Don't!"

"Don't what, Sheila?" He threw her arms down, but her last scream seemed to have affected him somehow. He looked scared, like a little boy, his eyes darting, filled with embarrassment or perhaps shame. Then as quickly as the vulnerability came, it left, his bravado resuming. "You think I'd want to touch you? Rape you? Don't flatter yourself."

He spat at her, barely giving her a chance to clench her eyes as his saliva sprayed into her face. She didn't deserve this, didn't deserve to be treated like some animal. Even as she held her ripped blouse around herself, an indignant rage lit inside her. "You coward. Does it make you feel good to do this? To beat a woman? Humiliate her? Does it make you feel like a real man?"

A nauseating smirk appeared on his face. "No, it doesn't, Sheila, but it feels great to do it to you. By the way, the torn blouse was compliments of Boreman." He tapped upon his cheek with his index finger, just below the eye. "He's experiencing all of this in real time."

So Boreman was involved in this, as well. The disgusting old creep. How could he want to do something like that to her? To see her suffer and scream? Bradley's reaction made sense now. He was no rapist—he was just following his boss's orders, as usual. His boss was the truly depraved one. Hot tears fell on her cheeks, tears filled with her seething rage.

"You sicken me, both of you," she said. "I just gave you a second chance to save this company, and you two flush it down the toilet. All you care about is trying to save your own necks by vilifying me. Go ahead then, ruin my name, blame it all on me. But the truth will come out. Just you wait. Both of you are going to pay for what you've done to me."

"Stand her up," Bradley said.

Two of his men rushed to her side, lifting her, their hands digging into her arms as they brought her to Bradley's eye level.

"You're finished, Bradley," she said. "Can't you see it? When that negating agent is released, Gentec will crumble and you'll all go down with it. I actually look forward to it now. Do your worst, little boy. I don't care anymore."

She meant it too. If this was to be the end, then so be it. She had made her choice. She had tried to resolve things rationally, but you couldn't rationalize with beasts that weren't human. Beasts like Boreman and Bradley.

She thought about Macey, wished he were here. Wished she could watch him crush Bradley the same way he had Troy. Why on earth did she leave him? It seemed so ridiculous now. Even if Macey did end up choosing Virgil over her because of his religion, it would have been better than this, better than dying at the hands of this monster. At least he'd have been here to protect her. She trembled as she prepared to face her fate.

"Go on and kill me, Bradley." Her heart thundered in a drum roll. "Go on."

He eyed her wordlessly. Finally he shook his head, smirked. "Aw, come on, Sheila." He ran his hand across her cheek. "Don't you think I could have finished you off already if I had wanted to do that? Ten times over."

She jolted her head away from him. What else could he possibly want from her? A taped confession? "Don't toy with me."

"Wouldn't dream of it. But there *is* something you can help me with . . ."

The sound of her breathing filled the silence as she grilled him with a stare. "What?"

"Your boyfriend." He grinned at her idiotically. "You didn't think this was all about you, did you? You think we'd leave a guy like Macey alive, knowing what he does?"

"What are you babbling about?" They had to leave Macey out of this. It no longer involved him.

"He's out there looking for you right now, and when he finds you, he'll find us."

"So?" Was Bradley playing with her again? Or could Macey really be looking for her? The possibility caused her heart to sink and soar at the same time. She hoped he had changed his mind, had chosen her over Virgil. But by running had she set him up for a trap? She had left him hoping to spare him from her situation, not get him killed over it.

She had to warn him somehow. She tried connecting to him through her comm, but the signal was blocked. By Bradley, no doubt. She fought to not let her anxiety show. She needed some way to get Macey out of this mess she had put him in.

"You don't know anything about him," she said, twisting her face into what she hoped resembled a convincing scowl. "Macey isn't even on my side anymore. He's dropped the case. Didn't you know that? You'll be lucky if you ever see him again."

Bradley narrowed his eyes, piercing hers. "You need to learn how to lie better than that."

"You think I'm lying? Why do I need to lie to you? Aren't you going to kill me anyway?"

"You're lying to protect him, but it won't work."

Maybe she had tried too hard, overacted.

Bradley sneered. "We know he's on his way here."

Her heart froze. "What?"

"Don't try to act surprised. You're not that convincing. But don't you worry yourself—we'll have a proper welcome for him when he gets here."

She heard a metallic *chi-chack* and spun to see one of Bradley's men cocking a black rifle that looked bigger than she was. Big enough to kill Macey.

"Wait, please. You can't kill him. He . . . he's . . ."

"He's what?"

She closed her eyes, praying Macey would forgive her. She couldn't think of any other way. "Macey knows Virgil, the guy who has the negating agent Jules made. They've known each other for years. Virgil isn't going to release the agent yet. He's waiting for Macey to join him in his cause. That's why I thought I had time to make this counteragent."

"This is really pathetic."

"Bradley, I'm telling you the truth. That's why I left him. I didn't think Macey would help me anymore. I thought he went to . . . to join Virgil."

Bradley held her stare.

"I'm serious!" Her mind raced. What else could she say to convince him? "Look, if you do away with Macey now, then Virgil will probably release the agent, but if you don't . . ." She could barely bring herself to say the next words. "If you don't . . . I'm sure you could get Macey to stop Virgil from releasing it altogether."

"And he'd do that for me, would he?"

"He would . . . if you had me."

Bradley flicked his eyes to the side in thought or perhaps in conversation through his neural net. After a few moments he looked back to her. "Let's go. We need to get set up. You're going to be part of the welcoming committee."

"What? Wait! Didn't you hear what I said?"

"I don't have time for your games, Sheila."

"No." She couldn't believe it. "You're doing it again. You're throwing away yet another chance to save everything. You idiot!"

He let out a chuckle. "You just keep on thinking that."

That was it. She'd had enough of Bradley and his ignorance. Enough of all of this. She looked to Bradley and his men, little toy soldiers all of them. What was she thinking? They'd be no match for Macey, no match for his power, his strength. She didn't need to try and save Macey at all. It was Bradley who would need the saving.

"You have no idea what you're in for." A smile crept on her lips. "Macey's going to go crazy when he sees what you've done to me . . ."

"Oh, don't worry." He grabbed her swollen jaw again, stared into her face. "Once Macey sees you I'm sure he *will* go crazy. In fact . . ." he squeezed tighter, the madness dancing in his eyes causing her to fear she had just made yet another terrible mistake . . . "I'm pretty much counting on it."

CHAPTER TWELVE

MACEY SHIFTED THE BUELL into top gear as he pulled onto the deserted streets of the old warehouse district. He pegged the throttle, accelerating till the scream of the engine drowned in the hurricane howl of the buffeting wind. The bike ate up the road like a ravenous beast. Buildings and side streets flashed by in a blur.

He needed to concentrate at this speed, but he found his mind drifting to Sheila. He prayed she would still be all right, that he would find her safe, unharmed. He remembered his promise to God, to put Him before all else. What if he truly *had* given her up? He shook the thought away. Was his faith so fickle?

His disgust in how quickly he could let doubt creep in caused him to push the throttle further, taking his self-loathing out on the road. God was still in control. No matter what happened, his faith would not waiver.

Not this time.

He made the last turn onto the side street that dead-ended at Hague's lab. He eased off the throttle and let the Buell cruise to a stop. Even at this distance he could tell something wasn't right. The garage door lay wide open. Granted, it could have been left open from the last time, but it didn't seem likely. And if Sheila had gone inside, surely she would have closed it for security's sake. Then he spotted the black sedan parked alongside the warehouse.

Testing his neural connection, he found the telltale signs of jamming. Was he too late? He needed to be calm, investigate the situation.

He nudged the Buell off the road and worked his way along a back alley, hiding behind whatever cover he could find, old buildings, even a couple of trees and an abandoned truck. He feathered the clutch and worked the throttle lightly, keeping the engine noise down.

He had moved the equivalent of a city block and remained about the same distance from the warehouse, but he didn't need to get any closer. He removed his helmet and focused on the doorway with his enhanced vision, the magnified view appearing in the corner of his eye. He zoomed close enough to see inside. His iris adjusted, turning the inner darkness to light. He examined the lab hastily to spot her.

And when he did, his mind came undone.

Sheila was teetering on the balcony railing, stripped to her underclothes, her hands bound behind her back, tiptoeing oddly. He zoomed in more. A noose looped around her neck.

The balcony shook and she stumbled, wobbling on the railing. The noose pulled taut as she leaned forward, her toes nearly breaking contact with the balcony. Macey's heart leapt into his throat. Suddenly her weight shifted back, allowing her to regain her precarious balance. The railing shook again and he looked across from her to see Bradley Thomas preparing to give it another healthy kick.

Perverted little sadist. Making her suffer before he killed her.

He forced himself not to react emotionally. His mind raced to formulate a plan. He could try shooting the rope, but even with his enhanced targeting his pistol didn't have the range for it, not to mention he'd have only one shot at it. After that his presence would be known. Bradley could easily just shoot Sheila with his own gun then.

Surprise held his only advantage now. He had to strike while Bradley preoccupied himself with his sick little game. He could head the rest of the way on foot and sneak into the lab, but that would take time he didn't have. Even if he ran at top speed he couldn't get there fast enough to avoid Bradley noticing him, or before Sheila fell.

Macey looked down at the Buell. It was an option maybe, but the thing was just too loud. Then again, it was also quite fast. Fast enough to get him inside before Bradley reacted? Possibly—the bike could pull zero to a hundred in a handful of seconds. With that kind of acceleration, he could cover the distance in a heartbeat.

Bradley kicked the railing again and one of Sheila's feet slipped free.

His mind spun. No more time to think.

Revving the engine, he popped the clutch and launched the Buell toward the lab at breakneck speed. The engine wound up like a jet turbine as he powered through first gear and shifted into second. Relentlessly, he closed in on the open garage door. Bradley's head snapped toward him, but he was less than a hundred feet away now and traveling at a speed he didn't want to know.

He barely touched brakes before leaping from the motorcycle. It tumbled and flipped to the side in a cornucopia of sparks and flying plastic, slamming into the garage door. Macey fell on the pavement, rolling with an impact that felt like he had been hit by a truck. He forced himself to ignore the pain as he caught sight of Sheila dangling on the noose, her other foot about to slip off.

He clambered to his feet as he slid inside the warehouse, propelled by his fall. Without trying to stop, he surged toward her, yelling her name, praying he would catch her in time, praying he could grab hold of the rope as well as her body, so his momentum would break it and not her neck when they collided.

"Sheila!" he cried again as he soared toward her. She was gagged, her mouth covered with tape. Then he saw her eyes, her gorgeous violet eyes. Wide open, staring back at him.

She screamed muffled words he could not hear, but her eyes spoke for her: panic–stricken. But there was something else there. It was as if she were trying to tell him something, something he should—

A weight crashed into him from above, slamming him with the force of a falling building. It snatched him from midair and thrust his body onto the garage floor with a crack of concrete.

He found himself pinned to the ground, covered by a net of thin wires that bit into his skin. The net tightened, the wires constricting his movement until all he could do was lie flat on his back, his arms outstretched.

He forced his head upward so he could keep Sheila within sight. She was still balancing on one foot, screaming beneath her gag. Her bloodshot eyes accentuated her reddened face, now swollen and bruised. He thanked God she was alive, but he could only imagine what Bradley must have done to her.

Bradley stepped next to her, a sick grin on his face. "Did you like that, Macey?" he called out from the upper level. He took hold of Sheila's legs, steadying her on the railing. "I hope I didn't scare you too much, but judging from your entrance I think I must have."

He untied the noose and hauled her down from the railing. She bucked furiously and Bradley responded by landing two blows to her ribcage. Her muffled cries went off like gunshots in Macey's ears, sent him straining against the net again, his anger summoning every ounce of his strength.

"I wouldn't do that if I were you," Bradley said. "That mono-wire will slice through even your body if you push hard enough."

He was right. Mono-molecular wire could cut through the toughest alloy, so long as you applied enough pressure. That's what made it so dangerous. He was strong enough to break the wire, but his body wasn't hard enough to resist it. He'd burst through the net all right, but come out in a hundred bite-sized chunks on the other side. That prospect stilled him. He needed to stop reacting and start playing the game.

He had made a mistake in underestimating Bradley. The guy had managed his intelligence well, dug up enough about his relationship with Sheila to manipulate him into this trap. He had never even spotted the net, which he could now see had sprung from the roof and was anchored at the floor. He had fallen for the bait, placed himself right in the kill zone. No more.

Bradley had used Sheila to lure him here and restrained him. The only thing he didn't know was why. Was he merely taking his time to murder both of them? Possibly, but not likely. If anything, Bradley hadn't demonstrated himself to be overly hasty. No, he wanted something else. This was the setup to some deal, and Bradley had arranged things to ensure he had absolute leverage in the negotiations.

The creep leaned toward Sheila and whispered something, cocking his own ear toward her as if she could whisper something back. "What's that, Sheila? Oh, you want to say hello? All right then, go ahead." He tore the tape from her mouth, making her yelp, revealing bruised and bloodstained lips.

"Macey! I'm sorry I did this to you. Just—"

"Sheila, keep quiet," Macey bellowed over her.

Another trap: Bradley trying to stir his emotions again. He wouldn't allow it. He remained silent. It was Bradley's turn to make a move, and he would force him to do so.

The balcony was a good twelve feet above the garage floor. A set of metal stairs at the far end provided access up and down. Toward the rear he spotted the bloodstained concrete pillar where Hague had breathed his last.

Dead silence took hold, and it had the effect he had anticipated. Bradley was no doubt waiting for him to plead for Sheila's life along with his own. But he had nothing to plead for. Bradley could either kill them or not, and by his hesitation he'd already shown his hand. Subtly the scales tipped in his favor.

"You know, you can thank Sheila that you're still alive," Bradley said. "I had planned on taking you out as soon as you got here."

Still he said nothing.

"What's the problem? Don't feel like talking?"

"You haven't asked me a question yet. Save for that one. See how it works now?"

Bradley scowled and then turned about, sucker-punching Sheila in the stomach. She groaned and doubled over, causing Macey's blood pressure to soar. He strained against the wire without thinking, but its bite brought him back to reality. He forced himself to ignore what he had seen, refused to call out her name. He spoke to her instead with his eyes, pleading into hers, which were now watering and drowned in despair.

"Let that be a lesson, Mr. Macey." Bradley rubbed his fist. "If you don't behave, Sheila will pay the price. Understood?"

Stay calm. Don't let him get to you. "I understand."

"Good. Now I do have a question for you. Sheila says you're old comrades with this Virgil character, the cyborg that has the negating agent. Is that true?"

Sheila shook uncontrollably, seemed on the verge of sobbing, unable to look at him. The sick freak must have beat the information out of her. He wished he could somehow communicate with her, tell her it was okay, that it didn't matter. But that would have to wait. Right now he had to keep playing Bradley's game, and he was already one step ahead of the clown. He knew what Bradley wanted. But he had to make him say it. "Yeah, it's true. That important to you for some reason?"

"She also said he's delaying the release of the negating agent on your account. Is this true?"

"What if it is?"

"It's a yes or no question. I expect your answer to be one of them. Which is it?"

Megalomaniac. "Yes."

"And why would that be?" Bradley leaned against the railing with both hands. "Explain to me why a terrorist would be willing to put his plans on hold just for you."

"You wouldn't understand. You'd have to believe in God for that. Judging by the way you like to hit women, I doubt you respect any sense of decency at all, much less a higher power."

Bradley froze, and he could tell he was fighting the urge to hit Sheila again. His cool was slipping nicely. "You be careful," he said with a prod of his finger. "I wasn't joking about being ready to take you out."

Next to him, a form shimmered into view and, in a multicolored burst of light, a gunman appeared—holding a 20mm rifle in his arms. The rifle and gunman hardly surprised him, but the optical camouflage did. Bradley had already proven he had access to some fairly impressive military gear. Now it only seemed to be getting better. Enhancing his vision, Macey switched to an infrared spectrum to see who else might be hiding out. He spotted the heat signature of at least two more spooks near Bradley, plus a third near himself.

"I'm going to assume you're telling the truth," Bradley said. "If that's the case, my employer is willing to offer you a deal."

"You want me to recover the negating agent for you, is that it?"

"Partially. The agent won't do me much good by itself."

"What do you mean?"

"Your friend Virgil. He comes with the package."

Macey hadn't expected this. It definitely wasn't a direction he wanted things to go.

"You deliver him and the agent, ready to be handed over to the authorities, and we have ourselves an understanding."

Macey forced a snort of nonchalance. "And what makes you think I can convince Virgil to hand himself over to you? I haven't seen the guy in fifty-odd years until yesterday. We're no more friends than you and I."

"That should make it all the easier."

"I don't see how." But already he knew his bluff hadn't worked.

"Look, I'm not telling you how to do it. I'm telling you what I want." Bradley leaned over the railing further. "I don't care if you have to beat him to a pulp and bring him to me in chains. The media and the police are involved now, and someone has to take the fall. It might as well be the guy who's actually responsible. Anyway, it's either him or Sheila, so take your pick."

"Macey, don't do this!" Sheila shouted. "I didn't know—"

Bradley wheeled and struck her hard across the face, dropping her to her knees.

"All right, enough!" Macey had to end this. "What happens if I do what you want?"

"Simple." He yanked Sheila back to her feet. "The authorities would have both cause and culprit for Ms. Darling's death. Gentec's name would be cleared. The charges against Sheila would be dropped, and her life would return to normal."

"No hard feelings, huh?"

"That's right. And to smooth things over we're even prepared to offer you both a sizable compensation package."

"Sounds like a sweet deal. Nothing like Sheila's original plan at all." He gritted his teeth to stop himself from saying something he didn't want to. "Now what happens if I'm not stupid enough to believe you'll deliver on your promises?"

"This offer comes with no surety. You either deliver or you get to see Sheila hang again. For real this time. The choice is yours." He gazed upward wistfully. "You know, my employer is being quite generous offering you this deal. Personally, I wouldn't, so I suggest you take it."

"Macey, don't," Sheila said.

He made eye contact with her, tried to convey with a penetrating stare that he knew what he was doing—that there was only one answer he could give, only one way to get them out of this predicament. He had already made his decision to stop Virgil, but his plan didn't include turning him in. Was he, after all this, still going to have to sacrifice Virgil to save Sheila? He couldn't bear to think about it, not now. God had spared them this far. He would see them through.

"I'll do it," he said. "I'll bring you the negating agent, and Virgil."

Sheila went limp and a symphony of emotions played across her face: relief, regret, guilt, shame, he couldn't tell exactly what. She no doubt thought he'd done it for her sake. He wanted to tell her not to feel responsible, that he had already made his decision about Virgil, but the less Bradley knew about everything the better.

"We're doing the right thing, Sheila," he called up to her.

"Glad you're so fired up about it." Bradley took hold of her and pushed her down the metal stairs in front of him. "But then you probably should be. After all, wasn't it your job to arrest terrorists?"

He felt like knocking his bloody teeth out.

"I'll give you six hours to make the delivery. I'll contact you with an exchange point."

"I'll be sure to keep my comm open."

"The counterweights holding down that net will release in thirty minutes." He sauntered past, holding Sheila by the arm. "I suggest you use the time to consider what will happen to Sheila if you don't come through on this."

He could see Sheila clearly now. She looked a mess, her angelic face contorted with bruises and pain, her body shivering. But her eyes still shone brightly as she looked down at him. He didn't want her to say anything, didn't want her to expose any more of their relationship. But inevitably she did.

"I'm sorry, Macey," she said with a rasp. "I didn't mean for things to turn out this way. I should have tr—"

"We'll be out of this soon." He had to fight back tears of anguish as he stared into her eyes. He wanted to say so many things to her, but prayed his eyes conveyed what his lips could not. He stared into those violet pools for as long as he could before Bradley finally marched her out of his sight.

Moments later, the slamming of car doors preceded the start of the sedan's engine outside. Tires spun in loose gravel as it pulled away.

Thirty minutes.

At least he wouldn't have to do anything until then.

Virgil rolled the glass canister within his palm, marveling at the magnified image of his fingers through the clear goopy liquid. Finally. The item he had waited so long for. It seemed ridiculously small for the greatness it would accomplish. But then, God always used the smallest of things to do His best work. Israel, David, Jesus. This was no different.

It had come at a price, though, and more than mere money. It had cost several lives as well. Gordon Pool's, for one. That still troubled him. If only he'd been able to get through to Gordon before it was too late. Sadly, such would be the fate of many who would trust in this Miracle Treatment. Fooled into believing they could cheat death until, like Gordon, their lives would be snatched away from them before they could repent. But he could prevent all that now.

Now that he had this.

Virgil stared out across the expanse of the desolate city of Pomona from his perch high atop a long deserted construction crane. The noonday sun beat down upon the ruins like bleached bones in a desecrated graveyard. Even from here the agent could be released.

He could break the glass at any time and be done with his mission. In truth, part of him wanted to, to have it all over with. But he had made a promise to wait. God had a way of throwing surprises at you. Communicating with Macey again after all these years was certainly one of them.

His old friend, his brother. Would he finally come to serve God again? He prayed so, more than anything. Even more than this mission to destroy the Miracle Treatment, he longed to reunite with his brother. He rolled the canister one last time before securing it in his overcoat pocket. Its use would have to wait until Macey's arrival, however long that would take.

"Father, protect Macey, guide him. Show him the path of truth. If it be Your will, I pray that we will once again be brothers. Guide me also, Father, that I will not stumble, but will forever do Your will. Guide us both on the path of Your truth. In Christ's name, Amen."

• • •

Macey limped back to his apartment in the Hills on what was left of the Buell. It was a miracle he could ride the thing at all. The handlebars and footpegs were now bent at extreme angels, and it needed a new paint job and fairing, but it managed to get him home via the back streets, albeit at an unbelievably slow pace.

By the time he keyed open his entrance gate and rolled into the driveway, the sun was perched high in a cloudless sky, radiating heat like a broiler. The shade inside his own garage provided welcome relief as he pushed the Buell inside.

He parked the motorcycle in the near-empty garage and contemplated giving himself a new nickname. Vehicle Violator had a nice ring to it. He had only the BMW left, unless he wanted to bug Hector for yet another car to demolish. Perhaps God was sending him a message about his materialism.

He passed through the inner door into his apartment and went through his usual routine. He checked the surveillance system and his external memory server. Finding those in order, he headed straight for the bathroom mirror to assess the damage to his body.

His clothes were a wreck and he had some abrasions from his fall. A few cuts where the mono-wire had sliced through. But overall, mostly superficial.

Nothing at all like the wounds he had seen on Sheila's body.

He let loose a sigh and ran fingers through his hair. How could things have turned so bad in such a short time? Had God left him already? He shook away the lament. He knew enough about God not to try and put Him in a box, to pull Him out like some lucky rabbit's foot only when he needed help. To praise Him when things went well and claim abandonment when things did not. God promised ease to no one, not even those who followed His path. And clearly, the path that lay before him was anything but easy.

He stripped to examine the rest of his wounds. He had some bullets implanted in his back from Bradley's first hit outside Grant's kitchen, a couple more in his chest from Pooly's rooftop gang.

Then he noticed a patch of scalp hair missing. From Troy's little stunt at Jackson's, no doubt. That one irritated him the most. The bullet had punctured the skin, exposing a bit of titanium skull underneath. He'd have to get that repaired eventually, but at least he could cover it up for now. Still, cyborg maintenance wasn't cheap, especially as he had to pay for it out of pocket nowadays.

Maybe he should send Troy a bill.

He cranked the shower and dragged himself inside. The warm water soothed his body and he let his mind loose. Bradley had given him no choice but to stop Virgil from releasing the negating agent now. Granted, he'd already planned on doing that, but he wasn't mentally prepared for the consequences. Originally he'd planned on handling things through Paul and CDI to ensure Virgil's safety. But handing him over to Bradley or the police was a death sentence. Betray Virgil and set him up for execution, what a laugh.

And that'd just be the easy bit.

All this time, he'd been proclaiming his intentions to stop Virgil as if it were nothing, a simple task, a mere precursor to ending Sheila's dilemma. As if Virgil would accept his reasoning and toss aside his own ideals like some lapdog. The truth was that Virgil's convictions were as strong as his own. Stronger.

In Jasper, they'd stay up late many nights: sipping coffee, cracking jokes, until inevitably the conversation would turn to the standoff surrounding them. And then they'd start at it, the same old debate. The Law of God versus the law of man and what the Christian's response should be when the two diverged.

Should man be allowed to choose his own law, no matter how ungodly? Or should man, despite himself, be forced back to God's Law, for his own good and salvation? Macey knew which side of the fence he stood on, and so did Virgil. They'd argue away the whole night: horn-locked, quoting Scripture, spouting philosophy, shouting insults, banging tables, until neither of them had the strength or will to continue. And then they'd laugh, shake hands, and agree to disagree.

Fifty-plus years later and here they were, back at the table again. Only this time there'd be no coffee, no laughter, no handshake, no agreeing to disagree. The debate would finally be settled, once and for all.

And he had to ensure that he won it, no matter what.

"Beat him to a pulp and bring him back in chains." That little punk Bradley had no idea how close he might have come to the actual truth. As much as he hated to admit it, to prevent Virgil from releasing the agent he would probably have to stop at nothing short of a physical confrontation.

And if it did, there was no sense being ill-prepared.

He stopped the shower and lumbered out. With just a towel-dry, he proceeded toward the basement, a trail of damp footprints following him down the creaky wooden stairs to the cinderblock-lined vault below.

The solar converter lay in the center. Around it lay piles of junk he had amassed over the years, covered in olive-green tarps. He didn't remember what lay underneath them and was almost tempted to look, but he had no time for that. No more distractions.

He fixed his eyes on a concrete hatch in the corner. It was roughly two feet square, recessed into the concrete floor. It protruded perhaps a half-inch, just enough for him to get his fingertips around. Pressing inward, he gripped both ends like a vice and lifted it out of the recess. He had designed it this way. No handholds. Only himself, a crane, or another cyborg would be able to lift the two-hundred-pound slab.

He dropped into the hole, landed on cold tile flooring some twelve feet below, and keyed on a light. The closet-sized room illuminated, and the mustiness of dust and old leather filled his nostrils.

On one wall hung a collection of rifles and handguns. Also some sentimental artifacts to commemorate the highlights of his career: a silver-plated pistol he'd found on an officer in Iraq, a ceremonial katana gifted to him by the Japanese Government after a six-month joint counterterrorist op he had conducted in Hokkaido, and a fully functioning M5 rifle salvaged from a naval base in Guam.

On an opposite wall hung placards of his medals and insignia from his days as a gold-bar lieutenant and upward. A shame he couldn't display them any longer, at least not all three of them together. There was a set for each of his careers in the military. One from when he had first retired from CDI after Virgil left, another from when he had rejoined and then retired again twenty years later, and the last from when he retired about a year ago, handing everything over to Paul. He wondered how long he would stay out this time or if he would rejoin at all. A bit of a moot point, though. So long as he had this body, he would always be in the military.

Larger weapons hung on a third wall: heavy ordnance, some of which would probably make even Bradley jealous. But he hadn't come for them. Leafing through a clothes rack full of uniforms set against the last wall, he withdrew a set of tropical print camouflage fatigues.

At least, that's how they would appear to most people. In actuality, it was a combat frame—armored clothing designed specifically for cyborg use. The fabric wasn't fabric at all, but tiny ceramic plates linked with artificial muscle fibers, the same stuff that made up his body. At a thought, he could make them solidify into a rigid, bullet-resistant sheet.

Moreover, the frame tied directly into his nervous system, augmenting his strength and reflexes. He could even accelerate his synapses to inhuman levels with something called a cynetic burst. It was a risky maneuver though, like replacing a blown fuse with a penny. It would get more power through all right, but you could fry your entire nervous system doing it.

The frame's last feature: enhanced mobility, via snap thrusters. The *snaps* worked by concentrating the frame's power supply to a pinpoint, creating a burst of plasma the size of a golf ball along with a snap-like explosion that propelled the wearer in a given direction. The thrusters could also be used as weapons, increasing the velocity of punches and kicks.

Memories of combat training sprang to life as Macey continued to gaze at the frame. Endless hours of hand-to-hand and acrobatic exercises intended to maximize its potential. It was the weapon of choice for a cyborg, really, whose strength already lay in mobility and imperviousness to small-arms fire.

No need to hide behind walls and shoot with a rifle when you had this thing on.

A cyborg in a combat frame could lay waste to an entire platoon with frightening ease. Get in close and take people out with bladed weapons, mono-wire, or just the frame itself. The only time a cyborg even needed to use ranged weaponry at all was against armored vehicles or tanks. For that, the advantage of using a frame came in the ability to wield weapons so large they would kill any normal human if he tried to fire them—like the 30mm assault rifle on the wall behind him.

In 2050 the Geneva Convention had deemed combat frames inhumane and had banned their use. But Macey knew that it hadn't been just skill that had allowed Virgil to dance across the rooftop against those rotary cannons, and sure enough those weren't regular combat fatigues he wore, either. If he hoped to even stand a chance against Virgil, he would have to employ the same.

He suited up, donning the frame legs first, the cold armor against his bare skin a grim reminder of what his body truly was—a living weapon, an illegal implement of devastation. Soon he would face off against the very same—Virgil, his friend, his brother in Christ, his fellow weapon of destruction. They would battle over the ideals of God, as they'd done so many times in the past, but this time they would have an outcome, a resolution in whatever form it took.

Macey only prayed that, somehow, they would both survive it.

CHAPTER THIRTEEN

THE EARLY-AFTERNOON SUN poured through the windshield of the BMW in a blinding beam of light. Macey had to squint as he ascended the overpass. Even with the air-conditioning on full blast, he was overheating. The heavy overcoat he wore to conceal his combat frame didn't help matters. Even though the frames resembled clothing—in this case, camouflage fatigues, boots, and gloves—a man his size wearing one could turn heads, and he didn't need the added attention.

He was half an hour outside LA, headed east on the San Bernardino freeway. The ruins of Pomona City blurred by to his right. Pomona City had the dubious distinction of being ten miles from the epicenter of one of the most powerful

Californian quakes in recent history. Magnitude 8.2 officially, although some experts claimed it had been even higher. But the quake alone wasn't all that plagued Pomona.

North of the city, the San Antonio Dam provided flood control for the Santa Ana River Basin, where Pomona resided. The quake had hit in mid-February, the height of the rainy season. That year, Pomona had been experiencing record rainfalls. The quake and the already elevated stress on the dam combined, and the dam gave way. The two disasters resulted into a calamity that rocked the city to its core. Thousands died.

Macey recalled spending just over a year in the relief and clean-up effort. But now, almost ten years later, the city still hadn't recovered. The downtown area was a ghost town, devoid of even basic infrastructure. No power and no water, save for the springtime floods that pervaded the repaired but only semi-functioning San Antonio Dam.

Although major accessways like the freeway had been repaired, many of the local streets remained damaged. Money had been in short supply, partly due to the seismic predictions of another quake of similar magnitude within twenty years. Government foot-dragging had left the rebuilding of Pomona in limbo. It had become a derelict graveyard long before it had been officially written off by the state.

The only people who lived in Pomona now were the worst of what humankind had to offer: career criminals, serial killers, cyber-gangers, terror-cell members—anyone wanting to drop off the map of civilization.

No surprise that Virgil would be among them.

Macey glanced at the old map of pre-quake Pomona in his lap and correlated it with the traffic satellite image in the lower corner of his vision. Not far now to the address Virgil had given him. He left the freeway and maneuvered the BMW through the asphalt trails that used to be streets, navigating a maze of concrete debris. Whole buildings lay toppled, blocking the roadway. In several places, the road itself dead-ended in open chasms.

All around, he felt the eyes of Pomona's residents on him. He drove slowly for safety, but a BMW idling though the middle of Pomona was like an unattended slot machine hitting the jackpot in the middle of a crowded Las Vegas casino. It was drawing attention he didn't want. Already he could see a group of opportunistic cyber-gangers preparing to pounce.

There were at least thirty of them, strolling into the street ahead of him. They were from his favorite crowd too: the Blitzers. Their vacuum-tube hairdos glinted in the late afternoon sunlight, contrasting with the black vinyl trench coats most of them wore.

They had to be roasting in this heat. But Blitzers weren't known for their fashion sense. The assembly had gathered right in front of his destination, a fifty-story building that had been under construction when the quake hit. It was one of the few tall buildings left standing in Pomona. A tower amidst the ruins, looming like a symbol of tyrannical control. Ironically, its technically advanced foundation had probably helped it survive the quake, but for what? Today it remained a skeleton, no walls or windows. It was a concrete layer cake with a cherry-red crane stuck forlornly at the top, never to be brought back down again.

When he looked back, the cyber-gangers had grown in number to over a hundred. He stopped the car. Where had they all come from? The building perhaps? Was it some sort of base or refuge for them? Probably. Like kicking an anthill.

A string of fluorescent-green graffiti on the second floor confirmed his suspicions.

131i7z3r5 > 411 > u 50 50D 0ff!

It was intended to be a warning. A debauchery of the English language was more like it, replacing letters with numbers in an attempt to look intelligent or hacker-savvy. To him it just reinforced their reputation of being idiots. But he could understand well enough what the message said: "Blitzers are greater than all, which is greater than you, so sod off."

He smirked at the British slang. An attempt to identify with their South London roots, and no doubt why the bartender in Club Miracle had spoken with that ridiculous phony accent.

Any other time, he might have been apprehensive about running into a hundred or so cyber-gangers out on the take, but today he just wasn't in the mood.

He tapped the gas and rolled the BMW right into their midst. The pack surged and hollered as he jammed to a stop with another screech of rubber.

"Oy! Watch it, yah bloody wanka!" one of them shouted as he opened the car door.

"Nice Beemer, Guv! Fancy if we nick it?"

"Look at that tosser! Got some bollocks to come 'round 'ere but!"

Their irritating lingo was probably ripped from some cheesy download-vid. Their jargon varied so widely between Scottish, Irish, and Cockney English that they could probably span all three accents in a single sentence and not know the difference. They probably couldn't even find South London on a map, much less ever lived there to pick up a proper accent.

Macey got out and slammed the door. He locked the car and several more gangly Blitzers crawled from the building and came toward him. White trash mostly, with a few Latinos. Most of them didn't look a lick over twenty-five. Stupid kids.

The black vinyl mass circled him, their accented chattering reminding him of a pub in London where he'd once tried to watch the World Cup. He could sense their anticipation, riling themselves up, about to charge in, topple him over, slice him up, and celebrate their newly gained prize.

Or so they thought.

Drawing back the sleeve of his overcoat, Macey raised his gloved hand and hit the snaps in the center of his palm. With a crack, twenty Blitzers collapsed to the ground, convulsing.

The snaps created a mild electromagnetic pulse, nothing serious, but the Blitzers' light-bulb setup created a perfect route for the pulse to travel straight to their nervous systems.

The other gangers backed away. As the fallen ceased their convulsions, silence fell. Their gang buddies probably thought they were dead. They would come to in about an hour, but he wasn't about to tell them that. Macey stood in their stunned calm like a wizard on some fantasy battlefield, surveying the ruin wrought by his dark magic.

"I expect this car to be here and in one piece when I come back," he said, his voice echoing off the concrete ruins. He gazed up at the unfinished building, still not making eye contact with any of them. "If it isn't, I'll hunt down every last one of you and make sure you share your friends' fate. Understood?"

"Crikey! He's just like that bloody Moses bloke, ain't he?"

Moses. So that's what they called Virgil here. Fitting.

"You with the horns." Macey pointed at the freak who had spoken, a Latino kid with two bulbs protruding from his forehead like devil horns. "I'm making you responsible. Anything happens to this car, you die first."

"W–what?"

"And I'd work on that accent of yours, *mate.* That one's Australian, in case you hadn't noticed." Crouching, he sprang into the air and hit the snaps.

He took off like Superman—not that these punks had ever heard of classic comic books. They gawked up at him like football fans watching a kick-off. He cleared about fifty feet before hitting the snaps three times. His body jerked with rapid acceleration as the wind pressed hard against his face, leaving three puffs of smoke behind him, a hundred feet between each one. If they hadn't been in awe before, they were now.

Halfway up the building, he slowed his ascent. His foot touched the lip of one of the floors and he bounded off it again, straight up, this time without the aid of the frame. He could have hit the snaps another time, but using them in such rapid succession produced a lot of heat. He'd have to let the frame cool or risk burning it out.

He soared a few more seconds, kicked off from another floor, and hit the snaps one last time. The suit propelled over the building's top ledge. He tucked into a somersault and glided at the apex. From here, some five hundred feet above, he had a gorgeous view of Pomona. The cerulean sky was an incongruous background to the sun-bleached concrete of the half-demolished buildings below.

He touched down on the roof, his knees bending like shock absorbers as he dropped into a crouch. The structure trembled with the weight of his cybernetic body.

He straightened, the wind flagging his overcoat. He probably looked like some combat superhero, had anyone been there to appreciate it. Oy, it felt good to blast the snaps again.

He surveyed his surroundings. The sun had bleached the roof nearly white, as it had the roofs of the buildings arrayed below. Junk littered its surface: a cement mixer, a gang-box, I-beams, a shipping container—all rust-red from years of exposure to the wind and rain.

At the center, the tower crane extended another hundred feet into the blue. The crane had once been red, but now its trusses were dulled and bubbling with rust. He checked the operator cab, the hundred-foot-long boom extending ahead of it, and the shorter counter-boom with its concrete weights extending behind. Overall, it looked structurally sound.

A gust of wind buffeted him and he pulled his overcoat tight. He saw no sign of Virgil, but one look at the crane cab told him exactly where he would be. He vaulted upward, hitting the snaps for good measure. He overshot the top of the crane boom, soared some fifty feet above it. The view of the ground with both crane and roof far below him was a spectacular sight. It was times like this he truly appreciated his body's capabilities. How many people could say they could actually fly?

Glancing downward, he lined himself up with the narrow beam of the crane boom, his arms spread to guide him. As gravity took effect he plunged toward it, his speed increasing. Would ten years of disuse leave it capable of supporting his landing? Maybe. Before his feet touched, he activated the snaps, sharply slowing his descent. He landed on the boom light as a feather.

Slow clapping filled the air.

Virgil stood on the boom, near the crane's center mast, a tennis court-length distance away. He must have climbed up out of the cab while Macey was in midair. "Very nicely done," Virgil said. "I barely felt you land."

His mirror shades gleamed like diamonds in the bright afternoon sun. His white overcoat fanned out like a cape, exposing his camouflaged combat frame beneath. Macey's own overcoat pressed against his back by the wind, clinging to his body like a wetsuit, his coat-tails whipping forward. He placed his hands in his pockets to keep himself balanced.

"Welcome to my home, Macey." Virgil gave him a pearly smile.

"This is some castle you got here, man. I especially like your tenants on the ground floor. Real classy bunch."

"The Blitzers?" He let out a laugh. "They are quite unique, aren't they?"

"Did you know they call you Moses?"

Virgil chuckled. "I keep trying to get them to stop that. Some of them are coming around, though. One or two might even come around."

"Come around? You mean you're trying to evangelize them?"

"Why not? Their souls are no less precious than yours or mine, are they?"

True enough, but he wondered if Virgil had intended that as a slight. Spreading the Word of God had always been one of Virgil's strong points, yet one of his weakest. Virgil had the courage to preach the gospel to anyone, even those Blitzers. As a Christian, Macey knew he should have the same courage. No not courage, wrong word . . . . Compassion. Virgil had once called him *Jonah* because of his lack of evangelistic zeal. Had he just displayed the same trait again—running away from God's command to preach to the "wicked"?

"Macey?"

"What?" He glanced up.

"You all right? Looked like you were about to fall off the crane."

"I'm fine." Why was he thinking about that Jonah stuff right now? Already he could feel his confidence slipping. Virgil knew him too well, that was the problem. Knew exactly where his weaknesses lay. He had him on his back foot already.

"We need to talk," Macey said finally.

"I was fearing this." Virgil hung his head. "You haven't come here to join me, have you?"

"Let's talk about why you're doing this."

"No," he said, taking a step forward on the beam, "let's talk about why you're not. You still in love with that girl? Still want to put her before—"

"Shut up." The bluntness of his reply surprised even himself. But Macey was more sure of himself now, and Sheila had endured—and was still enduring—enough without Virgil taking potshots at her. "You don't want to know what's going on with Sheila right now. But this isn't about her, understand? You leave her out of this."

"Interesting, the way your anger seethes at the mention of her. Why do you think that is?"

He could be so bloody self-righteous at times. "Let's concentrate on what this is really about, Virgil. Man breaking God's Law and you wanting to exact vengeance. Isn't that right?"

"What?" Virgil's voice rang with genuine indignation. He had gotten his attention with that one. "Vengeance? You think I'm acting out of vengeance? This is about setting things in proper order again. Have you forgotten that all life must die? Didn't you agree we've both lived far too long?"

"We're past that argument. This isn't about life and death. This is about you making people's choices for them."

A strong gust blew, swaying the crane boom beneath their feet.

"I think it's more about you making the choice to save this woman over serving God," Virgil said.

"I warned you to leave her out of this. I'm not going to say it again."

"Is your heart still deceiving you? Are you truly—"

"I've made my peace with God, Virgil. I've repented and regained my faith. You can't use that against me anymore. I can see clearly now. It was wrong of you to manipulate me with guilt, 'brother.' Will stopping you save Sheila? Sure it will. But even if it didn't, even if I'd never met Sheila, I'd stop you anyway. Because what you're doing is wrong. Dead wrong."

"You've truly regained your faith, Macey?" He lifted his chin. "Honestly?"

Did he not believe him? "Yes, I did. All right?"

A smile carved its way onto Virgil's lips and he threw back his head, released a howl of laughter slapping his hands together. "Praise be to God, Macey! My prayers are answered. Today I have regained my brother."

Macey hadn't been expecting a reaction like that. "Look, I'm touched you're so thrilled about my repentance, Virgil, but now isn't the time to be celebrating. We got major outstanding issues to work through here."

"Then speak, man, speak!"

What a turnabout. He hadn't anticipated his regaining the hope of his salvation would bring on a change like this. Perhaps now Virgil would listen to him more openly. Perhaps he'd donned his combat frame for nothing. At least he hoped so. But they weren't exactly on the same page yet, either.

"Virgil, I agree that the Miracle Treatment should not exist." The gusty wind stilled a moment, and he lowered his tone. "The same way I agree the Freedom from Deity Act should not exist. But by man's will they both do exist, and it's not our place to reverse what man has already decided."

"The Deity Act?" Virgil spoke the name like a curse word. "Are you really going way back there, Mace?"

"You can't deny it. This is Jasper all over again."

"What are you talking about, man?"

"You want to undo the Miracle Treatment, just like the people of Jasper wanted to undo the Deity Act. But they proved you can't fight against something like this. You can't undo what's already done. Mankind has made a choice and departed from God's path—but we've been doing that since Genesis."

Virgil flipped both hands in the air with disgust. He took a step back and leaned against the crane cab, folding his arms. "And we're supposed to just stand by and let it happen? Let mankind slip into the bowels of ungodliness while we sit on our moral high horses and shrug our shoulders? Are they not precious souls, Macey? Are they not worth us making the effort to save them?"

"Oh, no, you don't. This isn't about me not having compassion, okay? Don't pull that Jonah stuff on me again."

"Jonah stuff? What are you—"

"You think I didn't catch that earlier? What you said about saving the Blitzers' souls?" He couldn't believe he was denying it now. "You're some piece of work, man. If anyone needs to come down from their moral high horse, it's *you*."

Virgil grew quiet. Maybe his words had been harsh, but he spoke the truth. Someone had to pull Virgil back down from his high-and-mighty throne.

"I honestly meant nothing by what I said," Virgil said after a while. "But if you insist on bringing it up . . ."

"I don't."

"But why don't you want me to bring it up, Macey? Because it's the truth? A guilty conscience speaks volumes. Why wouldn't you want to help lead people to the truth by destroying this lie? This Miracle Treatment, this false hope of eternal life. When eternity truly falls, what do you think will happen to them?"

Virgil stepped away from the cab, hands in overcoat pockets, shaking his head. "But you don't really care about them, do you, Mace? You'd rather see them all find their eventual place in hell than to make an effort to reach out to them, wake them from their slumber. Like those Blitzers down there. Jonah indeed, my friend. Jonah indeed."

"That's not true." His gloved hands curled into fists. He hated how wrong and right Virgil could be at the same time. "You're putting words in my mouth. I may lack compassion, I admit that. But we're not talking about me: we're talking about principles. God gave us free will. The ability to love Him or not. If the world chooses not to love Him, then we can't grumble like spoiled brats about it. And we can't try to force people to love Him. Not even God himself does that.

"Despite what the rest of the world does, our duty is to remain faithful as an example to others. Don't you think God could make everyone obey Him? So why doesn't He? I'll tell you why: because God doesn't want forced obedience. God wants love, and love involves choice. Every human being needs to choose *for himself*."

Virgil scoffed. "These people can't be trusted to make their own decisions!" He swept his hand across the ruined city. "Look at the decisions they've made already. The Freedom from Deity

Act? They spit in God's face with that, and you expect them to be able to make a righteous decision now? We need to lead them. Show them the right path. Decide for them, if we have to. It's our responsibility."

"No, it's not," Macey said. "We're not God. We've been given no such responsibility from Him. We have no right to decide what people should or shouldn't do."

"You're right, we're not God, neither one of us is. But look at us!" Virgil spun about and took hold of one of the steel trusses making up the crane mast. He pulled, and a three-foot section of the steel broke free like a dry branch. He tossed it through the air, the beam sailing well over a city block before landing on a rooftop far below. "Can we really consider ourselves mere humans?"

Mere humans?

"Look at us." Virgil spread his arms wide. "Look at where we're standing right now. Look at how we got up here. Look at how old we are. How wise we are. How moral we are. Are we not so much more than these sinful humans who exist today?"

A shudder ran through him. He knew Virgil had strong convictions, but could he be delusional as well? Was he suffering from some kind of dementia?

"Virgil . . . we're human, okay?" He spoke slowly and deliberately, making certain his words sank in. "Ain't nothing special about us. Nothing. We're just two geriatrics in a couple of really souped-up wheelchairs. That's it!"

Virgil threw his head back, squawking with glee. His laughter felt so genuine, so strong, it was almost enough to make Macey join in. If not for his fear that it might be a maniacal laugh of insanity.

Virgil bent over at the waist, rested his hands on his knees until the laughter subsided. "You know, Mace, you always did have a way with words. But come on, think. God made man just a little lower than the angels, didn't He? And us, you and I, we are certainly a little higher than man. What do you suppose that makes us?"

He resisted an urge to sputter. "So you think we're angels now? You're crazy."

"Give me more credit than that, man." He waved his hand as if shooing away a fly. "I know what we really are. But haven't you wondered about God's purpose in it? Why we turned out like this? Haven't you ever considered that God put us in this situation, preserved our lives this long, so we could bring guidance to this dark generation? A generation darker than any we've ever seen.

"These bodies give us tremendous responsibility. We can't sit back and observe the world like we used to when we were a part of it. We died back in Jasper, Macey. Our lives were forever changed. We became something more than human, for God's purpose. So if you want to get right down to it, then, yes, I suppose I do consider us angels. God's messengers—is that not what the word 'angel' means? Is that not our mission: to spread the message of God?"

Okay, so maybe Virgil wasn't insane, at least not totally, but he was still wrong. "Our responsibility is to encourage people. Not force them."

"And what greater encouragement is there than death?" He slammed his fist into the crane booth behind him, shattering glass and steel with a massive *smash.* "It's a catalyst. A clock on the wall. A reminder that one day you're going to have to wake up and make a choice. Didn't that same logic encourage you to regain your faith? Aren't you a testament to the saving power of death yourself?"

Macey looked down at the wobbling crane boom beneath his feet before looking up again. "Yeah, I am. And yes, the fear of death did wake me up. But that's only because I already believed, once. It encouraged me to *remember* my faith, return to God. But someone who's never believed, what do you think this will do for them?

"Take Steven Grant, for instance. How long did it take for him to find God after he'd had the Miracle Treatment? Twenty years? Without the Treatment he could well have died long before then, and then where would his soul be? Isn't that proof that this Miracle Treatment could all be part of God's plan?"

Until now he hadn't considered the idea himself. "I mean, how many things has God allowed that man first took for evil but that He meant for good? Couldn't this be one of them? If anything, the Treatment has saved at least two souls who were destined for hell without it. How is that not God's will? And how many more could it save? Maybe by giving people more time on Earth, it will give them a chance to reconsider, exercise their choice, to understand what life's really about. Maybe it's like . . . grace."

Silence fell over them. Virgil's rigid posture was proof he had struck a chord. He had struck a chord within himself, for that matter. Could this Miracle Treatment truly be a miracle? A gift of grace to the people who would choose to use it? The powerful and wealthy, the vain and arrogant. People who would probably never even consider God, unless they lived long enough to realize there had to be something more to life than fun and games? The same way Steven Grant did? The same way Greta Darling did?

Emotions swelled through him rapidly, mightier than the renewed gusts of wind so great he feared he might fall. Was

God so powerful, so prescient, so farseeing as to use something that at first glance would draw people further away from Him, but in truth would end up drawing more people to Him?

"No," Virgil said suddenly.

"What?"

"I can't be wrong about this. I won't let you dissuade me, Macey. I know my purpose has to be true. This lie can't be allowed to exist." He reached into his overcoat and withdrew a glass container. "It has to end now." He raised the jar over his head, as if to smash it.

"Wait. You don't understand. Virgil, no!"

He felt powerless to stop him. Virgil had acted too suddenly and was too far away, but he had to do something. His mind reeled as Virgil's arm began to descend.

He initiated a cynetic burst.

Adrenaline-charged lightning surged through his body and his mind raced at inhuman speed. Milliseconds become seconds. The world slowed.

The frame fused directly to his nervous system with no limiting controls, accelerating his neural transmissions a thousandfold. His brain could fry from it, but there remained no other way. The cynetic burst would last only a second, but it would give him a chance to react before Virgil did.

In the distance he saw Virgil, perched atop the boom, his overcoat swaying behind him, his arm lowering gradually as if in slow motion. He was in mid-throw, about to wing the vial down to the roof below.

Arching his back, Macey fired all his snap thrusters at once, producing an explosion that rivaled a cannon blast. His world blurred as he zoomed toward Virgil like a bullet, covering the hundred-foot boom span in a blink of an eye.

Virgil's arm had barely moved by the time he reached him. He grabbed the canister, twisted his body to pull it out of his hand, and directed his shoulder into Virgil's chest as they collided.

The cynetic burst ran out. The world returned to normal speed in a flash of commotion, sound, and pain.

Macey plowed into Virgil like a missile, sending both of them careening into and through the steel mast of the tower crane as easily as if it were made of tin foil. His world spun. They went over the edge.

He barely heard Virgil's scream above the grinding of metal as they tumbled end over end. Ground and sky spun by in rapid glimpses: ground then sky, ground then sky.

Macey tried to fire his snaps, but they didn't respond. He had lost all control. The overload from the burst must've frozen his body. Had he fried himself?

The concrete rushed toward them. They were still above the roof of the building, but they wouldn't be for long. Their combined momentum would carry them beyond it.

His only thought was of the fragile glass canister clenched in his hand: prayed he wouldn't crush it when he landed.

With a spasm he regained control. He could move, though barely.

He and Virgil continued falling. He could see straight down to the ground now, some six hundred feet below. Even with their bodies, it wasn't guaranteed they could survive such a fall. They had to maneuver to the safety of the rooftop before they plummeted past it.

In the air next to him, Virgil looked unconscious, his limbs flailing.

Macey reached out, grabbed him by the arm, and angled back toward the roof, firing the snaps full bore.

The roof neared, but they weren't over it yet. He fired again. Another thirty feet to go. With a sudden roll, he fired one last time, tossing Virgil toward an open spot on the roof and cradling the canister against his chest.

He crashed into the roof on his back. His head slammed into the concrete, and he lost consciousness.

He came to, and found he was still sliding with the momentum. Virgil bounced across the concrete rooftop next to him.

Macey skidded to a stop just before hitting the rusted shipping container.

He heard a low groan from Virgil. He had to get up first. Struggling to his feet, he praised God that the canister remained intact within his hands.

He spotted Virgil twenty feet away. He was crouched on all fours, slowly rising. How would he react? Would he try to take the canister back? Attack him? No sense taking chances. He had to protect this thing, no matter what. Whipping off his overcoat, Macey wrapped the precious vial within, his eyes scanning the roof for a place to secure it.

"Give me that canister." Virgil's voice sounded like gravel. His mirrored shades were gone. For the first time, Macey saw his eyes. Two obsidian spheres stared back at him, devoid of all emotion, save anger and hate.

He heard a popping sound: Virgil activating his snaps. Macey barely had the chance to raise his arm in defense as Virgil barreled into him. His overcoat went flying from his grasp. The canister with the negating agent remained wrapped within it.

His back thudded into the rooftop as Virgil slammed on top of him, his arm drawn back to strike. Macey jerked his head to the side just as Virgil's fist drove into the concrete beside him, exploding in a shower of debris.

"Stop!" He pushed his knee upward into Virgil's chest, grabbed his arms, and threw him over his head. He used his snaps to propel himself from the floor in a single swift motion, spinning.

He came about just in time to see Virgil performing the same maneuver, pulling out of the throw and landing on his feet. They squared off, battle-ready.

Their eyes traveled to his fallen overcoat.

Virgil dove for it.

Macey lunged forward with a low kick augmented by his snaps.

He connected just under the ribs. He drove his foot upward, spinning Virgil like a top. Surging forward, he snatched up the overcoat just as Virgil powered back with a punch.

He ducked, clutching the overcoat to his chest. Virgil's fist blew by with a crackle of plasma.

"Stop! Listen."

"Listen to what?" A series of swift roundhouse kicks cut the air. "Death is supposed to exist, Macey. The Miracle Treatment has to be destroyed."

Virgil somersaulted and charged downward with a powerful hatchet kick. Macey dove out of the way, and Virgil's heel hit the rooftop in a spray of plasma. The concrete sundered with a bang. His foot traveled straight through, sparks flying as the reinforcement rod sliced like butter. The surface shook, cracks radiating outward in a spider web.

Then Virgil's foot struck a piece of support steel. With a metallic ring, the concrete roof gave way beneath them.

They fell through to the floor below, the twelve-foot drop ending in a jarring collision of concrete and twisted steel.

Macey landed on his back on top of the piece of roof that used to be under his feet. Dust plumed, giving form to the sunlight beaming through the wide hole above them.

Had that kick connected, Virgil would have killed him. They were playing for keeps now.

Movement across from him in the rubble. Through the dust, a pair of black eyes flashed open.

He had to get out of here.

Springing from his prone position with the snaps, he leaped up toward the roof, performing a back flip to give himself more distance. As his head came around he saw Virgil zooming upward out of the hole.

He had no time to react. Virgil pegged him with a downward punch to the shoulder that sent him slamming back into the roof, creating a small crater of his own.

He shook off the attack and performed a scissor kick, the momentum spinning him up and onto his feet.

No sooner had he steadied himself than Virgil flew on top of him, charging at him with a flurry of snaps-powered punches and kicks. "Macey, give me that canister!"

It was all he could do to jump backward and stay clear of Virgil's blinding feet and fists, his snaps popping like a machine gun firing. Fast, too fast. Had he just performed a cynetic burs—

Virgil's foot struck him in the head and spun him around. More blows rained down on him until Virgil caught him with a sidekick that sent him sailing toward the shipping container, slamming into it. Dinner plate-sized sheets of rust showered on him as he scrambled upright, trying to get a fix on Virgil.

He was still in the same spot, some ten yards away, his hollow black eyes wide and furious. "I said, give it to me." He rushed forward, hitting his snaps again.

Macey gripped the overcoat and hit his own snaps, darting to the side. Virgil plowed into the container, shattering more rust and debris.

Macey took the opportunity to gain some distance. He couldn't fight properly while trying to protect this canister. "Listen to what I'm saying, Virgil. The Miracle Treatment can save souls. You saved two yourself, don't you remember?"

Virgil emerged from the container, wielding a six-foot piece of rusted angle iron like a sword. Macey thought he was about to say something, but with a yell Virgil leapt forward with a horizontal strike.

Macey ducked under the swing, but the second stroke caught him on the side. A third landed in his stomach, dangerously close to the canister. He fell to the ground, cradling the canister in a fetal position. The blows kept coming as Virgil let loose on him, howling.

"What are you doing? Stop!"

"Shut up!" He sounded on the brink of tears. "I've got to destroy that thing. I'll go through you if I have to. Get out of my way."

Metal clanged as the angle iron fell to the rooftop, twisted into an 'L' from Virgil's forceful blows. He grabbed hold of the rusted gang-box, his fingers digging into its metal sides as he lifted it over his head.

Had Virgil lost it? Was he really going to kill him over this?

"Don't do this," Macey shouted at him, crouched to his knees. This couldn't be happening. They had gone through too much together to be fighting each other like this. He had to stop it. He wouldn't fight back; he couldn't anyway. Somehow he had to try and break through to him. "With the Miracle Treatment we're giving people a chance to repent." Virgil closed upon him. "A chance they might not have without it. Don't you want them to have another chance? Aren't you the one being Jonah now?"

Virgil stopped. He stared down with obsidian eyes bleeding tears. Nostrils flaring, the gang-box hovering dangerously over his head.

"Think, Virgil. Right now, is it still conviction that's driving you? Don't you think these people are worthy of God's grace?"

Virgil released a cry and Macey braced himself as the rusty box flew down on top of him. A breeze cut past Macey's ear but nothing struck him. He glanced up to see Virgil still gripping the gang-box. He spun it three times as if performing a hammer throw, then let the box slip from his grasp with a grunt, hurling it off the roof.

Silence fell between them as the gang-box soared two hundred feet before dropping out of sight. He had the ridiculous urge to see where it would land. He sure hoped it wouldn't kill anybody when it did. Or hit his car.

Virgil collapsed onto his haunches, the expression on his face unreadable, especially with those hollow black eyes.

Macey thanked God that Virgil had stopped attacking him, but had he really gotten through to him? "Virgil?"

Slowly he faced him. "What?"

"You tell me, man. You're the one who threw the box."

"Do I have to spell it out for you, Macey?" Virgil rose to his feet. "You win, all right? Keep your stupid vial."

He stood. Slowly, as if with an aching back. As he started to walk away, for the first time since their reunion Macey could recognize his old friend. Virgil was a proud man and he never liked to be wrong. No one did, but for Virgil it seemed especially difficult, probably because it didn't happen too often. But when it did, his temper could flare something awful trying to convince himself and everyone else that he was right.

Finally, Macey understood what was going on inside Virgil's head. He wasn't really trying to kill him. He was just ticked off, probably more at himself than anything else. He had tried to break that canister just to take his frustration out on the closest target. And when he didn't succeed with the canister, he went for the next closest target—him.

He glanced at the newly formed hole in the roof and thanked God he had survived it. Two grown men fighting was bad enough. But two cyborgs going at it in combat frames was bordering on insanity. It was a wonder the building still stood.

"So what happens now?" Virgil's back remained turned.

"What do you mean?" But he knew exactly what he meant. He just wasn't prepared to deal with it yet.

"You'll take me in now, won't you?" He swiveled to look over his shoulder. "That's what you came to do, right? Hand me over to CDI?"

He didn't answer, but the way he dropped his head to avoid Virgil's stare probably sent the same message. Yes, he had come to bring him in. Not to CDI, though. But why did admitting it feel like the most shameful thing in the world?

He wasn't sure what to say. Minutes went by, neither of them moving, talking. Macey burned with humiliation, remembering.

Wars, mostly. Battles in deserts and jungles. Horror and pain. How many times had he and Virgil suffered through it all together? How many times had Virgil saved his life? Too many times.

Was he prepared to sentence to death a man who had saved his life? Not just his life, but his very soul?

And yet, how had Bradley put it? "It's either him or Sheila, so take your pick." Some choice.

Virgil's massive shoulders shook as he suddenly sobbed, his cries echoing to the heavens. Macey froze. He hadn't expected Virgil to have a breakdown. But it was comforting in a way. He was glad to see him finally let down his mask of arrogance and superiority, glad to see him reveal the human being trapped inside that prosthetic shell of his.

"Virgil?"

He didn't respond right away. The wind whistled across the rooftop, conjuring up dust devils from the mass of concrete debris surrounding them.

Finally, Virgil gazed upward toward the scorching light of the mid-afternoon sun. "Earlier I prayed to God for His guidance. I prayed for both of us, but especially for you." He smiled sadly. "I never considered that His guidance would come from you. I thought you were the one needing correction, not me."

Macey couldn't think of anything to say. Maybe he didn't need to. Against all odds, he had convinced Virgil it would be wrong to release the negating agent and destroy the Miracle Treatment. But as Virgil had put it, what now? Was he supposed to deliver him to Bradley in the hope that he'd live up to his side of the bargain?

Carefully, he slipped his overcoat on and secured the vial in a pocket. He stepped toward Virgil tentatively, close enough to rest a hand on his shoulder.

To his surprise, Virgil slapped a hand on top of his, clutching it. "I'm sorry, Macey. I'm sorry about everything. About Jasper, about Sophia, about leaving." His black eyes glistened with tears, transformed from pits of darkness into wells of sorrow and despair. "I've been such a fool about everything. All those years I turned my back on you. On my own family. On everybody. I've been the loser all along. And now this Miracle Treatment. Look at what it took to stop me believing I was right. I nearly killed you."

"Yeah, but you didn't. And for the record, I knew you weren't really trying to kill me. Afterwards, anyway." He added the last bit to lighten the mood, but it didn't seem to do much for either of them.

Virgil kicked some concrete chunks into the hole he had made. "Don't let me off lightly. I could make perfect sense of what you said about the treatment, but I still wanted to smash that canister anyway. Didn't want to believe I could be so wrong about this whole thing. Like you said, I should have stuck to how I did it with Steven and Greta. Let them come to the decision, let them choose."

He rubbed his temples and released a sigh. "But I got this crazy idea to rid the whole world of the Miracle Treatment, all at once. Then I spent close to a year deceiving myself into believing it was the best thing to do. Now look at the damage I've caused. If not for me, Gordon Pool would still be alive today, giving me more chances at saving his soul. Not to mention all the trouble I've caused for Gentec. And your lady friend. Sheila, was it?"

The mention of her name caused Macey's mood to sour. He still had a decision to make. Virgil or Sheila, who would he save? Would it be right for him to force Virgil to pay for his crimes, handing him over to Bradley so Sheila could be released? No guarantee of that. Bradley could end up killing all of them.

In the end, how much culpability did Virgil bear for all this? He hadn't created the negating agent—Dr. Julian Hague had. Virgil's only real crime was attempting to use it on a massive scale, and he had already repented of that. Boreman and Bradley had escalated everything, making Sheila a target. If they hadn't done that, then this ordeal could have been over at this very moment, with Virgil's surrender.

"Do whatever you have to do to make this right," Virgil said. "I don't care if they lock me up, or worse. I deserve whatever's coming to me."

This truly was the real Virgil, his old friend, talking now. He felt ridiculous for ever doubting his ability to come around.

"You got nothing coming to you." Macey grabbed him by the arm, pulled him to his feet. "You understand?"

The blankness on his face said he didn't.

"I'm not going to turn you in. You've got no major crime to pay for anyway."

"You can't be doing this, man. You'd be risking too much trying to help me now. I've messed up too big to be—"

"Too big for what?" He eyed him sternly, then lightened his expression with a grin. "Too big for God's forgiveness? For mine? What kind of guy do you think I am to not forgive my own brother?"

"Mace, I don't deserve this."

"None of us do. That's why it's called grace, remember?" He jabbed him in the shoulder. "Now stop playing such a martyr and accept it."

The ebony eyes curved into half-moon smiles as Virgil began to laugh. Then he grabbed him by his overcoat and pulled him into an embrace. "Thank you, Macey. I mean it, man. You've been more of a brother to me in the last five minutes than I've been to you the last fifty years. I love you."

"I love you too, brother." He glanced over his shoulder at the rusted container, now sporting a Virgil-made hole to match the roof. "Man, I'm glad no one's up here to see us right now."

Virgil laughed, slapped him hard on the back. Laughing with him, Macey felt he could almost cry. He had forgotten what it felt like to embrace family. And right now, Virgil was about the closest family he had. He thanked God for healing their relationship. It was the best outcome he could have possibly imagined, yet the one he thought least likely to happen. Once again, he had underestimated God's power to work in incredible ways.

"All right, all right." He eased himself from the giant's crushing embrace. "You still trying to kill me, or what?"

"Man, I've missed you, Mace."

"Same here."

"Fifty years. We got a lot of catching up to do."

"Too much." He dropped into a crouch, overlooking the edge of the building. The wind gusted against his face, as refreshing as the view. The uncertainty and dread he had felt earlier today when he had crawled back to his apartment had now long dissolved. The path that lay before him was clear. There'd be no deal with Bradley—not the kind he expected anyway. His brother was now here to aid him. And the possibilities seemed endless.

"You know, if you really feel bad about beating me up just now, there *is* something you can do to make it up to me."

"I owe you for a whole lot more than that. Anything you need from me, you name it."

Macey sighed, realizing how ridiculous his next words would sound. "Would you help me save my girlfriend?"

The look on his face was priceless. "Your girlfriend? Are you serious, man?"

He nodded with a wide grin, causing Virgil to burst out laughing.

Exactly the reaction he had hoped for. He used to pride himself on being able to make Virgil crack up over just about anything. Thank goodness he still had that gift. Revealing the seriousness of Sheila's situation could wait. For now, he enjoyed the simple pleasure of being able to make his brother laugh again.

"Oh, man, this is rich!" Virgil wiped a tear from his eye. "I can't believe you, Mace. A young girl like that at your age? You must be taking that stuff . . . remember what it was called? Um . . ."

"Viagra?"

"Yeah that's it. Viagra!"

By the time they stopped laughing, they both had tears in their eyes. Two geriatrics in souped-up wheelchairs indeed.

Boreman and Bradley wouldn't know what hit them.

CHAPTER FOURTEEN

SHEILA GROANED IN RELIEF as the truck finally came to a halt. She sat in the cargo hold with one of Bradley's men, hands bound behind her back. Her shoulders strained as she leaned forward on the hard metal benches lining the truck's sides. She wasn't certain how far they had traveled, but while on the road a cool breeze had blown through the overhead canvas top at least. Now that they had stopped, she was baking in the stagnant air.

The lab coat they had given her was already dripping with perspiration. She'd love to remove it—if her hands were free—but she could hardly do so, seeing as she was almost nude underneath. More than a little degrading in the presence of a male guard.

With all that black military gear, he looked to be sweating even more than she was. He was the same guy who had cracked that joke about her too. Thankfully, he hadn't said anything else to her—or tried to touch her. Apparently only Bradley had the gall, or the permission, to beat her up.

The thought of that jerk caused her to tense, then wince. Her ribs still ached from where he had punched her. Her face felt even worse.

Sadly, this wasn't the first time she'd been hit by a man. Of course she'd been a lot younger then, just a kid really, and the "man" had been one of her mother's boyfriends. That wimp had proved nothing compared to the sadist Bradley had turned out to be.

But . . . it was only pain. *Shrug it off, Sheila. You're a big girl now.*

She'd find a way to settle the score with Bradley. None of these jerks would get away with this. She'd make sure Macey would see to that. He'd make them pay with their very lives, if necessary.

Macey. She had dragged him into such a mess. And still he had come through for her. He had even agreed to give up Virgil for her. And then the guilt came back. She'd had no idea Bradley would demand that Macey turn Virgil in. What if he wasn't exactly willing to sacrifice his friend? What if he was doing it because of her?

She hoped not. But his decision was comforting in a selfish sort of way. It helped, knowing he was out there thinking about her, fighting for her, sacrificing for her. Now there could be no question of his loyalty. Christian or not, Macey had proved himself the same guy she had come to know: strong, caring, chivalrous to the end. Maybe there was some hope for the two of them after all.

What do you mean maybe? There had better well be after all this.

She glanced toward the back of the truck. She couldn't see outside, but the canvas door looked easy enough to push through. Perhaps she could make a run for it. She couldn't hear much noise outside, just the idling of the truck's engine. But wherever they were, there had to be someone close who could help her.

She contemplated the risk. Bradley and his goons still needed her to complete the deal with Macey, so what could they do to her? Beat her some more? Big deal, she could take that. She had to take the chance, especially if Macey was helping her for the wrong reasons. She wanted him to choose her because he wanted to, not because she had forced him.

She shifted her glance back to the guard. He looked so bothered by the heat that she could probably dash out the back before he even noticed. But that wouldn't work in reality. She needed to distract him somehow. She scanned the interior of the truck—and spied a plastic bucket that she figured had to be for her use. She wasn't sure exactly how she'd pull this off, but the bucket gave her a good place to start.

"Hey, what's your name?"

The guard barely looked at her. "What?"

"Name? You do have one, don't you?"

"Steve," he said and then looked away from her. "Now shut up."

"Look, Steve, I really need to use the bathroom."

"Is that right . . . ?"

"Well, I do have to go *sometime*. You going to help me out or what?" And she jutted her chin toward her hands tied behind her back. "I can't exactly take care of business like this, ya know?"

He huffed. "Just do it right there."

He had to be kidding. "In my seat?"

"Yeah, why not?"

What a charmer. "Oh, well. You're the one who will have to smell it."

He sucked his teeth and then peeled himself off the bench, reached toward the back of the truck to grab the bucket.

As he stepped back toward her, her pulse quickened, her heartbeat thundering in her ears as her moment of opportunity approached. He placed the bucket at her feet. The instant his eyes left hers she made her move.

Sheila pushed hard off the bench, throwing her body into him. Her forehead hit what she hoped was his nose, and a yelp escaped his lips.

The force of her blow knocked her back onto the bench and flung him into his seat as well. Her head throbbed as if a hammer had hit it. But one glance at Steve made the pain drain away. His hands covered his face, viscous blood dripped down his chin.

"Ow!" he managed to gurgle. "You stuffid—"

She jumped up and plowed her foot straight between his legs. With another yelp he collapsed into a fetal position. The kick felt so satisfying that she couldn't resist helping herself to another, and for good measure she heaved a nice wad of spit into his face. "Who's the stupid one now, Steve?"

She only wished it could have been Bradley, but maybe she'd get her chance with him soon enough. The thought of that sicko returned her attention to the exit. Had anyone heard Steve's yell? She hoped not. Luckily, it looked like her last kick had knocked the wind out of him. He rocked back and forth on the bench uttering a high-pitched whimper. She had to make her move now.

She dashed for the back of the truck and pushed her head between the heavy canvas flaps, into the somewhat cooler air outside.

A white blare of sunlight hit her—both from above and below. It took a moment for her eyes to adjust. Sand. Tons of it. They were in the desert, the sky a crystal blue, the sun searing. She spied a couple more trucks parked nearby, six or eight men clustered around them.

A hoarse yell rang out from behind her. Good ol' Steve had regained his breath and was alerting the others. She hadn't moved fast enough. The men turned toward Steve's truck and could no doubt see her head poking out the back. Aw shoot, it was now or never.

She leapt from the truck, trying not to land headfirst into the sand. She thudded onto the scorching sand and gravel that formed the dirt road. She broke her fall by dropping to one knee, then hauled herself up with a grunt and took off in a sprint.

Shouts rang out behind her as she ran. Her leg muscles burned. Now she wished she were in better shape. Her bruised ribs didn't help either.

She came to the base of a small rise. A couple of steps up it and she gained a better view. What she saw made her feel like stopping. The desert surrounded as far as she could see. A few shrubs and cacti were the only splashes of color against the orange-red of baked clay and gritty sand.

Where were they? And why had they brought her out here?

The ground trembled beneath her as heavy footfalls pounded from behind. It was useless to keep running when she had nowhere to run. But she ran anyway. What else could she do?

She ignored the bite of the rocks into her soles as she plowed up the hill and crested the rise. She hoped against hope to see a highway full of traffic beyond.

There was no highway. No traffic. But what she did see surpassed anything her imagination could conjure up.

Fifty feet below her in a gully stood Bradley and a couple of other men she did not recognize. They stood in front of something that looked like a giant mechanical ant. It was the size of a bus with six insect-like legs protruding from its metal body. Where the head would be was a snout-like gun, reminding her of those awful cannons Bradley's men had fired at her and Macey at the parking garage. What was this thing?

Bradley looked up at her and made to run for her. But before he'd taken a step, her pursuers tackled her from behind.

Her face hit the stinging sand. It flew into her mouth. They fell on top of her, someone's sharp knee in her shoulder blades.

"Who was watching her?" Bradley's voice, sharp and irritated, preceded him up the hill until he finally appeared and came to stand over her.

She braced for what would come next. A kick perhaps, maybe another choke-hold.

Instead he continued his rant. "I said, who was—"

"Me, sir," Steve's voice called from afar. He sounded like a stuffed-up elephant. Hopefully she'd broken his nose. That alone would be worth a kick in the side.

"Get her up," Bradley said.

Instantly, two pairs of arms hauled her off the desert floor. She came eye to eye with Bradley. He had changed into the same black military gear his guards was wearing, and was sweating even more than Steve was.

Bradley scowled, but the look wasn't aimed at her. It was directed at Steve, lumbering up the hill. "What happened?"

She almost wanted to laugh as he tried to explain.

"Man, she . . . that stupid—"

A pop-like crack caused her heart to leap and left her ears ringing. A red pinpoint appeared on Steve's forehead. A cloud of scarlet mist exploded from the back of his skull.

She screamed without hearing it. She hadn't even seen Bradley pull out his gun, though now she could it smoking in his raised hand.

Steve fell forward, dark blood seeping from the gaping wound in the back of his head. It stained the sand tar-black.

She shook as Bradley faced her. His stare was no longer leering and obnoxious, but cold, stern, businesslike. Earlier, she had questioned whether Bradley had the nerve to actually kill her or not. Now she knew the answer.

Judging by their expressions, his own men shared her shock.

"I'm not paying you clowns top dollar to act like a bunch of hired dopers, understand?" He holstered his weapon. "If you can't guard an unarmed, restrained woman, then you're a liability. A liability I can't afford to have on my team. Any of you screw up this badly, expect the same result."

His eyes swept over her, devoid of any expression save disgust. "I hope you're happy with yourself, Sheila. Your little stunt has cost a man his life. Keep it up and you might rack up a few more before sundown." He wheeled on his men. "Get her out of my sight."

They hauled her off as if their lives depended on it.

What had she been thinking? She felt like crying, but no tears would come. She almost wished Bradley had just punched or kicked her like before. But he seemed different now, like he wouldn't waste his time doing something so trivial now. Things had gone to the next level.

What if he had been holding himself back in the warehouse? All of it a show for that sick Boreman, something to get his rocks off as he experienced it through Bradley's neural net. What if this was the real Bradley Thomas? A corporate killer who could murder his own men in the blink of an eye? This Bradley wasn't the same brown-nosing twerp she had come to know from Gentec. He was a psychopath. What chance did she stand against that?

She couldn't get the images of Steve out of her mind, his body hitting the ground, blood leaking from his head. She might have felt justified in wishing them all dead, out of spite, but the reality of watching the murder of another human being, no matter who they were or what they had done, was anything but satisfying, much less enjoyable.

This wasn't some kick in the groin.

"I'm sorry," she said, unsure who she was apologizing to. To Steve? To the guards carrying her? To Macey?

"Keep it to yourself," one of the men said. "Nobody else is going to die for you, understand?"

She hoped he was right.

But what about that contraption down there? Had they come here to buy it or something? To test it out? Was this some kind of firing range?

She had a feeling it wasn't anything like that. If they'd brought her here and this thing was here and they were all expecting Macey . . . .

How many more people were going to die because of her?

She couldn't stop this. This wasn't a battle she could win, something she could push her way out of. No matter how headstrong she was, she wouldn't be able to overcome any of this. Not without Macey.

He held her salvation now.

Macey sat opposite Virgil inside the darkened virtual environment. In real life, they were still on the rooftop, sitting on a couple of concrete blocks. Here, they sat on nothing.

In between them a holographic cube displayed mountains of data from the CDI server, painting their faces with its multi-colored glow. Macey accessed the cube at lightning speed, performing something he should have done ages ago—background research on Bradley Thomas. With the urgency of protecting Sheila, he had bypassed the most basic of CDI protocols: before you do anything, do your research.

It was time to start thinking and acting like an agent again. For the past hour they had been hacking through Bradley's personal files, following traces.

"Interesting guy," Virgil said as he scanned through the documents. "Former Navy SEAL. Surveillance expert. Dishonorable discharge, but no details on the case. Probably a black ops fall guy. His bank account received a hefty government deposit afterwards."

"A payoff for his silence." Macey had heard of such things before. "Looks like he used the money to start his own security firm. Has ties to weapons manufacturers too. That'd explain how he keeps coming up with his equipment."

Virgil leaned back, releasing a sigh. "I doubt we can use any of this to anticipate his actions."

"Why do you say that?"

"From the looks of it, this guy is a professional. Works for a living. He's acquiescing to the wishes of his employer rather than following his own agenda, don't you think?"

"That's true." Macey accessed the cube again, pulling more files. "Boreman could be the one calling the shots, though I doubt he'd allow Boreman to make a mis-maneuver. If I were in Bradley's position I'd probably get Boreman to make a clean slate of this whole thing. Get the negating agent, then start tying off loose ends. Eliminate me, you, and Sheila and be done with it. The way they got rid of Dr. Jules Hague. Boreman though . . . . I don't know, he might be pushing for this deal to actually happen. Bradley did mention that it was his 'employer' offering the deal, not him."

"Do you think he might anticipate us teaming up in a double-cross?"

"Not sure. I didn't let on that we were close friends, but he seems sharp enough to prepare for every possibility."

"So let's take that as a worst-case scenario and create our strategy from there."

"Sounds like a plan." Macey rocked his jaw from side to side. "Something's still nagging at me though."

"What's that?"

"Why would Boreman hire a guy like Bradley in the first place?"

Virgil shrugged. "To deal with the situation, I suppose?"

"No, he was hired long before all this Miracle Treatment sabotage stuff kicked off." He checked the records. "Almost a year before. I'm wondering if he doesn't have more to do with this whole thing."

"In what way?"

"Like maybe he helped put it all together."

Holographic numbers scrolled across Virgil's face as he thought about it. "Didn't you say that doctor guy, Hague, started all this?"

"Well, he created the negating agent . . . ." Something still wasn't making sense to him. "Virgil, how did you find out about this negating agent in the first place? How'd you get linked up with Pooly and all that?"

Virgil rubbed his forehead. "That's going back a while now, Mace. I think it was through a guy named Kestler, a broker who works out of this nightclub called Miracles."

"Yeah, I know him." He cracked a grin. "In a roundabout way he helped me track you down."

Virgil chuckled. "Sounds like him. He's quite the informant. Anyway, he said he knew someone who had a method of removing the Miracle Treatment. That's when he introduced me to Gordon."

"So you didn't go looking for someone to make this negating agent for you?"

"No, Kestler came to me. I only wanted to help those Club Miracle people forsake the lifestyle they were living, bring them back to God. But I admit, after hearing about the negating agent, it sounded like something that could help me achieve my . . . larger aims, so I pursued it."

"Okay, consider this." Macey severed his connection to the CDI server. The cube disappeared and was replaced by a blue, two-dimensional utility screen, waiting for the next command. "Julian Hague made this negating agent with the intent of destroying Gentec and Sheila, but he didn't strike me as the kind of guy to be running in the same circles as a broker like Pooly."

"Fair enough. But what if Hague went straight to Kestler with it?"

He pondered. "Yeah, I can see him maybe running into the likes of Kestler in that club, especially if he was out there trying to advertise his new product. But if that were the case, why didn't Kestler act as the go-between? Why would Kestler involve Pooly at all?"

"Maybe Kestler found the deal too hot and handed it over to him."

"Possible. Kestler did seem a bit skittish, but this was a pretty sweet deal. I don't think he would hand it off to someone else so easily. It'd make more sense if Pooly was the one who contacted Kestler to try and find someone who had a use for the negating agent. Because, as far as I know, Pooly was Hague's only contact."

"So there you have it, then." Virgil shrugged. "Hague found Pooly, Pooly found Kestler, and Kestler found me. That's not beyond possibility."

"I don't know." It still didn't feel right. "Seems like too much of a coincidence that Julian Hague, a geneticist with no underground ties, would run into a guy like Pooly, a street broker who happens to know Kestler, who happens to know you. And you happen to be a guy who'd be inclined to use this negating agent for some purpose. There seems to be an unseen force pulling these wants and needs together—a missing link between Hague and Pooly."

"There's one way to find out for sure." Virgil rose to his feet, standing in the virtual darkness.

"How's that?"

"Ask Hague or Pooly."

Macey shook his head as Virgil began chuckling. "Very funny, man."

"It wasn't really a joke. I was just pointing out the obvious."

"Which is what?"

"That it doesn't really matter, Mace. So what if Bradley turns out to be your missing link? It doesn't change the present situation. We know all we need to know. We got a worst-case scenario, so let's set up for it."

"Yeah, but if Bradley was involved in setting Hague and Pooly up, then maybe Boreman not only knew what Hague was doing, but aided him. Maybe they were both out to take Gentec down?"

Virgil shook his head grinning. "Great speculating, super-sleuth. You do CDI proud, but you got three problems. One, you have no proof. Two, why would the Gentec CEO want to take down his own golden goose? And three, even if you did have evidence and motive, it in no way changes the fact that this deal you made with Bradley to save Sheila has to go down in a hurry."

Virgil was right. The who and why could wait. Bradley had given him six hours to deliver the negating agent and Virgil into his hands. He checked his chronometer. They had three hours left.

"Time for a little role-playing, Virgil." Macey accessed the utility window, opened up a fresh data file. "If you were

Bradley Thomas and—worst case here—you knew there was a good chance that two combat cyborgs would be double-crossing you in an upcoming hostage deal, what precautions would you take?"

"A tank?"

"It's quite necessary, sir."

Roger Boreman rolled his eyes. He felt the situation slipping even further out of his control. "Look, Bradley, I'm not comfortable with this. I want this whole thing over with and soon. That's it."

"It will be, sir." Bradley's voice bore a hint of irritation as it came through the landline—voice only, piped through his holoterminal. What did he have to be irritated about? It was his foul-ups that had caused this mess. If anything, *he* was the one who should be ticked.

Boreman felt his office closing in on him. His bonsai trees attacked him from both sides. His Japanese rock sculpture was now a pile of burial stones. He would go mad before all this was over.

"I don't think I can approve this, Bradley." Boreman spun his chair away from the holoterminal to face his floor to ceiling window, briefly enjoying the sense of freedom provided by the sixtieth floor view. "I didn't sign up for this kind of business. This is going too f—"

"Might I remind you what you *did* sign up for?"

"What did you say?"

"Mr. Boreman, my original contract was to investigate Julian Hague. After I supplied you with the details of his intentions to destroy Gentec, it was *you* who decided to expand my scope to include consultation on how to best take advantage of the situation. When you did that, I asked you to give me your three highest priorities for success. Do you remember what you told me?"

"We don't need to be playing these games at a time like this."

"No need to remember, sir, I have your three priorities right here."

Boreman heard his own voice played back to him through the line. "Number one, whatever happens I want to get out of this thing clean, no culpability whatsoever. Two, I want to make as much money off this deal as possible. Rise or fall, I'm not going to take this kind of risk if I don't get paid extremely well. And three, I want Sheila Dunn destroyed by this thing. By whatever means possible."

His voice was replaced by Bradley's. "There you have it, sir. Your three top priorities."

Boreman's heart raced in a heated mixture of anger and fright. "What is this, blackmail? Why are you recording our conversations?"

"They're my personal notes. Come in mighty handy at times like these. Every so often I have to remind my clients exactly what they asked for."

"Oh, yeah? Well, so far you haven't delivered a single useful thing. None of this was on my original agenda."

"Mr. Boreman, the details of the plan may change slightly according to circumstance, but all is in order to achieve your three priorities."

"What do you mean 'change slightly'? This is nothing like the original plan. We were supposed to help Hague accelerate his distribution of the formula, remember? We were going to ride the stock down when the news hit, let Sheila take the fall, and then invest in Hague's new company when he started it up. *That's* what I agreed upon."

"Sir, we agreed upon your priorities for success, not an actual plan," Bradley said coolly. "True, the original plan was simpler, but unforeseen events made it impossible to follow through. For one, Pooly's unexpected killing of Hague cut the net income of this deal by more than half. Not to mention he's no longer able to create a new Miracle Treatment if this one is negated.

"So if we both want to keep on living and living, the recovery of the negating agent is now a priority. Another setback was Sheila hiring Macey. Throughout this operation he's thwarted our assassination attempts on her. He, sir, is the greatest barrier between you and achieving your number-one priority."

"How so?"

"Come on, Mr. Boreman: he's a CDI agent. Even if we initially pull away clean, he'll keep investigating until he digs everything up. The only solution is to eliminate him."

"I understand that. You were supposed to have done it already. But now you insist on getting rid of this other guy too. This—"

"Virgil. He's the third anomaly to bust this whole deal apart. First, he decided to mass-release the stuff. That wasn't part of the original plan, but it didn't hurt us. Not until Pooly killed Jules. That meant we had to be more sensitive to the stock plunge in order to catch it. But I took care of that. In fact, you're already quite rich from this whole transaction. I'm also fairly certain that Macey believes we want to avoid the negating agent's mass release in order to save ourselves and Gentec, which gives more credibility to tonight's deals."

"What do you mean?"

"I mean there's a good chance Macey thinks we want this deal to happen cleanly."

Boreman blinked out the window. "Well, don't we? We need that negating agent."

"Yes, we want the agent, but obviously we don't want a clean exchange. We want Macey dead. Sheila too. And the other one. Macey doesn't know any of that, but he might still suspect an attack. We need to be prepared for either scenario. That's why I shifted gears when Sheila told me he and Virgil were friends."

"What does that have to do with anything?"

"I've researched the both of them. Not only are they both cyborgs, they're both CDI agents. They go back over fifty years together. Some coincidence. If I didn't know any better I'd swear something was stacking the deck against us. Anyway, I didn't buy that story from Macey about them not being close. Soldiers become like brothers on the battlefield. Believe me, I know.

"You don't survive two wars fighting next to somebody and not have some kind of loyalty. Trust me, if we take out Macey and leave Virgil, the result will be the same. Virgil will keep digging 'til he finds out exactly how it all happened. And that means he'll find out the truth about you. Final verdict, Virgil has to go as well."

Boreman sighed. "So now you need a tank. Unbelievable."

"Yes, sir. And I wish I could have two or three."

"Are you—" He rubbed his forehead. "What's this going to cost me?"

"Thirty million. A fairly decent price for this kind of equipment."

"Thirty million? Are you out of your mind?"

"Sir," Bradley said, sounding exasperated, "you stand to make over a hundred times that amount. But it'll all be for nothing if you end up spending the rest of your *eternal* life in a prison. This is your 'get out of jail free' card, Mr. Boreman."

"Yeah, thirty million sure sounds free to me." You bloodsucker. "This thing can do the job this time, right? Not like those stupid guns you got before?"

"I've already performed a personal inspection of the equipment. This 'thing' can take out combat cyborgs, sir. That's what they are designed for. The Fireant has heavy armor, rapid mobility, stealth capability, and jamming. The AI is fully—"

"I don't care about the details. I just want an end to this fiasco."

"And you'll have it, sir. With the Fireant, it can all be over hours from now. Trust me, this is the only way your priorities will be met all in one go. Zero culpability, filthy rich, and Sheila Dunn destroyed." He paused. "I'm waiting with the suppliers now, Mr Boreman. You know I had to cash in a few favors to get this thing delivered short notice without any money up front. You *really* need to make a decision."

Boreman grunted. His "partnership" with Bradley Thomas had had its share of ups and downs, but lately it seemed he was no longer the one calling the shots. It was necessary, he supposed. He didn't know anything about this nasty business and Bradley did. But it was becoming harder and harder to trust him. All he seemed to do was ask for more money and then change the plan on the fly. But what choice did he have? Either way, Bradley shared his guilt, if not more so. He wouldn't do anything that would cause them to fail. At least, he hoped not.

"All right, Bradley," he said finally. "Get your tank."

CHAPTER FIFTEEN

<TWO MORE HOURS.> Bradley Thomas's voice sounded through the comm. *<I'll give you the coordinates again, nice and slow. Wouldn't want Sheila dying because you got the address wrong.>*

Macey grimaced as Bradley repeated the location of the exchange, the contents of the message annoying him as much as the voice delivering it.

<I'll be there.> He disconnected the comm before Bradley had a chance to say anything else. He glanced across the roof to Virgil, who was still seated on the concrete block, snacking on an energy bar.

"It's going down in the Mojave Desert." Macey reached for an energy bar of his own from the box Virgil had brought down from the crane cab. "About twenty miles east of LA."

"You got coordinates?"

He wired them through and searched the sky for satellites overhead. After taking a few bites of his chocolate-flavored snack, he located a satellite in geosynchronous orbit over the target area and pried through its security using his O-6 CDI clearance. As soon as he had a feed, he piped it over to Virgil so he could share the view.

His internal eye display gave them both an aerial view of the exchange location. Zooming in, he spotted several black trucks, starkly contrasting against the tan desert floor. Closing in further, he saw a couple of figures beside the trucks and, finally, the figure he wanted to see most—Sheila.

God truly had blessed him thus far. His reunion with Virgil, his renewed faith, his chance at love again. But his ultimate challenge lay before him.

From the steep angle the satellite provided he couldn't see much of her, just enough to identify her razor-straight bob, her slender nose, and high cheekbones. But even this quick glimpse filled him with longing and anxiety. As if to punctuate his emotions, the man guarding her looked upward, giving full view to his face. It was Bradley Thomas, leering at him inanely.

"Arrogant little punk." He almost spit out his energy bar. "He knows we're looking at him."

"He probably knew this would be the only satellite in orbit above the site." Virgil finished his own meal before tucking the wrapper away in his pocket. "He most likely figured we'd try and get a peek of him, so he tapped a direct feed to the bird ahead of us and waited for us to hack it. A psychological tactic—trying to make us think he's in total control. One step ahead. I wouldn't pay it too much attention."

Macey didn't. Neither did he bother performing a sweep of the satellite's connections to verify whether Bradley was watching their signal. Obviously he was. He disconnected the link. "So what do you think of our rendezvous point?"

"Well, it's a big open area. He'll probably have snipers. Maybe he'll use something aerial too. To be honest, I don't like it too much."

"No kidding." He'd already lost the taste for his artificial meal but he forced it down anyway. Although their bodies had an internal power source, their brains needed calories, especially when performing extreme maneuvers like cynetic bursts. "At least we don't have to guess about Bradley's intentions. This setup is pretty obvious. He's ready to attack."

Macey looked out over the horizon. The sun was well on its downward swing toward it, late afternoon already. Its rays were still bright, but far less scorching than they had been at noon.

"The door swings both ways." Virgil gnawed a chomp out of a second energy bar. "He'll know we can recognize a kill zone when we see one. So in a way he's letting us know that he's also prepared for a counterattack from us."

This was starting to look like a Mexican standoff. "So how do we approach this? No cover. No way to mask our entrance or egress. With this scenario we're pretty much open targets."

"I say we up our sophistication." Virgil swallowed the last of his cyborg-friendly meal in a healthy gulp and then donned a new pair of mirror shades he had retrieved from the crane booth.

Macey appreciated that. As much as he loved his brother, his obsidian eyes could be a bit unnerving. "Up our sophistication?"

"We saw what manpower resources he has, right?"

He recalled the satellite images from his memory and studied them in his internal vision. "Four hired guns, at least. Probably all well-equipped. Plus he'll no doubt have some kind of weaponry big enough to nullify us."

"Big enough to fit on a semi?"

"What?"

"About half a mile north. A semi truck parked with a flat-bed trailer. Looks to be nothing on it."

Macey scrolled upward and saw it as well, partially covered beneath an outcropping of rock, its identification unmistakable. "Well spotted. You think they brought something with them we aren't seeing yet?"

"Could be. And I think I see what looks like walker tracks heading toward the exchange site."

"Walker tracks?" His stomach tightened. If those were indeed walker tracks, then Bradley was going all out to kill them. The situation had taken another turn for the worse. "What do you think they belong to? A mobile gun platform? A tank?"

"Who cares?"

"Who cares?" Macey shot him a stare. "This is serious stuff here."

"Tell me, Mace." Virgil folded his broad arms. "What's stopping us from running in there and taking them all out before they even have a chance to react?"

"Are you kidding?" Macey stood from his concrete block, kicked a shard of broken plaster into the skylight Virgil had made. "Besides the fact that Bradley might have a tank that can take us out from over two miles away, there's Sheila to worry about. We can't go barreling in there with a frontal assault, man."

"Exactly." Virgil snapped his fingers, as if proving some great point. "Even if they do have a tank or even an attack jet, that's not our main concern, is it? Our main concern is Sheila. It's her that's our weakness and Bradley knows it. He's using her as a shield. So, if we were to remove Sheila from the equation, that would change things, wouldn't it? Then it would boil down to pure combat. And if you asked me, we got the edge on these rookies, no matter what kind of gear they got."

"Okay, but how does that help us? That's like saying to become a millionaire all you need to do is get a million dollars. Of course the situation would be easier if Sheila wasn't involved."

Virgil unleashed a chuckle. "Indeed, it would be."

"What's your point then? This is a hostage situation. She's under close guard. We can't just stroll in there and grab her."

Virgil looked extremely proud of himself. "I say we can."

Macey tossed the remainder of his second energy bar across the roof, irritated. "You're not making any sense, man."

"Misinformation manipulation, my friend." Virgil grinned broadly. "Fool their senses. Remember how I hacked your neural net on the roof earlier? We do the same thing to them."

He hadn't been thinking that far ahead. His whole perspective of the situation shifted. It was literally a Godsend to have Virgil back by his side, lending encouragement and strength, brainstorming ideas. Thinking outside the box was certainly one of his talents, but in this case he wondered if Virgil wasn't thinking a bit *too* outside. "You want us to hack them? All of them? At once?" He couldn't believe what he was suggesting. "An omni-hack-delusion mask. Are you serious? Do you have any idea how illegal that is?"

"Come on, Mace, it's not like we're trying to brain-fry them or anything like that. All we're going to do is temporarily hijack their senses. We paint the picture we want them to see, then achieve our objective under complete cover. Besides, it's not like we haven't done this sort of thing before."

"I just don't like the idea of using these methods. Not now." A stray cloud passed overhead, granting a few seconds of shade. "This isn't wartime, you know."

"You think Bradley isn't using military tactics against us? You think those aren't soldiers out there? And those sure enough look like walker tracks to me."

What could he say? Although he didn't like the idea of invading other people's neural nets, what Virgil was proposing did have the potential of giving them an incredible tactical edge, an edge they desperately needed—especially if Bradley *was* using a tank. If Virgil's plan proved successful, they could get in and out literally unseen, but the process wasn't without its problems. "Okay, overlooking the legality and morality of this for a moment, how realistic is it? We got nowhere near the support we need to pull something like this off."

"I beg to differ."

He raised a brow. "You got a military broadcast satellite I don't know about?"

"Not quite."

"Even if you did, the signal wouldn't get through. Remember that localized jamming I told you about? Bradley always uses it."

"Yeah, I do remember. In fact, that's what gave me the idea. I've been trying to figure out a way to overcome it. The solution is sitting right downstairs."

"What are you talking about?" But he already had an inkling as to what it was, an inkling he hoped was wrong. "You got some kind of transmitter stashed away, right?"

"About a hundred of 'em, if you look at it that way. They can send and receive far faster than any other transmitter and have a frequency sensitivity greater than any receiver made by man. Plus, they're mobile."

His inkling was correct. "Use the Blitzers? Virgil, are you nuts?"

"Well, it's not like we're going to get hold of a broadcast satellite anytime soon, are we? Trust me, the Blitzers will be willing to help us. They don't call me Moses for nothing."

"No way. We're not getting cyber-gangers involved in this. Have you considered their safety even? It's probably going to turn into a war zone out there."

"They don't need to be that involved, Mace. Just get within range of the jamming, maybe a couple hundred meters or so." He counted on his fingers as he laid the plan out for him. "We only need one of them to help, first to take care of the jamming and then to set up the transmission of the omni-mask."

He had to admit, Virgil still had it, he was as razor sharp as ever when it came to tactical planning. He hadn't gotten around to asking him yet, but he wondered if he hadn't stayed active while down in South America. Dozens of potential employers would have been eager to hire a man of his talents.

"All right," he said finally, giving in if only for curiosity's sake. "So how's this all going to work?"

"First the jamming. Once our Blitzer gets within close enough range to detect the jamming frequency, he copies the signal and rebroadcasts it out of phase."

"Use him as a wave guide and cancel the signal out against itself." A pretty good idea, though he had some serious doubts about its execution. "You expect some Blitzer off the street to be able to do that?"

"He won't be doing it, we will. He just needs to be there as the hardware. I got an M-class server we can use as an operations platform to patch into him. Same goes for the omni-hack mask. Once the jamming is canceled, we do a broadcast sweep and pick up however many neural net nodes are out there. Then we start accessing them one by one and hack through the security encryption for a direct feed to the sense receptors. Once we get through, we leave the channels open, and when all of them are prepped we launch our delusion mask simultaneously to all the targets, then move in."

It sounded good so far. He especially liked the use of the external military class server. Not only would it allow them greater hacking capability, but also provide a level of security. If they hit an offensive firewall, its protection hardware would shield them from a potentially deadly burn-back.

"And what if someone on Bradley's team doesn't have a neural net?"

Virgil stiffened as if it were a joke, then slowly he shook his head laughing. "Guess it's a risk we'll have to take, but come on, Mace, we're in the U.S. here, not some backwater. Who doesn't have a net in this country? Besides, you really think this Bradley guy is pro enough to prep for something like this?"

"Just saying . . ." True, these days there was only a small chance of someone not having a neural net and thereby being immune to the hack, but it remained a point worth considering. Some Special Forces units even specifically employed non-cybered operatives for just that reason. In the field they called it an 'Emperor's New Clothes' scenario. As in the fairytale, all it would take was for one person to not have a net and thus be able to see through the delusion mask in order to nullify it for everyone else.

Hopefully Bradley's lust for superior firepower was strong enough for him not to weaken his team with a non-enhanced member. But the possibility remained. "Okay, even without the potential of a New Clothes scenario, hacking all those neural nets isn't going to be a walk in the park. Even civilian-level encryption is some tough stuff to crack these days."

"I say we can do it." Virgil stood from his concrete block. "We got M-class cracking software on that server. All we need to do is work in parallel and back each other up."

"Yeah, yeah piece of cake," he said dryly with a lackluster roll of his eyes.

"You're not rusty, are you, Mace?" Virgil shot him a grin.

"Don't get cocky just because you got lucky in hacking me earlier." He raised a finger in warning. "I can still hack circles around you."

"Come on then. Let's get to it."

"Hold on. I've got to be honest with you, man. I'm still not crazy about using one of these Blitzers like this. This isn't their battle. Plus they can get killed a lot quicker than either of us can. We can talk realistically about going up against a tank, but come on . . . these guys are flesh and blood."

"I hear you." Virgil cradled his chin within his palm, released a sigh. "I'm not interested in getting any of them killed either, Mace, trust me. But if we do this right, you know we can get in and out without a single shot being fired. Anyway, I agree, we'll leave them to choose of their own free will. We tell them the risks and see who volunteers. How's that?"

It wasn't perfect, but it'd have to do. "It's times like this I wish I were still active. With CDI authority we could pull in an arsenal, even a real military satellite if we wanted to."

"Not wanted to." Virgil raised a finger of correction. "If the situation deemed it necessary, we could possibly *request* such equipment. Besides, we've already gone through that route. With the evidence you have, CDI can't do much for us. Especially with me being the main suspect."

"I know." He had already made his call to HQ and had gotten a sympathetic, but ultimately helpless response from Paul. Still, Paul had promised to send some kind of support if he could find some justification for it. At least he was understanding about the situation with Virgil and held off pursuing him.

Perhaps it was just as well. He didn't want to spook Bradley with a full-blown CDI response team. Who knew what he would do if confronted with something like that. This way they had a chance of outsmarting him without raising his guard. And as much as he'd rather not use them, the Blitzers were indeed the only ones with the capabilities they needed to pull it off.

"Okay, let's do it," he said finally. "On condition we make their safety a priority."

"Of course." Virgil extended his hand. "Wouldn't have it any other way."

Macey gripped it, and together they bowed their heads in prayer.

• • •

With their snaps popping, Macey and Virgil touched down on the pavement twenty feet from the BMW.

It was parked right where he had left it. Perfectly unmolested.

The Blitzer with the devil horns was leaning against it. Apparently the kid had taken his warning seriously. As they ambled toward him, he straightened, his eyes widening with what looked like excitement.

"I bloody knew it," the kid said with a wide-mouthed grin. "I knew you blokes were the same!"

"How are you, Bobby?" Virgil said.

"Oy, who's this with ya then, Moses?"

"This is my brother. You can call him . . . Jonah."

Macey rolled his eyes as Virgil enjoyed a laugh.

Bobby joined in despite it being an inside joke. "Ha! You blokes bloody own, y'know that?" His laugh was near maniacal. "All your base are belong to us!"

<*Was that a compliment?*>

<*Think so.*> Virgil shrugged. "I need a volunteer, Bobby. I got a dangerous mission I need some help with. No games this time. This is serious. Deadly. Round up some guys who might be interested, will you?"

<*This time?*> Macey cocked a brow.

<*Don't ask.*>

"Oy, I'm interested, mate. No need to ask those other sodding mugs. See how well I took care of your Beemer for you then, don't ya?" Bobby glowered. "I'm your man, Moses. What you got for me then?"

"There's a good chance you can get killed doing this, kid," Macey said to him. "We can't guarantee your safety. This is no joke."

"Don't care 'bout dying. I already owe Moses me life. If I lose it helpin' him, we'd just be square. So what I gotta do, then?"

Virgil glanced over at him. <*Your call, Mace.*>

<*I'm not even going to ask how you've managed to foster this kind of loyalty, Virgil.*>

<*The power of God, man. What else can I say?*>

"All right fine. You're hired, Bobby." He strode toward the BMW. "Let's get moving. We have to make a pit stop before we head out."

"A pit stop?" Virgil said.

"To my apartment." He unlocked the car doors. "I got a little stash you might be interested in. Could come in handy for whatever Bradley has hidden out there in the desert. We should have time. Little over an hour now before the exchange."

"Bloody straight!" Bobby exclaimed, whipping open the back door of the BMW and plopping down inside. "This is what I'm talking 'bout! High rollin' with the big boys, finally! Let's crack some friggin' 'eds, mates!"

<*You sure know how to pick 'em, Virg.*>

<*Yeah, Bobby's a trip.*> Virgil tucked himself into the passenger seat, grinning.

Macey couldn't help but chuckle.

Inevitably, obliviously, Bobby joined in as well, cackling his head off as he poked his face between the front seats like a dog going for a ride.

The kid was a trip all right—Macey liked him already.

• • •

Bradley Thomas checked the chronometer in his eye just as the sun kissed the edge of the earth in an explosion of strawberry-orange hues. It was nearly time.

Behind him stood one of the trucks. The others were parked adjacent to it, forming a rough semicircle of the jet black machines. A couple of his men stood beside him for show. The rest lay in hiding, monitoring the perimeter. The location he had selected stood in the middle of a natural cul-de-sac, an abandoned dirt road that dead-ended at the foot of a canyon. A perfect setup. The vehicular access was well controlled and, more importantly, the Fireant had an elevated attack position atop one of the outlying dunes.

In less than an hour it would all be over. The entire messy operation wiped clean in one blast from the Fireant's main gun. As soon as he had the negating agent in his hands, that was. That would be the only challenging part. But he was prepared to handle it.

<Vehicle approaching.> One of his men reported through the comm. *<One click out. Silver BMW. Two occupants.>*

<Make sure it's not a decoy.> He was wary of such tactics. If only that fool Pooly hadn't gotten so greedy and killed Hague. If Hague were alive, he'd already be working on the new Miracle Treatment and the release of the negating agent would be of no consequence. In that scenario, he would have been able to take out Macey and Virgil at first glance. But now he was forced to make this deal to secure the negating agent. At least, he needed to appear to make this deal.

He just hoped they weren't planning to rush him at close quarters. No way could he stand up to two combat cyborgs. He had given strict parameters to the Fireant to lay down the hammer if anything like that did happen. Still, trusting his personal safety to an AI tank was nothing less than nerve-wracking, especially considering the odds he would soon be facing.

He opened all his comm channels, making sure the tank could hear his instructions as well. *<As soon as we get confirmation on the ID, everyone get into final position.>*

<Copy.> A host of replies sounded through the comm, along with a positive response from the tank's monotone-voiced AI.

He'd much rather be inside the tank's cockpit calling the shots. But he needed to be seen by Macey. Play the face-man. If he wasn't in plain sight, Macey might suspect an attack. But even without the tank's fire support he wasn't totally defenseless against the cyborg duo.

"Get her out here," he said.

His men hurried to obey his command. They retrieved Sheila from the passenger seat of the middle truck. To his surprise, she didn't come out kicking and screaming. Maybe she was using her brain for once. They placed her beside him, still bound at the wrists. And now also at the ankles. No running this time.

"It'll all be over soon, Sheila." And, in truth, it would be—for her. "Just don't try anything stupid like before."

He didn't expect a response from her. Her gag, also new, wouldn't allow one. He could understand now why Boreman hated her so much. Sheila Dunn's mouth made her one incredibly annoying woman.

<Confirmation on both targets traveling within the BMW, sir.>

<Good. Final prep, everyone.> He took hold of Sheila's arm, clutched his human shield securely. *<It's showtime.>*

• • •

Macey rolled the BMW along the dirt road that led to the exchange site. He could see Bradley and Sheila already, but he was in no rush to reach them yet.

Virgil rode shotgun next to him. Literally. Except in this case the shotgun was a 30mm cyber-rifle he had selected from the vault, now loaded with High Explosive Anti-Tank (HEAT) rounds.

In the back, Bobby huddled on the floor to remain out of sight. It was strange seeing his curly head and vacuum tubes just below the level of the seat. Like some kind of robo-dog.

All three of them were connected to each other via hard-wire, patched through Virgil's military server, which rested atop the handbrake. So far Macey was impressed by Bobby's networking capabilities. He certainly was no novice.

But he wasn't a soldier, either. Though they had gone over the plan at least a half-dozen times, including a contingency plan in case everything fell apart, Macey remained ill-at-ease about Bobby's presence. He prayed for the kid's safety.

<*Anything yet?*> He posed the question at Bobby through the comm as he inched the car forward.

The kid glanced up at him, his hair matted with perspiration. They purposely had the windows up and the AC off—to raise the internal temperature of the car so as to mask Bobby's heat signature. He didn't put it past Bradley to scan them with IR, and they couldn't give away their ace in the hole. He and Virgil were immune to the heat, which by now registered well over a hundred degrees, but poor Bobby felt it all. He was a real trooper though, and hadn't complained, not once.

<*Nothing.*> Bobby breathed in short, shallow breaths. <*Keep going forward.*>

Macey complied until Bobby yelled out, "Stop!"

That same instant Macey's neural connection to his remote memory server severed, as did his comm lines, his net spewing blaring red error messages. "We hit the jamming."

Virgil looked over his shoulder at the young Blitzer. "Did you capture the sample, Bobby?"

The kid didn't need to answer. He reacted to the jamming as to a dentist's drill, his body jittering at ultrasonic speed. "B-b-bloody right, man. H-h-h-hurry it up! This h-h-hurts!"

"I'm on it." Virgil bowed his head in concentration.

Macey overlooked the operation through his hardwire patch to the military server. The integrity of Bobby's connection had destabilized due to the jamming signal permeating his horns, but this was what they were counting on. With every quiver and shake of the kid's net, the jamming signal revealed its telltale frequency signature.

It wasn't constant. Its ever-changing amplitude seemed to bombard all channels at once. This was high-grade military jamming. Virgil ran several utility programs, taking samples from the signal. Only a few seconds later he isolated a base frequency and began analyzing the pattern.

"I think I got it," Virgil said.

Something that looked like a mathematical formula written in machine code popped onto the window in Macey's internal display.

"I'll transpose it now."

Virgil began coding an algorithm that would apply the phase shift while anticipating the frequency changes of the jamming and matching it within a fraction of a second. Computer code and equations flew across the screen so quickly that Macey could barely keep up with them.

"Got it. Preparing to broadcast. You ready, Bobby?"

"D-d-dying here!"

Virgil keyed the last command.

In an instant the blaring red error messages within Macey's comm turned green. His status reverted to "online."

"Counter-jamming successful." Macey glanced back at Bobby, who was now a disheveled wreck. "You did good, kid. Real good."

"No worries," Bobby said sardonically with a droopy smirk. "You two never said it was gonna bloody well 'urt so much."

"Time for phase two." Virgil hit a few keys on the server. "Keep your speed up, Mace."

He glanced at the dash. The BMW was barely crawling along now. He tapped the gas again, regaining momentum. They couldn't make their approach seem too obvious. He was a quarter of a mile from where Bradley and Sheila stood in front of the parked truck. He would close that gap to about thirty yards before he stopped.

But before then they had to have completed the omni-hack. "Go for it, Virgil. I'd give us about two hundred seconds."

"Roger." Virgil eyed Bobby. "Get ready." He shut his eyes. "Sending ping."

With all three of them patched back into the military server, Macey had a multi-windowed display of Virgil's handiwork. A window resembling a radar screen appeared. A wave swept across the display, and eight green dots flashed into view.

"Those are the neural net nodes present in the vicinity," Virgil said. "You take half, I'll take half."

"Roger," Macey said, locking on to one of the dots. He opened another window and began his hack.

The security he encountered seemed standard. Difficult, but not impossible, to break through. The cracking software on the server worked like a dream. He ran several of the algorithm programs simultaneously, probing past the top-level encryption and breaking through to the user interface. A tinge of guilt ran through him as the full senses of the person he hacked fell into his complete command. It was the ultimate form of personal invasion.

He could watch, hear, and feel every second of another person's life in real time if he wanted to, and many sick people dreamed of doing just that. It nauseated him. Every moral bone in his body screamed for him to sever the connection. But he couldn't. He needed to do this.

He isolated the sensory channels and prepped them to be overlaid with the fake reality they would soon concoct.

"One down," Virgil said.

"Same."

Macey kept pace with him as if in competition. The race helped keep his mind off the ethics of the situation. The process became mechanical, detached. Another one done, then on to the next. It was a familiar process, one he hadn't induced in a long time. The emotional detachment that wartime brought on.

"Crikey! You two are fast!" Bobby exclaimed. "Never seen anything like it in me life."

"Mace, we got a problem. I need your help."

The alarm in Virgil's voice nearly caused him to botch his own hacking job. In a few seconds of tense concentration he managed to finish it off before glancing in his friend's direction. "What's wrong?"

Virgil's face was creased in a mask of intense focus. "I think I might have found whatever it was Bradley brought on that semi. This is some serious military-grade encryption. Deeper even than the jamming. Must be a tank or something. Offensive firewalls everywhere, plus a semi-sentient AI. Take care of the rest while I hold it off, then come help me."

Macey didn't pause to think. He accessed the last of the nodes and began hacking them. They had discussed how they would handle the possibility of a tank, but Virgil's reaction suggested it was a far greater threat than they had anticipated.

Virgil was on the edge, dodging detection by the tank's AI by fractions of a second. If the tank's computer had the slightest indication of a hacking attempt, the entire jig would be up.

Finishing the last hack, he turned to assisting Virgil. Two seconds in, and he knew they were in trouble. The AI was aggressive, an advanced model designed for the rigors of cybercombat, where such hacking attempts would be as commonplace as bullets hitting its armored hide. He began attacking from an opposite angle, taking advantage of the distraction Virgil caused.

"Don't bother with that," Virgil said. "It's too late. We need to launch the mask."

Macey glanced up to see that they had nearly reached Bradley already. "Not good."

"Just make the connections to the cameras and run the feed. We'll have to keep running interference. Bounce the AI between us and hope it doesn't catch on."

Not the original plan. Running the mask would be hard enough, but simultaneously fending off a military AI? It bordered on impossible.

"We might need your help, Bobby." Macey opened a portal to the tank's mainframe, a dense matrix of security code streaming onto the military server's screen at a mind-boggling rate.

"Never seen code that thick before . . ." Bobby's accent had dropped away. But he sounded more impressed than concerned. Maybe he didn't know how close they were to a fiery death. Macey decided it wasn't the best time to educate him.

"I'm going in, Bobby," he said to the young Blitzer. "Back us up."

CHAPTER SIXTEEN

GLARE FROM THE BMW'S WINDSHIELD hit Sheila's eyes. It drew closer and came to a stop. Her heart thundered with anticipation. Finally, the driver's door swung open, and like a vision of salvation, Macey emerged.

He looked taller than she remembered. He wore a flowing overcoat atop what looked like military fatigues. She gazed at him longingly, waiting for him to turn in her direction. When he did, their eyes met for only a moment, but it was all she needed. His gaze held strength, confidence, and security. Instantly the anxiety gnawing at her insides quelled.

It took all her might not to cry out to him, something her gag wouldn't allow anyway, but she restrained herself nonetheless. She didn't need Bradley knowing how desperate she was, and even a muffled cry would signal that.

As if he had read her thoughts, Bradley tightened his hold on her arm. "Good to see you, Mr. Macey. Did you bring what I wanted?"

Macey stepped around the front of the car to the passenger door and flung it open. Something fell out with a thud. Muffled moans echoed from the ground. Macey emerged from around the car, dragging a man whom she barely recognized as Virgil. He looked as if he had been pulled from a train wreck. His body was twisted, his limbs mangled. Though the last time she'd seen him she'd wished for him to look like this, now she winced at the sight of him.

"Is *this* what you wanted?" The harshness in Macey's voice caused a shudder of guilt to run through her soul. It was as if he were speaking directly to her. Had he needed to almost kill his best friend because of her?

"That's half of it," Bradley said. "Where's the negating agent?"

"Right here." Macey dipped his hand into his overcoat pocket and raised a glass canister. "How do you want to do this?"

"Move toward the center, then I'll let Sheila walk out to you. Leave the agent with Virgil. Then Sheila can leave with you."

"Just like that?"

"Just like that. But don't push your luck. I got 20mm rifles with armor-piercing rounds aimed at your head . . . and hers."

"I wouldn't doubt it." Macey snorted. With his free arm he grabbed Virgil by the collar of his tattered overcoat and hauled him across the sand.

"Sheila."

She flinched. Was Macey calling her? No, it couldn't have been. He remained a fair distance away and the voice had sounded close, almost directly in front of her. She recoiled at the recollection of Bradley's attack on her in Jules's lab. Was the same thing happening now?

"Don't worry," the voice said again, but this time she wasn't sure it was Macey's. It sounded deeper, coarse. Then in front of her stood a man. He not so much emerged as appeared, as if he had been standing there the entire time and she just hadn't noticed.

She lurched backward, her heart dancing in her throat.

The towering figure that was Virgil gazed down upon her. His arms cradled an enormous gun, bigger than the one Bradley's men had used against Macey at the lab. She released a muffled cry against her gag, fought to get away. He was here to kill her. But how could he be here at all? How could Virgil be right here, when Macey was still dragging him toward them?

Her eyes darted back to Macey. Virgil was no longer with him. In fact, Macey was not even walking toward her, but at a standstill, his eyes closed in what looked like intense concentration.

Her mind whirled with vertigo. Her heart pounded with fright. Nothing was making sense. She looked back to Virgil and then to Bradley, who seemed oblivious to both Macey and the near-seven-foot giant standing in front of her.

"I'm undoing your bonds," Virgil said. He stooped and broke the fiber-weave bindings as easily as if they were thread. He repeated the process with her hands, then removed her gag.

Too stupefied to speak, Sheila shifted her eyes back to Bradley. He was still focused on Macey, his fingers digging into her arm. By the time she regained enough sense to formulate a question, Virgil was already speaking to her.

"Don't move. I need to make an adjustment."

"What's going on?" The most intelligible thing she could manage. "How can you be here? What are you planning to do to me?"

"I plan to help you," he said. "As for what's happening, you were experiencing a delusion. Everyone else is experiencing the same thing—watching Macey drag me toward you. I've pulled you out of it. Now you're seeing the real world again."

This had to be some kind of weird dream.

"You can talk freely, no one else can—" Virgil winced, rubbed his temple as if something had struck him there, but within a few seconds he regained his composure. "Sorry. We don't have much time. Macey and I are both under an incredible amount of mental strain. While I'm doing this, he's holding a conversation with Bradley. He probably won't be able to talk to you . . ." He grunted. "There, now Bradley won't notice you leave his side. Come with me."

He reached his hand toward her.

She still couldn't compute what exactly was going on, but she knew well enough not to accept things happening as they were. "Wait. Why are you helping me, Virgil?"

"There's no time to explain. You have to come with me."

Was he for real? "You've got to be kidding. You've destroyed my life and now you want me to trust you?"

"Here, maybe you can trust this." Something cold and smooth pressed into her hand. She looked down to see the glass canister that Macey had held.

"This is the negating agent. I really can't explain now, but know this: I'm truly sorry for the pain I've caused you, Sheila.

I'll do everything within my powers to rectify the damage I've done. And that starts with getting you to safety. Please take my hand."

Could this really be happening? Could this be the same Virgil who'd been bent on destroying her Miracle Treatment? Could he have changed so drastically? "This can't be right. You . . . you were trying to destroy the Treatment. How—"

"Macey and I are brothers. There's nothing we wouldn't do for one another. I know he cares for you, so I'm helping him save you."

He was doing this all because of Macey? Was this Macey's plan? What choice did she have but to go along with it then? At least Virgil wasn't trying to blow her head off, or hang her. Slowly, apprehensively, she reached out to him.

He smiled and gently clasped her hand. As he began leading her away, Bradley's grasp on her arm released, but he didn't react to it. He just stood there, arm raised as if still gripping her.

"I don't understand." She looked up at Virgil as they walked across the sand. "Where are you taking me?"

"To the car. But not the one you can see over there. That's part of the delusion."

She studied the BMW. It certainly looked real enough. As she turned to face wherever Virgil was leading her, she saw another car, identical. "This is freaking me out. How are you doing this?"

"It's complicated." He winced, pain creasing his face again. "Can you see the real car yet?"

"Yes."

"Good." He stopped and let go of her hand. "Get in. Drive out of here as fast as you can. You'll find a young man named

Bobby in the back seat. He's a friend. But he looks a little strange. Get both of you to safety as fast as possible. "

"What? Wait! I still don't understand. Why are you doing this? What's made you suddenly want to help me?"

Virgil stared down at her, his mirror shades reflecting the fiery streaks of the setting sun. "'Two are better than one, because if they fall, the one will lift up his fellow; but woe to him that is alone when he falleth, and hath not another to lift him up.'"

"The Bible, right?" She couldn't help but roll her eyes. "You really are just like Macey. Try English, okay?"

He winced again, his voice straining. "I can see why he likes you. You remind me very much of his wife."

How was she supposed to take that?

Virgil exhaled suddenly, as if a great weight had dropped from his shoulders. "That's better—got it chasing its own tail for awhile."

"Got what doing what?"

"Never mind. Sheila, I made a terrible mistake. Macey helped me see it. He lifted me up when I fell."

"So that's why you're helping me? Because he helped you to . . . to . . ."

"See the light?"

"I guess." She stared back at him, unable to think of anything better to say. Was that how things were between Macey and him? Did they both take the Bible so literally? Could they change so quickly, based purely on what they read within it? She looked again at the car behind Virgil and then back toward Macey, still standing in the same position.

"If Bradley and his goons can't see us, why don't we all just leave?"

"We can't. Macey can't even move because of the concentration he needs to maintain this delusion, which is linked to the kid in the car. We need to stay here and keep up the mirage. Once it drops, Macey and I will be able to hold off Bradley long enough for you to get out of range. Now please hurry."

"All right." She was still unsure but she started to move toward the car anyway. "Wait! I saw Bradley with this big machine thing that looked like a huge . . . mechanical ant or something. I think—"

"It's a tank. That's why you need to get moving. We've managed to fool its senses as well, but that's what's causing us so much strain. We're going to have to drop our connection to it shortly. We can hold it for about ten minutes more, maybe less. You need to get out of its range before then."

Her heart pounded. Was she going to have to leave Macey out here with that thing? What was going to happen to him? To both of them?

"He and I will be fine," Virgil said, as if reading her fears. Or perhaps it was her expression he had read. "We can handle Bradley, but we won't be able to do that until you get to safety."

Ignoring the anxiety and uncertainty building in her stomach, she turned and gazed up at Virgil one last time. "I don't claim to know everything that's going on here, but all I can say is . . . I'm glad you're on our side now. Thank you."

"Thank God. He's the one who made it all possible."

She didn't know how to respond to that. She still wasn't sure if there was any such thing as God. But by the way Virgil and Macey operated, God was certainly real to them. "I . . . I don't believe in God." She forced the words off her tongue, unsure why she had said them. Maybe because she was speaking to

Virgil and not Macey. A way for her to test what kind of reaction Macey might have if she revealed the same truth to him.

"I think you will believe eventually, Sheila." And he pointed to the glass canister in her hand. "Once you run out of things to live for in this life, you'll start seeking something to die for. And when you do, you'll have a fine teacher to show you the way."

His words caused a shudder to run through her. She wasn't sure what he meant by them, but she couldn't deny the anxiety they brought on.

"See you soon," Virgil said with a nod. Then, as quickly as he had appeared, he vanished.

His words danced inside her head. Too much to think about right now. She jogged for the BMW but couldn't resist glancing back in Macey's direction.

He was still standing there, eyes pressed shut in concentration. So strong, so unyielding. She could only imagine what he was going through for her sake. How she longed to stay with him, run to him, embrace him, tell him how sorry she was, how much she cared for him. But, no. Macey had a plan and this time she would trust it.

To the very end.

Bradley Thomas awaited his moment of opportunity. Macey still dragged what was left of Virgil toward him. Perhaps he had misread the relationship he and Macey had shared. Macey seemed to have taken his advice literally. He could only imagine what kind of battle had raged between the two of them to produce the mangled cybernetic body that was now Virgil.

But he wasn't about to lower his guard. When Macey reached the halfway point, he held up a hand. "Far enough, my friend."

Macey stopped.

Although Bradley had the upper hand, Macey was still a combat cyborg. The only thing keeping Macey in check was Sheila. He clutched her arm tighter within his palm.

Both Macey and Virgil were already in the kill zone. Now all he needed was to get the negating agent to safety so he could signal the Fireant to attack. "Move five paces forward," he said. "Set Virgil and the negating agent down, and back away. Then I'll let Sheila move toward you."

"Fine." Macey stepped forward as instructed, taking five slow, deliberate steps. He dropped Virgil's twisted body and set the canister upon the desert floor before backing away. "All yours."

Indeed, it is. But now came the hardest part, forcing Sheila to play her role. Hopefully she wouldn't try anything stupid like making another run for it. Things could get messy then. He wanted the tank to make a nice clean shot of all three of them, concentrated in a single group. If she made a run for it, the tank would have to spray a haphazard stream of 30mm rounds, trying to fix a lock on them. Ducks in a barrel, clean and easy—that's how it would be.

A message flashed through on his comm. He barely perceived its transmission.

<*Say again?*>

After a pause he heard it again: <*Vehicle exiting mission area. Request commands.*> It was the Fireant.

<*Explain.*>

Eventually the AI repeated in its monotone voice: <*Vehicle exiting mission area. Request commands.*>

Bradley scanned left and right for movement. Was another vehicle approaching? But no, the AI had said exiting, not entering. <*Fireant, qualify your last message. What vehicle?*>

Again, no reply.

"Come on," Macey called across the desert expanse. "I don't have all night."

He barely acknowledged him with a cut of his eyes before sending another message to the tank. <*I said, give me more details. Do you copy me?*>

Dead silence, until finally he heard it again. <*Vehicle exiting mission area. Request commands.*>

What was going on? He checked his comms—and was met a wall of error messages. "A delusion mask?" he whispered. But how?

He glanced about, unsure if what he saw was real or not. He had no way to tell. His heart pummeled within his gut.

Macey appeared to be a good twenty meters from him, but in reality he could already have his hands about his throat. Wily old cuss. He had pulled a fast one on him. He'd had no idea Macey was capable of something like this. He would have to act fast to regain the advantage.

Checking his connections, he found them intact. Macey had hacked his neural net, feeding false information to his senses, but he had merely disconnected the comms—another slick move. If he had tried to disable them, his neural net would have more easily detected the hack. A fact he could now use against him.

"I'll send her when I'm good and ready," he said to Macey, stalling for time. His only option was to strike while Macey still thought he had the upper hand. "Back up some more. I don't want you too close."

Working the internals of his neural net, Bradley brought his comms back online and entered the global address of the Fireant's comm link, secured a connection. Within a few seconds the tank's AI accepted his security clearance and a channel opened.

<*Greetings, Mr. Thomas*> The tank's monotone AI voice acknowledged him. <*Vehicle exiting mission area. Request commands.*>

<*Send me a visual feed.*>

Within his vision, a window opened displaying Macey's silver BMW charging along the dirt road, kicking up a cloud of dust. His pulse throbbed within his temples. Had Macey made a complete fool of him? <*Close in your visual on the occupants.*>

The view zoomed and his mind reeled.

<*Sheila?*>

<*Confirm IR signature of one female. Commands?*>

Impossible. Why wasn't anyone else seeing this? And where were Macey and Virgil, if not in the illusion before him and not in the car? A chill ran down his spine as it finally hit him. <*On my mark, send an offensive counter-jamming measure.*> He could still hardly believe it. <*I think we're under an omni-hack mask.*>

<*Will comply.*>

He turned to fix his eyes upon Sheila standing next to him, finding it hard to believe she wasn't really there. <*Prepare to wake everyone up.*> He readied the command. <*We must stop that car.*>

• • •

Something was wrong. Macey sensed it.

Bradley was taking far too long to act. From the corner of his vision, Macey saw his BMW starting down the dirt road toward the highway. Sheila had moved as fast as she could, reversing haphazardly and darting away. Could they give her enough time to get out of range?

The tank's AI proved far sharper than they had anticipated. She should have been well out of sight by now, but twenty seconds had passed since they were forced to drop the tank's delusion mask, and the BMW remained within its range.

Tension filled him. Maybe they should have changed the game plan once they knew the level of the tank's security. Sheila might have been better off remaining hidden in the car instead of trying to drive it away. Now she was a highly visible target, a moving bull's-eye the tank's guided munitions could easily hit. He cursed himself for it. Sheila was more at risk than ever.

He had one last hope of keeping her safe. Once the tank fired, it would briefly reveal its position. He prepared himself for it, ready to pinpoint its location. His thoughts edged a hair-trigger away from releasing a cynetic burst. If he could spot the tank, act before it did, he could—

His head exploded in an ear-piercing shrill of pain.

His vision blurred, fading to a mind-numbing white. He collapsed to his knees, hands cupping his ears, falling to the desert floor, spinning, trying to get a handle on what had happened.

The blaring noise continued, like a drill sergeant's whistle blowing in his ear. Something crashed into him from the side, something fast and powerful that sent him tumbling end over end until he fell onto his face, his mouth dragging open, tasting sand. A second later another sound filled the air.

The familiar din of a rotary cannon.

"No!" he cried, desperate to drive the blaring whiteness from his eyes. The car. Sheila! He struggled to rise but something heavy pressed on top of him. He kicked it off.

<*Mace, stop!*> Virgil's voice reverberated inside his head. <*It's me, man.*>

His vision cleared and he could make out Virgil's form kneeling next to him. "Virgil, the car. Sheila—"

<*It's not firing at her.*> He darted his head to the side. <*Move!*>

Virgil hit his snaps, powering into the air. Macey followed suit. The sand beneath him liquefied as another blare from the tank's rotary cannon assaulted his ears. He balked at the destruction it caused, thanked God it had fired upon them and not the car. No way would Sheila survive a hit like that.

But why? Why didn't it take out the car?

And then suddenly, it made sense. He railed at himself for being so stupid. He needed to take a step back, stop viewing the situation from within his own head and start seeing it from his foe's. Of course Bradley wouldn't waste the tank's firepower taking out Sheila when he had two combat cyborgs to worry about.

In mid-flight, Macey reoriented himself, getting a fix on where the shot had come from. Tracing the line of fire, he isolated it. The multi-legged tank loomed a hundred yards away, set high atop a sand dune covered with the khaki of desert camouflage. He couldn't clearly make out its designation, but his neural net did what his eyes alone could not. In an instant the IFF spilled a weapons profile onto his internal display.

<*An MLT8-A Fireant. Autonomous model. No wonder that AI was so tough.*>

<Forget the AI. We need to worry about staying ahead of that cannon.> Virgil barely touched down before hitting the snaps again, and with good reason. The cannon fired once more, leaving a smoldering hole where he had just been.

Macey headed off in the opposite direction, giving the tank two targets to try to hit. They needed to take it out quickly. That 30mm cannon wasn't its only weapon. *<Virgil, draw its fire with your rifle. I'll try and get in close.>*

<Don't worry about it, man. You need to go protect Sheila.>

He scanned the desert for her, hitting his snaps to gain altitude. His BMW was still heading toward the highway, a good distance off now, a rising dust plume in its wake. She had almost reached the highway. A wave of relief washed over him. They had pulled it off. Soon she'd be out of the tank's range. Soon she'd reach safety.

And then he saw it. Not a quarter mile back, a black truck was gunning down the road after her.

"Bradley," he whispered the name like a curse. The tank was just a distraction.

<He's trying to get his bargaining chip back, Mace. You go take care of it. I'll handle the tank.>

<Alone?> He swiveled his head toward his brother in arms, now several hundred yards away from him, bounding ahead of the Fireant's blazing main gun. He was working in a spiral pattern, and with each landing he dropped into a crouch, shouldered the massive 30mm rifle and took a shot. The rifle went off with a massive *whump* and sent a visible shock wave racing across the desert.

<That model is armed with surface-to-surface smart missiles.> Macey relayed the designation information to him. *<If it target-locks you, you're dead.>*

<Then hurry up and deal with Bradley so you can get your tail back here to help me.>

Despite the urgency, he hesitated. Virgil was prepared to try a solo attack against the tank. Together, they stood a good chance, could trade off its attacks, pincer it. But alone, it was only a matter of time before the tank would win. *<Virgil, you can't—>*

<Just go, man!>

Hitting the snaps, he sped toward the dirt road. His brother was risking his life to give him the opportunity to protect Sheila.

An opportunity he had no choice but to take.

Sheila ignored the burn of the leather seat on her skin as she pressed the accelerator to the floor. The BMW surged forward, the steering wheel bouncing within her palms as the car ate up the dirt road ahead of her.

Free. She still couldn't believe it. Maybe it was too soon to believe it anyway. She wasn't exactly free yet. Bradley still lurked out there somewhere. She would only truly feel safe once she reached the highway. Then, other issues awaited. Even her own safety wasn't true freedom from this ordeal.

She had merely swapped places with Macey. Now he was the one at risk. What a sick world it would be if she survived only to have him die. Her gut twisted at the thought of it. To be so utterly cheated by life. To have all their efforts shattered so vainly while people like Boreman and Bradley got away unpunished.

Almost enough to make her really wish there was a God. Or to become utterly convinced there wasn't.

A groan emanated from behind. In her rearview mirror she saw the vacuum tube kid in the back seat waking up. What had happened to him? When she'd clambered into the car he'd seemed in a trance, his head wired into a portable computer. The next thing she knew, he'd screamed and the computer had popped open like a toaster, complete with burnt toast in the form of charred circuit boards.

"You okay back there, kid?" She tried to make eye contact through the mirror. She had no idea what role he played in all this, but at this stage she didn't care. It was part of Macey's plan and that's all she needed to know.

The kid's bloodshot eyes focused on her. "You must be the sheila called Sheila. Bloody right, you live up to your name, but. No wonder Jonah's got his 'ed all knackered up over you."

"Uh . . . huh?"

He chortled. "Name's Bobby," he said fiddling with something in the back. "Crikey, this thing's bloody fried. What 'appened?"

"Don't ask me. I'm just—"

The rear window shattered.

Sheila screamed and jammed on the brakes. Her eyes flew to the rearview mirror, which now displayed the frostlike pattern of the broken back windscreen pierced with a single bullet hole dead in its center.

"They're bloody shooting at us!" Bobby cried. "What you stopping for?"

The roar of an engine came from the side. She nearly drove off the road trying to avoid Bradley's black truck. It zoomed next to her and swerved into her path. The steering wheel pulled from her grasp as the BMW careened with the impact.

She grunted, struggling to keep the wheel straight. The car swerved side to side. Jamming the accelerator, she released a cry as she swung the car back into him, metal on metal screaming as she plowed into the side of the truck.

Another gunshot rang out. The front windshield exploded into a mosaic of shattered glass. She cried out, her screams matching Bobby's in a shrill pitch.

Then from the side she saw Bradley veer toward her again. The truck slammed into her and the steering wheel spun her hands loose.

The BMW careened off the road. They struck something and the car lurched upward, the world spinning as the car launched into a roll.

When the car was on its side, and still rolling, the glove compartment popped open and the glass canister flew out of it. Sheila's breath left her as she desperately reached to grab the vial, the one thing she cared about more than her very life. As the car bounded and jostled, her fingertips grazed the glass canister containing the negating agent, now bouncing chaotically off the passenger seat.

She grasped again, then her entire world went black.

Macey soared through the desert sky, powerless as the BMW tipped onto its side, rolled onto its roof and began to slide. Anxiety surged through him, charged with anger and hate. Is she dead? Have they killed her? Blasting the snaps, he jetted downward, blazing toward the BMW and taking aim at the black truck charging after it.

Releasing a cry, he slammed full force into its side like a meteor, unleashing every ounce of his rage.

The truck flew sideways, still in forward motion, its tires biting into the ground so violently it flew into a flip of its own.

Macey didn't waste time to see what became of its occupants. Far greater concerns pressed upon his mind. Touching ground, he slid to a stop and raced toward the BMW, which was now overturned and at a standstill.

"Sheila!" He dove into a crouch to rip open the door with a creak of metal. He pulled it free and flung it behind him. There she was, hanging upside down, unresponsive, affixed to her seat by her safety belt. He grabbed hold of her, tore apart the belt, and pulled her out.

He checked her vitals. She was still breathing, thank God, but the stream of blood dripping down her forehead wasn't good. He rested her gently on the ground, careful to cradle her neck.

Then he remembered Bobby.

He rushed to the car again, peering into the back seat. He wasn't there.

Through the busted back windshield he spotted him, and panic tore at his soul. The young Blitzer had been flung from the vehicle and lay face down at the edge of the road, motionless. The vacuum tubes were both smashed.

"No," he whispered. He couldn't be dead. No one should have died over this. He called out to him, bracing himself to leap.

An explosion sounded and his left shoulder felt as if it had burst into flames. The impact slammed him into the car. He tried to turn to face his attacker, but another blast came. He fired his snaps to avoid it, diving toward Sheila to shield her, outstretching his arms to break his fall.

He saw only his right hand in front of him. The other was gone, a tangled mass of shredded muscle fiber sprouting where his left bicep should be. He broke his fall awkwardly, landing on his one hand and careening onto the ground. He pulled himself into a roll and wound up on his knees, hovering over Sheila.

He stared blankly at his missing arm. What had he been shot with? A 20mm, at least. The destructive power of the weapon up close sobered him. Even his combat frame did little to stand up to the armor-piercing rounds.

"You're finished, Macey." Bradley's voice called from behind him. "I thought you were an honorable man, but it seems I've misjudged you. You'll pay for your treachery."

Bradley was talking. But why talk? He could have killed him already.

"I didn't bring my wallet," he said wryly. "You take IOUs?"

Bradley answered with a metallic *chi-chack* of the 20mm being re-cocked. "I'll settle for a pound of flesh."

He had let his guard down. Let his emotions get the better of him again. Bradley had gotten a clean shot. One glance at his blown-off arm confirmed that, but his limb could easily have been his head.

Slowly Macey faced him. Bradley stood flanked by two other men. All three toted 20mm cyber-rifles. They paced forward from the wreckage of the black truck, which teetered on its side. Bradley had a gash in his thigh, and one of his men limped.

"Where's the negating agent?"

So that was it. He didn't know himself. Virgil was supposed to have given it to Sheila. He prayed it remained intact. But from the state of the car, that was questionable. "Probably dispersed, thanks to you."

The muzzle of Bradley's rifle flashed and the 20mm round hit what was left of Macey's shoulder, showering sparks as his body whipped backward with the force.

On the ground, Macey severed the tactile receptors for his entire arm to prevent the pain sending his brain into shock.

"I'm not playing games," Bradley said. "Now where is it?"

Below him, Sheila let out a moan and her head fell toward him. Then her eyes flashed open. He had expected her to come to groggily, confused, but she was completely alert, her violet eyes piercing his own. She'd been awake, for how long he did not know, but obviously long enough to get a sense of the situation and to decide to play possum. She mouthed two words.

My pocket.

He scanned the length of her body, saw her hand tucked into the pocket of the lab coat. And within it: the gleam of the glass vial resting in her palm. She mouthed one more word.

Catch.

He barely had time to comprehend before she spoke aloud.

"You want it, Bradley?" She rolled to her side, pulled her hand free from her pocket. "Take it!" She flung the negating agent in a high arc through the air.

All eyes followed the spinning canister. Sheila's distraction was brilliant and gutsy, but he couldn't let it distract him too. He had to risk one more cynetic burst.

He fired the synapses and his world slowed. The canister slowed to a near standstill at the apex of its ascent.

Time to finish this.

Launching from his kneeling position, Macey covered the short distance between Bradley and himself in a single leap. He landed in front of one of his guards, disarmed him with a quick strike to the 20mm's barrel, which snapped its stock in two with a shatter of plastic and steel.

He let his momentum carry him into a sweeping roundhouse kick that connected with all three heads in rapid succession. He knew they were unconscious before his foot hit the ground, but he followed through on Bradley just in case, executing a spinning hatchet kick that hammered his left collarbone. He drove the kick downward, dropping Bradley to his knees in a crumpled heap.

The burst would run out soon. Arching his back, he vaulted into a reverse somersault to get a rapid glimpse of the sky behind him and to see where the canister would fall. It was about to hit the ground, a yard or so away. He fired the snaps just as the burst faded.

The world sped to real time again. In a flutter of confusion and pain, the cool glass canister fell into his palm. Then he slammed into the desert floor, rolling onto his back. Slowly he returned to his normal senses and hauled himself to his feet.

A glance over his shoulder displayed his handiwork. Bradley and his men were indeed unconscious, collapsed where they'd stood. He had attacked with finesse rather than force, which had spared their lives. After all, he needed them as suspects. More importantly, even someone like Bradley deserved a chance at God's grace. Virgil had taught him that much. Granted, once he did wake up, the punk would probably need wires in his jaw and a full-body cast.

That'd be just fine too.

"Macey!" Sheila cried.

Before he could turn, her slender body crashed into him, nearly taking him off his feet. Her arms thrust about him, crushing him in a vice-like embrace as her head nuzzled into his chest.

"I'm so glad you're here. I'll never leave you again."

He cradled her with his one arm. "It's all right. It's over now."

She pulled back from him and gazed upward, her violet eyes dampened but her face glowing with exuberance and relief. "I love you," she said, her eyes darting back and forth, searching his. Then she let loose a nervous laugh, breaking their gaze. "I'm sorry. I know that sounded stupid. I promised myself I wasn't going say that but as soon as you—"

He cupped her chin and kissed her on the mouth. Deeply, soulfully, losing himself in the magic of their reunion. Until reluctantly he relinquished her lips and caressed her cheek with his thumb.

She blushed, then the radiant smile dropped from her face and she ran her hand over where his arm used to be. "Does it hurt?"

"No, there's no pain."

"Oh . . . good." She ran a hand through her hair as she stared at Bradley and his men. "This has been a nightmare. I can't believe it's all over so quickly. One second I was watching the canister in the air and the next you had it in your hand and Bradley was on the floor. Is he dead?"

"Nah. He'll be more than fit to stand trial for all this." He held the negating agent toward her. "What *I* can't believe is you throwing this thing. What if I hadn't caught it?"

"I knew you'd catch it somehow." She swiped it from him with a beaming smile. "I got faith in you, Macey."

"Reckon you oughtta with a bloody throw like that!"

He glanced over Sheila's shoulder. "Bobby?"

"In the flesh, mate," the Blitzer said, coming around the back of the upturned BMW.

Macey thanked God he was alive, albeit with a limp and a pair of shattered horns. "You all right?"

"I ain't the 'appiest bloke, I tell ya." He leaned against the trunk. "But I guess for being slingshot out a windshield, I got no worries. Where's Moses then, eh?"

"Moses?" Macey's heart all but froze. Virgil was still out there fending off the tank. *Alone.* "I have to go."

"What about us?" Sheila said anxiously.

"You both need to get out of here. There's no telling what can happen with that tank. I don't want it coming after you if we fail."

Her face drained. "Fail?"

Macey stepped briskly toward the BMW. Maybe he had said too much, but failure started to play on his mind. Knowing the classification of the tank, failure wasn't beyond possibility. Bradley had done his homework again. The Fireant was built to take down cyborgs—and a completely autonomous AI wouldn't stop until it did so.

Stooping, he grabbed hold of the BMW beneath the roof and thrust upward with his one arm. The car flipped onto four wheels with a crash.

Bobby whistled appreciatively. "Noice."

"See if you can get this thing working again." From his pocket Macey withdrew a handful of restraining locks and tossed them toward Bradley and his crew. "Secure those guys and take 'em with you. You know how to use those, right?"

Bobby limped over to pick them up. "Not exactly. But I've had 'em used on me enough times to figure 'em out."

Macey glanced back to Sheila. She looked on the verge of tears. "I'll come back for you, Sheila. I promise."

"I know," she said unconvincingly and returned a forced smile. "Go save your brother, Macey."

The way she said it, he couldn't tell if she was being supportive or merely expressing dejection. But he couldn't worry about that now. Virgil's life was on the line, and every second he wasted could mean its forfeit.

"Take care of her, Bobby," he said, and turning sharply he hit his snaps full bore and sailed into the twilight sky.

Virgil rocketed through the hot desert air like a missile, the 30mm cyber-rifle shouldered and ready to fire. In mid-jump he reacquired his target: the lower leg joint of the Fireant's front right side. From three hundred yards, he lined up his shot. His feet hit the sand and he squeezed the trigger. The recoil of the rifle sent his shoulder flying back a foot.

Seven hundred milliseconds, he told himself, and jumped, hitting his snaps in the opposite direction he had leapt, throwing him backward. A stream of depleted uranium rounds from the Fireant's main gun sprayed in front of his face. He figured as much. The AI was trying to anticipate his actions, but luckily he could misdirect it. For how long, he did not know.

The temperature on his frame was soaring. He'd been using his snaps constantly and hit cynetic bursts every chance he got. Speed was his only defense against the tank. One slip and it could destroy his body instantly.

Seven hundred milliseconds—that was how long the Fireant's targeting computer needed to get a lock on him. Once it did, no amount of misdirection could save him. He could outrun the sluggish turret controls of the main gun, but not the visual ID lock of a guided missile.

Merely running wasn't enough either. He had to keep attacking as well. If he went 100 percent defensive, the tank's AI would stop seeing him as a threat and would perhaps go after Macey.

Re-shouldering the rifle, he touched ground and squeezed off another shot. The 30mm HEAT round flew true to its target. With a flash of sparks, the front leg joint of the Fireant exploded and the tank toppled to one side. But it was far from dead.

Virgil hit his snaps again to avoid the target lock.

Nothing happened. He didn't move.

An error message flashed into the corner of his vision. The frame had overheated. His snaps were gone. His time was up.

From over two hundred yards away a puff of white smoke emanated from the Fireant's rear missile hatch.

Checkmate.

<Sorry, Macey.> He sent his final message through the comm. *<I'm not gonna make it.>*

Macey screamed his brother's name through the comm, powering forward at full sprint. In the distance he saw Virgil at a standstill, frozen like a deer in headlights. Opposite him stood the tank, its missile hatch jetting a stream of white smoke into the sky.

<I was too slow. Get out of here while you can.>

<Shut up and move!> He closed in on the tank, its multi-barreled main gun moving to take aim at Virgil. *<Move, man! C'mon!>*

He fired his snaps in rapid succession, burning them like a string of firecrackers. The desert skirted below him as he flew over it, stirring a massive sand cloud in his wake. He dove straight for the tank.

As he had hoped, the Fireant's cannon swung toward him, but he had already closed the gap. Firing one last volley of snaps, he sprung to the side as the cannon fired, setting ablaze the ground next to him. Not letting up, he changed direction again, leaping and soaring above the tank.

He cocked his arm back and plunged downward, firing a punch directly into the turret. His plasma-charged fist hammered the base of the turret, sparks flying as the tank's reactive armor blew off. The armor disbursed most of the energy from his strike, preserving the cannon, but he had accomplished his goal, taking the heat off Virgil—for the moment anyway.

Pain shot through his body and brilliant arcs of electricity bolted over the tank's surface. His teeth ground together, pulsing with the surge of current.

<Mace, get off that thing. It'll fry you.>

<Too late for that.> But Virgil was right, the Fireant was using one of its anti-personnel countermeasures designed to keep ground forces from clambering on top of it. A normal person would have been killed by the electrified hull, but Macey's cybernetic body could absorb the damage to a far greater extent. Still, he wasn't indestructible.

Already he could smell the burning of metal and synthetic skin as his body began to cook. But he had scant time to worry about that. The missile was in the air.

Scanning the horizon, he sought Virgil, saw him running along the sand dunes as the cannon blazed back to life. This close to the muzzle the chainsaw buzz deafened him.

Virgil barely dodged the barrage with a rapid jump, a short-lived triumph with the missile still on its way. Tracing the pillar of smoke, Macey saw the missile had reached its initial firing apex at about two thousand yards and was now streaking downward, seeking Virgil's position.

It was fast—supersonic, at least—but in this case its speed would work to their advantage. They were at close range and a missile was a long-ranged weapon. It would have to take a slow, wide-arced turn to make its way back to their proximity. That meant more time, but only forty or fifty seconds tops.

<Mace, get out of here. It's got a lock on me. I'll kite it to buy you some time.>

Macey knew what he meant. He would trail it behind him while he ran. But that wouldn't work. He couldn't outrun it. Even if he'd had his snaps and was moving at top speed, it'd hit him. There had to be another way.

<Virgil, try to snipe it.> If Virgil could stand still long enough, he could try to take out the missile with his rifle. But to do that, Macey needed to make the cannon stop chasing Virgil.

Ignoring the waves of current singeing his body, Macey grabbed hold of one of the six cannon barrels of the Fireant's main gun and wedged his arm between it and the electrified hull. Sparks flew and the cannon fell silent.

<I got the cannon disabled, Virgil. Stand still and take the shot.>

Virgil complied, landing on a high dune and pointing his rifle toward the sky. Predictably, the turret swung toward him and Macey braced himself for what would follow.

The multi-barrel spun, slamming his elbow hard against the tank's hull. His forearm creaked with the force. The barrel kicked backward and a fierce humming came from the cannon's servo motors.

Macey fought against the barrel's rotation, metallic bangs pinging from the overstressed steel as the gun's turning mechanism began to break. He scanned the dunes for Virgil.

He wasn't there.

The tank shook and Virgil's booted feet landed next to him, crackling with white-hot arcs of lightning.

"What are you doing here?" he shouted up at him.

"Get clear, Mace." Virgil's voice reverberated with the flux of current flowing through him. His body began to smoke, his overcoat charring, the same way his own must be doing by now. Oblivious, Virgil shouldered the 30mm rifle and fired rapidly into the sky. "Go now."

Macey understood what he was trying to do. He couldn't allow it. Virgil had used the opportunity of him stalling the cannon to make his way to the tank. Now, even if he missed the missile with his rifle, it would home in on him and take out the Fireant in the process.

"I'm not going anywhere. I won't let you martyr yourself."

"Keep distracting me and we'll both end up martyrs." Virgil let fly a volley of 30mm rounds. He followed their path toward the missile that corkscrewed about two thousand yards above them. None hit.

"Keep trying." Macey risked a cynetic burst, slowing time. Even so, the missile descended rapidly. Fifteen hundred yards . . . nine hundred.

Virgil fired again, letting off two rounds in quick succession. Macey followed their arcs.

Three hundred yards.

One of the rounds sailed true.

The missile exploded in a brilliant flash.

Macey raised his voice in cheer, but then saw Virgil's shot sail straight through the already exploded missile, disappearing into the shrapnel. What had just happened? Had it predetonated somehow?

And then he saw it.

Some thousand feet above them, hundreds of individual micro-bomblets materialized from the exploded missile, radiating like a burst of fireworks.

A cluster bomb.

In seconds each bomblet would fire downward in a rain of high-explosive death that would destroy the tank and themselves.

"Virgil, run!"

Virgil seemed paralyzed, stuck in the pose of his last shot. Then Macey remembered he was acting within the cynetic burst. Virgil probably couldn't even see the bomblets, much less know to avoid them. Macey needed to get them both clear and fast.

He released the tank's main gun barrel and dove toward Virgil, plowing into him like a linebacker. He fired his snaps as the burst ran out and his world blurred into a barrage of explosions, light, and sound. Intense heat consumed him. And then, nothing at all.

He came to while still in motion. The back of his head plowed into the sand as he skidded over it. He jarred to a stop, hitting something so solid he nearly blacked out again.

Hazily, he could make out the Fireant. It was a hundred feet away. He had gotten them clear of the bomblets that peppered the tank's armored hide like torrents of rain, setting it ablaze. His ears dampened automatically, cutting the din to a minimum.

He turned to the thing he had struck, his eyes taking a few moments to focus.

It was Virgil.

He lay face down in the sand. One of his legs had been blown off at the knee. His clothes and combat frame and skin were all but gone, revealing a charred endoskeleton of artificial muscle and bone.

"Virgil!" He shook him.

He didn't respond.

Macey struggled to his knees, crawled closer to study his face. His shades were gone, his dark orbs open, glassy, fixed. "Virgil?" No, he couldn't be dead. He couldn't lose his brother again. Not now. Not like this. "Virgil!" he screamed, shaking his body more frantically. "Don't you die on me, man! Move!"

Then Virgil's eyelids fluttered and his head turned to face him. Black eyes blinked. "Will you stop hollering at me? I'm right here."

He stared, stupefied. "You're all right?"

"'Course I'm all right." Virgil struggled to heave himself onto his elbows. "You'd think after what we just went through I'd be allowed a little 'blackout' time."

"Thank God." He still couldn't believe it. "I honestly thought you were gone."

"Do I look dead to you?"

He laughed. "You want an honest answer?"

"Shut up."

"Let's just say I think it's time you invested in some new eyes, my friend. And a new . . . pretty much everything."

Virgil snorted before letting loose a hearty chuckle. "Let's get out of here." He tried to get up, but he rolled onto his side and sucked a breath through his teeth in disgust when he noticed his leg was missing. "Cheap Middle Eastern bodies."

Macey performed a body assessment of his own. Part of his lower left torso was missing, but he still had two legs and an arm. Not bad after taking on a battle tank. "Let's go." He pulled himself to his feet and extended a hand, supporting his brother.

Virgil slung his arm over his shoulder and together they turned to view the tank. It was completely in flames, the armor destroyed and the actual metal burning now. The heat that was thrown from it seared them even at this distance.

"Praise God." The flames reflected in Virgil's dark eyes. "I guess we did it, Macey." He turned toward him. "Where's Sheila and Bobby?"

"Safe. I sent them off in the car."

"Nice . . . . And Bradley?"

"Awaiting trial. Sleeping now, though."

Virgil chuckled. "So, since you sent away or destroyed all the vehicles for a hundred miles around, how *we* getting home?"

Before he could crack a grin, a silent explosion ripped from the tank, pluming fire fifty feet high. A split second later the shockwave hit, nearly knocking them both to the ground. "Whoa!"

"We'd better get going before the rest of the munitions go up."

"Good idea." Macey began limping away, hauling Virgil from the battlefield with him. They advanced another hundred yards or so before the next explosion went off.

Against the blood-red horizon, Macey made out someone running toward them.

"Is that who I think it is?" Virgil said.

He could only smile in response. There was Sheila, running down the slope of a sand dune to greet them. Her hair and lab coat flew haphazardly as she lost balance, falling backward onto her hands and rear to slide the rest of the way.

Behind her, Bobby strolled, hands in pockets, taking deep, carefully placed strides. The Blitzer cupped his hands about his mouth and yelled. "Sorry, blokes. She made me turn 'round. I couldn't bloody stop 'er, mate!"

Virgil let out a chuckle. "You sure know how to pick 'em, Mace."

"Macey!" Sheila called, dashing toward them—and then stopping dead. "Oh, my . . ."

He could only imagine what the two of them must look like to her—horrific. Most of his frame and skin were gone. Like a Terminator, endoskeleton only. He just hoped enough was left on his face to preserve his human façade. "We're all right. We just need a new paint job, that's all. But you might wanna hold off on any hugs. Don't know how hot my body might be."

"That's true." Virgil grinned at her. "You know, I think I might—"

A weight pulled Macey to the side.

He turned to see his brother's eyelids fluttering, his body falling. With his missing arm, Macey couldn't support the weight, and Virgil hit the ground, a stream of crimson flowing down his neck. "He's bleeding."

"Moses!" Bobby cried, dashing forward to drop down beside him.

"Is he going to be all right?" Sheila asked.

"I'll be fine," Virgil said in a slur. "Don't you worry. I'm in good hands."

Macey fell to his knees, checking where the blood came from, but there could be only one place. Tilting Virgil's chin to examine the back of his head, he soon found the wound. "He took shrapnel to his braincase. Try and keep him still. I'll get a medivac out here ASAP."

"You better do no such thing."

Macey blinked. "What?"

Virgil stared up at him, tears filling his obsidian eyes. "One hundred and twenty long years I've waited for this moment, Mace. Eternity's here, my brother. Finally. God's calling me home at last. You–you really want to stop that from h–happening?"

"Don't do this. Don't give up."

"Hey . . ." Virgil extended his hand. "God brought us back together for a reason. To have me s–save your soul and you save mine. We're brothers again. All my prayers have been answered. I have nothing left to live for in this life. I'm . . . ready to get moving to the next one."

Macey took his hand, gripped it solidly, felt it trembling. Tears burned his own eyes now. He wanted to save Virgil, tell him he had so much more to live for. But he had no right to say that, nor was it even true. They both knew he had far more to gain on the other side than here. "I just wish we had more time together."

"We had enough, and it was good. So don't you dare start crying for me. I'm the one getting off light here. You're the one that's gonna be stuck down here after I'm g–gone." He chuckled softly.

Macey managed a smile. "Early release for good behavior, huh?"

"Something like that, but don't try following me too quick. You got fifty years of slacking off to . . . make up for."

"Don't remind me."

"Ah, well." He looked toward Sheila. "At least you got someone special to spend it with now."

Macey nodded and turned to her. "That I do."

"I'll see you when you get here, Mace." His gaze encompassed Bobby and Sheila. "I hope to see you all here someday . . ."

"We'll work on that," Macey said, and Sheila pressed a smile through her tears. "I promise."

"'Til eternity falls, brother." His grip grew weak. "I love you, man."

"Love you too, brother."

Virgil's lips curved into a wide grin and Macey couldn't help but smile back at him. Then the grin faded and Virgil's hand fell limp within his own.

Macey released a sob as he felt his brother's spirit pass. He pulled his hand to his face. Sheila's hands fell upon his quaking shoulders as she knelt beside him, pressed her body close to his in embrace.

His brother was gone. Sorrow, envy, grief, joy—he didn't know which emotion filled him most. He broke down, weeping, unable to contain any of them. He comforted himself within Sheila's loving hold as hot tears streamed down his face.

"I'll see you soon, brother . . ." He rested Virgil's hand upon his chest. And silently he whispered a prayer to God—praising Him, thanking Him, and, as Sheila's warmth glowed next to him, reveled in how truly he had been blessed.

From the moment this had all started, from the instant he'd seen Virgil's name in that Bible, Macey had hoped that somehow he would be able to face his brother again, to face God again. In the end, he was not only able to do that, but so much more—he'd regained his faith, reconciled with his brother, and found a woman to love. God had blessed him more than he could have ever imagined.

"It's okay." Sheila soothed him with a gentle rock. "I'm here for you. Everything's going to be all right . . ."

He reached back, taking her tender hand within his own, and squeezed it. "I know," he said, and a smile of joy emerged through his tears. "I know."

EPILOGUE

CRISP DECEMBER AIR frosted Macey's breath as he approached the pristine doors of the Gentec headquarters. He drew his tan overcoat taut about his body as he bounded up the concrete stairs, the action more from habit than for warmth.

The overcoat was a snug fit, same as the uniform he wore beneath it. He had opted for a slightly larger build this time around, but unfortunately he hadn't had the chance to upgrade his wardrobe to match.

He stopped just outside the double glass doors of the main building entrance and leaned against the white marble wall. He checked the chronometer in the corner of his vision. He had a few minutes to kill. Suit-clad office types went in and out as Macey let his mind drift, his thoughts venturing to the same place they always seemed to these days.

Virgil.

Since his brother's death, life had been chaotic. The last three months felt like an entire year had been compressed within them. After grieving for Virgil and embracing the joy of his departure into God's hands, his first ordeal had been to replace his own damaged body.

Sheila had wanted to buy him a cloned one, of course, but in the end that had pushed him to make the decision he was leaning toward anyway. After a week in the hospital, he'd reenlisted in CDI. Why not let the government pick up the tab? It had turned out to be a good move, considering the price tag. He'd even gotten a promotion out of the deal. His old buddy Paul was once again his subordinate.

His next challenge had been Sheila's trial. Just the thought of it knotted his stomach with tension—the endless hours in the courtroom and on the stand. Glad that was all behind them now. Bradley had cut a deal the first chance he got, turning state's evidence against Roger Boreman, which had reduced his sentence from life in prison to thirty years. Not bad odds for a user of the Miracle Treatment. Boreman, on the other hand, got life. But he ended up serving less than a week.

On the morning of his third day in prison, he hung himself.

Apparently, for Boreman, eternal life was only worth living when filled with comfort and ease. Ironically, that was the truth. Whether it be in this world or the next, an eternity of suffering and agony was too much for anyone to bear. That was the truth Greta Darling and Steven Grant had come to know.

Unfortunately, Boreman hadn't been as open to choosing the same path when offered to him.

Macey grimaced as he recalled the encounter.

Maybe it was a bit of Virgil that had rubbed off, but he actually managed to suck up his pride and pay Boreman a visit before his sentencing. Despite the Bible lesson, Boreman chose death as his escape from an eternity in prison, but failed to accept the grace of God that would've kept him from entering a more permanent one.

The way of the world, he supposed. Free will, God gave it to everyone. Wasn't that what this was all about? Inevitably, some would use the gift of choice to reject God rather than follow Him. Sheila might even follow the same path.

He prayed that would not be so. But saving her wasn't something he could force. Teach and encourage, that was all he could honestly do—all any Christian could do. The rest would be up to her. Same for the rest of the world.

But there was hope. He had gotten her to come to church with him last month and, although he was sure she didn't quite *enjoy* it, she had paid attention and asked questions at least. He wasn't about to give up on her. After all, what sense would it make to save her body and not her soul?

Macey checked the time again. Late, as usual.

After being named Gentec's new CEO, Sheila had turned Doctor Julian Hague's negating agent into its newest product. Golden Respite, she called it.

The response from the clientele had proved phenomenal. Eventually she'd incorporated it into the overall design and cast a new image for the Miracle Treatment. No longer was it simply a live-forever pill, but the key to living a healthier, happier, more fulfilling and complete life—or so the ads said anyway.

The proof of Sheila's genius rested in the sales. A far wider range of people now opted to buy the Treatment, knowing it would make them healthy up until the point when they chose to stop using it.

Gentec rebounded in a matter of weeks.

A flurry of movement caught his attention through the glass doors. Macey saw what—or rather, who—he'd been waiting for.

Like a vision of déjà vu, there was Sheila, the spitting image of when he had first met her, striding powerfully amidst a bevy of well-dressed lackeys clamoring for her attention. The sight was almost enough to make him laugh.

He stood to the side as the doors swept open. A chorus of voices emerged as she exited the building. She passed right by him, swarmed by what looked to be a camera crew, along with her usual entourage. A female reporter in a neon blue power suit walked in stride with her, shooting questions, although he couldn't discern about what. It wouldn't matter anyway, not in a few seconds.

Sheila stopped, halting the ten or so people keeping pace with her. "Just a moment," she said and then cocked her head to the side. "Speak."

<How many times do I have to tell you to stop talking when you use your comm?>

"Macey?" She glanced about. "How did you—?" Finally she caught sight of him, her face twisting into a mock scowl as he let loose a chuckle. *<What are you doing here?>*

He took a step forward. *<I've come to take you to lunch.>*

<Sorry, hon, but I can't. I got this stupid TV show thing to do, remember?>

<Do you now?> He grinned and stopped just short of the crowd.

All eyes turned to him as they followed Sheila's gaze, which now darted with uncertainty and a fair bit of apprehension.

<Macey, what are you doing?>

"I'm sorry everyone," he said aloud. "I'll need to borrow Ms. Dunn for about an hour."

The TV crew and her staff balked at him in silence. Finally the reporter stepped forward. "Excuse me, and *you* are?"

"General Rick Macey with the Department of Civil Defense and Intelligence." He swept aside his overcoat to reveal his uniform and triggered the newly upgraded ID tattoo on the back of his hand to display his rank. "I need to speak with Ms. Dunn regarding a matter of some importance. I hope you understand."

<Macey!> But her smile betrayed her protest. *<You are so crazy sometimes.>*

"Ms. Dunn, if you'll come with me please?" And he extended his elbow to her.

She radiated a blush, then straightened herself and addressed her team in a deathly professional tone. "Sorry, everyone, but I certainly don't want to violate any mandatory compliance laws. We'll reschedule this interview after lunch."

<Very well said.>

<I learned from the best.> She grinned.

Her hangers-on burst into a din of confusion as she passed them, taking the crook of his elbow. *<I'm so going to do this to you at your job one day, Macey.>*

He cracked a grin as he departed with her in tow. "You know, you're going to have to start calling me by my first name."

"Rick?" She raised a brow. "Seriously? I don't think I've ever heard anyone call you that."

"No one does." He slid his hand into his pocket. "Well, actually, there is *one* person."

She pursed her lips. "Who's that?"

He answered her question with a smile.

"My wife."

LaVergne, TN USA
23 November 2009
165013LV00001B/32/P